THE APPEARANCE OF ANNIE VAN SINDEREN

Also by Katherine Howe

Conversion

The Physick Book of Deliverance Dane

The House of Velvet and Glass

The Penguin Book of Witches

THE APPEARANCE OF
ANNIE VAN SINDEREN

KATHERINE
HOWE

G. P. PUTNAM'S SONS

G. P. PUTNAM'S SONS
an imprint of Penguin Random House LLC
375 Hudson Street
New York, NY 10014

Copyright © 2015 by Katherine Howe.
Interior images © after6pm/Shutterstock, Mi.Ti./Shutterstock

G. P. Putnam's Sons is a registered trademark of Penguin Random House LLC.

Library of Congress Cataloging-in-Publication Data is available upon request.

Printed in the United States of America.
ISBN 978-0-399-16778-2
1 3 5 7 9 10 8 6 4 2

Design by Annie Ericsson. Text set in Minister.

For Charles Susman and Marion Magee,
who went until the wheels fell off

Who knows, for all the distance, but I am as good as looking at you now, for all you cannot see me?

—Walt Whitman,
"Crossing Brooklyn Ferry"

PROLOGUE

The café in the basement of Tisch, the art and film school at New York University, was redecorated this year. After entertaining a number of ambitious design proposals, including one with a water wall illuminated from within by pulsating LED lights, they decided to go with a retro–New York theme that featured subway-tile walls, stained mirrors, large filament glass lightbulbs, and hand-weathered bentwood chairs. They revamped the menu, too, adding old-school New York deli food, like huge pastrami sandwiches on rye, hot potato knishes, and half-sour pickles the size of a freshman's forearm. Everyone seemed pretty confident that the redesign would make the space more inviting for students than when it had a 1990s look, with grunge band posters and retro shag carpet and papasan chairs. Nobody ever went down there then.

They decided to dress up the wall behind the salad bar with silk-screened reproduction newspaper articles, all collaged together. For some reason most of the collaged newspapers documented long-forgotten tragedies, like the Draft Riots in 1863 or the Astor Place Riot of 1849. The decorator's assistant whose job it was to find and silkscreen the newspapers, they found out too late, had kind of a macabre sense of humor, and had been rejected by NYU.

She's since been let go.

Fortunately, nobody ever bothers to read the articles.

On the lower left part of the wall, overshadowed by the metal rack that holds the cafeteria trays, is the following story. There's a smear of ketchup across the title, but it's so low down on the wall that no one has noticed, and the bloodred stain has been allowed to stay.

The New-York Star Sentinel
October 28, 1825

TRAGEDY STRIKES CANAL JUBILEE GRAND AQUATIC DISPLAY

Dozens Feared Lost as Barge Sinks amid Cannonade

New-York—
The celebration of the marriage of the waters between Buffalo and the Atlantick reached a tragic climax off the Battery yesterday during the celebration of the Grand Canal Commemoration.

The day's revels began as a grand cannonade announced the entry of the Erie Canal boats into the waters of the Hudson River. There they were joined by steam-ships carrying representatives of the Canal Corporation flying flags of the City, escorted by pilot-boats, barges, and canoes with Aborigines from Lake Erie to see them safely to the waters off New-York. Upon passing the North Battery the flotilla's arrival was heralded with a National Salute, and it proceeded to round the island and traverse the East River as far as the Navy Yard, where it was met by a Frigate flying the flags of the City, which fired another National Salute.

The officers of the Navy then joined the Corporation and their guests on the flotilla proceeding to the Battery, where the Grand Aquatic Display met with the Mayor and the Governor, together with representatives of the Mechanics, Merchants, Military Officers, Citizens, Tradesmen, the Students of Columbia College, the College of Physicians and Surgeons, and all the Societies for the Grand Procession throughout the City. All ships and vessels were splendidly decorated, festooned with flags and pennants in celebration of the honor of the day.

By special order of the Canal Corporation the Evening Celebration began with the ceremonial illumination of City Hall beginning at seven, together with all Theatres and Public buildings similarly illuminated with suitable bunting and decoration. As the illumination neared its apogee, a grand display of fireworks of entirely novel design ignited over City Hall, with echoing fireworks and Cannonade bursting over the flotilla moored within sight of the Battery's many thousand spectators. The standers-by agreed such a sight was never before seen in the City of New-York, and when the barge nearest land erupted in a roar of great blue-purple flames, many were heard to remark that the Fire Brigade of the Seventh Ward had outdone themselves with their sponsorship of such a fine display.

However, the tragedy of their mistake was soon apparent, as screams pierced the night from the unfortunate barge, which carried distinguished family and guests of the Canal Corporation. Several pilot-boats approached to render assistance, but in vain, driven back as they were by tremendous heat and rains of sparks. As the flames licked into the night sky, the silhouettes of the unfortunate souls trapped aboard could clearly be seen, their hands rending their clothes as they were burned to cinders.

Within minutes all that remained of the unfortunate barge were some few charred logs slipping beneath the nighttime surface of the harbor, and the screams of helpless onlookers echoing through the night, as elsewhere in the city the spectacular Grand Commemoration concluded amid applause and universal acclaim when his Excellency the Governor ceremoniously united the waters of Lake Erie and the Great Rivers of the World with the Ocean.

The New-York Harbormaster refused to speculate as to the cause of the barge's conflagration, only suggesting that an errant spark had ignited the bunting hung thereon. This correspondent, however, observed what appeared to be anti-slavery sloganeering on the doomed barge, possibly the result of radicalism.

The United Brotherhood of Luddites has notified this paper of an imminent statement of responsibility.

The Canal Corporation has declined to comment on the record.

PART ONE

WES

CHAPTER 1

I've been having trouble with time lately. But I must have been thinking about her even before Tyler said anything.

"Would you tell her to sit down?" Tyler hisses.

He's squinting through the eyepiece of the camera that we've signed out from the AV department supply closet. It's a 16 millimeter, so it's not like there was a waiting list or anything. I'm not even sure they'd notice if we forgot to bring it back. In fact, it's possible Tyler's not planning to bring it back. Pretty soon they're going to be collector's items. I wonder what one would go for on eBay? A lot, I bet.

"What?" I whisper back.

"Her. That girl. She's blocking the shot."

"What girl?" I crane my neck, looking, and the hair on my arms rises. At first I don't see who he means. It's too crowded, and I'm too far back in the corner.

"*Her.* Look."

Tyler gestures for me to come look with an impatient crook of his finger.

The room we're in is not much bigger than my bedroom back

home, and crossing it without accidentally groping somebody is going to be tough. It's packed with, like, twenty people, all milling around and turning off their cell phones and moving folding chairs to get close to the table in the center. Red velvet curtains cover the walls. It should be bright, because the picture window faces the Bowery, but the window has a velvet curtain, too. Even the glass door to the town house's stairwell is taped over with black construction paper. There's a cash register on a counter off to the side, one of those antique ones that rings when the drawer opens. And there's a door to nowhere behind the cash register, behind a plastic potted plant. That's where Tyler's set up the tripod.

The only light in the room comes from candles, making everything hazy. A few candles drip from sconces on the wall, too. Other than that, and a cheap Oriental carpet latticed with moth holes, there's not much going on.

I don't know what Tyler thinks is going to happen. We're each supposed to make our own short film to screen in summer school workshop, and Tyler's determined to produce some masterpiece of filmic experimentation that will explode narrative convention and reframe visual media for a new generation. Or else he just thinks using Jurassic format will get him an easy A, I don't know.

I pull the headphones off my ears and nest the boom mike against the wall behind where I'm standing, in the corner farthest from the door. I'm worried something's going to happen to the equipment and Tyler will find a way to make me pay for it, which I cannot under any circumstances afford. I'm disentangling myself from headphone cords and everything and accidentally bump the back of some woman's head with my elbow. She turns around in her seat and glares at me.

Sorry, I mouth at her.

I keep one eye on the microphone, as if staring hard at it will prevent it from falling over, as I edge around to where Tyler's waiting. The air in here has the gross, wet summer feeling of too many people all breathing in a room with no air-conditioning. My hair is slick with sweat. I can feel the dampness in my armpits, too, a fetid droplet trickling every so often down my side. I really hope I don't smell. I didn't start wearing deodorant 'til sophomore year of high school, when one of the coaches pulled me aside for a talk so mortifying I don't know if I'll ever get over it.

It's a more diverse group than I'd expected in this room. Mom types in khakis, a couple of panhandler guys in army surplus jackets and weedy beards, a girl with tattoos snaking around her neck and straight 1950s bangs, and at least one guy in a suit, like a banker. There's a black guy in a Rangers jersey and saggy jeans. One really young girl with a hard-gelled ponytail, here with her baby. I'm surprised she'd want to bring a baby here, but there's no telling with people sometimes. Some of them exude the sharp pickled smell that people get when they've been drinking for a very, very long time.

I'm climbing monkeylike around the room, trying and failing not to get in everybody's way, and the woman sitting in the middle, who owns the place, gives me a sour look because I'm being so disruptive.

"The angle should be fine from where you are," I whisper to Tyler when I reach his corner.

"Yeah, no kidding, but she's completely blocking the shot." Tyler pops a stick of gum in his mouth, which he does whenever he wants a cigarette but can't have one. Or so he says. I don't think he really smokes.

"We're going to begin," the woman in the turban intones, and all the people start settling down and putting their phones away.

The camera's on a tripod, angled down over the circle of heads, right at the center of the table. The table itself is like a folding card table, but everyone's crowded around it, so at least a dozen pairs of hands are resting there. It's covered in a black velvet cloth, and between the knotted fingers are a couple of crystals, one polished glass ball that looks like a big paperweight, a plastic indicator pointer thing from a Ouija board, a dish of incense, and some tea lights. The incense is smoking, hanging a haze over everything, like the smoke that drifts after Fourth of July fireworks.

It's a total firetrap in here. I don't know why I agreed to come. But Tyler was dead set on getting footage of a séance for his workshop film. I don't know why we couldn't have just staged one with some kids from our dorm. That would have been easier. And he's not a documentarian, anyway.

Not like me.

"Spirits are fragile beings," the woman in the turban continues in a fake-sounding accent, and everyone but us leans in closer to listen. "They can only hear us when they're ready. When the right person goes looking for them. We must be very serious and respectful."

"Look," Tyler insists, plucking at my T-shirt. The woman glares at him, but he doesn't pay any attention. He comes down off the footstool that we brought and gestures with a lift of his chin for me to confirm what he sees.

"I'm telling you, man, I'm sure it's fine," I whisper as I step up on the stool and screw my eye socket onto the eyepiece of the camera. But when I look, a weird crawling sensation spreads across the back of my neck. It's so intense, I reach up and rub my hand over the skin to get rid of it.

At first it's hard to tell what I'm looking at. We've put a Tiffen Pro-Mist filter on the camera, for extra artistic effects or something, and my pupil dilates with a dull ache when my eye goes from the orange glow of the room to the softened pastel outlines in the filter. It looks like Tyler might have framed the shot too narrowly. He's aimed the camera right on the woman's hands in the middle, so it should be showing me her knuckles wrapped around a glass ball, next to a tea light ringed in halos of pink scattered light. But all I can see is what looks like a close-up of the black velvet tablecloth.

"Can we talk to, like, anyone we want?" the girl in the gelled ponytail asks at the same time that I say, "Dude," while reaching up to readjust the angle. "You're in way too tight. That's the problem."

"Bullshit I am," says Tyler. "She got in my way."

"Shhhhh!" One of the mom types tries to shush us.

"Who did?" I ask Tyler.

I zoom out about 10 percent and then pan slowly across the tabletop, using the tripod handle like Professor Krauss taught us, expecting any second to stumble across one of the crystals magnified to the size of a truck. Tyler thinks he knows how to use this equipment, but I'm starting to have my doubts.

"I *beg* your pardon," the woman in the middle interrupts us. "Are you boys almost finished?"

"Just about," Tyler says, raising his voice. "Thirty seconds." To me, he hisses, "Don't screw up my shot, man. I've got it all set up."

Like hell you do, I think but don't say.

"Spirits who are at peace cannot be disturbed," the woman goes on, trying to talk over our whispering. "Anyone we reach will have a purpose for being here. It's our job to determine what that purpose is. To help them. Bringing them peace will bring us peace, too."

"So we can't just ring up Elvis, huh?" the banker jokes, and a few people laugh uncomfortably.

I've panned the camera slowly across what I thought was the velvet tablecloth, but I come to rest on a small satin bow. I pull my face out of the viewfinder and look up, squinting through the candlelight to find what the camera is looking at. But I don't see anything. The table looks the same, crystals and Ouija thing and whatever. No bows anywhere. The person nearest the line of camera sight is the guy in the Rangers jersey, who's bent over his cell phone and not paying any attention to us.

"But I, like, wanted to talk to my nana and stuff," the girl with the gelled ponytail complains.

"Huh," I say.

"See her?" Tyler asks.

In the camera, outlined in eerie art-filter light, I find the satin bow again. I adjust the focus and zoom out very slowly.

The bow proves to be attached to the neckline of somebody's dress, in the shadow of lace against pale skin. I adjust the lens another hairsbreadth. I inhale once, sharply, the way I do when jumping into the lake by my parents' house for the first time at the beginning of the summer, when the water hits me so hard and cold that it makes my heart stop.

Tyler's right—there's a girl blocking the shot. A girl like I've never seen.

"I see her," I say to him, covering my sudden irrational panic. "It's not a problem."

"We can reach her, *if* your nana needs to be reached," the psychic explains with apparent impatience. "If she has something in this world holding her back."

"Told you," Tyler says to me.

"What, you saying my nana's not at peace, and it's my fault?" the girl's voice rises.

"I'll take care of it," I say to Tyler.

"No, no," the psychic backpedals. "That's not what I meant."

"You can trust Madame Blavatsky, sweetie." One of the mom types tries to soothe the girl with the baby. "But you should let her get started."

The weird crawling sensation spreads across my neck again, but

6

I can't rub it away because I'm busy climbing back around the periphery of the room to reach the girl with the satin bow. She's just standing there, not talking to anyone, looking down at her hands. My heart is tripping along so fast, I'm having trouble catching my breath. I don't want to make her feel weird or anything. I also kind of hate talking to people. But more than that, she's . . .

"Yes, we really can't wait any longer," the woman in the turban says. "Spirits only have limited time, once summoned, to resolve their unfinished business. If we don't act quickly, we risk damning them to an eternity in the in-between."

The medium's starting to get pissed off. I'm not positive, but I think Tyler's paid her for letting us film. Which we're not supposed to do for workshop, but whatever. She sounds really annoyed. I don't blame her. *I'm* kind of annoyed. At Tyler, mostly, for dragging me along to do sound when I could be working on my own film. *Should* be working on my own film, especially considering how much is riding on it. In fact, all I want is to be working on my own film. But I find myself pulled into other people's stuff a lot. I get caught up.

"What do you mean, limited?" asks the guy in the Rangers jersey. "Like, they on the clock or something?"

Tyler thinks he's going to be the next Matthew Barney. He's doing an experimental film of people in what he calls "transcendental states," using all different film stock and filters and weird editing tricks that he's refused to reveal to me. I don't think we're going to see much in the way of transcendental states in a palm reader shop upstairs from an East Village pizzeria. But we already spent the afternoon with the AX1 filming drummers in Washington Square Park. I think he's running out of ideas.

"Or something," the medium says, and when she says it, a sickening chill moves down my spine.

7

The girl with the satin bow on her dress is standing on the opposite side of the room from the camera, not far from where I stashed the mike, looking nervous, like she's doing her best to blend into the wall. She's awkwardly close to the edge of the table. Nobody seems to notice her, a fact that causes my ears to buzz.

Now that I've seen her, I feel like she can never be unseen. She looks . . . I suck at describing people, and *beautiful* feels especially pathetic. But the truth is, I don't understand how I haven't been staring at her the whole time we've been here. As I edge nearer, my blood moves faster in my veins and I swallow, a fresh trickle of sweat making its way down my rib cage. I can feel her getting closer. Like I can sense where she is even when I can't see her. She's not paying any attention to me, her head half turned away, looking around at the walls with interest.

The girl is so self-contained, so aloof from all of us, that she seems untouchable. Watching her ignore my approach, I wonder how you become someone that other people make room for, whether they know it or not.

She's wearing one of those intense deconstructed dresses they sell in SoHo. My roommate, Eastlin, is studying fashion design, and he's got a sweet internship in an atelier for the summer. He took me to the store where he works one time and showed me this piece of clothing, which he said was a dress, which was dishwater-gray and frayed around the edges, covered in hooks and eyes and zippers and ribbons. I couldn't really understand what the appeal was. To me it looked like something I'd find in a trunk in my grandmother's attic. When he told me how much it cost I dropped the sleeve I was holding because I was afraid I'd snag a thread and have to take out another student loan.

I'm definitely afraid to touch this girl's dress. Seeing how she

8

wears it, though, I begin to understand what Eastlin's talking about. Her neckline reveals a distracting bareness of collarbones. Her hair is brushed forward in curls over her ears in some bizarre arrangement that I think I saw on a few hipster girls in Williamsburg when Tyler took me out drinking there. She must sense me staring at her. Why won't she look at me? But she's finished her examination of the curtains, and if she's noticed me approaching her, she's not letting on. As I move nearer, near enough that I can practically sense the electrical impulses under her skin, she steps back, retreating from the edge of the table into the red curtain folds along the wall. I glance at Tyler, and he waves to indicate that she's still in the shot, and I should get her to sit down already.

My heart thuds loudly once, twice. Up close, her skin looks as smooth as buttermilk. Milk soft. Cool to the touch.

I want to touch the skin at the base of her throat.

This thought floats up in my mind so naturally that I don't even notice how creepy I sound.

"Hey," I manage to whisper, drawing up next to her. It comes out husky, and I cough to cover it up.

She doesn't hear me. At least, she doesn't respond. My cheeks grow warm. I hate talking to people I don't know. I hate it more than going to the dentist, I hate it more than taking SATs or doing French homework or stalling a stick-shift car with my dad in the passenger seat.

"When everyone is *seated*, we'll finally begin," the woman in the middle of the room says pointedly. A few eyes swivel over to stare at me trying to talk to the girl, and my flush deepens.

"Listen," I whisper in desperation, reaching a hand forward to brush the girl's elbow.

The instant my fingers make contact, the girl's head turns and she stares at me. Not at me—*into me*. I feel her staring, and as the lashes over her eyes flutter with something close to recognition it's like no one has ever really seen me before her.

Her face is pale, bluish and flawless except for one dark mole on her upper lip, and twin dark eyebrows drawn down over her eyes. As we gaze at each other I can somehow make out every detail of her face, and none of them. When I concentrate I can only see the haze of incense smoke, but when I don't try too hard I can trace the curve of her nose, the slope of her cheeks, the line where lip meets skin. Her eyes are obsidian black, and when she sees me, her lips part with a smile, as if she's about to say something.

I recoil, taking a step backward without thinking, landing my heel hard against the boom. The microphone starts to fall, and I fumble to catch it before it hits the girl with the gelled ponytail and the baby, and I nearly go down in a tangle of wires and headphones and equipment.

"Dude!" Tyler chastises me from behind the camera.

He's laughing, and some of the people around the table are joining in. The guy in the Rangers jersey pulls out his phone and snaps a picture of me glaring at Tyler. The girl with the neck tattoo smiles at me out of the corner of her mouth and starts a slow clap, but fortunately nobody joins in and after a few slow claps alone she stops and looks away.

"It's fine," I mutter. "I've got it under control."

"Whatever," Tyler says, pressing his eye to the viewfinder and panning across the people's faces. They've started to join hands.

Once I've gotten the headphones back on and the boom mike hoisted over my head, balanced unobtrusively over the table so I can pick up the soft breathing of all the New Yorkers in this second-floor room on the Bowery, I check to see if the girl in the deconstructed dress is still hiding against the velvet curtain.

10

I don't see her.

The woman in the turban has blown out all but the candles in the sconces on the wall, plunging the table into an intimate darkness with everyone's face in shadow. In my headphones I hear Tyler whistle softly under his breath, and I imagine that the scene looks pretty intense through the softening filter.

"Now," the woman breathes. "We shall invite the spirits to join our circle, if everyone is ready."

I get a better grip on the boom, balancing my weight between my feet and settling in. The woman in the turban told us it would only take about forty-five minutes. But forty-five minutes can feel like an eternity, sometimes.

CHAPTER 2

W ell, that sucked," Tyler says. He pulls on the gelled tips of his faux hawk with irritation.

"No kidding," I agree, fastening closed the audio equipment case with a final click. People are filing out all around us. Some of them look embarrassed. The banker guy was the first one out the door.

"I don't know how they expect us to make an art film when nothing interesting ever actually happens here," he continues.

"Tyler," I mutter to him.

"What?" he says.

I glance pointedly at the woman in the head scarf, who can absolutely still hear us. She's tidying up all the objects on her séance table, pretending like she can't. The crystals clink together in her hands.

"Whatever," Tyler dismisses me. "We should've done it on skateboarding. Those guys are always easy to find. And they love being on film. It would've basically directed itself."

"Uh-huh," I say. Because what the world needs is another student film about skateboarding as a transcendent state. That's definitely the most interesting thing happening in New York City right now. As if.

"I'll wait for you outside," he says, shouldering a bag of equipment and pulling out his phone.

I nod, not looking at him while he leaves. I'm waiting for him to go. I want to try to talk to her. If I can work myself up to actually doing it, that is.

Some of the other people are loitering, too, like they want to talk to the woman in the turban. I know I should be going. We've signed up for the editing room tonight to work with Tyler's digital footage, but it closes at eleven, and the sooner I can get this project finished, the happier I'll be. I pretend to reach into the box to adjust the coils of wire inside. Really, I'm listening, and looking under my eyelashes to see where the girl with the hipster-curled hair is. One of the khaki mom types is talking to the woman in the head scarf in a low voice. The girl in the gelled ponytail eyes me, jostling the baby over her shoulder. I was pretty impressed that the baby didn't cry, what with the dark and the chanting and everything. Especially when all the candles went out. That was a pretty cool trick. I wonder how the woman in the head scarf did it.

I glance sidelong at the ponytail girl, quick so she won't notice. That girl has got to be like three years younger than me. That must really suck, having a baby in high school. She's petite, and the baby is just a little guy, who'll probably be small like she is. I let my eye roam down her body, which is tight and young. She's in those uptown jeans, the ones that make a girl's ass look really high, and she's wearing huge gold hoop earrings. The baby has his fist around one of the earrings, gumming it. I guess I can see how it would happen. But even so. God. A baby.

"The hell you lookin' at, huh?" the girl snaps, glaring at me. She shuffles the baby onto her other hip, freeing the earring as she does so.

Dammit.

"Nothing," I mutter, looking down fixedly at the audio equipment box. "Sorry."

"That's right," she says, turning her back to me.

Well, that's just great. Caught checking out the unwed underage teen mother. I am an asshole.

My hands rush around to finish packing the audio equipment. I figure it'll take Tyler and me about two hours to edit the digital footage into a rough cut tonight, and then over the weekend I can slap on some transitional music and headings or whatever, and he'll get the 16 millimeter film back from the developer early next week and we can edit it in with the digital and then get this over with. Then I never have to see any of these people again.

"Busted," whispers a young woman's voice not far from my ear.

"Huh?" I glance up and find the girl with tattoos and Bettie Page bangs standing directly in front of me, her arms folded.

I struggle up to my feet, trying not to look at anyone. I definitely don't want to catch myself looking at my accuser's tattoos. She has starkly inked black laurel leaves coiling over her chest and up her neck, and the fold of her arms makes her breasts swell a little under her tank top. I swallow, looking fleetingly at her face, and then hard at a spot six inches above her left shoulder.

"Don't feel bad," says the tattooed girl. "I was staring, too."

Someone pulls open a cheap velvet curtain, exposing the picture window overlooking the Bowery. The window lights up with the orange chemical glare of the streetlights below, tinted red by the neon sign advertising the medium's services: PALMISTRY CLAIRVOYANT PSYCHIC TAROT $15. Outside, taxi horns, and the wet roll of tires through streets hot with tar.

"Bye, Madame Blavatsky," someone calls on her way out the door. The bell overhead jingles.

I look more curiously at this girl's face. Under all the eyeliner and black lipstick and tattoos she's actually pretty. Younger than I thought at first. My age, basically, so, like, nineteen. She has a snub nose and pale eyebrows, which suggest that the black dye in her hair hides an agreeable dirty blond. The red light from the neon sign makes her skin look creamy and pale.

"Yeah," I say, because I'm really smooth like that.

More of the people are filing out around us. The guy in the Rangers jersey left like ten minutes ago, never looking up from his phone. I glance over the tattooed girl's shoulder, searching for the girl with the deconstructed dress. I haven't seen her since the lights came back on. I don't know where she could have gone, since Tyler's tripod was blocking the only other door.

"So what did you and your friend think?" she asks.

"Um . . ." I hesitate.

The truth is, I thought it was a waste of time, and I'm pretty sure Tyler thought so, too. Everybody held hands and chanted, and the medium said some stuff and then all the candles blew out. But then there was a long wait and as far as I can tell nothing happened. One of the moms started crying. Then the medium busted out some matches and lit all the tea lights again and then there was a little more chanting and then it was over. I didn't see anyone in what Tyler might call a transcendent state. The atmosphere was spooky. I was ready to be freaked out. But then, nothing.

I'm on the point of saying this to the punk girl, but I stop myself. What if she comes here all the time? Maybe she takes it seriously. I don't want to hurt her feelings. I peer at her face, probing it for clues, trying to read what she wants me to say. But besides a lip piercing that I didn't notice before, all I see is a girl's warm smiling goth-made-up face.

"I guess it was interesting," I hedge. "I mean, I hadn't been before, so I didn't really know what to expect. But it was kind of cool,

I guess. I liked when the candles all went out. That was freaky. What did you think?"

"Eh." She shrugs, hoisting an army surplus backpack over her shoulder. "I don't really care. I just come here to sleep."

"What?" I blink.

"It's okay," she says, taking my elbow. "Madame *Blavatsky*"—she gives the name ironic emphasis—"never remembers me."

I was going to ask the medium to sign the release form that Professor Krauss told us to use for any projects that we want to put on the web—and I know Tyler's going to put this on his Vimeo, because he won't shut up about it—but this girl is dragging me by the elbow and anyway the medium's busy talking to the girl with the baby. I hesitate. I don't want Professor Krauss to tell us we can't use the footage without the release. But then I think, *Screw it.* It's just a summer school project. Nobody cares. It's not like anyone's ever going to see it anyway, besides at workshop.

"I find it hard to believe she wouldn't remember you," I say, and immediately wish I hadn't.

The tattooed girl gives me a coy smile over her shoulder, takes my hand in hers, and leads me to the door. I'm dragging my feet, because I haven't seen the other girl yet, and I really wanted to talk to her. I thought for sure she'd . . . I mean, the way she looked at me, I thought . . . But I guess, if she wanted to talk to me, she'd have stuck around.

I'm weirdly disappointed. I mean, I didn't even talk to her. Not really.

"That was a nice line," the girl with the bangs says as she drags me down the stairs to the street. "Almost like you didn't even plan it. Come on. I'll let you buy me a slice."

The first floor of the psychic parlor's building houses a no-name pizzeria, one of those places with Formica counters and fluorescent lighting and a good-size plate of garlic knots for a dollar. I spot Tyler on the sidewalk outside, our camera equipment heaped around his feet while he looks at his phone. He hasn't noticed us come out.

"Okay," I say. Pizza is good medicine for disappointment.

It's a hot night, damp from summer rain, and the pizzeria doors are propped open to the street to capture any passing breeze. I don't even realize how hungry I am until the smells of cheese and garlic hit me. Saliva springs to my mouth, and I'm instantly starving.

We spend a minute staring slack-jawed at the menu board overhead, and then we're at the front of the line and a guy in a stained apron is yelling at us. He chucks our slices into the oven, jerks his thumb at the lady behind the cash register, and by the time she's taken my ten bucks the slices are out, paper plates and puddles of orange grease and fistfuls of tissue-thin napkins.

She gets pepperoni and garlic. Two slices. She doesn't even make a thing of getting two. My high school girlfriend was so weird about food, it drove me crazy, but I was always too afraid of ticking her off to say anything about it. I like that this girl eats garlic. And I like that she doesn't seem to care if I like that she eats garlic.

I get the same, and we pick two seats at the counter facing the street. The window is open, but the air is dead.

"So what were you guys doing up there? Are you making, like, a movie or something?" the girl asks through a mouthful of pizza.

Outside the window Tyler spots me and throws his hands up in a what-the-hell-man? gesture that I've come to know pretty well over the past month.

"Kind of. I guess," I say while chewing. "It's for school. Like a project?"

"Oh yeah? Where do you go?"

17

"NYU," Tyler says, appearing at the counter between us. "I'm doing an experimental film. It's a non-narrative, multimedia, post-visual exploration of transcendent states. He's just helping me out."

Tyler reaches across us and helps himself to my second slice with a superior grin of acquisition. I glower at him.

"Um." The girl with 1950s bangs suppresses a smile. "You don't say."

She eyes Tyler, and I watch her take in his skinny black jeans and faded Ramones T-shirt that he probably got at Urban Outfitters. I look down at my own utterly nondescript polo and cargo shorts from the Target in suburban Madison, Wisconsin, and frown.

"NYU, huh? That's great," she says in a way that suggests she doesn't necessarily think it's great.

"I . . . ," I stammer. "I don't really go to NYU. I mean, I want to. But it's just summer school."

"He thinks if he makes a good enough film, they'll let him transfer." Tyler smirks. "Then he can go for real."

My ears flush purple. Dick. It's true, though. It's the one thing I want most in the world.

"Oh yeah? You any good?" she asks me.

I start to answer when Tyler interrupts through a mouthful of my pizza. "We should get going, dude. We've got the lab starting in twenty minutes."

"Right," I say. But I don't make a move to leave. I want to tell her that yeah, actually, I am pretty good. But I'm afraid if I say that out loud the universe will hear me, and then I'll be jinxing myself.

"Well," the girl says, toying with a crust. "Thanks for the pizza, anyway."

"Sure," I say. "No problem."

Tyler sighs loudly. "I'm Tyler," he says to the girl. "And this is Wes. And Wes has got to be going now. Come on, man."

I glare at Tyler in a way that I hope will set the gel in his hair on fire, but nothing happens.

"Well, Tyler and Wes," she says. One pale eyebrow arches at me. "It's been real."

"I . . . ," I start to say. There's got to be a right thing for me to say, right now. Nothing good comes to mind, though, and Tyler is already outside with half the bags, flagging down a cab.

The girl pulls out a phone and snaps my picture. I'm embarrassed. I always look weird in pictures. My hair sticks up in this wavy way that I hate, and pictures make my nose look huge. Plus I'm too tall, so in group pictures the top of my head is always cut off.

She smiles mysteriously at me and whispers, "I see you, Wes."

A strange shiver travels around behind my ears when she says this.

"I've got to go. Sorry," I mumble.

"Sure." She smiles that one-sided smile again, looking at her phone instead of me.

"But, listen," I say in a rush of unaccustomed courage. "Can I know your name?" I'm not about to make the same mistake twice in one night, and not ask. Not even I am that stupid.

Her smile spreads, lighting up her eyes, and she leans in close to my ear.

"I see you, Wes," she whispers again. Her lips hover so near to my ear that I can feel her breath on my skin. It makes my ear tingle.

"What?" I whisper back, confused.

"Dude!" Tyler hollers from the corner. "Come on, let's go!"

Her smile goes sphinxlike.

Baffled, I gather my stuff, keeping one eye on her as I sling bags over my shoulder and toss a crumpled dollar bill onto the counter. With a last glance at her, which she meets with a slow, silent wave, I turn and lope out of the pizzeria. Tyler's loading equipment into the trunk of a cab when I arrive puffing next to him.

"Hey, you see that girl come out?" he says to me.

"What?"

"That girl. The one who was blocking my shot. Did you see her come out?"

I glance back at the pizzeria and observe the tattooed girl with 1950s bangs collecting my pizza crusts and dollar tip and loading them into her backpack. Weird.

"No." I pause.

The girl continues to sit at the counter facing the street, fiddling with her phone. She smiles to herself, unaware that anyone is watching. I glance up at the windows above the pizzeria, but the velvet curtains have been drawn closed again. Thinking about the first girl makes the pizza weigh heavy in my stomach. The pizza of dismay.

"No, I guess I didn't," I say.

"You've got to make her sign one of Krauss's releases, you know, to cover my ass. This is so going on my Vimeo channel when it's done."

"Uh-huh," I say.

Then we're in the back of the cab and Tyler is giving the driver the address of the film lab. I turn and look one last time through the rear windshield. It glitters with droplets of hot summer rain.

The chair where the tattooed girl was sitting is empty, and there's nothing but some greasy napkins and plates to show she was ever there.

Upstairs, behind the neon of the psychic medium sign, the velvet curtain twitches. I press my cheek to the taxi window, squinting up at the façade of the building.

A vertiginous rush knocks me sideways. I'm almost certain I glimpse the pale outline of the girl's face with hipster hair curled over her ears. The face is looking down at our taxi in the street, and she's

20

smiling. That perfect mouth with its perfect mole. The eerie feeling spreads across the back of my neck again, and I close my eyes against it. It's almost sickening. The taxi jolts as it pulls away from the curb, jostling me against Tyler and shaking loose the weird sensation.

But when I open my eyes again, the girl is gone.

CHAPTER 3

I'm so tired I haven't even bothered to take my sneakers off. I root my face in my pillow, feeling myself just beginning to float off the surface of my bunk when there's a soft click, and a triangle of light cuts into the room.

"Jesus. What happened to you?" a male voice says. It's deep and gravelly, unmatched to the young, slender guy it actually belongs to.

I moan, draping my arm over my eyes to block out the light.

"What time is it?" I ask, my voice thick with sleep. I belch, and the stale taste of pepperoni and garlic pizza fills my mouth.

"Beats me."

Springs creak as Eastlin flops onto his bed. Soft sounds of sneakers being unlaced. A click as he turns on the desk light. The lamplight hammers into my brain. Tyler took me out after we hit the editing room, to say thank you, I guess. God. It's not like we don't know how to drink in Wisconsin. But I can't drink like Tyler. And he magically seems to know all the places downtown that don't card.

"Man, come on," I whine.

"What? It's only two." Eastlin is laughing at me.

I peek under my arm at my roommate and see him leaning over

a mirror on his NYU-issue desk, wiping his face with a moist ball of cotton.

"Two? God."

"Yeah. It's early!" Eastlin grins and chucks the dirty cotton ball at me. It hits my forehead with a wet *splap*. "I wouldn't even be home, except for the DJ sucked, and this guy wouldn't leave me alone."

"What guy?" I ask.

"Some twink. He was *thirsty*." Eastlin shakes his head with pity.

"Yeah?" I say.

"Old, too."

One of Eastlin's dirty socks comes sailing toward my face after the cotton ball, but I bat it away in time.

"Sounds rough." I try to commiserate. My gay friends back home don't go clubbing. Or if they do, they don't tell me about it. Which makes me pretty sure they don't. My high school friends are more the beer and batting cages type.

He laughs, leaning an elbow into his pillow while pulling out his phone. "And was your night as good as it looks?" he asks without looking up. He stretches a bare foot out, spreading the toes until they crack.

I groan, staring up at the ceiling. Acoustical tiles. There have been moments, this summer, when my solitude has been so deep that I've caught myself counting the divots in them.

"Tonight was the palm reader, right?" he prods me.

"It was. Tonight was the *palm reader*." I add ironic emphasis to the words, though the truth is, I kind of had my hopes up about it. Tyler was so enthusiastic, when he described it to me. I wanted it to be cool.

"Somebody should really tell that guy that nobody watches art films anymore." Eastlin pauses. "In fact, I'm pretty sure nobody *makes* art films anymore."

"It's going to suck," I inform him. "It's going to suck so hard I don't think I'm going to let him put my name on it."

"Tyler? He probably wasn't going to, anyway."

"Yeah," I say, thinking.

"Now, see this guy?" Eastlin flashes his phone at me, showing a profile picture from some cruising app that he uses. I catch a glimpse of a clean-cut guy our age with a lopsided grin and a backward baseball cap. He looks like a lacrosse player. "Why couldn't he have been there? He probably doesn't go to clubs."

"Actually—" I start to say.

"He probably doesn't have to. Meets everyone he wants at the polo matches or whatever. He looks like you, if you, like, knew how to dress."

Eastlin thinks I'm a slob. But then, Eastlin thinks that most guys who wear cargo shorts are slobs, even though cargo shorts are a completely normal thing to wear.

"Actually, you know. It wasn't bad. It was okay," I say. I don't know why I want to defend my night to him. But I sort of do. I mean, it's not like I was just sitting here by myself playing Minecraft. Which is what I would've been doing, if Tyler hadn't made me go out.

"Bullshit it was. You look like you've been hit by a truck."

"Yeah. Except . . ." I hesitate. "There was this girl there."

I regret it the moment I've said it.

"Oh, reeeeaaally?" My roommate's phone has immediately disappeared and he's zeroed his eyes on me. I've taken no end of crap from him about my failure to bring a single girl back to the room in five weeks. More than once he's pointed out that I'm squandering ridiculous opportunities in the privacy offered by his active nightlife. It's become a joke.

"Elaborate, please," he says, resting his chin on his hand.

I close my eyes, my mind's hand reaching forward to brush the elbow of the girl with the curled hipster hair and the bottomless black eyes. My scalp starts to tingle.

"She was—" I begin.

"Was she hot?" Eastlin likes to cut to the chase. Or rather, he likes to cut to the end of the chase.

I consider the girl's face. That cool, opalescent skin. The mole above her upper lip.

"Hot isn't the right word," I say.

Eastlin's eyebrows move slowly up his forehead, and he breaks into a smile. His front tooth is chipped, I don't know from what, but it means that he doesn't smile widely all that often. "You think she's beautiful," he tells me.

"Come on," I say, rolling my eyes.

"You do. I can tell."

How can I explain her to him? Not because he won't understand, but because something about her fails me. She's impossible to put into words. There's only the feeling.

"I don't know how to even tell you," I say, helpless before the idea of her.

"What did she look like?" he presses me.

"I don't know."

"Light? Dark? Big tits? Little tits? Come on. Give me something to work with."

"Light hair. In this kind of weird, complicated curl situation. Dark eyes."

"What was she wearing?"

"Actually," I say, looking at him with new interest. "She was in some crazy deconstructed dress thing. It looked like something you'd have at the store."

Eastlin's eyes light up. "She was wearing Abraham Mas? Which one?"

"What do you mean, which one? I don't know. A dress. With a bow at the neck. Sleeves."

"Which *piece*. They all have names. Each design is unique."

My roommate is clearly trying to be patient with me, but it's hard for him, living with such a rube. They apparently don't have rubes in Connecticut, where he's from.

"You've got to be kidding," I say.

"Would I kid you? With this face? Come on." Eastlin smiles.

"I don't know. Maybe it wasn't from there. Looked like it, though. That lace trim, kind of torn, but, like, on purpose? Heavy. Expensive. I've never seen anything like it before."

"Lace trim?" He brings a fingernail to his mouth and gives it a meditative chew. "We did lace two seasons ago. Stained in tea."

"She was . . ." The right words won't come. The right words usually don't, for me. I mostly experience the world in images. I wish I could show Eastlin the film I took of this girl, in my mind. It unspools before my eyes, rolling forward like a silk ribbon falling out of someone's hand, and I see the girl in the deconstructed dress smile.

"If she shops at Abraham Mas, I probably know her," he offers.

A funny fluttering thing happens inside my chest, and I have to clear my throat to get rid of it. "She was young," I say helpfully.

"Young." He tears off the offending nail, examines the bare fingertip, and spits the nail out on the floor. "Most Mas girls are Madison Avenue types. You know. Lunch. Their hair, my God. Three hundred dollars a week, for the color. At least."

"I think you'd recognize her," I say, surprised at the urgency in my voice. I want him to know her. I want him to tell me who she is. "Definitely."

Just then the pocket of my cargo shorts vibrates twice. I fish inside and pull out my phone. It's got a huge crack in the glass from where I dropped it in the subway last week, but it still basically works. A bird icon informs me that someone's mentioned me on Twitter.

"Huh." Eastlin starts in on the next nail. "Well, at the very least, she'd be in the store system. We can stalk her."

"Come on," I say, peering at my phone.

The tweet is from a profile I don't follow.

It says, **I see you, @wesauckerman.**

And it links to a picture of me on Instagram. In the picture my mouth is half open, like I'm in the middle of saying something. My hair is sticking up, and there's pizza grease on my mouth. The glare of the fluorescent lights has been softened with a filter. I'm smiling.

I laugh, tugging on the forelock of my hair. The profile belongs to someone named Maddie, with no identifying details other than "NYC." The profile picture is a cartoon unicorn galloping on an ocean of stars. The girl with 1950s bangs is webstalking me. Maybe it wasn't the pizza that helped push away my disappointment.

"Look at you," my roommate says, getting to his feet and tossing a towel over his shoulder. "She text you just now?"

"What?" I say, weighing whether or not I should respond.

She must have found me from an image search. I guess I know people can do that, but it's not like it ever occurred to me to try. What should I say back to her? I should say something funny. But I'm not sure what Maddie will think is funny. I hesitate.

Maddie. Maddie who has Bettie Page pinup bangs. And a *neck tattoo*. My high school girlfriend thought all girls with tattoos were sluts. She could be kind of a bitch, though. What do *I* think of girls with tattoos?

"Pathetic," Eastlin remarks as the door closes behind him. A second passes before the door opens again, and his head sticks back

27

inside our dorm room. "And you realize I mean that in the worst possible way."

"Asshole," I say, laughing, and chuck his own sock back at him. With a grin he shuts the door and the sock misses by six feet.

I stare at Maddie's profile, ruminating. There's not much to it. Lots of retweets of joke memes. Her Instagram is mostly pictures of diner food, glistening French fries or hamburgers in primary colors. There are a few arty shots of corners of New York City. A curl of pilaster. A puddle. A pigeon with a gnarled foot.

I stuff my phone back in my shorts pocket without responding. I need time to think of something good. My fingers interlace behind my head, and I stare up at the ceiling tiles.

"You're going to have to put the effort in, Wes," my dad's voice plays on a tape in my brain. I hate that I can still hear him from a thousand miles away. "You can't just hide behind your video camera all the time. Watching life happen to other people."

I frown and roll onto my side, away from him.

My dad came to the Village when he was my age, determined to be the next Bob Dylan. He dropped out of UW, panhandled bus fare, and showed up in Port Authority with nothing but a change of boxer shorts, thirty-six bucks, a jean jacket, and a guitar. I think he was surprised there wasn't a committee of folkies waiting to welcome him with open arms and a bunk in a commune squat. Nobody told him that by 1975, it was already too late. Not even Bob Dylan wanted to be Bob Dylan anymore.

Dad lasted a month sleeping on some girl's floor before he ran out of money. She let him stay on another couple of weeks after he went broke, and his mouth always twists in a funny way when he gets to that part of the story. After a while the girl met somebody else, and Dad called home collect to beg Gran and Grandpa to wire him some money. Then he packed up his guitar and took a bus back to

Madison. He hasn't been back to New York since. It's not the same now, he likes to point out. It's nothing like what it used to be.

When I applied to come here for summer school, I started hearing this story a lot. Before that, he never seemed to know what to talk about with me. I never tried to play guitar. I never talked about wanting to go somewhere else, and he never shut up about it. He never understood that getting out of Madison was easy for me. I spent most of junior high deep in World of Warcraft, erecting complex pixelated walls between myself and reality.

But I didn't feel like I was hiding. I felt like I was watching.

I started getting into filmmaking in high school. Anime, at first. I wanted to learn how to program video games. I'd make little movies on my phone and stuff, too. But then my mom gave me a Sony HDR CX900 for my eighteenth birthday. I found the real world was more interesting than I thought. When I looked at life through the camera, I felt like I could finally see it.

I'd thought about applying to NYU for college, but Dad didn't think I could handle it. I never got a straight answer on what part he didn't think I could handle. Whatever. Most of my friends and my girlfriend were going to UW anyway.

UW doesn't have a film school, though. I do communications arts, which is basically the same thing. But sometime freshman year, I just . . . I don't know. Okay, the breakup was part of it. Seeing Instagrams of her with some guy in the dorm two doors down from me basically ripped out my soul. But around that time, too, I started feeling detached from myself. Like no time was passing. Every restaurant and café, my friends' dorm rooms, my ex-girlfriend's parents' driveway, all were haunted by versions of myself that I was done with. Walking around UW, eating at Dotty's, seeing the same people from high school, made me angry at myself.

I applied to NYU for summer film classes on the last day before

29

the deadline, never thinking I'd get in. But I did. I had to borrow the money from my grandparents, which was embarrassing. Grandpa is pretty out of it now, so he probably hasn't noticed that I'm gone, but Gran seemed pleased with herself, when I called her about it. Like she'd been waiting.

"We'd have given it to your father, you know, if he asked," she whispered in my ear the day she slid me a check. I pocketed it without opening it.

I was wearing Dad's sport coat, which is too big. It makes me look like David Byrne.

I pushed the bloodied steak residue around on my plate. I didn't much like asking for what I wanted. There was something undignified about it. Maybe Dad didn't like asking, either.

Dad made it pretty clear that he thought I was going to screw it up. In Dad's mind, New York was for people too hungry for life to be anywhere else. I wasn't hungry enough. I was too safe, behind my camera. I would never just show up in Port Authority without a place to stay. I wouldn't play guitar in the subway for spare change. I wouldn't take up with some girl I met on the street and spend my summer afternoons tangled naked in her sheets, waiting for her to figure out that I'm using her before she kicks me out and I have to take the bus home like Bob Dylan. I see a girl who makes my head swim and I get so freaked out at the thought of even talking to her that I can barely touch her elbow.

Even when I think I'm living, I'm still just watching.

But I have a plan. I have a plan, to start living.

I count 932 divots in the dormitory ceiling tile before I drift off to sleep.

CHAPTER 4

I rub my fingers over my eyes and indulge in a ten-second fantasy of punching Tyler in the face. I mean, I wouldn't really. I've only really ever been in one fight, when I was eight. And I lost. Big-time. But today I let myself get really detailed, imagining my fist connecting out of nowhere with the bridge of Tyler's nose. I can feel the wet splintering under my knuckle when the bone breaks. I can feel warm blood coursing from his face.

It's pretty satisfying.

"Look at this crap," Tyler says for the tenth time in as many minutes. "We can't use any of this. The hell did you do to my settings, man?"

We're back in the editing room, and it's ten thirty at night, which means we're getting kicked out in half an hour. Tyler's just gotten his 16 millimeter film back from the lab. For the past week he hasn't shut up about it. This, I'm to understand, is what's going to really set *Shuttered Eyes* apart from all the other Scorsese-rip-off crap our classmates will be showing at workshop. He wants to edit together his color video footage from the park with the soft-filter night film stock we took on the Bowery, and somehow that's all going to come together in a visual tone-poem about the state of the human soul in transcendent meditation.

I guess. God, I don't know.

I still have to get the music dubbed into my documentary, which is due in a week, for the second workshop screening. I'm calling it *Most*. It's people of all different ages, on the street or at school or in restaurants or wherever, talking straight to the camera, confessing what they want most. It's actually turning out better than I thought it would. It never ceases to amaze me what people will say to a camera that they won't say to a regular person. All that's missing is a couple more interviews, the title sequence, and the transitional music. I'm not worried about it, exactly, but in the back of my mind I have this idea that if I can just make it good enough . . . Maybe . . . If the film professors really like it . . .

I'm too superstitious to think about that right now. So far, it's going okay. And I'm not quite the artiste Tyler is. I can work on my laptop in the dorm. Tyler needs capital *E* editing equipment. Sometimes I want to get him jodhpurs and a beret, he's so invested in his "directorial persona." I think that would tick him off, though.

"I didn't do anything," I say, each word deliberate, so that Tyler will hear how pissed off I'm getting.

"Well, somebody did something. Look at this."

He speeds through the film again on the Steenbeck, and the filter shots of tea lights and crystals smear into an indistinct blur.

"What did you expect it would look like?" I ask, leaning my head in my hands. "We used a filter. And the light was lower than we planned for. Of course everything's going to be hard to make out."

"Bullshit, man. You talk like you've never seen that Paris Hilton video."

Okay. I have to give him that one. That was, like, the defining moment of sixth grade. I'm basically scarred for life now.

"Come on. That was digital," I point out.

He stops the film with an irritated punch of a button and then scrolls it forward in slow motion. I peer over his shoulder into the viewfinder.

The frame looks grubby from smoke and low light, just as I remember the room. I see my own shape in the background, fiddling with the microphone. I can pretty much make out most of the people I remember being there—the guy in the Rangers jersey, the banker dude, the teenage girl with her baby. The focus hazes in and out as Tyler adjusts the lens. The camera zeroes in on the tabletop, with its hunks of crystal and its plastic Ouija pointer thing. Then the frame vibrates, and I see Tyler's shoulder move into the frame, gesticulating to me.

I narrow my eyes, watching. Me-on-film rolls his eyes, leans the boom mike in the velvet curtains, and climbs around the edge of the room. This is all how I remember it. The camera stays on the tabletop, where not much is happening. All at once an eye looms into view, and Tyler stops the film.

"See?" he says, as if the source of his irritation should be obvious.

The eye—Tyler's, I can tell by the almond shape, short lashes, and the heavy liner—hovers in an angry blur, staring at us.

"I don't see what the problem is." I yawn and check my watch.

"Wait," Tyler says.

He starts the film again. The eye disappears. The camera moves a little, as though someone is fiddling with the tripod under it. In the edge of the frame, the medium—Blavatsky—winds a scarf around her head, and people start finding their seats. I notice Maddie, wedged at the table between two khaki moms. She gives a knowing smile to the camera, and then she looks away. A finger twirls in her hair.

"Listen," I say, my mind on my own workshop film, and also on a seven-layer burrito from Taco Hell. "It's getting late."

33

"Here," Tyler says, not listening. He stops the film again. "Look."

It's me, moving back around the table. There are so many people gathered around that it's hard to see me through the crowd of bodies. I come to a stop, leaning forward. So far, I'm not seeing anything weird. Then, the medium dims the lights, throwing the room into candlelight.

"See?"

"Tyler." I'm getting sick of this. My stomach growls in agreement. "I'm gonna go."

"Hang on." He fumbles with the Steenbeck, and the film starts spooling again through the reels.

"The film is fine. Everything looks fine. You just have to decide what you're going to use. I can't keep sitting here waiting for you to make a decision."

Tyler glowers at me. I don't think he's used to me not going along with his vision.

"But I can't use *any* of it," he insists.

I stand up, slinging my backpack over one shoulder. Outside the editing room, someone snaps off the light in the hallway. The building has that dead feeling that buildings get when they're emptying of people. Distant voices, and footsteps receding.

"What are you talking about?" I ask him, unable to keep the irritation out of my voice.

"The forms, man." He punches stop again, and the frame freezes.

"You have all the forms."

"I don't have *hers*," he says, lifting his chin at the image on the screen.

When I see it, my scalp tightens, the hair on my arms stands up, and I drop my backpack on my foot with a thud. I realize, too late, that my video camera is in there.

There, hovering in freeze-frame, half obscured behind the velvet

34

curtain, stands the girl with the hipster-curled hair. That milky skin. God. She's so beautiful that for instant I'm afraid I'm going to be sick.

She's peering around the curtain like a little kid playing hide-and-seek. Her hand holds the curtain next to her cheek, and I can just see a pale shoulder where her dress is slipping down. The crease of flesh at the top of her armpit is showing, and the contrast between collarbone and swell of girl flesh momentarily distracts me. Her dark eyebrows are arched, and she's looking at something just offscreen. Her face looks curious, maybe even surprised. She's standing just behind Maddie, who sits in frozen attention, bent over her phone.

"What's she looking at?" I ask. My voice sounds hollow in my ears.

"Who cares?" Tyler says, flicking his fingers against his thumb as though tossing away an invisible cigarette butt. "The point is, I can't put this online unless I have her release. And you didn't get it."

"What?"

"*You didn't get it.* You were too intent on buying pizza for some skank."

I glare at him, a hot burst of rage exploding in my chest. I work my jaw, and my molars grind together.

"You can still present at workshop. Who cares?" I point out.

"Who cares about fucking workshop?" Tyler yells. "Listen, I know this is just, like, summer school for you, or whatever, but you are aware that this is important to me, right?"

I'm surprised and annoyed by how upset Tyler seems. When we met the first day of class he'd made a big thing about how he actually grew up in the city. He called it that, too: *the city.* As if there were only one in the entire world. He knew all the subway lines, and he knew how to hail a taxi, and he taught us not to take the black cars 'cause they'll rip you off, and once he got us into a nightclub by being on the list. And he wasted so much money on film stock, it was ridiculous. I mean, who doesn't shoot digital? You might as well get a thousand dollar bills together and light a campfire with them at the lake. So from the first week I'd assumed he was some rich Manhattan kid who was parked in summer school so his parents could get him out of the co-op while they got divorced in peace. There're people like that in Madison, too. I just wasn't friends with any of them.

Tyler fixes me in a stare that is boiling with rage, and then looks away. Swallowing my own anger, I lower back into the chair next to him.

"I'm sorry," I manage to say. The words feel sour in my mouth.

Tyler doesn't look at me. He shrugs a dismissive shoulder.

"No, you're right," I force myself to continue. "I said I'd help you with the sound and the releases. You're right. I'm sorry."

I wonder if this will be enough to get him to chill out. I wonder if I will ever have the nerve to put my own work ahead of other people's. I wonder why I let myself get pulled into these situations over and over again.

Tyler meets my gaze. For a second I'm worried he's going to cry, and the possibility makes me panicky because I don't know what I'm supposed to do, and because I know he'd be angry at me for seeing that, and he'd be a dick to me afterward.

He takes a long breath.

"Okay," he says at length.

"Okay," I agree, though I'm not entirely sure what I'm agreeing to.

"At least she wasn't blocking the whole shot like I thought," he goes on, wiping his eye with a fist. "She doesn't turn up until that part at the end. It means I can use all the table shots for transition."

"Yeah." I nod. Something vaguely bothers me about this. But I'm not sure what.

"My workshop's in three days, so you should have plenty of time."

Tyler slides a blank form across the table to me. The frozen image of the girl with hipster-curls hair hovering in the editing deck view-finder seems to be looking at me. Her mouth is open as if she's about to say something, or like she's trying to get my attention.

"I should have plenty of time? I mean, I have a bunch more interviews to do and I've gotta dub in my music and stuff, but yeah, I'll finish." I eye the form without picking it up.

"No," Tyler says slowly. "Plenty of time to find *her*."

"How the hell am I supposed to do that?"

"How should I know? Ask the medium. She had to pay, right? Maybe her name's on a receipt. It's up to you."

There's no way I'm going to do that. I stand up again, leaving the form on the table.

"Tyler, I said I was sorry," I say. I pick up my backpack and feel around inside it to make sure the camera is okay. It is. No shards, anyway.

"I heard you." Tyler glares up at me.

"Come on, man. What else can I say? You were right. Honestly, I don't see what the big deal is."

"The big deal . . ." He's clearly getting super-pissed at me. It occurs to me that he might have been indulging in fantasies of crushing my nose at the same time that I was fantasizing about crushing his. "Is that I've got a shot at gallery representation. Okay? Do you have any idea what that means?"

I actually do have some idea what that means. Not that I believe him.

"You're kidding."

"Do I look like I'm kidding?" Tyler stares up at me, hard.

"What kind of gallery representation?" I ask with suspicion.

I'm not about to go combing the streets of New York City just so that he can have his crap experimental film shown in some basement art space owned by the daughter of one of his dad's banker friends.

I'm sick of propping up his fantasy life. We both know Tyler's going to go back to school in the fall and switch his major to business administration and stop wearing eyeliner and that's going to be the end of it. Then he'll use the fact that he once majored in film as a way to pick up PR girls when he gets off at night from his i-banker job. I've only been in New York for, like, five weeks, and I already understand how Tyler's life is going to unfold. I'd put money on it.

Sometimes, I hate him for it.

"I met this girl who works at Gavin Brown, okay? Last week, at this opening. I was telling her about *Shuttered Eyes*, and she said she wants to see the cut when it's done. She needs to see it *on my website*." He stares at me with begging eyes.

"Gavin Brown?" I say with surprise. "Are you serious?"

Tyler nods.

"Like, *Gavin Brown*, Gavin Brown?"

I can't hide that I'm impressed. That's a real place. It gets people in the Whitney Biennial. Art collectors, real ones, actually buy stuff at Gavin Brown. And they want Tyler's art film? How is that even possible? I catch myself wondering if maybe Tyler has some talent that I haven't seen. But by looking at him I can tell that Tyler knows this is real. This is probably the most real thing that has ever happened to him.

Sometimes, it's hard to know opportunity when it happens, Gran said when she gave me the tuition money. At the time, I thought she was kidding.

Slowly Tyler holds out the image-release form to me.

"I have so much left to do, Wes. For serious. I have to edit all the different film stocks into one file and I haven't even picked my music yet. As it is, I don't think I'll be sleeping between now and workshop. I'm gonna run out of time. But you've got a week longer than me before yours is due. Please? I won't make it otherwise."

He looks truly pathetic. Wheedling, almost.

I hesitate.

Then I take it.

"No promises," I say.

"Thank you," Tyler says, relief flooding his face. "No, seriously. Thank you."

I shake my head, loathing myself for being such a pushover. But one thought flickers at the edge of my consciousness, and mollifies me as I stuff the release form into my backpack.

Her, whispers the thought, and a delicious tremor travels up my spine.

That girl. With the dark eyes. That untouchable girl.

Now I have a reason to find her.

CHAPTER 5

I feel pretty pleased with myself for trying the image search, I'm not going to lie. So it's a real letdown when it doesn't work.

I spent the rest of that night dubbing in The xx to *Most*. There's a wonderful yearning quality to that band, so even though it's pretty old, I wanted to use it anyway. One of the people in my documentary is an old guy, Charles, who I found playing chess in the park. His face is incredible. Deep lines, like troughs on either side of his mouth. Sunburned to the color of mahogany. He's in a knitted wool hat even though it's July. What he wants most is to fly on the Concorde, which is impossible since the Concorde doesn't exist anymore, except for the one you can visit on the pier next to *Intrepid*. But the way he talks about it, the speed, the pointed nose . . . Charles thinks about flying on the Concorde every day. He hunches over the chessboard in the park, winning twenty dollars a game, and in his ears all he hears is a sonic boom of the impossible. I edit and edit, earbuds in, and it's not until I pull the earbuds out of my ears and hear the sleepy chirping of sparrows in the ginkgo trees outside my window that I realize it's five in the morning.

"Oh my God." I moan.

I lean back in my desk chair and rub my forehead with my fingers.

Eastlin hasn't come home. I consider texting him to make sure he's okay, but then I remind myself that Eastlin is totally ripped and is probably safer cruising guys in clubs than I would be trying to buy a pierogi at Veselka by myself. Whatever, I text him anyway, a quick **Everything cool?** And then I loll my head on the back of my desk chair, staring at the ceiling.

Divots. Acoustical tile. God, I'm so tired.

That form. Tyler.

That girl.

How in the hell am I going to find that girl?

I pull out my phone again and stare at it for a long minute, thumbing through different apps. When my thumb hovers over Twitter, I feel a lurch in my chest.

Maddie.

Maddie probably knows the hipster-curls girl. Right? Maddie said she goes to that palm reader all the time. To sleep, she said. Which is a weird thing to say, now that I think about it. Maybe she was joking.

I chew the inside of my cheek, thinking.

I haven't messaged Maddie back, and it's been a week. It's not that I didn't want to. I did want to. A lot. I just couldn't think of something funny to say. I fully intended to text her back within a couple of hours, as soon as I could think of something good. I thought of just saying *Hey*, but that didn't seem good enough. Then before I realized that was happening, three days had gone by, and then five, and then it was just way too much time and I felt like an asshole. This always happens to me. I put off something that I want to do because I want it to be really awesome, and I'm afraid of getting it wrong. I want it to be awesome so bad that I mess everything up by waiting.

I consider texting her a photo of something, and look around my dorm room. What, I'm going to text her a picture of Eastlin's skinny jeans in a heap on the floor? Yeah, no.

I can't ask Maddie.

But thinking about Maddie reminds me how Maddie found out who I was.

I see you, Wes.

I see you.

"Okay," I say aloud to myself. "That's what I'll do."

After three hours of fitful sleep on my face I finally drag myself out of bed and over to Tisch. I'm already waiting for the elevator when I notice that I'm still wearing the same clothes as yesterday. In fact, it occurs to me that I'm not 100 percent sure when I last changed them. Or showered. I eye the security guy who checks our IDs, and when he's distracted by his copy of the *Post* I take a surreptitious sniff of my armpit.

Oh, man. It's bad.

"Morning, Wes," says a voice while my nose is still in my T-shirt collar.

"Oh!" Dammit. I pull down the tail of my T-shirt and cross my arms over my chest. Hopefully that will keep the worst of the funk under control. "Morning, Professor Limoncelli."

The head of the film department flares her nostrils at me. I'm not sure if she can tell I slept in my clothes.

"You ready for documentary workshop next week?" she asks lightly.

God, it's already Wednesday. I am so screwed.

"Um," I stammer. She intimidates the hell out of me. "Yeah, I think so. Just about."

"What's yours called again?" She gazes up at the elevator the way people do when they think they can hurry it along by mental telepathy.

"*Most,*" I tell her. "It's kind of a documentary meditation on desire? Where I, you know. Talk to people? And they tell me what they want the most."

I think she's suppressing a smile, but I can't tell if that's really happening or if I'm just being paranoid.

Could the elevator be taking any longer? I thought getting here by eight I'd avoid everyone. But the elevators here are famous for being slow. Already some grad students have come shuffling in with their huge Starbucks cups and a few other professors are milling around looking at their watches and Professor Limoncelli is smiling at me like she can tell I was up editing all night.

"Sounds interesting," she says, turning back to gaze up at the elevator numbers as they fall one at a time. All at once I realize that I'll have to stand next to her all the way up to our floor if I get on the elevator. That is completely impossible. That will make me completely freak out.

"Thanks!" I chirp. "Me, too. I, um. Actually, I realize I forgot something, so . . . yeah."

I start edging away. The elevator arrives with a ping and everyone starts loading on.

"Okay." She smiles. "See you Friday."

"Yeah! Yeah. See you."

The second the doors ding closed I turn on my heel and run for the stairs. I catch the security guard laughing behind his newspaper.

I'm winded when I get to the hall outside the editing room, where the student lockers are, and it takes me a second to remember the combination to Tyler's locker. After some yanking and fumbling I get the lock open and then his 16 millimeter film is in my hands.

I don't have a lot of experience with actual film. I shoot all my stuff digitally, since it's so much cheaper. But Tyler thinks it's a "more authentic encounter with memory and consciousness," or so he said on our first day in class. Pretentious ass. He probably got that out of a back issue of *Film Comment*. But God, Gavin Brown. Damn. A part of me feels envious. A large part, if I'm honest. I mean, it's not like I came to New York thinking I'd bust my way into the art scene. Then again. Can it hurt, if you're a documentary filmmaker, to have a friend big in the New York art scene?

Assuming Tyler is my friend.

I load the film into the Steenbeck and spool it forward, slowly, rewatching all the footage that Tyler showed me last night.

Just before the end, I freeze frame the film and sit back in my chair, staring.

There she is. I can just see her in the background, drawing the curtain away from her face. Looking off to the side, like she's trying to get someone's attention.

I wonder what she's looking at.

I nudge the film forward another frame or two, trying to get the angle of her face just right. It takes a minute of tinkering back and forth.

There. After the séance is over and someone turns the lights on in the parlor, I can see her best. That pale skin. The little mole on her upper lip. The curls over her ears are glossy and thick. Her face is turned partway toward the camera, and her mouth is open like she's calling out to someone.

I pull my phone out of my shorts pocket, hold it as steady as I can, and snap a picture. A film still.

"Okay, hipster girl." I say to myself in a fake Bond-villain accent. "Let's see who you really are."

I share the picture to Google on my phone and hit search.

The waiting circle spins for what seems like forever while the results load. While I wait, I start rewinding Tyler's film with a punch of buttons and a whir of tape. The girl with the hipster curls blurs out of existence.

I've tucked the film reel back into its canister and am about ready to leave when I check my phone for the search results.

And the results are—nothing.

Well, not nothing, obviously. The results are hundreds upon hundreds of pictures of random girls, none of whom even remotely look like the girl with the hipster-curls hair. I frown, scrolling through all the glurge spat out from the farthest reaches of the internet. How can there not even be one? No Facebook? No Instagram? No drunk selfie with a bunch of other girls dressed like slutty witches on Halloween? Nothing from high school, even? My Facebook is like a permanent repository of all my worst high school moments— bad hair. Zits. My ex-girlfriend, who tags everything to make sure I see it. That's one reason I never check it anymore.

"Huh," I say aloud.

I sift through pages of anonymous girls grinning into cameras, arms around each other's necks, fingers flashing peace signs. So many girls, and none of them are the girl with the hipster-curls hair.

Deep into page six of the search results, I almost recognize someone. I squint at the phone, trying to figure out where I know her from. This girl is blond, and grinning into the camera like all the others. She's pink-cheeked and fleshy in an appealing, healthy way. She looks really young, like fifteen. It's from a defunct-looking Facebook page that is all set to private except for the profile picture. The girl's name is Malou, which seems like a name I'd remember if I'd ever heard it, which I haven't. I know that I recognize her, though. Not from Madison. I just can't put my finger on where I've seen her before.

I save Malou's picture to my gallery and flip back to the film still.

When I look at it, there's a strange heaviness that comes into my chest, and for a minute I'm worried I'm going to cry, which is stupid because there's nothing wrong. The girl hovers there, an image of an image, looking off to the side like she desperately wants to catch someone's attention.

Someone who's just out of shot, to the right of the frame, trying to stay out of the camera's way.

Someone who, I realize in a dizzying rush of certainty, is probably me.

CHAPTER 6

The Bowery looks different during the day. Maybe it's because I was up all night, and it's still pretty early, but I have the hallucinatory feeling that I'm floating above the sidewalk as I walk. The thin light of summer morning brings things into sharp relief that I never noticed before. A restaurant with overturned chairs on the tables. A taxi, light on, idling by the curb. A lumpy sleeping bag rolled up against a doorway, with two dirt-crusted feet sticking out the end.

My dad told me that I shouldn't go to the Bowery. He said that's where all the flophouses are, the ones where homeless men pay five bucks to sleep in chain-link enclosures, caged like animals. He told me about his one night of glory playing CBGB, sitting in with some guys he met through the girl he was crashing with. He saw Television and Blondie play in person.

I guess Dad really hasn't been back to the city in a while, because other than the line of homeless guys snaking out of the mission waiting for breakfast, the Bowery looks pretty plush to me. Fancy bars I can't afford. High-end furniture shops. There's even a Whole Foods.

I reach the corner of Bowery and Bleecker, and hesitate. Nothing looks familiar. The night I went along with Tyler I just got in the cab with him and our film equipment. I was so worried about forgetting something that I didn't pay any attention to where we were going.

A leggy girl prances by, still dressed up from the night before, probably on a walk of shame, not that she looks ashamed. Her makeup is all sex-smudged. She eyes me but doesn't say anything as she passes.

"Hey, excuse me?" I call out to her.

She pauses, far enough away that I have to raise my voice. City girls are wary. I guess I don't blame them. She doesn't know I'm not a skeeze.

"Um. Do you know where there's a pizzeria around here?" I shout.

"Are you serious?" she says. Probably because there's a pizzeria across the street from us. Just not the right one.

"Yeah, sorry. Not that one. The one I'm looking for has a palm reader upstairs from it?"

She doesn't even dignify that one with an answer, just shakes her head in disgust and walks away.

"'Kay. Thanks," I call to her retreating back.

I wander south, watching as the city around me begins to shake off sleep. A guy comes out of a bodega on the corner and starts hosing down the sidewalk. From the steam rising up where the water runs into the gutter I can tell it's going to be hot today. Sticky hot.

When I get to First Street, I pause.

There it is. It's not actually on Bowery, turns out, it's just off it, around the corner. I don't know why I didn't remember that.

The no-name pizzeria is still shuttered for the night, metal security gate down and padlocked, zigzagged with faded graffiti tags that read LUDDITZ 4 EVA. The z looks like a lightning bolt. Upstairs in the picture window the neon sign that says PALMISTRY CLAIRVOYANT PSYCHIC TAROT $15 is lit, but that doesn't necessarily mean anything.

I guess I should have called or something to see if they were open. That didn't even occur to me.

I'm so busy worrying about whether or not the place is open that I'm basically standing right in front of it before I notice that there's someone sitting on the stoop.

It's a small person, a girl, curled in a ball, arms and face tucked behind updrawn knees. All I can see is the stark-white part of her hair, her knees draped in what looks like a nightgown, two slippered feet sticking out from under a frayed hem, and her rounded back. The figure is rocking back and forth softly, sleepily, and she doesn't seem to notice that I'm there.

"Hey," I say as I approach.

I'm on the point of asking what time the place upstairs opens when the figure raises her face and stares at me.

The eyes are formless puddles of black.

It's her.

"Oh!" I exclaim. I take a step backward in shock, my scalp tightening, and the hair on my arms stirs with electricity.

She looks exactly as I remember her, the curls over her ears, the pale cream skin. The mole, God, that mole! But in the morning light she looks even more . . . It's like she captures the light. Like it moves through her, and gathers within her, and makes her exude a fragile glow. I swallow and realize that I'm staring, and I haven't said anything, and that's totally weird, and I'm probably freaking her out. When I open my mouth to speak I discover I've been holding my breath.

She looks at me. Confused, like she's been asleep. Or maybe she came out to get the paper, and forgot her keys, and she's locked out. She obviously wasn't planning on talking to some guy on the stoop before she's even had any coffee. She blinks, and the tiny movement over her eyes shakes me loose from myself and I get it together to actually say something.

"Hey! Hi!" I say. Smooth, Wes. You are so, so smooth. You are so smooth, you could give glass lessons.

What? What does that even mean? I think in a panic.

At first she looks taken aback. Like I surprised her. When I speak, though, her face brightens. She even smiles. When she smiles, it unlocks a beam of light in my chest, like I've leveled up in a video game I didn't know I was playing.

Her lips are the color of dried rose petals, and the minute the thought crosses my mind I marvel crazily that I would even come up with a metaphor like that.

"Herschel?" she says.

"Huh?" I ask.

I look around behind me, thinking maybe she's talking to someone else. But the street is empty, save for the guy hosing down the bodega corner and an elderly woman in orthopedic shoes pushing her grocery cart down the sidewalk across the street.

"Oh!" Her eyes grow confused. She shrinks behind her knees.

"Hey, no. I'm sorry. I'm Wes. From the other night. Remember?"

"Wes," she says slowly. She gives me a long, steady look. Studying me. Those dark eyebrows knit over her eyes. A little wrinkle forms between them, and it might be the most enticing wrinkle I have ever seen. My mouth goes dry.

"Yeah. Um. I was here with that other guy? Filming the séance. Last week?" My eyes search into hers. She has to remember.

"The séance," she repeats, thinking. It's like she doesn't know what to do with the word I've given her. Then her black eyes glimmer with recognition, and I feel my pulse thud in my throat. "Oh yes! I remember. Of course."

She sounds uncertain, though. There's definitely something off about her. Like she's saying the right things because she's practiced, not because it's what she really means. It crosses my mind that maybe this girl is hiding something. Maybe she's like Maddie. Maybe she goes there to sleep, too.

Or maybe she's, like, *on* something.

I peer at her more closely, and she smiles prettily up at me. The eyes are definitely bottomless, but not in a druggy way. When she smiles, her mouth looks like a bow on top of an expensive present.

"Are you okay?" I ask.

"Okay. I was just waiting," she says, tipping her head to the side as she looks up at me.

"I was actually hoping I'd see you again," I say without thinking it through first.

"You were?" Her smile widens. She's blushing, and it makes me dizzy, that I've made her blush.

"Definitely," I say. "In fact, it was absolutely imperative that I find you. Did you know that?" I wonder who this guy is, who's flirting so effortlessly with a hipster New York City girl. Because it's definitely not Wesley Auckerman from Madison, Wisconsin.

"Aw," she says, eyelashes lowering over those black eyes. "You're teasing me. You're not really here."

"Sure I am," I insist. I plop myself down onto the stoop next to her, my knees drawn up, too, my sneakers alongside her slippers. I nudge her with my elbow. She feels firm, fleshy. In that fleeting pressure my elbow finds room between her ribs, and I dig it in gently, to tickle her. She giggles.

"See?" I whisper.

Her tentative smile breaks into a huge grin. She laughs and nudges me back. Her elbow is sharp in my side, but I like it.

"So how did you find me?" she asks. "Wes." She rolls my name around in her mouth, like an unfamiliar flavor.

"It wasn't easy," I confess. "Given that I don't know your name."

She doesn't pick up my gambit. One of her eyebrows draws up into an inquisitive arc.

"Wes," she says again. "Is that a nickname?"

"Maybe," I say, arching my eyebrow back at her.

She bites the inside of her cheek, waiting, but two can play at this game, and I don't pick up her gambit, either. We wait a long beat, daring each other with our eyes. She nudges me in the ribs again, and then we both laugh. When she laughs, her whole face squinches up until the bridge of her nose wrinkles, and I can feel her shoulders shaking where she's pressed against my side. The curls over her ears vibrate from the energy of her laughing, and it's all I can do not to put my arm around her shoulders and pull her to my chest and bury my nose in those curls. But that would be completely crazy, and so I don't.

"So, listen," I say after our laughter subsides to eruptive snorts. "This may sound really weird, but I did have to find you."

"Weird?" she echoes.

"I mean. It's not a big deal or anything," I rush to reassure her.

I go to pull out Tyler's release form from my bag. She watches me rummage in my backpack with interest. I finally find it, smooth it out on my leg because of course it got all crumpled up while I was carrying it around, and then pass it to her.

"I just need you to sign this. I'm sorry. I should have done it when I was here before." I'm feeling foolish now. Like she'll think that I'm just flirting because I want something from her. When actually, I want . . . I want . . .

She looks the release form over, a baffled expression on her face. Then she glances up at me, questions in her eyes.

"I mean . . . ," I fumble. "I'm just as glad I didn't. Remember to get you to sign it, I mean. Before. Because then I had to . . ."

I trail off, staring at her. A long moment falls between us. She's watching me. I can't tell what she's waiting for.

"Anyway," I say, looking back into my backpack as a flush reddens my face. "Here." I hand her a pen.

She takes it gingerly, weighing it in her hand.

"Sign?" she says at length. "But what is it?"

I don't know why she looks so worried and confused. In a flash I wonder if maybe she's famous. What if she's some cable-show teen sensation and I don't know? What if I've been so into my video games and documentaries that she's someone everybody's heard of except me, and people bother her to sign stuff all the time, and I'm being a complete jerk? It would explain the funky hair. And the expensive, high-concept dress. But as soon as the thought blooms into being, I discard it. She would have shown up on my image search, if that were true. Even if the funky hair is new, Google would have found that face. That perfect mole.

God, that mole.

Then I wonder if maybe she's in trouble. Maybe she's run away from home and doesn't want to let on where she is. She certainly wouldn't want to be in some art film on the internet, in that case. That must be it. Maybe I should offer to help her? I could protect her. She's younger than me. Someone as young as her shouldn't be on her own. I bet she has nowhere else to go. That's probably it. She's in trouble. She needs help.

"Seriously. Is everything okay?" I ask gently.

Those black eyes turn to me again. "Is . . . everything . . . okay," she repeats, in the same way that she repeated my name. Like she's trying it out, in her mouth. "Oh. Kay."

"Is it?" I press. I drop my voice to a whisper and say, "You can trust me. It's okay."

She blinks once, twice, and then smiles again. The smile fills her face with light, and I see that I've guessed wrong.

"It caps the climax," she says with a grin. "Got any ink?"

"Um. What?" I'm confused. I don't even understand what she just said.

"Ink?" She peers at the pen, dandling it in her fingers. "You want me to sign it, don't you?"

"Well, yeah, but . . ." I'm not sure what I'm supposed to say at this point and am about to ask her what she means, when she freezes, ears pricking up, listening.

"Are you—" I start to ask her, but she shushes me, pressing her fingers to my lips. My skin tingles where she touches my mouth, and I feel myself growing light-headed. Her fingertips are warm and soft.

"Shhh," she whispers.

She listens intently, her gaze moving to the façade of the building where we're sitting. All I can hear is the faint buzzing of the neon clairvoyant sign, and the abrupt shutoff of the bodega guy's hose at the end of the block. There's a long minute of listening silence, and then her face twitches with recognition, as if she'd just heard someone call her name. But there's nothing. Only the hot summer wind ruffling the pear tree leaves.

I'm about to ask her what's going on when her fingertips disappear from my lips and she leaps to her feet, her dress bunching in her hands. Her ankles look skinny and pale above the slippers on her feet.

"I'm sorry," she says in a rush, dumping the release form and pen in my lap. "I'm sorry, Wes, I've got to go. That's my mother."

"Your—what?"

She's already dashed up the town house stoop and opened the door and started up the stairs that lead to the palm reader, and then I guess to the couple of apartments up above. But I haven't heard anyone. The building is silent, still lost in morning sleep.

"My mother. I'm sorry, I have to go," she calls from inside the vestibule.

"But—" I get to my feet, palms sweaty where they're crumpling the release form. "Hey. Listen. I'm sorry, look, I know you don't know me, but I really need your help with this."

She hesitates on the inside stairwell, one hand on the banister, staring back at me.

"Help?" she says in a small voice.

But then something startles her, and she looks up with urgency to the curve where the stairs disappear into the dark.

I can't stand to let her leave. I want her to stay here on the stoop with me, sitting close, making private jokes and elbowing each other. I mount one of the steps on the stoop, reaching a hand toward her.

"Please?" I say. I'm trying not to beg. It's so not working, though.

"I . . ." She hesitates, torn.

She clearly feels bad about ditching me like this. But she is going to do it anyway.

"Look," I say. "If you have to go right now, I can just wait. Okay? You go do whatever, and I'll just wait down here. It's no big deal. I mean. You won't be long, right?"

"Um . . ." She's almost persuaded.

What else am I going to do with my morning, anyway? Maybe I can hang out in the pizzeria, find a couple more people for *Most.* That would be pretty cool. Maybe she'd want to be in it. Maybe she'd let me film that bowlike mouth with its perfect mole talking, and talking, telling me what she wants most in the world.

"Please?" I say, more softly this time, my eyes pleading.

She chews her lip, hand still on the banister, considering. All at once, she relents. I can see it in her face. I have to suppress the urge to fist-pump in the air.

"All right," she whispers. "Wait down there. I'll be back as soon as I can."

"Okay," I say. I'm grinning like I've just won Powerball. "Okay. I'll be right here."

She smiles at me and turns to hurry up the stairs.

"Wait!" I call out, and she stops, looking over her shoulder.

"I don't know your name. What's your name?" I don't even care if I sound desperate. I can't let her get away again.

She hesitates, but only for a second, and then she smiles.

"Annie," she says. "I'm Annie."

Then she's gone.

CHAPTER 7

I think what I'd really like is my own place," the pixelated kid says. "I been living with my moms since I got out of school, right? And she's just . . . You know, she's on my case all the time."

The frame is tight on his face, his nose the same aquiline one I've seen on ancient Roman sculpture busts at the museum uptown. Heavy eyelashes, wavy dark hair. I zoom out about 20 percent so I can show the pizza ovens behind him and get the deadening quality of the fluorescent light. His white T-shirt is soft from washing.

"Where would you live?" I ask. "When you move out from your mom's."

He shrugs and his eyes slide to the right, over my shoulder. "I mean, the city, right? I'd like to get out of Jersey. You know. Get some sweet place downtown, like a loft? With a doorman, yo. Then when I roll up in my Lambo, with some tight little model, you know? I just throw him the keys. Forget about it."

The kid smiles, gazing into his daydream. The digital video camera whirs softly, and I zoom back in, very slowly.

"Hey!" the older guy at the register hollers. "You got people waiting. What's the matter with you?"

Shaken out of his reverie, the kid's face darkens. He looks down, then back up at me.

"We done?" he asks, with a new challenge in his eyes.

"Yeah," I say, shutting the camera off. "We're done. Thanks. That was awesome."

"You gonna put that on TV or something? Am I gonna be famous?" The kid grins. He's kidding. Mostly.

"As if anyone wants to see you, on the television. This guy," the older man behind the register says to a woman he's ringing up for a soda and two slices. She rolls her eyes.

"Nah," I say. "Sorry. It's a project. For school."

"Oh." He's hiding his disappointment, and now I feel guilty for filming him for *Most*. Like I shouldn't have gotten his hopes up.

"I mean," I stammer. "It's hard to say, you know?"

"Oh yeah." The kid shrugs me off. "Sure."

He turns his back to me, ladling out tomato sauce in an expert circle of red on raw dough, showering it with cheese, placing pepperoni like punctuation marks to show that our conversation is over.

I check my phone.

12:32.

I blow an irritated sigh through my nose and lean my cheek against the pizzeria window for probably the thirtieth time, looking at the door to the apartments upstairs. I don't know how much longer I can wait here. I mean, I sat on the stoop for an hour 'til they opened, and I've been parked in here ever since. I've bought about a slice an hour, and now my belly is sticking out a little over the waistband of my cargo shorts. I still haven't showered, my hair is sticking up in all different directions from having been slept on, my chin is bristly, and I think I'm starting to look kind of sketchy, hanging out here all day.

But I told Annie I'd wait.

So I've been waiting.

"This guy," the register guy says again. I don't pay any attention. "What, he thinks real estate is free in New York?"

There's a pause, and then I feel eyes on my back.

"Huh?" I say.

"You gonna sit in here all day?" the guy barks at me. Having abused his underling enough, I guess now it's my turn. He must be really great to work for. Man.

"Um . . ." I pause, trying to come up with the right response. I guess it's whatever keeps my ass from getting kicked.

Dammit. I told her I would wait here 'til she came back. I can't stand the thought of breaking my word to her. Anyway, I need her to sign the stupid form. This guy is thinking about rearranging my face into a Cubist painting, and it's all for nothing.

"This is a respectable business, you know," the guy continues.

"Paul," the Roman-looking kid says, putting a hand on his sleeve. "He's been buying slices. He's okay."

I spread my hands in a what-can-I-do? sort of gesture, and smile my most apologetic, nice-guy-from-the-Midwest smile. I don't know if those really work in New York, though. Paul glares at me. So much for my big plan of interviewing Paul to kill more time.

"Sorry," I mutter. I pull out my phone, checking for I don't know what. Do I think she'd have texted me? It's not like she knows my last name.

Instead, I find half a dozen texts from Tyler, wanting to know where I am and what's happening. If I don't get the release he has to cut the footage she's in, and he's running out of time before fiction workshop, and he's going to kick my ass and I'd better text him back.

Great. Just really terrific.

I stuff my camera into my backpack, toss a dollar onto the Formica countertop next to my greasy napkins and stack of paper plates, and slink out of the pizzeria. But on the stoop I hesitate.

I mean, I can't just *leave*.

I try the door to the town house, but it's locked. Outside the front door there's a row of brass mail slots, the kind that open with a small key, and an intercom buzzer with peeling paper labels stuck next to each button.

I spend a long minute inspecting the buzzer, daring myself to push one of the buttons and get let in. There's one that says FATIMA, which I think is for the palm reader. Then there's one that says EIN-BERG, with the first letter missing, and one that says HERNANDEZ in pretty cursive. The other four are either blank, or whitened from rain.

I cup my hands around my eyes and peer into the stairwell, blocking out the yellow summer sun. Honestly, other than the palm reader on the second floor, it doesn't look like the apartments are occupied. No window-unit air conditioners jut out over the street. No window propped open with a spinning box fan. No catalogues on the floor. No menus.

I take a deep breath, roll my head back and forth on my shoulders to loosen up, and push my thumb against one of the unlabeled buzzers.

Nothing happens.

"Dammit," I say aloud, stepping back to look up at the indifferent façade of the town house. It stares back at me, giving away nothing.

I don't understand. She definitely hasn't left. I'd have seen her. I was sitting right by the pizzeria window. I had a clear view of the apartment building door. I watched the door the entire time, even when I was filming the Roman kid.

I push the buzzer labeled EINBERG.

Nothing.

"Ha," a voice laughs behind me. "Good luck with that."

"Huh?" I spin, startled.

I'm met with the amused expression of Maddie, in cutoffs and ripped fishnets and combat boots and tank top. Her bangs perfectly straight, hair braided into Princess Leia coils around her ears. She's laughing at me, and I'm gripped with irrational panic, like she's caught me doing something wrong.

"Making social calls?" she asks me, eyebrows arched. "I hope you've got a calling card. There's nobody here."

"What do you mean?" I ask, staring back into the depths of the stairwell.

"I mean, there's Fatima Blavatsky's. But the rest of the building's empty."

Her smile is getting mischievous, mainly by seeming to take over one side of her mouth more than the other. She shifts the grocery bag she's carrying onto her hip, cocking a combat boot out in defiance.

"Empty? Are you sure?" It comes out more suspicious than I mean. But I can't tell if she's just trying to mess with my head. I mean, I *saw* Annie go inside.

"Oh yeah," she says. "I'm sure."

Empty? So where did Annie go, if it was empty? If she wanted to brush me off, she could have just said no. I hear no from girls all the time. More often than not. My ex-girlfriend could say no like it was going out of style. Why would Annie pretend to like me if she didn't?

"How do you know?" I ask.

Maddie sighs and puts the grocery bag down at her feet, stretching her arms overhead. I can hear her spine pop when she stretches.

"I know," she says patiently, "because I was squatting here until three weeks ago. Then they came through and cleared everybody out."

"You were . . . What?" I'm confused. She seems kind of young to not have anywhere to live.

61

Maddie shakes her head, dismayed by how dense I am. "Squatting. I told you. Come on. I'll let you carry the bag, and then if you're really nice, you can buy me breakfast."

"But—" I start to protest.

Maddie's already picked up her grocery bag, which upon closer inspection mostly contains takeout boxes and spotted fruit, and started walking back down the steps to the sidewalk.

"Hurry up," she calls to me.

I glance one last time into the deserted stairwell, disappointment crushing the breath out of me, pulling my mouth down. I don't understand. I thought we were . . . I really . . . She must have felt it. How could she not have felt it, too?

I sling my bag over my shoulder, shake my head, and turn away.

For a minute Maddie and I trudge along together in silence. The street is busy now, crowded with people picking up lunch, striding with purpose from one place to another. In New York everyone's in a hurry all the time.

"I can't believe she ditched me like that," I finally grumble, unable to stop myself.

Maddie looks sidelong at me, and then snorts.

"It's a shocker," she agrees. "Me? I'm shocked."

"I'm so screwed. Now I can't get her to sign my thing. She just ditched me! God!" The complaints crowd out of me, one on top of the other, and only then do I realize I'm actually angry.

"What thing?" Maddie asks lightly.

We're walking south, gradually wending our way east. And then farther east.

"This stupid release form. It's not even my film! I don't know why I care," I spit. Of course, it's not the release that's making me upset. I feel stupid, letting Annie see how much I liked her.

"Show me," Maddie says, stopping by the gate to an austere cemetery. It looks like nobody's been in there for a long time. There's a historic plaque and everything. A marble angel with outspread wings watches our conversation between gnarls of ivy.

I prop my camera bag on my thigh, fish out the crumpled paper, and hold it out for her to inspect. In a glimmer the grocery bag is in my arms and she's holding the release form.

"Oh yeah. I signed one of these for that guy. Your friend. He was a real dick about it. Got a pen?"

"In there," I say, nodding at my backpack. The grocery bag is heavy. It smells like all different kinds of leftovers mixed together, Indian and Thai and collard greens and maybe matzoh ball soup. Glass bottles clink around in the bottom.

Maddie pulls out a pen from my backpack, which is somehow now over her shoulder instead of mine, and says, "Turn around."

Obediently, I turn my back to her.

"What's her name?" I hear the click of the pen.

"Annie," I say, and when I say it, something weird happens in my chest and then I'm embarrassed, as if someone might have seen.

"Annie what?"

"Um . . . ," I stammer, because I have no idea, and yet it seems impossible that I don't know.

"Oh, for Pete's sake. You're ridiculous." I feel the pen press between my shoulder blades, and then Maddie is waving the paper under my nose. "There. Happy?"

It says *Annie Cinders* in loopy cursive.

"How did you know her last name?" I ask, amazed.

Maddie gives me a coy look. "I didn't. That's *my* last name."

"Your last name? But what if . . ."

"Oh my God. WES. Nobody cares!"

63

Maddie shoves my pen in the pocket of her cutoffs and moves off down the street, hot summer sunlight painting white stripes across her shoulders and hair. Her hair looks even blacker in the day than it did the night I met her, like it swallows the light. I have to hurry to catch up. She's still carrying my backpack over her shoulder. From behind I can see the laurel leaf tattoo wrapping around her neck, coiling up under her hair.

"I guess Tyler won't know," I muse. "It's not like the gallery's going to check."

I fish my phone out of my shorts pocket and text Tyler a cryptic note that the paper is signed. Immediately the phone vibrates with a text returned that just says **K**.

"Tyler. He's the guy from the other night, right?" she asks.

"Yeah." I'm getting winded from how fast we're walking, but I don't want Maddie to notice.

"He seemed like kind of a tool," she remarks.

I laugh before I can help myself.

"Yeah, well," I demur. "He's got a *vision*. You know. He can't let little things like being cool to other people get in the way."

Now it's Maddie's turn to laugh.

"Oh yeah. Me, neither." She stops, noticing a pizza box on top of an open garbage can. Before I register what's happening she's opened the pizza box, discovered half a pineapple pie inside, and hollered, "Score!"

"What?" My stomach lurches with disgust as I watch her fold the pizza half in thirds. She pulls out a couple of paper napkins from her cutoff pocket, does a half-assed job of wrapping it, and stuffs the pizza into the top of the grocery bag.

"They probably just put this out. It's totally fresh!" She grins happily at me. Then she plucks at my T-shirt and says, "Come on."

We walk all Lawrence of Arabia style through the sweltering city, the stench of day-old pineapple pizza filling my nostrils. After all the pizza I'd already eaten that morning, I'm struggling not to retch. Why would she want pizza someone had thrown away? A sour belch rises in my chest and I swallow it back. The effort makes sweat bead on my forehead.

"Where are we going?" I ask after another avenue passes and we're still walking east. I didn't realize the island went this far east. We've passed the numbered avenues and are well into letters.

"Home. Ish. I've got to drop this stuff off, and then you can buy me a thank-you breakfast."

"Oh," I say.

"*Thank you, Maddie* is what you meant to say," she corrects me in a singsong voice.

"Um . . . ," I start to say again, because that is absolutely the way I usually am, with girls, when Maddie finally stops up short outside a decrepit brownstone on Avenue D, across from a huge housing project. The building is condemned, with a red rectangle with a white X sign in it plastered up to show that it's going to be torn down. The first floor has bars on all the windows, with plywood where the glass should be, and the front door is made of metal. It looks locked down tight. There's an orange sheriff department eviction notice stuck to the door.

She marches up the front steps and eases the door open with an elbow. Turns out it's not locked at all. The sheriff department seal is a fake.

"Honey!" she calls into the house. "I'm home!"

I hesitate on the stoop, clutching Maddie's scavenged groceries to my chest. I'm sweating, both from the heat, and from nerves. Am I really going to follow this girl into an abandoned house? Who knows what's in there. Mice. Rats. Homeless people. Slowly it occurs to me that if she's squatting, that means Maddie's probably homeless.

Homeless people make me nervous, which is the kind of thing it's not cool to admit, so I usually don't, but it's true. Anyway, I should be getting back. I've got to get my workshop film done for next week. And I'm exhausted and freaked out and crushed from Annie's ditching me for no reason and all I really want to do is sleep.

I look left. I look right. Nothing is amiss. A black kid pedals up the street on a low-rider bicycle, his knees rising and falling, one hand relaxed on the handlebars. Merengue plays on a radio a block away. A rush of miserable anger floods my chest as I think about Annie leaving me on the stoop. I don't understand why she didn't come back. What's wrong with me? I'm nice! Too nice, maybe. Letting people push me around. Letting people keep me waiting. Well, to hell with that.

Resolved, I set my jaw and march up the stairs and inside the abandoned building, bringing the bag of scavenged food with me.

CHAPTER 8

I t had been an actual house, I'm pretty sure. But now it's like I've stepped into a scene from *The Matrix*, except I'm in cargo shorts instead of a patent-leather trench coat and shades. This had once been a nice hallway, narrow, wood floors, with a skinny staircase stretching up to the second story. Huge patches of plaster have peeled off the lathing and fallen from the walls. Treads have been pried from the stairs, open to a black chasm beneath. Pale patches suggest places where architectural remnants—plaster trim, light fixtures, whatever—have been ripped off the walls and sold. A puffy-lettered spray paint mural winds up the stairwell, reading MADCINDERZ in wild style.

I'm gawking, I realize, but I hear footsteps in the dim room to my right, which I guess was once the living room. The windows are boarded up, so what little light there is struggles through chinks in the boards and walls. It smells old, like rotted wood. The light makes patterns of spots across the floor and the walls, and in those spots glitter clouds of dust.

"In here, Miss Madness!" another female voice trills from deep within the bowels of the house.

Suddenly I'm itching to be looking at this scene through my video camera.

"Maddie?" I ask the dim interior.

I follow the sound of footsteps and voices, creeping forward, worried about stepping on a nail. Or a mouse. Or God knows what.

"Check it out! Pizza!" Maddie cries to the other girl.

I round the corner to find Maddie and a wisp of a black girl in giant platform goth boots standing in a room furnished with a stained mattress, a 1950s aluminum kitchen table, a couple kerosene lanterns, a scented candle (grapefruit? weird), a turntable with one huge 1970s speaker, a milk carton full of record albums, a stained corduroy beanbag chair, and a hot plate. There's a naked lightbulb dangling overhead, fed by an extension cord that tangles across the floor and out a broken window, but the bulb isn't turned on. Someone's painted a huge anarchy sign on the wall in white house paint. It's a nice touch.

"Oooooh. And a delivery boy," the wisp says with a leer. She runs her tongue over her teeth as she smiles at me.

My backpack is resting on the kitchen table between them. Blood thuds in my ears with my sudden need to hold the camera safely in my hands. I walk up to them with the grocery bag like I do this kind of thing every day, set it on the table with manful authority, and pick up the camera. Maddie notices how anxious I am, though, and arches her eyebrow at me.

"What'd you get?" the wisp asks Maddie as she rummages in the bag.

"Couple forties. Muttar paneer. Drunken noodles. Oh, and, like, a totally fresh pineapple pizza." Maddie smiles at me through the dark.

"Killer," the wisp says through a mouthful of pizza. She cracks open a forty and swishes the malt liquor in her mouth, gargles with her head tossed back, then swallows.

"It's cute. I don't think Wes here's ever been Dumpster diving before," Maddie remarks.

"Wes, huh? What is that, like, a prep school name?" the wisp jeers.

"I dunno," Maddie says, eyeing me. "Maybe you should ask him."

"Screw him," the wisp says, rummaging deeper in the grocery bag.

While they make fun of me I've been wrestling my camera out of its case and I've fixed it safely to my eye with an exhale of palpable relief. Through the comforting pixels of digital video the scene becomes interesting, instead of scary. I zoom in on the wisp's face. Her hair is bleached a punk yellow-blond, and she wears it gathered into two heavy braids of dreadlocks on either side of her face. She's wearing so much eye makeup she looks like she's been punched in the face.

Or maybe, I realize, she's been punched in the face.

"So is it just you guys, living here?" I ask, hitting record. The camera whirs to life in my hands.

Her cheeks are so thin that I can see the food moving under her skin as she chews. The wisp completely ignores me, thrusting her arm into the grocery bag looking for more leftovers.

"Sort of," Maddie answers me. "We're kind of a collective."

"What kind of collective?" I ask.

My camera hunts for, and then finds, Maddie, who has settled in the beanbag chair, knees knocking together, looking up at me with her head cocked to one side. She's smiling in a way that suggests maybe I'm not as bad as she thought.

"Anarcho-syndicalist fregan," the wisp says through another mouthful of something that I don't want to see. She's started vamping for the camera now, sticking her tongue out, turning one shoulder this way and peeling an edge of T-shirt down to reveal a burnished expanse of tattooed skin.

"What's fregan?" I ask, zooming in to capture the vamping.

She fixes me and my camera in a glare so deadly the pixels seem to vibrate.

"You don't usually bring me such stupid delivery boys," she sniffs to Maddie.

Maddie laughs, hoisting herself out of the beanbag, comes over, plucks my T-shirt, and says, "Come on. You promised to buy me breakfast."

"I did?" I swivel my camera around and train it on her face.

"Yep. Don't you remember?" Her hand has closed over my upper arm with surprising strength, and she's started to drag me bodily away. I wonder if Maddie is rescuing me. Like she can tell how nervous I am.

"Bye-bye, delivery boy!" the wisp slurs. I guess the beer is hitting her. She's pretty small, after all. "Come back later and you can film me some more. If you know what I mean."

"Shut up, Janeanna," Maddie calls over her shoulder, hustling me through the vacant living room and down the hall. Through my camera lens everything is confusion and darkness, and then suddenly we're back outside under the hot summer sun.

Maddie hauls me along as my feet scramble not to trip and I try to stuff the video camera back safely into its bag. A taxi honks as we tumble into the street.

"Hey," I say. "Wait up."

"Hey, yourself," she says. "I want eggs."

"Eggs? Eggs aren't vegan." I'm pleased with myself. I hooked up with this girl in Madison for two glorious weeks last summer who was vegan. She didn't eat dairy or eggs. She wouldn't even eat honey.

It used to really piss her off when I teased her about caring for the feelings of insects.

Maddie rolls her eyes so hard I can almost hear it.

"*Fregan*, Wes. God."

"Yeah, but what's fregan? Nobody's told me yet," I point out.

"It means vegan, unless it's free. You're buying, so it's free. I want eggs. Also, this place is fair trade, so it's okay. Come on."

When I look up I see that we're now in SoHo. The sidewalk is six deep in tourists, skinny girls in little sundresses and huge bug-eye sunglasses. It's hard to believe the burned-out shell of Maddie's squat is five minutes away.

"Maddie?"

"Hmmm?"

"I didn't think they still had squats on the Lower East Side," I say. *It's all Disneyland now,* Dad opines in my mind. *A movie set for people who've watched too much cable television. You should have seen it when I was there.*

She laughs through her nose, steering me into a cavernous natural foods restaurant and then to a booth in the back. It's the first time today I've been in air-conditioning, and the sweat immediately evaporates from my skin, making my scalp tingle with relief.

"Yeah, well." She shrugs, propping her knees up on the edge of the table and looking with interest at the menu. "It's not really a squat, exactly."

"What do you mean?"

A quick scan of the menu reveals that buying breakfast for me and Maddie is going to set me back at least twenty dollars. A twist of anxiety lodges in my stomach, which is already full of pizza anyway.

I just won't eat, then. It's fine.

"It kind of belongs to Janeanna." Maddie shrugs. "Her dad's a developer? His company bought the shell. They're going to tear it down pretty soon. So we sometimes stay there. There's sort of a group of us that comes and goes. Everybody contributes. Everybody's welcome if one of us vouches for you. A collective. Like I said."

"Huh," I remark. "So Janeanna's, like . . ."

Maddie glances up at me with arched eyebrows under her bangs. "What?" she challenges me.

"Nothing," I say.

I was going to say *So Janeanna's loaded*, but that doesn't seem like the right thing to say. Gran always told me it was rude to talk about money. Though in New York it seems like money is all anybody ever talks about. For sure it's all anybody thinks about. I don't know what is the right thing to say, so I go with, "What's your dad do?"

Maddie flares her nostrils and focuses more closely on the menu.

"My dad," she says, "doesn't do a goddam thing."

I sit, watching her browse the menu with unnecessary attention, feeling the cool breath of the restaurant air on my skin, realizing that as soon as I think I understand something, I don't actually know anything at all.

"So what's your movie?" Maddie asks me. It's starting to feel normal, hanging out with her. We had an easy breakfast, laughing and making goofy smiles out of orange slices. She's not as bad as I thought. She's actually pretty cool.

We're back outside on the sidewalk, my wallet thirty bucks lighter, and I'm starting to get antsy. I want to get back and edit in the footage from the guy in the pizzeria, and the stuff I took of Janeanna, and Tyler's been blowing up my phone about something, and anyway, Maddie makes me self-conscious. I don't get why she wants to be hanging out with me. I mean, she's got a *neck tattoo*. She lives on her own in a squat. I'm just some guy.

"It's a documentary," I say, shifting my weight and trying to come up with way to escape.

"What kind of documentary? Can I see it?" she asks. She actually sounds interested.

I've pulled out my phone and I'm scrolling through all the messages I've missed. I come upon the film still I took of Annie and stare at it, not answering Maddie right away. Annie's hovering, gazing off camera at me. She's smiling, trying to tell me something. Something pulls at me, in my chest.

"Wes?"

"Huh?"

I glance up and see Maddie waiting for me to answer her, and she looks so genuinely interested and friendly that an immediate wave of guilt and remorse crashes over my head, drips down my body, and puddles around my feet. She's here, right now. She could've ditched me anytime, but she didn't. Instead she invited me to her weird hangout, and she rescued me from her dissipated rich friend, and then she wanted to have breakfast with me like a completely normal person. Annie's this girl in my imagination. But Maddie is real. She's realer than I am, even.

"Know what?" I say with a rush of inspiration. "I'll do you one better. Come on."

She giggles as I take her hand. We hurry together down the SoHo streets, elbowing aside people laden with shopping bags, dashing in front of a taxicab as it honks to a halt. We turn down Wooster, laughing, breathless, breaking into a run for no reason, and then I pull her through some glass doors and into a space that is gray and hushed and very, very expensive.

"Welcome to Abraham Mas," says a young male voice, and then Eastlin is standing there, looking first surprised, then pleased, and then kind of weirded out, presumably because Maddie and I are soaked with sweat and out of breath and laughing and are probably going to get him in trouble.

"Hey!" I grin at him. "What's up, man? How's it going? You never texted me back."

Maddie is stifling laughter behind her hand. A couple of Fifth Avenue blondes pause their browsing nearby long enough to scope Maddie up and down, exchange a look between themselves, and then turn their backs. Eastlin notices, and I see him notice, but he doesn't say anything.

"Yeah. Um. Not too much. Just working. You know." He eyes Maddie, and then sends me an inquiring look. I know he's asking if this is the girl I was talking about. I glance at her sidelong and then give him a proprietary smile, just so I can enjoy letting him think that maybe it is. Maybe I'll rise in his estimation from "pathetic" all the way up to "lame."

"Yeah. I thought you were gonna be in today. Listen. Is it okay if we film here?" I ask him, resting a hand on Maddie's shoulder. She smiles and shrugs at Eastlin.

"Film? You mean, for your workshop thing?" Eastlin looks kind of nervous. They probably have rules against that. You probably have to get permission from some central office, and fill out a bunch of forms, and pay them a thousand dollars an hour and promise Gwyneth Paltrow will be there.

"Yeah. I want to interview Maddie for *Most*. It'll take two seconds."

"I'm Maddie," Maddie says, helpfully, pointing a finger at her chest.

"Eastlin's my roommate," I explain to her. "He does fashion design."

"Coooool," Maddie approves, drawing the syllable out and nodding.

"Ummm . . . ," Eastlin stalls. He obviously wants us to go away. He scans the store, sliding his hands into his pockets and trying to come up with a reason to get rid of us. The Upper East Side blondes have moved deeper into the back, where they hang all the shirts made of little scraps of oyster-colored chiffon.

"I don't know, Wes," he says finally.

"Come on. Please? It'll be awesome," I plead, rocking on the balls of my feet and jostling my backpack over my shoulder so he can see how excited I am.

"Please?" Maddie echoes, folding her hands under her chin and giving him big, wet eyes like a Dickensian orphan. "What's *Most*?" she asks me out of the side of her mouth.

"Eastlin?" asks a huge, totally ripped guy with an earpiece and a plain black T-shirt that hugs his biceps who has just come looming up behind my roommate. He folds his arms and his chest seems to get twice as big. I have to stifle more laughter. "Everything okay over here?"

"Yeah, Duane. We're cool." Eastlin rolls his eyes ever so slightly, and then seems to make up his mind. To me, he says, "Right this way, sir. Let's see how I can help you today."

He leads us to the middle of the store, past racks of weird dresses that look to me like frayed flour sacks dyed deep eggplant and mauve. I spot Maddie peek at a price tag in the palm of her hand before dropping it like it's on fire.

Eastlin parks us in a dressing room, then closes the velvet curtain behind us and whispers to me "Okay, asshat. That better be her. Also? You owe me." Aloud he says, "Thirty minutes, then, sir? Can we bring you anything? Ice water? Champagne?"

"Thanks, man," I say at the same time that Maddie calls, "Champagne would be great, thank you!"

There's a leaden pause from outside the curtain. Then Eastlin says, "Right away, miss," and his shoes disappear.

"This place is crazy!" Maddie whispers to me, smiling.

"Yeah," I agree. "Don't worry, though. He's cool."

I'm nestling her on the stool in the corner, against heaps of fine netting and chiffon from the clothes they haven't put away yet. The light is perfect. I knew the light in here would be perfect. Some places have light that seems to make every woman more beautiful. I grab one of the flour sack dresses from the hook in the dressing room, and hold it under her chin.

"Know what? You should put this on," I say. It's not really appropriate for a documentarian to costume one of his subjects. But the color is so rich I can't help it.

The burgundy brings out the blue tones in her skin, making her lips look redder. And the texture is so matte and soft that it makes her hair look shinier. I'm so certain of the rightness of it that it's almost creepy. I look down at myself, and note with dismay that no amount of expert lighting can save my cargo shorts from sucking. Eastlin's influence must be rubbing off on me.

"Are you kidding?" She blanches. "Have you seen how much these things cost?"

"So what? We're not buying it." I grin at her. "Please? Pretend like it's a costume. For a play."

She smiles at me, uncertain, holding the dress in her lap. Then she gives in.

"Okay, fine," she says. "I'm going to sweat all over it, though. And you have to step out."

"I'm gone," I say, backing away with my hands raised to show I'm unarmed.

I duck out through the curtain and mosey up to where Eastlin's standing behind the counter at the front, fiddling on an iPad. A flute of champagne fizzes enticingly at his elbow. I can't even wrap my mind around shopping in a store so expensive that they give you champagne while you shop. For free.

Without looking up, he says, "You are not having sex with that goth chick in my dressing room. FYI."

"Don't worry," I reassure him.

"I'm not worried," he says, eyes still on the iPad. "You and I both know that, if necessary, I could beat you to death with your own arm. *I* have nothing to worry about."

He gives me a challenging look and holds it for a long minute. For a split second I can't tell if he's kidding.

Then we both burst out laughing.

"I should start going to the gym," I muse.

"You really should," Eastlin says with pity.

"Listen," I say, leaning my elbows on the counter and craning my neck to look at the iPad. "I've got a favor to ask you."

"Oh, goody!" He gives me a wicked look.

"Sorry." I smile and shake my head. "Not that."

"Don't knock it 'til you've tried it," he says drily. "So what's the favor?"

"Do you think you could try looking up that girl I told you about?" I say. "The one who shops here."

Eastlin glances at the dressing room across the store.

"That's not her?" he asks.

"No, that's someone else."

"I knew that wasn't her." He shakes his head. "I'd remember. God, I'm so over that nineties' torn-fishnets look." He pauses for a moment to regret the rest of the world's bad taste. "All right, fine. What's her name?"

"Annie," I say.

Saying her name out loud makes me light-headed enough that I'm actually glad I'm leaning on the counter. *Annie.* The word feels beautiful in my mouth. As soon as I think that, though, I get embarrassed, like Eastlin might have heard me think it. Is it lame, to look up one girl while waiting for another? It is, isn't it. But it's for Tyler's release, anyway. It's not like I'm trying to find her because I want to hook up with her or anything.

Do I?

"Annie what?" He's poking at the iPad screen.

"I don't know."

Eastlin sighs heavily and rolls his head back on his shoulders. "Wes. Come on."

"What? I didn't ask."

"What's the matter with you?"

"She had to leave in a hurry. I didn't have time to ask her last name."

"Wesley Eugene Auckerman—" he starts.

"My middle name's not Eugene," I interrupt.

"—need I point out to you that in a mere five weeks of roommating I have been laid eleven times, and you have been laid exactly zero?" To emphasize the zero, he holds his finger and thumb in an O shape, looking through it at me.

"Thank you," I say with mock earnestness. "Thank you for pointing that out."

"Anytime." He turns the iPad to face me. "These are all our Annies and Annes. But none of them is her."

"How do you know?" I ask, looking curiously at the list of names and addresses.

"Well, this one's on the board at MoMA, and this one is a director at Goldman Sachs. This one just landed a walk-on in that new paranormal witch movie, and this one . . ." He ticks them off one at a time.

"All right, all right. I get it," I groan. I bring my hands up to my face and rub my eyes with my fingertips.

He turns the iPad back to face him.

"The way I see it is, you have two options," Eastlin tells me. "I suggest the second, which is giving up."

"I can't," I say, and it comes out sounding sort of strangled and desperate, which is not what I intended. "Not possible."

"All right," Eastlin says, eyeing me. "Then we go with option one."

"What's option one?" I ask.

He fixes me with an innocent stare, and says, "Find her some other way. Duh."

"Excellent. This is a good plan. Simple, and to the point. Thank you." I stare at the countertop. I am the pizza of dismay.

He hands me the champagne flute and smiles. "You're welcome."

I start to make my way back to the dressing room, where Maddie is waiting. Maddie. That name feels kind of cool in my mouth, too.

"Seriously, dude," Eastlin calls out to my back. "There're cameras in there."

Back inside the dressing room, champagne stashed on an end table, lighting a perfect rose-colored scatter totally devoid of shadow, I pull out my video camera and train it on Maddie's face. Her eyes are closed, and she's rubbing a cheek against the silk of one of the dresses behind her. I creep nearer, zooming in without zooming in. I let the camera study her, traveling over her half-closed eyes. There's something. Yes. She's very . . . I get in so close that I can't see her Bettie Page bangs anymore or her neck tattoo, just the round planes of her cheeks, and a soft dimple where her smile deepens. She looks different, this close up. Younger. She looks . . .

A laugh erupts out of my mouth, and I pull the camera away from my eye and stare at her in surprise.

"What?" she asks, eyes flying open at the sound of my laughing. "Do I look weird?"

"No, no," I reassure her. "You look good. You look actually . . ." A smile pulls at my cheek while I decide. "Beautiful," I say.

Then I say, "Malou."

She stiffens, her feet scrambling over the dressing room floor as though she's thinking about bolting. But she doesn't. She just stares at me, hard, waiting to see what I'm going to do. I smile at her, and bring the video camera back to my eye. The pixelated image of her face in my viewfinder relaxes. Her cheeks are framed by tulle, and she gazes at me with heavy lids, watchful and steady.

Maybe it wasn't coincidence, Maddie turning up in my image search for Annie. Maybe I've been looking for the wrong girl all along.

"Guilty," she whispers, gazing down her nose at me.

"So tell me, Maddie Miss Madwoman Malou," I whisper, my camera moving over her skin, lingering on her mouth. "Tell me what you want most in the world."

CHAPTER 9

That Friday night, fiction film workshop night, the screening room is packed, and I've never seen Tyler so nervous. The guy is barely holding it together. He's dressed up, for him, in skinny black jeans with a rubberized wet-look finish and extra eyeliner. His black hair is gelled up higher than usual. And he keeps rubbing his nose, which looks red and raw underneath. He looks like the guitarist in a Japanese Sex Pistols tribute band.

"Are you okay?" I whisper to him.

"What?" he whispers back, distracted. "Yeah, sure."

His left knee jiggles so fast I can barely see it, and the jiggling is rattling the keys in his jeans pocket.

Tonight all the live-action fiction kids' projects get shown in front of the professors and the rest of the film students, including animation, whose workshop is Monday, and documentary—we're up next week. Up until this point we've seen snippets of one another's work, but nothing complete. Everybody's films have to have music, sound, credits, the whole shebang. Workshop is half of our grade, but more importantly, workshop is when we'll judge one another, silently. Taking the measure of one another is even worse than being graded.

I look around, scanning the faces of my classmates. A couple of them I know are going to pose a serious challenge, but it's hard to tell. Watchers, like me, don't always broadcast their talent to the rest of the world. And sometimes the ones who pretend to be geniuses are kidding themselves more than anyone else.

There aren't that many film students, only about thirty of us in total, about evenly split between girls and guys. Three workshop professors, each of them looking like she'd rather be doing anything else on a Friday night.

Only Tyler looks like he's on the brink of a total meltdown.

"Stop that," I hiss to Tyler.

"What?" he looks at me, irritated.

"Your knee. It's jingling your keys."

Tyler looks around, confused. "Huh?" Then he seems to hear the jingling for the first time, and puts both his hands on top of his knee. The jingling stops.

"Thanks," I say.

"Sorry," he says. As soon as we stop talking, the other knee starts jingling.

I groan and stare up at the ceiling.

More acoustical tile. I could count the divots, but I won't.

"All right then," Professor Krauss says. She's gotten up behind the lectern and is shuffling through some notes. "We're just about ready. Cleo? Are you ready on the lights?"

Tyler's head whips around, hunting through the crowd. It's pretty much just our classmates in the screening room, though there are a few parents, and some kids from other classes. One group of girls has brought poster boards that read DEEPTI ROCKS.

"Dammit," Tyler mutters. "They can't start yet. We've still got five minutes."

I check my watch, but Tyler's wrong—we're actually five minutes past.

"Who are you waiting for?" I ask.

"Nobody." Tyler frowns into his lap.

"Is the gallery supposed to be sending someone or something?" I ask, looking over my shoulder, too.

"No. Forget it."

I eye him, but the lights in the screening room start to dim, and whatever Tyler's thinking disappears in the gathering dark.

"All right," says Professor Krauss. "Let's get started. First up tonight is Deepti Chatterjee, with a narrative piece she's calling *Girl in the Park*. It's seven minutes, shot on digital video, and stars . . . I can't read this. One of the drama kids. Ready?"

The cheering section whoops, and one of the voices calls out, "Starring Laura Gutierrez!"

"Jesus," Tyler mutters under his breath next to me. "Grow up."

The screen flickers to life, and then we get seven minutes of the back of a girl's head as she circumnavigates Washington Square Park to the dubbed-in tune of "These Boots Are Made for Walkin'" by Nancy Sinatra. While the girl walks, she slowly removes one item of clothing at a time, dropping it carelessly behind her, until she's (apparently) totally nude. Except the camera never leaves the back of her head, so I'm reasonably certain that Laura Gutierrez was not actually nude in Washington Square Park. She's probably in swimsuit bottoms and pasties. Okay, I have to hand it to her for the pasties part. You wouldn't catch me going semi-naked in Washington Square Park, if I were a girl. Actually, you probably wouldn't catch me going semi-naked in Washington Square Park if I were myself.

Heads start turning as she passes strangers going about their everyday lives. Nannies with strollers. Office girls on lunch break.

Some dudes playing drums. Hare Krishnas. Once we start to get down to serious skin, the music changes to the Yeah Yeah Yeahs singing "Heads Will Roll," and a few people have started following Laura like supplicants. I can't tell if they're part of the film project, or just randos. If they're randos, that would have been pretty freaky. When the girl loses the last item of clothing, a pair of thong underpants, she comes to a halt directly under the Washington Square arch, then turns to the camera and winks over her shoulder at the very second the music stops.

The credits roll over a rehash of "These Boots Are Made for Walkin'," while Deepti's cheering section goes totally berserker, and everyone starts clapping.

"God, could that be more derivative?" Tyler says, arms folded over his chest.

"I don't know," I say. "Her editing was pretty tight, actually."

"Whatever," Tyler says.

"Okay," says Professor Krauss. "Nice job, Deepti. And Laura, too. That took . . . that took some guts. So. What would we say is the narrative thrust of this piece?"

"Um, I'd say it was about the inherent violence of the gendered gaze? And about a woman's control of her body in space?" calls one of Deepti's friends.

"Okay," Professor Krauss says. "Sure. And how is that story conveyed in a visual lexicon?"

I fade out from the class discussion of Deepti's piece. Maybe Tyler's right, it was kind of derivative. But I had to admire her technique. I don't think my sound editing is going to be nearly that sharp. Okay, *Most* is more complicated. It's got different scenes, different people, lots of different light levels and transition music. *Girl in the Park* is basically one long tracking shot, which if I want to be a jerk about it, I could point out it could've been done in one take, like, the day before yesterday. Then all she has to do is find music that's the right length. I mean, everybody loves tracking shots. I've probably watched that *Goodfellas* tracking shot where they go through the kitchen to get into the Copa, like, a dozen times. And in *The Player*, there's a whole tracking shot where they spend the entire time talking about tracking shots. The more I think about it, the more irritated I get. Deepti thinks having her friend get naked in the park is, like, some big artistic statement. Like, we'll all be so distracted by thinking about Laura walking naked through the park that we won't notice she made a crappy film.

Thinking about Laura naked in the park makes me shift in my seat, and I look around for a second to make sure no one notices. The lights are dim. I'm safe.

"All right," Professor Krauss continues. "Next up, we've got *Shuttered Eyes*, by Tyler Lau. Says here Tyler shot using both digital and sixteen millimeter—is that right?" she asks him, sounding impressed.

"Yeah," Tyler says, like, it's no big deal, and not something he's been obsessing about for weeks.

"Wow. Okay. So it was shot in both sixteen and digital, and he says it's a"—she squints at the paper—"visual tone-poem meditation on the . . . nature of . . . identity and . . ." Professor Krauss gives up, looks at the audience and says, "It's an art film. Let's go."

We're plunged into darkness, the numbered countdown begins, like I always imagined would roll before one of my films, and then the scene opens on Tyler's eye, filling the frame of the camera. Dissonant classical music plays that I don't recognize, but which Tyler told me a while ago is by some guy named Schoenberg. After a minute, I'm lost. But it's a pleasurable lost. The images tumble together in a way that makes me uncomfortable, but which manages to be beautiful. It's like a kaleidoscope, only it's telling a story. Here's a flickering candle, here's an eye, there's the baby gumming a quartz crystal and someone taking it away, then hands grasped together on the tabletop and holding perfectly still. There's the woman winding on her turban, there's me falling (oh, man, I can't believe he put that in), then back to a repeat of the woman winding her turban. Time seems to move both forward and back, and it's dizzying, but it's rhythmic and magical. I'm letting myself be pulled into the experience of it.

And then, in a flicker of light, it happens.

I see her.

Annie.

My scalp crawls, and a strangled gasp comes out of my mouth.

She's standing right behind Maddie, and staring straight into the camera. It's shocking, arresting. Her bottomless black eyes pierce into me, and her rose-pink mouth opens. Her hand reaches slowly forward, toward the camera, and the lighting is such that it almost looks like her hand is reaching out from the surface of the screen and into the space where we're sitting. I imagine I see her arm cast a shadow on the flat movie screen. For a second, I'm terrified.

Then just as quickly, she's vanished, the scene is the same—how did he do that?—it's just Maddie at the table, looking down, in fact now I can clearly see that Maddie is asleep (of course she's asleep). The phantasmagoria of images continues: candles, the baby, candles, the guy in the Rangers jersey crying (when did that happen?), the Ouija pointer moving with no one touching it (that totally did not happen), white screen with contrails of lights, quick cuts of color digital film of shapes that I can't make out, Tyler's eye again in soft filter, and then it's over.

There are no credits.

The lights go up, and for a long minute nobody does or says anything. I can see Tyler gripping the armrests of his chair next to me, can feel the anxiety clinging to him like sweat. I can almost smell it.

Then I realize that I'm gripping my armrests, too.

"Well then," Professor Krauss falters. "Who would like to comment first?"

There's another long pause, and then Deepti's hand creeps up.

"Deepti?"

"Um. I actually thought it was kind of derivative? Kind of like Stan Brakhage, if he, like, used real people?"

Oh, man. Here we go.

Rage vibrates off Tyler so hard it makes the hairs on my arms stand up.

"Deepti," Professor Krauss says slowly. "Have you ever actually *seen* Stan Brakhage?"

I raise my hand.

"Yes, Wes," says Professor Krauss.

"Okay, so, maybe I'm biased, since I did sound for Tyler, but . . ." I glance at him to see if it's okay, what I'm doing. His face is a mask. "But I thought it was kind of awesome."

"Can you elaborate?"

"Well . . ." I hesitate.

I'm not really an art film guy. Documentaries, I can talk about. I can talk about the Up series, I can talk about Michael Moore. The Maysles brothers. The only art film I've seen to my knowledge is *Cremaster 3*, and to be honest, I fell asleep halfway through and woke up with no impression beyond a vague desire to wash my hands. I am totally out of my element. But I can't back out now. I can feel Tyler waiting next to me.

"So," I start, "one of the things I really admired about it was its use of time?" I wait, wondering if I'm going to say anything else. Then I continue, "It managed to use non-narrative image structures to convey a simultaneous passage of time forward and backward. It made me really involved in the aesthetic experience of the film. And I thought the way he incorporated diegetic sound with the music was pretty tight."

A heavy pause deadens the room while everyone stares at me.

"I thought so, too," Professor Krauss say finally, looking at Tyler over the rims of her reading glasses. "Well done, Tyler. You made some bold visual decisions in this piece that really paid off. The transitions were a little clunky, but that's just a matter of technique. It'll improve with time. And I thought your homage to Kenneth Anger was wry and unexpected. Next time, don't leave off the credits. Okay. Up next, we've got Kanesha Wright, with a piece called *Summertime . . .*"

Next to me, I hear Tyler exhale long and slow. I glance sidelong at him and smile an encouraging smile.

"Thanks, man," he whispers to me as the lights start to drop for Kanesha's film. "That means a lot."

"No problem," I whisper back. "It rocked."

There's a long pause, and as Kanesha's opening music kicks in, I just hear Tyler whisper, "You really thought so?"

"Definitely," I say. But I can't make myself smile when I say it. I'm thinking about how it's going to be my turn, one week from today. One week. That's not much time. One week for me to make something that might get me the thing I want most in the world.

And I'm thinking about Annie's nighttime eyes staring out of the screen, straight at me.

I look up at the ceiling of the screening room to keep myself from tearing up. I count sixteen divots before it gets too dark to see.

CHAPTER 10

Toss it back! Do it!" a chorus of voices shouts, and a stream of tequila burns down my throat. The backsplash of it in my nose makes me cough, but then Tyler's shouting, "Bite it! Come on!" and my teeth are sinking into a lime wedge and the burst of acid rips away the tequila aftertaste and my eyelids fly open and Tyler shouts, "YEAH!" and pounds me on the back and then hollers to the bartender, "Same again!"

"Dude," I cough, laughing, "wait a minute!"

"No waiting!" Tyler cries, grinning. "You can't wait, that's the whole point!"

He licks the back of his hand, sprinkles it with salt, picks up the tequila shot, and vaults onto the bench alongside the scarred wood table where we're sitting in an old-fashioned East Village bar.

"To the two biggest film geniuses to come out of Tisch since nineteen-freaking-seventy-five!" he shouts.

Everyone in the bar cheers, Tyler hoists the shot glass over his head, licks the salt from his hand, tosses the tequila back in one slug, and chucks the empty shot glass across the room. There's a shatter and someone in the back shouts, *Hey!* but Tyler doesn't pay any attention. Now he's down off the table and biting a lime wedge next to me, leaving the rind in his teeth and giving me a green-rind grin while sliding a shot glass over in front of me.

Obediently I lick my own hand, sprinkle it with salt, and pick up the tequila shot. Tyler and everyone is clapping and cheering. I hesitate, take a deep breath, then in one motion lick the salt off my hand and toss the tequila back. I exhale the fumes with an "aaaaaah" and thunk the shot glass upside down on the table, pick up the lime wedge, and tear into it with my teeth. A warm patch starts to spread across the back of my neck.

"Yes! That's it. That's how we do it," Tyler shouts near my ear. "Now tell me again what Krauss said about *Most* at the reception. Verbatim. I want to hear it."

"Come on, man." I wave him off, but I'm grinning.

"Shut up, shut up. Listen. Do you know what Krauss said about this guy's documentary?" he shouts to a couple of girls who are jammed up next to us at the picnic table. They look at each other, giggle, and shake their heads.

"She said she's heard it's *powerful*, and she can't wait to screen it next week. Tell them," he instructs me.

"I'm sorry," I explain to the girls. "You'll have to excuse him, we've . . ."

"Powerful," Tyler says, jamming a finger into my chest, his arm over my shoulders. "That's serious film talk, right there. That's what that is." The girls are really laughing now.

"Are you guys, like, filmmakers?" one of the girls asks, half hidden behind one of her friends.

"Damn right we are!" Tyler hollers. "You remember this guy's face, because you're gonna be seeing us on TV. When we get our Oscars. I swear." He points to me, finger wavering from the tequila.

The girls all laugh, trying to figure out if they're supposed to know who we are.

"Dude," Tyler says, leaning in close to me. "You have to do sound on my next one."

"Your next one?" I slur. My eyes are having trouble focusing on one point all together. And my lips are feeling kind of numb.

"Totally! The woman from Gavin Brown wants to see another one from me by the end of the month. She said, at the reception. Do you have any idea what this means?"

He's grinning so wide, I can't help but grin back at him, even though I can't feel my mouth. His eyeliner's gone streaky with sweat, and his cheeks are flushed, and in the background one of the girls has taken a selfie with him and looks like she's posting it to Instagram, just in case he's famous.

"It means," he says, leaning in close, "that it's really going to happen for me, Wes. For serious. All this time, you know, and I think maybe it's finally going to happen."

"What is?" I ask, leaning into him in a conspiratorial whisper.

Tyler smiles and takes my overturned shot glass so that he has something to play with on the table. Without looking at me, he says, "You don't know me that well, do you?"

I'm taken aback. I mean, we've seen each other every day for five weeks. I feel like I have a pretty good idea about Tyler. I don't always like him. But he's okay, basically.

"Sure I do, man." I stumble to reassure him. "Come on."

Tyler shakes his head, smiling to himself.

"Did you know I had to work two jobs during the year to save up for summer school?" he says lightly. "My dad's dry cleaning shop. And a moving company run by some Russian dudes in Brighton Beach. Cash only, under the table. So sketch. That's how bad I needed this."

I turn and stare at Tyler. Damn. He plays it close to the chest. The art films. All that 16 millimeter film stock. The hair and everything? The nightclub with the list? My image of his plush Upper West Side life—of framed prints and polished parquet and a mother with a gambling problem—evaporates before my eyes. No, I did not know he was sending himself to school. I'm starting to think that maybe I don't see all that well into people.

He catches me staring and his smile shades uneasy. But whatever he's worried about seeing in my face isn't there. Tyler passes the shot glass back to me.

"Listen. I know I was being kind of a dick about stuff, before. It's just, my dad couldn't pay for it. And even if he could, there was no way he'd think art school was a good use of money, you know? He was kind of on the fence about college anyway. So I just really needed everything to be perfect. I had put too much into it to let myself screw it up." He's looking at me, needing me to understand.

"Your dad didn't want you to go to college?" I ask. This baffles me. If I'd tried to not go to college, my parents would've sold me for parts. And Gran, forget it. She'd have clobbered me to death with her handbag. The big, hard-sided one from the sixties.

"Nah. I mean, to be an engineer or a doctor, yeah. But my math grades sucked. He was all set I should be a plumber. Make good money, not go into debt. College is just an excuse to waste time that would be better spent supporting the family. According to him."

Tyler looks me full in the face, his eyes damp at the corners, and for the first time, I start to understand who the eyeliner is for. I nod.

"*Shuttered Eyes* had to be good," Tyler goes on, his hand tightening into a fist. "I mean, it couldn't just be good. You know? It had to be *perfect*."

"No, no. I get it." I rush to close the subject because we're both about to get uncomfortable with all this sharing. Later, he'll blame the tequila. Or more likely we'll both pretend this conversation never happened at all. "It's no problem," I continue. "God, look at Krauss! She loved it. Right? And that woman from Gavin Brown?"

I'm not normally Mr. Effusive. But I want Tyler to know that I get it. I really do. I watch him, wondering if I've persuaded him. Wondering if this means we're really friends now.

He weighs what I'm saying, and then his face splits into a delighted grin.

"Can you believe how freaking awesome this is?" Tyler cries, sweeping an arm out to encompass I'm not sure what. School, the workshop, the summer, maybe the entire city. "And *Most*? Seriously? It's art, man. It's freaking beautiful. I've seen what you've been doing. You're a freaking artist, Wes. Next week, Krauss is gonna lose her mind. Everyone will. I'm freaking serious."

Someone plunks two more tequila shots down in front of us and we look up in confusion, because we didn't order them. The tableful of girls next to us all giggle some more and wave.

Tyler and I exchange a wry look, pick up the shot glasses, and lift them in tribute. Then we clink them together and down the shots in one gulp.

Somehow my feet are moving, and I'm not sure where they're moving to, because all I can see is the blue screen on my phone. My thumbs aren't working quite right, but I'm pretty sure I'm texting Maddie, and I'm reasonably certain I'm telling her to meet me and Tyler at another bar. Tyler's got one of the girls who bought us tequila shots wrapped around his neck like a scarf, and they're stumbling along in front of me, singing a Taylor Swift song. Tyler started by trying some Velvet Underground, but the girl didn't know what he was talking about.

The phone vibrates in my hand.

93

Where R U right now? Maddie wants to know.

I stop, swaying on my feet, and look around. Everything is lights and taxi horns and the smell of hot summer rain, and I squint, trying to make out a street sign, but my eyes will. Not. Focus. I close them, inhale a long, ragged breath, and open them again, but it doesn't help.

"TYLER," I holler.

Ahead of me two figures pause in the blur of people, and then come swaying back to me.

"WHAZZIT?" he hollers back to me. The girl he's with keeps giggling and giggling.

"What street izzis?" I slur.

"Uuuummmmmm . . ." He squints also, looking around in a circle that makes me dizzy to watch.

"Second," the girl chirps. "We're on Second and Bowery. Who're you texting with?"

"My friend," I manage to say. "She's meeting us. Where're we going? I'm sposta giver the address where we're going."

"Give it here," the girl says, yanking the phone out of my hands. With lightning speed her thumbs fly over my smartphone. At first I'm okay with this, and then just as quickly I'm not. What's she telling her? This could be bad. I should get it back from her. I should—

But then she's handing the phone back and she says, "Come on! She'll meet us there. She your girlfriend or something?"

"No, she's just this . . . she's, like," I say, but nobody's listening, so instead of talking I shamble along behind them as we go another block and turn down a side street.

"Dude!" Tyler cries, stopping short. I trip over my feet trying not to run into him.

My heart collapses when I see where we are.

Her, my mind breathes. My hand reaches out for something to

94

steady itself against, and finds the bark of the long-suffering pear tree near the curb.

We're standing in front of Annie's house.

The pizzeria is doing a brisk business, kids hanging out along the counter open to the street, its windows folded back to let in the night air. There's music and the smell of garlic knots, and the kids inside are all laughing together, and Tyler and the girl are laughing together, and maybe it's the tequila pickling my brain, and maybe it's a mistake or I'm confused or overtired, but I have to bite the inside of my cheek to keep from crying, and I'm so glad it's dark and nobody's looking at me.

Not even the town house is looking at me. All the windows above the pizzeria are empty.

Tyler wraps his arm around the girl's waist and gestures up to Fatima Blavatsky's.

"This is where it all happened," he explains to her. "Did I tell you I shot it in sixteen millimeter *and* digital? I had to transfer the film to video and then edit it all together. This guy"—he gestures to me, where I'm sagging against the tree with my arms clutching my waist, as if I could hold the despair inside by force—"this guy is a sound genius, did you know that?"

"No," the girl says and giggles.

But I can't laugh along with them. The neon sign PALMISTRY CLAIRVOYANT PSYCHIC TAROT $15 is shut off, and the curtains are closed. I stare up at the indifferent face of the town house, a void of misery yawning open in my gut.

I was waiting for her. Where did she go? Couldn't she feel it? If she felt it, why didn't she come back?

"Come on," Tyler shouts, snapping me back to myself.

He and the girl are already halfway down the block, laughing and waiting for me. I'm here, right now. My life is happening, right now.

95

My life is waiting for me. I cast one last doleful look up at the silent face of the town house, and turn to go.

The next bar is right around the corner, and when we tumble through the door and into the throng of kids holding beer glasses, I spot her.

Maddie is already leaning over the edge of the bar, waving a hand and trying to get the bartender's attention. Her arms are pressed together, deepening her cleavage, and she's coiled her dyed-black hair into a huge beehive on the top of her head, finishing off her look with 1950s cat-eye glasses. When she spots me, she smiles and lifts her chin in recognition. I elbow through the crowd, and when I reach her side, my hands go around her waist.

"Hey," she says with some surprise. "Take your time, why don't you. I was just about to give up on you guys."

"Hey," I say, nuzzling behind her ear where the laurel leaf tattoo curls up into her hair. "Hey." She smells good. Like lemon. She smells real. She's warm, and soft, and real, and she's been waiting for me. Maddie is what's good. Maddie Miss Madwoman Malou.

"Whew." She mock-waves her hand in front of her nose. "What is that, tequila?"

Without answering, I pull her to me, and before she can say anything, I press my mouth to hers.

I love how soft girls are. Their skin. Their lips. The delicious fleshiness of their bodies, smooth and perfect under my hands, which always feel too rough somehow. Sometimes they're so soft I can't believe I'm allowed to touch them. Maddie's lips are so soft that at first I imagine I can't even feel them, they are just this impression of perfect warmth on my mouth. But then, responding to my pressure, her lips move, open, and I taste plummy wine and an underlying lemony sweetness. My hands wander, I'm not even sure where they're going, but when one moves up the back of Maddie's neck and into her hair I sigh with pleasure, because the nape of her neck is soft, and her hair, that glossy dyed-black hair, is tangling around my fingers, softer still.

Her eyes close, and she leans into me, impervious to the crush of people around us, the din of other kids clamoring for drinks, for music, shouting conversations. Her weight moves against me, and I feel the soft swell of her breasts press into my chest. The pressure of them makes my breathing go faster. My other hand moves around her waist, on instinct, finding the small of her back and drawing her closer to me with urgency. Her hands are in my hair, and my skin tingles where her fingertips touch me, along my cheek, behind my ears. Our lips move, hunting for each other, and the world starts to fall away.

"Nice!" Tyler shouts in my ear, shattering the perfect bubble of Maddie's kiss.

He claps me on the back and comes in for a high five, but stops short with a laugh when he sees our faces. Maddie and I drop each other and both turn back to face the bar, our cheeks hot and red. Maddie reaches up to adjust her cat-eye glasses, which have been knocked askew. I leave Tyler's hand hanging in the air, but he covers by dropping it to the girl's shoulder and giving her a brotherly shake. The girl claps, laughing at us.

"Scuse me!" Maddie calls out to the bartender, too loudly. "Can I get another Malbec? And he wants a tequila shot. Thanks."

The bartender grunts an assent.

Maddie's fingers drum on the top of the bar. She looks at the ceiling.

I clear my throat, trying to come up with something good to say. Do I acknowledge what just happened? It'd be cooler not to, right? God. I'm always so nervous, making the first move. And girls always want you to make the first move. The first time I kissed my ex-girlfriend, at this party in a friend's basement, I was so nervous I almost threw up.

A long minute wears by while we wait for our drinks with both of us pretending we weren't just making out in a bar. Tyler and the girl from the other bar crush in next to us, trying to flag the bartender down, both of them looking sidelong at Maddie and me and grinning. Finally, after what feels like an hour, our drinks plonk down in front of us. Maddie picks up hers and turns her shoulder to me, taking a slow sip and looking across the bar into the middle distance.

"Oh," I say, realizing what's going on, and I reach into my jeans pocket to fish out my wallet. "How much?" I ask the bartender.

"Twenty-two," he shouts.

"Christ," I mutter, and leave some wrinkled bills on the bar.

"Dude!" Tyler shouts, thrusting into the awkward dead space between Maddie and me. All I can think about is Maddie's skin, which is a relief because until five minutes ago all I could think about was Annie. But now I have to come up with a way to get rid of Tyler. "Did he tell you about workshop?"

Maddie eyes Tyler through her cat-eye glasses and takes a long sip of her wine.

"He's a freaking genius!" Tyler continues, and the girl he's with says yeah, which is weird, given that she wasn't there, but whatever.

"A genius, huh?" Maddie smiles at me from behind her wineglass.

I shrug in what I hope is a nonchalant way. I keep my gaze on her. I want her to feel me, looking.

"He didn't tell you?" Tyler's gotten served a beer, and the girl is holding a Cosmo. "Krauss is already telling everyone his film is *powerful*. Next week, man. Just you wait."

"Tyler. Come on. Jesus," I grumble.

Maddie's watching this exchange with a smirk. "I bet she'll like the footage of me best, though," she says.

It's true. The footage of Maddie is going to be the best part of *Most*. The guy with the Concorde obsession is also pretty awesome. But those few minutes of Maddie, draped in frayed burgundy silk, leaning her head back into ruffles with lidded eyes, under that warm perfect light in Eastlin's store; that's the part that makes me forget to breathe.

What I want most, is to be different, she says. *I want to make a new now. I don't want to be a name, or a place, or a story that someone else tells about me. What I want is right here. What I want is right now. That's why people come here.*

Then her eyes open halfway, and she gazes long and hard at my camera. At me. Into me.

What else do you want, Maddie? I ask offscreen.

But instead of answering, she fills her hands with burgundy chiffon and rains it over me and my camera, layer upon layer winding and falling and tangling together until I'm wrapped in so many gauzy layers that none of us can tell where the camera ends and the world begins.

CHAPTER 11

I should go," Maddie whispers.

    I can barely see her, in the dark. She's just a silhouette in the blue shadows of my dorm room on Waverly Place, her hair falling over her shoulders, propping her weight on one arm as she gazes down at me. My hand plays over her shoulder, tracing the laurel leaf tattoo up and down the side of her neck.

"Did that hurt?" I ask, brushing my fingertip along her skin. I can't imagine needles digging color into that perfect, kitten-soft skin.

"Come on," she says, brushing my hand away. "Give me my shirt."

I don't actually know what happened to her shirt. I remember peeling it off her shortly after we fell in the door, but that was a while ago. We've been tangled together on my twin dorm mattress for a couple of hours, exploring first tentatively, almost politely. Lips meeting, then tongues, and then pressing together, hunting for each other in the dark. Her breath gasping in my ear as my hands moved over her jeans, thinking about undoing the button, not having the nerve. At one point she bit my lip, but I'm pretty sure it was an accident.

"You don't have to go," I say softly.

All at once it seems impossible that she should go. She cannot possibly go. She must stay here, and lie next to me, and let me wrap my arm around her waist so that I can fall asleep with my nose buried in her musk-lemon hair. This is what's real. This is what's good.

"No, I really should," she says.

She trails a fingertip down my chest, which is lightly slicked with sweat. Her fingertip finds my happy trail, draws slowly down the skin of my belly, and circles my navel. It's exquisite torture. Eastlin's jibe of the day before yesterday replays in my head, and I wonder if I should leave some kind of note on the door to warn him. Or a tie, maybe, like my dad says they did in college in the 1970s.

A tie? Who am I kidding. I don't even own a tie.

She's sitting on the bed next to me, her feet drawn up. Her bra is black, all lace and ribbons like a Halloween costume. She tucks a hank of hair behind one ear and watches me. Slowly, the finger inches its way down, devastating, deliberate, almost painful in its insistence, until it reaches the waistband of my jeans.

I shift myself without meaning to, aching, straining for her to touch me.

Does she know? Can she tell?

She must know. I can just make out her eyes in the dark, watching me.

Please, I think.

I should say it, I think.

I want to say it. But I'm afraid. She probably thinks I've done this a lot. Or worse, what if she *doesn't* think I've done this a lot? What if she finds out I have no idea what I'm doing? My ex-girlfriend would never let us get this far.

I swallow, staring at Maddie, hard. She tugs on the waistband of my boxers, which stick up out of my jeans.

Oh my God.

"Please," I whisper.

"Wes," she whispers back. "I can't. I have to get home."

Her hand withdraws, and I see her silhouette move against the window, her back bending as she rummages on the floor, finding a tank top and pulling it over her head.

I groan in dismay.

A soft laugh reaches me through the dark.

I sit up, grasping for her. My hand finds her belly, soft and warm under her tank top. I bring my lips close to her ear.

"Are you sure?" I whisper.

Her hand closes over mine and removes it from her belly, placing it with resolve back on my own leg where it belongs.

"I'm sure," she says in her regular voice.

I flop back against my pillow with a resigned sigh, arms cradling my head, while she gets to her feet, picking up a sock here, a bag there, lifting her arms to roll some of her hair into a thick knot on the top of her head. I watch her, a lazy smile on my face.

She hops while pulling on a shoe, clonks into something, says, "Ow."

"Do you want me to put on the light?" I ask her.

A knee presses into the mattress next to my hip and then her weight is on top of me. Maddie leans down, her hands on my cheeks, which have grown stubbly in the past few hours. I feel her breath on my face, a loosed strand of her hair brushing against my shoulder. Slowly, deliberately, she moves her lips to meet mine. It's almost more than I can take, and my hands move to her hips, my kiss getting more insistent. Her weight feels perfect, on top of me.

"*Wes,*" she says, disentangling herself from my grip and climbing off the bed.

"Stay," I say. "Please? Nothing has to happen. We can just sleep."

Am I lying? I don't think I am. I hope I'm not. I swear to myself that I'm not lying to her in the same moment that I try to remember which desk drawer holds Eastlin's seemingly inexhaustible condom supply.

"You don't understand," she says.

There's a pause, and I wonder if she's going to tell me something crazy, like she has an STD or something. Or what if it's something worse? I flash to the girl in the uptown jeans from the séance the other night, the one with the baby, and my stomach makes a sickening lurch.

Instead, she sighs and says, "I have a curfew, okay? I have to get home."

"You have a . . . what?" I sit up.

"Look, can we talk about it tomorrow? I've really got to go." She's pulling her bag over her shoulder and rolling on some lip gloss and is clearly ready to leave.

"Oh." I can't keep the confusion out of my voice. How can she have a curfew? She lives in a squat with a rich, alcoholic gutter punk named Janeanna! Doesn't she? In a flash I realize that of course she doesn't. "Okay," I say, trying not to sound annoyed.

I get up, find her with some difficulty, and fold her into my arms. She stiffens against the embrace, but then relaxes into it when she senses I'm not trying anything, even letting herself lean her cheek on my shoulder for a long minute. I comb my fingers through her hair where it falls down her back.

Standing there in the dark, holding her, warm and soft and lemony, my eyelids start to get heavy. When she says, "Okay," and breaks free from my arms, I sway where I'm standing.

I don't think I've ever been this tired.

"Good night, Wes."

By the door, she hesitates.

"Good night, Maddie. You going to get home okay? Should I get you an Uber?" I ask her, running a hand through the floppy part of my hair.

"I'll get a cab," she says. "Don't worry about it."

I wrestle with the idea that I should see her out to the street and into a taxi. I should pull on my sneakers and put on a shirt and walk her down past the security guy and flag down a taxi on the corner and give the cab driver her address (Curfew? *What?*) and thunk on the top of the cab with my fist and wave good-bye to her, and I absolutely would do all of these things if it weren't for the solid wall of fatigue that has bricked itself up around me, insisting that under no circumstances will I leave this room.

Instead I say, "Text me when you're home, okay?"

And she says, "Okay. See you," and then the door clicks shut.

I crawl into bed, shaking with equal measures of frustrated desire and fatigue. With a groan of appalled surrender I peel my jeans off, grope for a tube sock on the floor, close my eyes, twist my body in the sweat-soaked sheets, and think of her.

A door opens and shuts, and light from the hallway spills into my dreams, causing me to twitch half awake. One eye cracks open just enough to ascertain that Eastlin has gotten back from wherever he was, and he's silently moving around our room, pulling off his clothes and gathering up his stuff for the shower. I consider asking him how his night was, but before the thought can fully form, sleep has wrapped its fingers around my mind and pulled me down, down, down into the dark.

I'm in the Village, walking down Bowery, but it looks different. At first there are tons of people there, and I feel like I'm supposed to know some of them, but nobody looks familiar, and there's no sound, it's like watching a silent film. Then there's a girl there, in the crowd, dressed in fishnets and cutoffs and platform boots, and I call out, "Maddie," but she doesn't hear me. She's far ahead, and getting farther away, so I run to catch up with her, because there's something very important I'm supposed to do, but the faster I run, the farther away she gets. She's getting swallowed by the crowd, but I can just see the back of her head, with her two hipster pigtails brushed forward over her ears. "Maddie!" I shout, but no sound comes out, and all these hands in the crowd are grabbing at me and holding me back so that I can't move, but I'm still moving somehow. I get closer, almost close enough to touch her burgundy frayed dress, and I stretch my hand forward, I reach out my fingers to touch her, but my hand grabs nothing, and she turns around and stares at me with her bottomless black eyes. *Wes?* I think she says, but her mouth doesn't move.

Wes?

There's someone in the room. I'm sure of it. I don't know why I'm sure of it, because I don't think there was a noise, but I'm sure of it. I listen. I hear breathing, and I tell myself Eastlin must have come back from the shower and I didn't hear him come in, and now he's here, he's asleep across the dorm room from me, we're in the NYU dorm on Waverly Place and I'm in summer school and we're all safe, and everything is okay, and there's no reason for me to be awake, except I am. Aren't I?

I listen harder.

I'm not awake. I must still be dreaming. I'm dreaming there's someone with me, and I'm supposed to do something. There's something I haven't done. I don't remember what. *Most*? No. Workshop's not 'til next week. Tyler? No. I don't remember. What am I supposed to be doing?

Wes.

I want to explain that I'm sorry I don't remember what I was supposed to do, but I can't see the people I have to explain to. I can't see who's talking to me. Someone is talking to me.

Wes.

Someone is saying my name. Someone wants something. It's not my dad. Is it? No, I'm not at home, I'm not in Madison, I'm in summer school. I'm in New York. I'm scowling, the sheets twisted around my legs. I can feel the pillow under my head. I'm soaked through with sweat, and my heart is beating very fast.

"What?" I say, or think I say, but I don't hear anything. I can feel someone close to me. Someone is breathing close to me.

Maddie is close to me.

No, Maddie left.

I bicycle my feet, kicking the sheets away.

"Wes!"

I don't know where the sound is coming from, if it's inside my dream or if I can really hear it, but there's someone in the room with me and I'm dreaming there's someone in the room with me and . . .

"Wes!"

"Arrrrgh!" I cry, muffled, my mouth full of pillow. I'm struggling in the sheets, fighting against something. I'm gasping for breath, but the pillow is there and I can't breathe and I try to reach up and pull it away.

Hands are on my shoulders, soft hands on my shoulders.

"WES, WAKE UP!"

Hands are shaking my shoulders, cold hands, and they're shaking me. They're really shaking me. They're really shaking me because there's a girl sitting on the edge of my bed with her hands on my shoulders, and she's screaming, "WES, WAKE UP!"

My eyes fly open, and I flail and twist out of her grip, scrambling back against the headboard, pillows and sheets spilling to the floor. My heart is thudding in my ears, and I can't hear anything but the rushing blood pumping under my skin.

"You're . . . you're . . ." I'm panting, my eyes dart left and right. It's still night. It's dark in my dorm room and I can just see the girl silhouetted against the blue light of my bedroom window.

"Shhhhh!" she shushes me, a finger pressed to her lips. Her bottomless black eyes plead with mine.

"But . . . how did you . . . ," I sputter.

The figure sitting on my bed reaches a hand forward for me, reaches for me, and she's in a frayed burgundy dress and I'm terrified. Instinctively I withdraw from her hand as it reaches for me in the dark.

"Wes," she says, and her mouth is moving this time, because this is real. This is really happening.

My breath is coming fast, and I gather the covers up to my bare chest as if that will keep me safe. But I'm awake now, I'm definitely awake, in the moonlit cinder-block dorm room I can see my desk, and Eastlin's desk, and a lumpen shape of Eastlin asleep in his bunk across the room from mine, and the blue window shade growing pale with early morning light, and the mechanical hiss of the air conditioner, and there, at the foot of my bed, tiny in a lace-trimmed dress with heavy sleeves gathered at her elbows and a perfect crimson bow nestled between the swell of her breasts, sits Annie.

Annie is sitting on the foot of my bed.

"What," I gasp, not sure why I'm so afraid. "What. How did you get in? How did you know where I . . . What are you doing here?"

She stares at me, with those eyes, that perfect mole on her upper lip.

"I'm sorry," she says.

This isn't what I expected her to say. I don't know what I did expect her to say, but it wasn't that.

"How did you get in here?" I whisper, mindful now of Eastlin's gentle snoring in the room with us.

"What do you mean?" she asks, looking genuinely puzzled. "But I told you I'd be right back."

"What?" I ask, confused. I must be still dreaming. I must still be asleep. She's not making any sense.

"Wes," she says, and she rests her hand on my foot under the covers. "Can you help me?"

I blink at her. Annie. She's sitting on the foot of my bed. Her eyes are boring into me. Her skin is whiter in the moonlight, almost supernaturally white. How did she get into my room? How did she even know where I was? And yet, through my confusion and fear, it's still there. The tug of her. Of wanting to be near her. Even as my heartbeat thuds with adrenaline I feel pleasure, and relief.

She didn't ditch me after all.

"Please?" she says. Her voice is small. "Could you? I'm sorry to have to ask, but . . ."

Now I remember. I asked her if she needed help. I imagined that I could protect her, that I could fold my arm over her shoulders and rescue her.

It was stupid of me. But I can't let her see that.

"What's going on?" I whisper.

She leans in closer, and for the first time I see that Annie is afraid, too.

"I don't know," she says, her eyes widening.

"What do you mean?" I ask. I place a hand atop hers. She's cool to the touch, her bones small and delicate within her flesh.

Her eyes hunt around my dorm room, as if the answer might be found pinned up on my wall next to the *Serpico* poster.

"I"—she falters—"I've lost my cameo."

She holds her other hand up in front of me, waggling her naked fingers. I don't know what she's talking about.

"You've . . . what?" I'm baffled. It's like we're having two different conversations.

"I don't know!" she cries, and then she hides her face in her hands with sob.

"Oh, hey, don't do that," I say, feeling horrible for making her cry.

I edge closer to her on the bed and put my arms around her. She trembles against my chest, burying her face in my neck, and I feel the spreading warmth of her tears soaking my skin.

"It's okay," I whisper, bringing my hand to cup the back of her skull. Her hair is soft. The curls over her ears are crushed into my chest, and she smells like dusty roses and something else . . . smoke. And wet earth.

She sobs. Her sob is so loud I glance over at Eastlin to make sure she hasn't woken him, but he lets out a rattling snore and I know he's dead to the world.

"What's going on, Annie?" I ask, one hand stroking her back. She's trembling, and her hands have coiled around my waist and hold me so tightly that it's hard for me to breathe.

"I've lost my cameo!" she wails.

"Okay," I say, unsure what she's talking about. "We'll find it. Okay? We'll find it."

She wipes her bubbling nose on my chest and looks up at me with red-rimmed eyes.

"I said I'd come right back," she says, obsidian eyes searching mine. "Why didn't you wait for me?"

I don't know what to say.

"Wes," she gasps. "I came right back."

PART TWO

ANNATJE

CHAPTER 1

I t's my mother's bedroom.

I think.

My ears are still ringing from the fireworks, and I rub my eyes. Behind my lids there's an explosion of colors as I dig in my knuckles, trying to rub away the confusion. There's an acrid smell in my nostrils, from the gunpowder, and I can tell that the stench of smoke is still clinging to my dress. It's on my skin and in my hair. Lottie will kill me for wearing this dress. The ribbons and lace make it so hard to clean. She was dead set I wear the other one.

When I move my hands from my eyes to my cheeks, the details of the room become clearer. Yes, it's definitely Mother's bedroom. In our house on First and the Bowery, not my aunt's in Hudson Square where we all went to be safe after the . . .

Anyway.

My hands fall to my sides and I listen.

The house is silent. Eerily so.

"Mother?" I call out.

My voice sounds odd in the room, dead and unechoing.

I stand still, ears straining.

The room looks the same as when we fled a week ago. Lottie's left sand on the floor, which will make Mother wild. She hates to see the residue of cleaning. The coverlet is pulled up over the bed, white knotted lace stretched all the way up over the bolster. Lottie's left the key in the bed frame, too, because Mother's always after her to tighten the ropes. Enamel bowl and pitcher on the washstand, empty. Knotted lace doily on the dressing table. On the doily, a pair of gloves, a silver hairbrush, and a cut-glass bottle of perfume. Mother's sampler from when she was a girl framed over the dressing table, with its alphabet and numbers and quote from Daniel 12:2 framed by laurel leaves.

And many of them that sleep in the dust of the earth shall awake, some to everlasting life, and some to shame and everlasting contempt.

I've always hated that quote.

The pale pistachio curtains are tied back, though, which is another error of Lottie's, as the white glare of the sun streaming through the windows will bleach the wallpaper. It occurs to me that I should close them. Or Lottie should. Someone should, anyway.

"Lottie?"

No answer.

There's no noise whatsoever, which is unsettling. Usually I can hear all the traffic on the Bowery from everywhere in the house, even upstairs. The wagon wheels creaking, the stamp and snort of horses. Right before we left I heard a woman and a man grunting in the alley next to the drawing room, and Mother hustled us upstairs. She doesn't know I've actually seen them, the bright-colored women who walk the Bowery now. There's a lot Mother doesn't know that I know.

I rub a slipper over the floor, and the familiar grate of sand on pine sounds even odder in the silence. It's hot in Mother's bedroom, because of the sun most probably. I don't remember the sun ever coming in this strong. Usually elm branches keep it shady on the front of our town house. Cool air and rustling leaves once you get a story above the dust and filth of the street. But now the sun is glaring so harshly along the walls and floor that the room seems filled with a pale white haze.

"I should close them," I murmur to myself. "Mother will be upset."

My voice sounds strange in my ears. I'm not certain if I spoke the words, or only thought them. When I start to walk to the window, my feet feel like they're sunk in sucking mud.

I stop short, looking down at my slippered feet. I wiggle one set of toes, then the other. I make like I'm going to take a step, but I can't.

"Oh, come now," I mutter. I reach down and wrap my hands round my thigh, trying to bodily pick up my limb.

It doesn't budge.

I can flex my toes in my slippers, and I can twist at the waist and touch my face and my hair, and run my hands down my dress, but I can't move from this spot at the foot of Mother's bed.

That's when I realize I'm dreaming.

The realization comes to me in a flood of relief. But *of course* I'm dreaming. That oddness, that deadness in the air isn't really there. I'm not waiting around in Mother's bedroom at all. I'm asleep under a quilt with a torn square in the spare room at my aunt's house, the one in the attic with the tiny rosebud wallpaper. There's a calico cat wrapped around my head, its paws kneading my ear. It's the night of the fireworks for the Grand Canal, and I've only just gone to sleep, and that's why my hair still smells smoky. In a minute I'll wake up, and everyone will be down at breakfast, and they'll tease me for sleeping so late, and none of it will have . . .

None of it will have . . .

I frown, trying to remember.

I rub my foot over the floor, and the sand scrapes again. It certainly feels real.

The sun seems to grow brighter in the room. It's so bright now I can't make out the curtains at all. I squint against it, holding my hands up to shield my eyes. When I do so, I observe the backs of my hands, and I hold them a little way away from my face, staring.

My hands are filthy. The palms are smirched with smoke, my arms blackened all the way up to my elbows, and the sleeves gathered over my elbows look oddly flat and gray. The lace is tattered. My fingernails are black, and when I look closer I see that they're crusted with mud. "But what . . . ," I start to say.

I flex my fingers, picking at the mud under my nails, and that's when I notice that the red shell cameo ring Herschel gave me last week is missing.

"Oh no," I whisper to myself.

My heartbeat quickens in my chest. I hunt around on the floor, thinking it may have slipped off. I look at Mother's dressing table and at the end table. I shake the folds of my skirt in case it's caught on a thread. I scrabble at my throat, digging a finger into the soft space between my breasts, because sometimes I pin it there, concealed inside the ruffles.

It's nowhere. Gone.

I decide I'm ready to wake up.

"Mother!" I call out, louder this time.

There's no answer, not a mouse skitter nor a finch peep. No voices below stairs, no one outside in the street. The sun whitens in the room.

I grip my skirts in a mounting panic.

"Mother!" I scream. "I'm ready to wake up now."

Nothing.

The only sound I can hear is the thud of my blood in my temples and the gasp of my breath. This dress is too tight. I'm growing out of it. It's squashing my breasts down as I try to breathe, like a dress made for a little girl, only I'm not a little girl anymore. I worry the finger where the cameo belongs, frantic. If I'm dreaming, then it's not really lost, I reason with myself. It's really on my finger right now. When I open my eyes, it will be there. I squeeze my eyes shut tight, bringing my fists to my temples, willing myself awake.

"Wake up," I whisper. "Wake up, Annie. Wake up wake up wake up wake up."

I open my eyes, but I'm still in Mother's bedroom. The light, though, has grown so bright that it's obscuring Mother's bed. I can only make out the barest outline of the posts.

"I'll wake up any minute," I assure myself.

I wrap my right index finger around the bare ring finger of my left hand, twisting where the ring should be.

"It's not really lost," I mutter. "No one knows. You'll find it."

I pause, looking around myself at the slowly disappearing room. The light rises and spreads, swallowing the washstand, creeping along the floor until it touches the toes of my slippers.

"You can find it," I whisper.

The sunlight moves over my feet, flowing like water until it reaches the hem of my dress. I recoil when I observe that the hem is ripped into tatters. I swallow, fearful of what Lottie will say. I'm afraid to see Mother's face when she learns the dress is spoiled. I'm always spoiling my good clothes, and I never notice 'til it's already happened.

Up and up creeps the glaring white. I feel the warmth of the sun reaching my legs through layers of silk and linen, and it feels good, like the blood is coming into them at last, like I might be ready to move. I lift my right foot and creep it forward an inch, farther into the sunbeam. This time, my foot goes where I ask it.

"You'll find . . . ," I hear myself say as the sunlight floods up my skirt to my waist.

I stretch my arms into the light, spreading my fingers and enjoying the feeling of them moving. But then, something interrupts me.

I pause, ears twitching. I hold my breath.

It's almost not there, but it's there.

A whisper.

Startled, I take a step backward, hunting around the room for signs of life, but the light is so bright I can't make out the dressing table or the bed anymore.

"Who's that?" I cry. My voice trembles.

The whispering continues, and I wrap my arms around my waist, cupping my elbows, eyes straining wide to see forms in the room with me. I can't see anything, but I can hear the whispering growing clearer.

It's a young man's voice. Somehow it sounds both very far away, and very close by.

In a strangled cry I scream, "Herschel!" before I can help myself. As soon as his name escapes my lips, I clap my hands over my mouth for fear someone will hear me, that I'll wake up with my aunt leaning down over my bedstead with that curious look she's been giving me all week.

The murmuring creeps nearer, but I can't make out the words. I knot my fists in my skirts to keep my hands from trembling.

"I know you're there!" I shout. "I can hear you!"

The sound seems to wrap around me, and along my neck I feel a breath of breeze. A shadow flits through the white sunlight of the window, and I spin, hunting for its source. My hands find the foot of Mother's bed, and I grip the post. The light is changing, getting whiter and yet dimmer all at the same time. On one wall, a candle flames to life, but it's not in a place I remember a sconce being.

My knees shake, and I can barely hold myself up.

"Please wake up, Annatje," I whisper as tears squeeze out of the corners of my eyes.

The voices grow more distinct, but I still can't make out exactly what they're saying. The hairs on the back of my neck rise.

"Please go away," I sob. "Please! Please leave me alone."

The sunlight collapses in on itself and more candles sputter to life, flames licking up the walls with tendrils of smoke. Though I know the wallpaper is pale pistachio, its color looks wrong. It looks somehow pistachio and red at the same time. I feel more breaths of air along my neck, brushing against my cheek, stirring the curls over my ears.

I shut my eyes, my throat closing as the tears run down my face. The voice is in my head, is in my ears, is behind me and around me and next to me and right in front of my face.

The voices are talking to me.

All at once the town house begins to shake, as though last night's fireworks for the canal celebration were shuddering anew over the Bowery. I hear the explosions and smell the burned gunpowder and soot. The walls and floor vibrate around me like the walls of a bass drum, and the last of the sunbeam is swallowed up by candlelight, pulling darkness along behind it. Under my hands instead of my mother's bedpost something soft springs into being, smooth like tufted velvet.

Without warning, I feel invisible fingers close around my elbow. My eyes fly open and my mouth releases a piercing scream.

And then I hear a young male voice very clearly say, "Listen."

CHAPTER 2

My scream is still echoing in my ears as I twitch, kicking my feet and fighting away phantoms of sleep, tossing off the coverlet, when I feel a soft hand flop against my cheek. My eyes fly open. I've soaked through my nightdress, and I'm damp and hot. The sheets are twisted around my legs. Gasping, I clutch the mattress and look crazily about myself. I'm awake. I'm not in the dream anymore.

I'm awake.

I'm in my bed. My own bed, at home. The horsehair mattress rustles under my weight. My face is pressed to my favorite pillow, the lumpy feather one that's been flattened 'til it's just right for my cheek. I feel soft breathing next to me, and the hand on my cheek coils itself into my hair, getting caught on the rags I use to tie my curls into place at bedtime. Slowly my eyes trace to the left, to the owner of the hand.

My sister's sleeping face rests on her own pillow in the bed next to me. The rag doll I sewed for her when she was a baby is nestled under her chin. One of its button eyes is missing, the empty socket erupting in frayed thread. She's too old for a doll, and Mother has tried to hide it from her more than once, but Lottie or I generally find it and smuggle it back to her. My sister's mouth opens and emits a soft snore.

Without moving, I let my eyes roam around the details of the room, suspicious.

I'm at home. I'm in the room I share with my sister, upstairs from Mother's room. This is puzzling, as I don't remember coming back from my aunt's. Did we come back here after the flotilla and the parties last night? But I would remember that, surely. I'd remember being loaded into a carriage in lamp-lit streets littered with cast-off bunting, laughing and heady with wine and our journey on the barge, and the carriage jouncing over the rutted streets uptown, tossing my sister and brother into me and Mother and Papa. I'd remember pulling up to our house, because I'd be relieved it was safe for us to come back.

Wouldn't I?

Anyway all our clothes are at Aunt Mehitable's house. I'd expected to awaken in Hudson Square.

I try to raise myself on my elbows, but my sister tightens her grip around my neck with a contented sigh and I'm trapped. I resign myself to waiting.

The light is thin, so it must be early yet. I hear the last tittering birds of the season in the elms outside the window, and someone's moving about downstairs. Mother is awake. Papa would be, too, much earlier, as he's in the Canal Corporation on top of his job at the bank downtown, and has been beyond busy. We barely see him. A knot of worry twists in my gut. Why would Papa let us come back again, without first . . .

But I can't argue with the fact that I'm in my bed. At home.

Everything looks completely the same.

The room that Beatrice and I share is on the third floor, with two tall windows looking over the kitchen garden and privy at the rear of the house, windows dressed in dark wool hangings now that the weather's turned cool. Mother is still choosing the furniture for the drawing and dining rooms, but she's already appointed her and Papa's rooms. Their beds are as heavily carved and draped as old Spanish galleons, topped with plumes of ostrich feather. Beattie and I share her old bed, which sags in the middle and has hangings that are kind of mothy, but still warm. A soft pop tells me that Lottie's already come in while we were sleeping and stoked up the fire.

Everything in our room is just as we left it. My own childhood sampler, complete with its crooked *S* and lopsided laurel leaves, is framed over the mantel. Beattie's sewing basket sits abandoned on the floor by the rocking chair. The washstand that always wobbles is in the corner. A shelf with my books, *Pilgrim's Progress* and *A History of New-York from the Beginning of the World to the End of the Dutch Dynasty*, together with a few others, is pushed against the far wall. The dead fern that I forgot to water is curling in a piece of cracked chinaware on the mantel. A faint, but sharpish, smell suggests that Beattie used the chamber pot in the night, and it's marinating under the bed. Even the shawl Beattie started knitting in August and finally abandoned in a heap, rests untouched on top of our dressing table.

"Beattie," I whisper, nudging her with an elbow.

She grunts in her sleep and presses her nose into my neck.

There's a clang in the room next door, and I hear a woman's voice mutter in annoyance. Sounds of something scraping against the wood floor, and then the door to the narrow hallway between our brother's room and ours swings open and Lottie appears, rolling a large, shallow metal tub into our room.

"All right, gals," Lottie barks. "Up and at 'em."

She's not supposed to roll the tub in on its edge like that, because Mother's concerned it will ruin the floors. I watch, my eyes widening in bafflement as Lottie maneuvers the tub to the foot of the bed, then tips it to its bottom with a metallic spang. She drops a cake of Pears soap into the pan and wipes her hands on her apron.

Beattie rolls over, her eyelids fluttering.

Freed from her arm around my neck, I sit bolt upright in bed.

"Lottie?" I ask.

"Water's on to boil," she continues in her brusque manner, paying me no attention. "I don't much care who's first."

I don't much care who's first.

I mouth the words as she says them, as she does every morning.

She trudges back out the door she came in, down the four flights of rear stairs to the kitchen in the basement where the kettle will be whistling with hot water for our washing.

"Beattie, wake up," I hiss, shaking my sister's shoulder with urgency.

"Huh?" She stretches her arms overhead, yawning. She smiles sleepily at me and cuddles her doll, her curls spread over the pillow.

"Beattie." I take her hands in mine. "Are you awake?"

"I'm awake," she says, rubbing her nose on her shoulder. "Morning, Annie."

"What day is it?" I demand.

"What day?" she echoes. Another yawn.

Before she can answer me the door to our room flies open and it's Edward, the youngest, skidding in on his stocking feet.

"Get up get up get up get up get up!" Edward bellows. He vaults across the room like a rabbit. Just last week he broke the bed and Mother was beside herself.

With a squeal of pleasure at being alive, my brother launches himself into the air just as I cry, "Eddie, wait! Not again!"

But it's too late, and my brother lands on us in a tangle of sheets and elbows and feet. My sister lets out a squeal of anger, diving to whack my brother upside his head, and for a long minute I'm pinned between their two struggling bodies.

In the midst of the struggle, I feel more than hear a dull snap, and our mattress lurches partway to the floor. My siblings pause in their struggle to register the destruction, and then resume their battle with renewed vigor.

Eddie broke the bed, again.

This all feels so . . . normal.

Slowly, deliberately, I hold my hands out in front of me, to look at them, just like I did in my nightmare.

They are perfectly clean. No smoke stains or dirt. My nails are pearly with health.

But Herschel's ring still isn't there. I hunt around in the sheets, but it's not there, either.

"I don't understand," I whisper, staring hard into space.

I have to think. I have to figure this out.

"Ow!" Edward whines as Beattie digs a knee between his shoulder blades and grinds his face into her pillow.

"I told you not to jump on us like that!" Beattie screams in his ear. "I told you and told you!" She said the same thing when he broke the rope last week.

"Annie! Help!" My brother's cries are muffled in the bedclothes, but I'm not paying attention. I'm staring at my hands, flexing my fingers in the dull morning light.

Why isn't Herschel's cameo on my finger?

"Annie!" Edward squirms out from under Beattie's grip and looks to me to adjudicate.

Ignoring him, I get slowly to my feet, still staring at my hands. I rub my fingertips against my thumbs, and the shiver of reality travels through my skin. Everything feels completely real. Completely normal. Everything is exactly as it was.

"But this isn't right," I say aloud, looking around. "This can't be right!"

The side door to Edward's room swings open again and Lottie grunts in under the weight of two hot kettles with wooden handles. Her face is red from the effort of hauling the water up the stairs from the kitchen, and she's out of breath. She drops them by the tub with a thunk at the very moment that the main door to our room swings open to reveal our mother. She's in a crisp day dress, and her skin is as smooth and flawless as cream, except for a smattering of tiny pox scars on her cheeks. Her hair is perfectly plaited over her ears and her expression is grim. We freeze. *What's all this, then?*

"What's all this, then?" she asks.

She watches Lottie, who is hunched next to the washtub and stacking a couple of towels by the rocking chair. The servant doesn't look up. She excels at evading Mother's active management. Then Mother's gaze passes over me, where I'm standing like a lost waif in my nightdress, stained with sweat and staring at my own hands like a madwoman. She comes to rest on my siblings in the collapsed bed.

Edward?

"Edward?" she prods.

My brother scrambles to climb out of the wreckage and straighten his clothes.

"He started it!" Beattie insists, struggling to stand up on the sloping mattress. "I told him not to jump on us, but he always does!"

"Beatrice," my mother says.

It's all she has to say.

She stares at them both for a long, cold moment, and then says, "Lottie, ask the boy to see to that when we're away this afternoon."

She doesn't remember. She doesn't mention last week.

Lottie grumbles, "Yes'm." She hates to speak to Mother. The "boy" is the Negro man Winston who does for us what Lottie can't. A man of all work. Mother hates to speak to him as much as Lottie hates to speak to Mother.

I'm observing this minor domestic scene, but I'm apart from it. I can't understand what's happened. This morning is unfolding just like the morning of the day Herschel gave me the ring. That day, last week, before the . . .

The day we fled to Hudson Square. I got up, and Ed broke the bed rope, and I dressed and breakfasted with Mother, and then he was waiting for me outside the theater, and we . . .

"Edward. Beatrice. Annatje. Breakfast will be served in half an hour," Mother informs the room full of reprobates, and closes the door to underscore her point.

"Annie," I whisper the correction out of habit. I hate that they gave me a Dutch name; it's so old-fashioned. I've been trying to get them to call me Annie for over a year, and everyone but Mother goes along with it. Even Papa. And Papa's mother was a Stuyvestant, as Mother never tires of reminding me.

Lottie starts pouring water into the tub, and says, "I don't care who's first. Ed?"

With a squeal of disgust my brother flees our bedroom. There's no getting him to bathe if he can possibly help it, and he usually can. Sometimes he goes so long without washing that his neck turns gray from grime.

"I'll go," I say, and my voice sounds strange and hollow in my ears.

Seeing that she needn't rouse herself 'til I'm done, Beattie flops contentedly back into the bed, resting her doll on her belly and making faces at it.

With a shrug Lottie stomps over and starts helping me out of my sweat-stained nightdress. The bedroom is cold, not winter cold, but there's an uneasy autumn chill in the air, and my skin crawls with gooseflesh when the nightdress is lifted away. I wrap my arms around my nakedness with a shiver.

I perch on the edge of the shallow tub, dipping the washrag into the warm water that Lottie pours around my feet, and I soap myself as quickly as I can. I hang my head. Lottie wrings a towel out, pouring tepid water over my head, and it drips down my cheeks and runs off the tip of my nose. A few tears make their way into the rivulets of water, trickling off my face, but Lottie affects not to see them. She mutters, in identical tones that I remember her saying last week, "That Edward'll be the death of me."

"What's going on?" I whisper softly under the sound of the water plashing over my shoulders and into the tub.

"Where's my cameo?"

CHAPTER 3

I have to find Herschel.

He'll understand what's happening.

Well, maybe he won't, but even if he doesn't, I mind less the things I don't understand when I'm with him. And this doesn't make any sense. False retrospection only lasts a moment. Mornings don't just repeat themselves exactly. Not like this.

I dress myself hurriedly, annoyed that the bodice on my day dress is too tight. I have to rearrange my breasts with a scoop here and there so that they don't feel painfully squashed. I need new clothes, but Mother doesn't see it. Or doesn't want to see it. I should just ask Papa, now that the celebration is over. Papa won't be as distracted as he was.

"It's cold!" Beattie whines as she eases her feet into the bathwater.

"Then you should've gone first," Lottie points out. "*I* don't care who goes."

Beattie whimpers under the scrubbing of the washrag, but I can't worry about her right now.

Rushing, I hop as I cram one foot into a slipper and nearly topple over onto the wrecked bed. I don't know what day it is. If it's

Saturday, I won't be able to see him. And if it's Friday, I won't be able to see him at night. In fact, I can almost never see him Fridays, as that's the day they have to get ready for Saturday. And on Sundays, he generally can't see me. But it's not Sunday.

Of course, he's not supposed to see me at all.

He's usually at his uncle's shop on Pearl Street, not far from the Brooklyn ferry landing. He calls it a *schmatte* shop, which I guess is supposed to be sarcastic, but it's just dry goods as far as I can tell. There're a hundred shops like that one. Maybe more than a hundred.

When I go there, I buy thread.

I've bought so much thread in the past few months that I couldn't hide it in the house anymore. I filled Beattie's overlooked sewing basket. I bribed Lottie with it until she started getting suspicious. I gave it to Winston to carry home for the freedwomen in Seneca. I even started secreting it under the stockings and bloomers in my drawer, but then I worried Mother would find it and so I threw it in the privy. That made me feel guilty, though. Now I give it to beggar women that I pass in the street on my way home. They're always shocked and grateful. I try to choose the ones with sucking babies or small children. Sometimes they remember me from the last time. One even argued with me once about the color, and followed me cursing down James Street for two blocks, and tried to throw a brick at my head.

I don't walk down James Street anymore.

I'm excited to see Herschel, and tell him about the flotilla last night. So many fireworks! I'd never seen so many. And the music playing! And the military salutes, and . . . and . . .

I frown.

Anyway, I can't wait to see him, and tell him we're back home. I'm sure that the minute I see him everything will click back into place and I'll feel like myself again. The thought of seeing Herschel sends

129

a shiver of pleasure through me, and I close my eyes, recalling his particular smell, and the tickling texture of his young beard against my cheek.

No one can see into me the way Herschel can.

Behind me, Lottie is struggling to scrub behind Beattie's ears and Beattie is whining that the water's too cold. If I slip out now, they'll think I'm just going down to breakfast, and no one will notice me leave.

I hurry over to look at myself in the glass on the dressing table, to pinch my cheeks and fluff the curls over my ears before rushing out of the house.

I step in front of the mirror, fingertips at my cheeks.

But instead of my reflection, the mirror reflects a hideous apparition back at me, with bony fingers on its cheeks. Before I can stop myself, I scream in horror and clap my hands over my eyes.

In the glass, this horrible thing leered at me, a desiccated creature of teeth and skin and bones. Hair like seaweeds sprouting from its head. Eyes empty and bottomless, just pits where the eyes should be. The thing was like the specter of a witch, or a demon out of Cotton Mather. Something evil and wretched and unthinkable.

"Annie?" Beattie calls from the washtub. I hear water slosh as she stands up.

My hands are still over my eyes, and I'm trembling.

Horrible. Too horrible. A nightmare thing that somehow crawled out of my dream with me when I awoke.

"Annie?" I hear my sister's bare feet pad over to stand behind me. A gentle hand comes to rest on my shoulder.

"I . . . I . . . ," I stammer.

I don't know what's happening.

I don't understand.

"It's all right," Beattie says.

I'm hiding behind my hands, unable to look, and so instead Beattie pulls me to her in an embrace. She's damp and cold from the bath, and the sweet smell of Pears soap fills my nostrils as I breathe in my sister. I crush my face into her hair and shudder. Beattie's only twelve, but she has a reassuring wisdom at times. I've even thought of telling her about Herschel. I can't tell anyone, but I yearned to show her the cameo when he gave it to me.

But I can't.

I can't tell anyone.

No one can know.

"Here now," Lottie chides us from the other side of the room. "You'll catch your death."

Beattie releases me and I screw open my eyes. I see the concerned look of my sister, who's wrapped in a damp towel and staring at me curiously. Over her head, in the oval dressing table glass, I spy our twin reflections. My face is paler than usual, almost sallow, but the monster has vanished. I wipe my eyes with my wrists and suck the tears out of my nose and down my throat.

"It's Ed's fault, for waking us up like that," Beattie says soothingly. "You're just overtired."

She gives my arm a squeeze and then returns to the tub where Lottie's waiting.

I nod.

I can't tell her that I was already awake, before Ed. Long before Ed.

Lottie gives me the briefest of glances, and then looks away while rubbing the water off Beattie.

"Well," I say to the room. "I'll just go downstairs, then."

I hurry to the door to the front stair, avoiding catching either of their eyes,

"Tell Mother I'll be down in a trice," Beatrice calls after me.

On the landing outside our bedroom I smell cooking bacon and beans, and strong coffee, and my stomach rumbles. I start down the curving staircase, my hand tracing the banister. This house is much more comfortable than my aunt's, though she finds our neighborhood remote and unfashionable. Her house is drafty. I spent every night in her spare room shivering under the quilt with the torn square.

As I descend the stairs, the smells of food intensify, changing in a just perceptible way. There's a sharpness to the smell, and it makes my mouth water.

What could Lottie have done to the beans? I wonder. It smells so good that I'm regretting my plan to sneak away to see Herschel and miss my chance at breakfast. I am planning to buy something in the street on the way, hot corn or something like that.

Downstairs I hear voices in conversation from what sounds like the drawing room, animated voices so loud that I wonder if Papa's in there having another argument with some of the Canal Corporation men, like I caught him having last week.

They mean to do it, I'd heard my father shout. *Don't you see? They can still ruin everything.*

The other man had said something I didn't understand. They were both on the committee for the Grand Aquatic Display to be held when the canal finally opened, the party that we went to last night. A whole flotilla wending all the way from Buffalo to the Hudson, and down to New-York, over a period of weeks, and when we heard word that they were only a few days away, the city leapt to preparations. Papa and all his business associates readied to receive them amidst fireworks and music and martial displays, all the newspapers there and Governor Clinton pouring water from Lake Erie into New-York Harbor, along with water from the Ganges, and the Nile, and the Amazon, and the Mississippi, and all the greatest waterways in the world, though Ed had wondered aloud how they really knew that's where all the water was coming from, after all, doesn't all water look the same?

I hesitate on the stair, straining my ears. The voices grow louder, but somehow not more distinct. I can't tell what they're saying. Usually Papa is downtown by now. He hasn't breakfasted with us in weeks. Always rushing off to planning meetings, being picked up outside the town house by different carriages. Strangers rapping at the door and asking for him.

The morning light is streaming into the first floor hallway, pouring like rays of heaven through the transom window over the front door, glinting off the hall-stand mirror. I squint against it, and descend another step. Usually the morning light is soft, orange and muted, since more buildings have gone up on this block. But today the light is harsh and white.

I bring my hand up to shade my eyes, peering into the glare.

The whiteness is so bright it's almost a haze. It fills the hall, lightening the dove-gray walls and swallowing the floorboards.

I descend another couple of steps, and the light glows so bright that I can't see where I'm stepping. My feet hunt about for each stair tread, and I grope for the banister, but I can't find it. My hand plunges into space, grasping nothing.

Finally my foot lands hard on the floor, and the carpet runner is missing, and my foot makes an unfamiliar sound in the front hallway. Voices are all around me. Their murmurs rise and fall, like music, or like the crowds of people outside the African Grove Theater on Bleecker, a clamor of voices and sounds and smells and everyone talking at once, but somehow never to one another. I can't make any of them out, and none of them seem to be talking to me, but they buzz around to my ears like bees, close enough that I struggle to bat them away.

"Papa?" I call out.

The brightness of the morning sun is making my eyes ache.

"Order up!" someone shouts close to my ear, making me jump.

"What?" I say, looking left and right.

I can't see anyone. I'm alone, but somehow I'm surrounded by people and smells and I can hear a bell jangling, but I can't tell if it's the bell Mother uses to summon us for meals or if it's something different.

"Mother?" I try this time, wondering if she's serving breakfast in the drawing room for some reason. Perhaps she has guests? But she wouldn't entertain at breakfast. And she would have made sure Beattie and I dressed up.

A whiff of air brushes past my cheeks, and I spin where I'm standing, but all I see is the outline of the front hallway filled with pure white light.

I move nearer to the drawing room, reaching a hand forward to where the sliding door should be, but my hand keeps going forward in space, deeper into a void, not meeting anything.

"Keep it moving, keep it moving! Whatchou want, huh?" someone barks on my left.

My eyes wide with terror, I spin again, hunting for the speaker.

"Who said that?" I raise my voice. "I can hear you!"

Nobody answers me, but still I hear the voices, talking amongst themselves, little snippets of conversation that I can almost understand, but not quite.

Another whiff of air brushes past my other cheek, and I close my eyes, feeling whatever it is pass through me as though it were a summer breeze.

"What is this?" I ask myself. "What is this?"

When I open my eyes again, I'm standing in the middle of the drawing room, but it's not the drawing room. It's overlit with glaring white lights that hum overhead. Most confusingly of all, it's packed to the gills with total strangers.

They're gathered around small tables I've never seen before. All Mother's carefully chosen fixtures are gone, the horsehair sofas and the occasional chairs and the hulking marble mantelpiece with the gilt-framed mirror. Or rather, there's a mirror where the gilt-framed one used to be, but it's spotted and chipped, and someone has written on it, what looks like a long list, with words that don't make any sense to me. Like Latin, but not Latin.

Calzone. Pepperoni. Mortadella.

The oil chandelier is gone, and instead it's as though the whole ceiling were lit from within by white light that flickers, but not the way a candle flickers. The smell of food is mouthwatering.

But who are all these people?

I stare at them, and none of them pay any attention to me. They're all different ages, dressed in the most bizarre way. Some of them look like they aren't even dressed at all. Girls in camisoles lean over tables, their bodies loose, their hair flowing down their backs. They're with boys, most of them, and they're all eating with their hands. It's like a kind of savory pie, only without a crust. They all act like it's completely normal that they're there, eating breakfast in my mother's drawing room.

Panicking, I grip my skirts in my fists.

Where did these people come from? Who said they could be in our house?

"Who ARE YOU?" I scream.

Nobody answers me!

"Tell me who you ARE!" I bellow, rushing up to one of the tables.

There's a girl sitting there, one of the ones who's left the house in her nightdress as far as I can tell, and she's bending forward and laughing, and I can see all the way down her bodice. She's completely unlaced, and if Mother knew this prostitute was in her drawing room, I don't know what she'd do. She'd call Papa, and she'd call Winston, and if they didn't come she'd beat the girl bloody with a fireplace poker herself.

"You can't be here!" I shout in her ear.

The girl just keeps laughing and talking, chewing with her mouth open.

I put my hands on the table between them, leaning into their conversation. The boy is just as bad. He reeks like a French waterfront whore, and his hair is so short it looks like he's been lately shaved for lice. Neither of them takes the slightest notice of me.

"Get out of my HOUSE!" I scream at the top of my lungs, and I take hold of the table where they're sitting, grab it with both my hands and make ready to hurl it away, crashing it across the room in a righteous fury.

"Annatje?" someone says softly.

I look up, my eyes crazed with violence.

Mother is standing by the sliding door of the drawing room, her hand resting on the burled walnut that she chose for the wainscoting. She is giving me a curious look.

Panting, I look down at my hands, and find that they are resting on the card table that Mother left out from Papa's whist game last week. No one has been in the drawing room since then. There's a round stain where one of the corporation men left his sherry glass without a coaster. It looks dried and gray in the morning light.

"Is everything all right?" she asks me lightly.

I release the edge of the card table and smooth my hands down the front of my day dress.

"Of course, Mother," I say with some difficulty.

"I thought I heard you shout, just now."

I level my eyes at my mother's face and smile prettily at her.

"Shout?" I echo, as mildly as I can.

"Yes. I thought I heard you raise your voice, a moment ago."

It's not like Mother to press the issue. Usually we maintain a tacit agreement that we will each pretend I do what I'm supposed to do, virtually all of the time. It's easier on both of us.

"I'm so sorry, Mother," I say. "Perhaps you heard someone out in the street? A peddler? They're getting louder and louder, aren't they?"

She watches me for a long moment.

"Indeed they are," she says after a time.

We stare at each other across the length of the drawing room, each wondering who is going to call me on my bluff.

At length she says, "Well. Beatrice is down. We're about to eat."

"All right," I say.

She's on the point of leaving, when she gives me a last long look and says, "Are you quite sure you're all right, Annie?"

Her unaccustomed use of my preferred name takes me aback, and I have to lean on the card table.

"I . . . I think so," I say.

What I want to do is run to her, and have her hold me and tell me that I'm just having a bad dream within a bad dream. I want her to tell me that it's probably on account of my having too much Madeira, which I shouldn't have accepted from Mrs. Dudley at the corporation dinner, and it serves me right for indulging too much, and it's just this sort of thing that's made her consider joining the Temperance Society. I want to tell her that my cameo's missing, and beg her to help me find it, and I want to tell her that it was Herschel who gave it to me, and why.

"I think . . . perhaps, there's something the matter with my head," I finish.

I bring my hand to my temple.

"Hmmph," my mother sniffs, and her dismissal fills me with relief, as it is exactly what she would do, if we were really having this conversation. "In any case, there's coffee on the breakfast table."

She whisks away down the hall, and I can hear the rustling of her skirts as she goes.

I lean myself ever so slightly to the left, so that I can see farther down the hall and confirm that she's really gone.

And then I grab up my skirts and run for the front door.

CHAPTER 4

"Herschel," I breathe as I blunder down the front steps of our town house and flop into the street. A carriage rattles by, and I throw myself out of its way. The horse, a bay mare with a grizzled muzzle, rolls its eye at me as it trots past.

I round the corner from First to the Bowery, into the morning crowds of the avenue. The traces of last night's revels have vanished, which is odd—I'd expected wet bunting and a stench of spoiled beer. Well, the stench of beer is there, but it usually is. Beer and urine and the salty smell of seawater, even though we're well inland from the waterfront. At least we're far enough in that it doesn't stink of fish.

Men stroll by in twos and threes, some women, too, and in front of the butcher shop a puppy steals a ham trotter and endures the abuse of a pigeon for his trouble. The day is cool and windless, and the sky is an unbroken palette of white.

"Hot corn!" a yellowish mulatta waif hollers to the men bustling by. "Hot corn, piping hot! Fresh out of the boiling pot!"

She's carrying a huge covered basket that smells enticingly of boiled maize ears. A few sporting bloods pause to notice her as she strolls by. One gentleman in tight lacing and a tall hat lets his eye roam down her body in a frank, appreciative leer.

She stops, returning his look with just as much frankness.

"Hot corn, sir?" she asks him. She reaches into the basket, finds an ear browned in its husk, and holds it out to him.

"How much?" he asks, leaning nearer.

A knot of other men passes by, remarks on the exchange, and laughs. The tight-laced man straightens, red-faced, and lifts his hat to the passing men. Their laughter becomes an uproar.

The hot corn girl looks annoyed. They're going to cost her her business. After all, she's really selling two things. Already the tight-laced man is moving away as if they weren't in the midst of a negotiation.

"Here, I'll buy it," I say to her. I'm hungry anyway.

The men all think this is a marvelous turn of events, and hoot and applaud like they're at a disreputable theater. A bright-colored woman in plaid happens by, an actress or someone pretending to be one, and joins in the merriment. One of the men puts his arm about her waist, and leans in to hear the price she whispers in his ear. It'll be more than the hot corn, I can tell.

"Fine," the corn-selling girl says, ignoring them. I fish a penny out of my skirt pocket and press it into her palm. She hands over the ear.

As I take it, I look at her. She's shorter than me, about Beattie's size, but I can see that she's older than Beattie. Maybe older than me, but not by much. Her cheekbones are so sharp I can see them clearly through her skin, and her eyebrows and hair are wiry.

"Thanks," I say to her with a nod.

"Hmmph," the girl grunts, uninterested in my charity. She turns away, and resumes her cry of "Hot corn! Piping hot! Hot corn!"

I peel the husk back and take a bite, wandering south on Bowery. It won't take long for me to reach Herschel's uncle's *schmatte* shop. I have money for thread. The corn is rich and sweet, and I chew contentedly, pausing every so often to spit corn gristle into the sewer along the center of the avenue. I'm starting to feel better. It must have been the Madeira, honestly. I didn't realize I'd had so much. Mrs. Dudley kept refilling my glass over and over, teasing me about when I'd get married, and tickling me to make me tell her about my beaux, and I was so afraid I'd say something to give myself away about Herschel that I kept reaching for my wineglass so I wouldn't have to talk. And then it was time to dash for the dais, and . . .

I pause, looking at the overlapping posters pasted up on the brick wall of a haberdasher. Ads for theatrical productions, sheet music, lumber, cigars, rum, molasses, rewards for slaves run away, a notice for a political meeting. I take another big bite of my corn and chew, wiping my lips with the back of my hand as I look closer.

STOP THE MARCH OF TIME, it reads. Underneath the heading there's a rough engraving of a barge in flames. Then there's a time listed for a meeting, and the signature of the notice reads UNITED BROTHERHOOD OF LUDD—

The rest is torn off.

I frown.

"And how are you today, my dear?" whispers a voice in my ear.

I turn and spy a man with a huge round belly straining at the buttons of his waistcoat and spindle legs, his mustache growing into the hair on his cheeks. He's looking at my chest. All the blood vessels in his potato-nose have burst long ago.

With a sigh of disgust I throw my corncob into the street and start to walk downtown.

"Hey," the man says, trotting after me. "I'm askin' you a question."

I hunch up my shoulders to make my chest smaller, and walk faster.

"Hey! Girlie!" He's catching up. I can hear his breath huffing through his hideous nose.

"Leave me alone!" I shout, and a few heads turn from passersby noticing, and then deciding not to intervene.

"Look here," he says, reaching for my elbow, but before he can get his hands on me I break into a dead run.

"Hey!" he hollers. "Why'd you walk so slow, if you didn't wanna talk to me?"

A few people scatter in the street, opening a path before me in surprise. A dog barks and nips at my heel, tearing away a mouthful of lace from my underskirts.

My arms pump, my breath coming hard and fast in my chest, and even though the cool autumn air whistles through the cross streets, mixing air from the river into the city miasma, a sheen of sweat beads on my forehead as I run, skirting rickety stairwells and wives out marketing and bands of frock-coated bloods lounging in the doors of victualing houses with oyster shells heaped at their feet.

Herschel, I think, my eyes smarting with tears. *Herschel, I have to see you.*

I run faster and faster, and the Bowery blurs around me, faces and horses and barrels and baskets and hanging hunks of meat for sale and theater marquees all smearing into an indistinct mass as I fly past.

I gasp for breath in the rhythm of his name, *Her* on the inhale, *schel* on the exhale, and as I run the pale morning sky descends slowly, transforming by degrees into a fog rolling up the streets. I almost trip over a rut in the cross street, my skirt ripping on the heel of my slipper when I catch myself, but I keep running. The fog coils thicker, so thick I can feel it against my face. Before long the path by the shopfronts is completely swallowed with mist, and the sounds of the street life have deadened.

I slow to a walk, my hands pressed to my ribs against the painful stitch that's digging into them. My breath comes in short gasps. The fog rolls nearer.

I stop walking.

There's no one on the street. I'm alone, completely enclosed in a veil of fog. I strain my ears, listing for the telltale calls of pineapple sellers, children scavenging the trash heaps for bits of rope and broken nails, peddlers' carts creaking past, black fortune-tellers selling numbers for policy, whores hustling the men coming out of coffeehouses.

There's nothing.

I rub deeper into my rib cage, frowning.

I'm surrounded by dead silence.

"Well," I say aloud to myself. "If that don't beat all."

I wait for what feels like a long time for the fog to lift. These fogs happen sometimes, though usually not this far uptown, and usually not this far from the wharves. This is oyster-selling fog. Ocean fog.

The stitch in my side finally subsides, and I smooth my pigtails back into place and wipe the sweat from under my eyes. Lottie will kill me, with the sweat stains I'm leaving on this dress. I bend down to inspect the damage to the hem, and find it not too bad. A roll and a few stitches, and it'll be too short for me, but Beattie can wear it. It's too small for me anyway, and we've let it out twice already.

I start walking again, with some care, as the fog is so thick I'm having trouble telling what direction I'm going. But I know the way to Herschel's store as well as my way to Hudson Square, or to the ferry landing, or the Battery. I know it as well as I know the path from our room to Ed's, or from the kitchen door to the privy. I'll find him.

I keep walking.

My feet carry me for a long time. I'm not sure how long, as the fog stays heavy, but I feel myself begin to get tired. And the corn hasn't held me hardly at all. I want dinner. I want Herschel to give his uncle some kind of excuse so that we can slip off a few blocks away and find a beer hall that serves cured ham. Course, Herschel can't eat ham.

Well, Herschel will have to go despite himself. Ham is what I'm hungry for. Or bacon! I should've stopped for some bacon before leaving. I don't know why I was in such a rush, only . . .

My ruminations on dinner are interrupted by the thinning of the fog, ever so slightly. I peer ahead, trying to make out where I am. I should be at Chatham Square by now. Or past it, even. Well past. I could have walked all the way to the water, by mistake, though you can generally hear the rigging and the seagulls and the ships creaking, between all the hubbub of the wharves and stalls and junk shops.

I can almost recognize where I am. I hurry forward, into the thinning patch that is opening before me.

It's the stoop of a town house, that much I know. There's no one about on the street. The block is deserted and silent. I squint, trying to make out more details of the house. I walk faster, picking my skirts up in my fists, then dashing up to the stoop to stare at the building's face.

It's my house.

"But how did I . . ." I trail off.

I spin about where I'm standing, but there's no one there, and just outside the periphery of the front stoop, the fog is just as thick.

I scratch in my curls.

"I got turned around," I explain to myself. "In the fog, I got turned around someways."

I stand on the stoop for a long minute, chewing my lip. The truth is, I'm feeling awfully tired. It was a long night, after all. All that Madeira. Perhaps it would be wiser to go inside and rest. Perhaps I should look for the cameo in my room, and rest, and collect my thoughts, and perhaps I can bribe Winston to carry a message to Herschel, to meet me at a theater we've gone to before, where we can sit in a corner and kiss and no one cares. Winston carries messages for me sometimes. Winston excels at never letting on, when he sees things. Willful blindness is almost as good as trust.

I mount the steps to the house and try the door.

It's locked. I don't have my key, of course, but someone's always home.

I rap on the door with my fist first, and when that doesn't work, I take hold of the brass knocker and give it a good loud *knock knock knock*.

I wait, listening for the telltale shuffle of Lottie's feet on the stairs. There's no answer.

I try again. *Knock. Knock. Knock.*

The house has a dead sound, as though it were completely empty, not only of people, but of furniture, and all hint of life.

"Hello?" I shout up to the windows. "Ed?"

My brother's room looks over the street, since my parents are less concerned with the modesty of an eight-year-old boy than with their potentially wayward daughters. If he's upstairs playing or at his lessons, he should certainly hear me.

"Ed! I'm locked out!" I scream at the top of my lungs.

The house makes no reply.

Muttering, I hurry down the front steps and around the side alley, through the gate to the kitchen garden in back. I exhale a long sigh of relief when I spy Winston chopping wood next to the chicken coop. Mother likes to keep chickens because it reminds her of when she was a girl, in Connecticut. But it'd be cheaper just to buy them.

"Winston?" I call out.

Winston doesn't hear me. He lifts the ax overhead with an air of barely restrained rage that even I can see, and seeing anything about him is difficult, as the fog is thicker back here. He brings it down with a grunt, and the log splits. Winston's saving up money to buy his wife, who labors as a housemaid for a man at my father's bank. She costs ninety dollars. So far he's saved seventy-one.

He hoists it out of the stump underneath, and lifts it overhead again, and brings it down with a thwack. Over and over and over and over and over again. Like Sisyphus, pushing the boulder up the hill. The woodpile never seems to get smaller. The chopped pile never seems to get larger. The chopping of wood will never end for a man of all work with an indentured baby daughter and an enslaved wife.

"Winston?" I try again.

I edge nearer, and see that it's not the fog that's making Winston hard to see. Winston is hard to see because Winston almost doesn't seem to be fully there. He lifts the ax overhead, and I can see through the ax head to the fence beyond. He brings it down, and the curve of Winston's back blends in with the chicken coop beyond. My eyes widen.

As I watch, Winston seems to fade, like a newspaper bleached and curling in the sun. He keeps lifting and chopping, lifting and chopping, but with each blow he gets less visible, until even the sound of his chopping drifts away. Presently Winston retreats to the barest outline of himself, as if drawn in watery ink, and then on a passing breeze he blows away.

I stand for a long time in the kitchen garden, staring at the spot where he used to be.

I'm alone.

The vegetables are all gone. The fat gourds and pumpkins that we usually have in October are gone, the garden bricked over and desolate, interrupted only by the rustle of dead leaves.

I wrap my arms around myself, hugging tightly. The wind picks up, blowing my skirts against my legs and my curls into my mouth.

Slowly I turn and walk back down the alley to the front of the house.

As I round the corner onto the street, I spy a dark figure at the front door. He's young and slight, and I can't see his face, but he's holding a knife.

"Hey!" I shout. "What are you doing?"

The figure turns to stare at me with a start, stabs the knife into the wood of the door so hard it sticks, and flees down the stairs.

"Wait!" I yell, running after him. "Wait! Who are you? What do you want?"

Whoever he is vanishes into the dense wall of fog just beyond the circle made by the front stoop of my house. I'm on the point of following him, but I'm loath to step into the fogbank again. What if I get lost?

What if I can't find my way out?

I stare at the carved wooden door of our house. The knife jutting out from the door pins in place a folded paper fastened closed with a red smear of sealing wax. I mount the stairs to rip the offending paper off the door and observe that the seal in the wax is shaped like an old-fashioned spindle.

It's the note. The one we found on the door last week.

The same note.

Papa wouldn't let anyone see it when it came.

He crumpled it in his hand and cried, "Eleanor!" in a way that I had never heard him address my mother before. And more importantly, she'd come. They'd spoken not more than five minutes and then Mother had emerged from the drawing room, handed a folded paper to Winston to carry to Hudson Square and said to me brightly, "Well! Better pack."

This is the note that sent us running to my aunt's house.

It's not the day after the Aquatic Celebration.

It's the week before.

My blood thuds in my ears. I slowly mount the steps of our town house and reach my hand forward to pluck the note from the knife.

But before my hand can touch the paper, something strange happens.

The door begins to melt.

It looks like the door is sculpted of mud, and a sudden hard rain has come up. The door dribbles down itself under my hand, the knocker and the handle and the carving sliding down the surface of it and pulling apart while I watch. In moments our heavy wooden front door is gone, and the note and knife vanished with it. The slurry runs into crevices in the brick, pouring down the steps and oozing around my feet. Speechless, I take a step backward and nearly topple off the top step. I catch myself by grabbing on to a cheap metal railing that wasn't there before.

Behind our door is a glass one that I've never seen. It has a metal handle, and I can see through it into what had been our entryway, but I don't recognize anything inside. Our wood floor has been replaced with some kind of odd-looking tile, and our curving stair is gone. Next to the glass door stands a row of little brass cubbies with names written on them. And to the right, jutting out where our front gated garden used to be, is a wall of glass, lit with that glaring white light I saw in our drawing room before, with the same little tables and stained mirror. Behind the tables I can see a long counter, with racks of pies covered in cheese. But all the people are gone.

"This isn't happening," I explain to myself, and I'm pleasantly surprised by how reasonable I sound.

I turn around, keeping perfectly calm, and proceed down the steps with my head held high.

When I reach the walkway, I break into a dead run and flee into the fog. I run and I run and I run and I run, not caring where I'm going, not turning corners or looking, seeing nothing, until my chest is bursting and my stitch is back and I have to stop, leaning over, my hands on my knees, panting like a dog in summer.

The fog parts, and when I look up, I find myself back in front of our house again.

I roll my head back on my shoulders and laugh aloud.

"All right!" I scream at the top of my lungs. Screaming feels really good. I never get to scream. And none of this is really happening anyway, so why not?

"ALL RIGHT!" I bellow, and my voice echoes deadly off the face of my home. "I give up! Are you happy now?"

I don't know who I'm talking to. Myself, I suppose.

Chuckling with relief, I walk over and plop down on the stoop.

Obviously, one of two things is happening. One, I've gotten yellow fever and I am at this very moment lying-in in my aunt's house, out of my head with delirium. This is a distinct possibility, as yellow fever rips through Herschel's tenement in the Sixth Ward every summer. It's a wonder I didn't get it sooner, frankly. I probably danced too much at the Aquatic Display, and certainly drank too much, and the fever took over and I collapsed. In which case, this will all be over soon, because I will either recover, or I'll be dead.

The other possibility is that I've gone mad.

I'm less persuaded by this possibility. People don't go mad all at once, do they? Isn't madness more of a gradual kind of thing? Maybe you wake up one morning not quite yourself, and the next morning you're even less yourself, and then before you know it you're not yourself at all. I've seen mad people, of course. They take them in at the almshouse, which is why most sane paupers would sooner live with eleven strangers in a wet cellar. They turn up in the street, too, roaming about, muttering to themselves, getting beaten with a walking stick when they steal a bread crust from a coffeehouse table in the open street.

Of course, if a body goes mad, perhaps one doesn't know it? Perhaps it's the persuasion of sanity that truly marks a madwoman. I muse on this idea for a long while, my fingers knitted over my knees, leaning back against the step and gazing up into the blank white sky.

149

If I am mad, in a sense, it could be fun. My parents will still have to care for me. They'd never cast me out, certainly not while Papa has his political designs. I won't be responsible for myself at all. I can do or say whatever I like. I can go see Herschel and not have to pretend I'm not!

At the thought of Herschel, though, my face darkens.

He'd never want to be with a madwoman. Who would?

Herschel's not allowed to be with me, anyway. His family won't allow it. They don't marry outside their *schul*.

I look down at my hands, at my naked finger where my cameo ought to be.

If I'm reliving the day the note was stabbed to our door, then it's the same day Herschel gives me the ring. Perhaps that's where my cameo is. Perhaps he hasn't given it to me yet. But how can he give it to me, if I'm trapped here?

How will anyone ever find me, in all this fog? If nobody ever finds me, what will happen then?

I shiver, huddling within myself and pulling my arms to my chest behind my updrawn legs. I sink my head down, resting my forehead on my knees.

I have to think.

I have to figure this out.

A long time passes, I don't know how long, before I hear a young male voice say, "Hey! Hi!"

I look up, my eyes dazzled with hope. I've been found!

"Herschel?" I say, my voice catching in my throat. My heart thuds twice in quick succession.

The fog has thinned just beyond the stoop where I'm sitting, and I can barely make out the figure of a boy slouching toward me. There's something familiar about him, but I can't see his face.

"Huh?" the boy says.

He pauses inside the thickest edge of fog, and I can tell by his movements that he's looking around to see who I'm talking to. I stare hard at him, trying to see him clearly. But it's not who I thought it was.

"Oh!" I exclaim, my heart sinking. I withdraw behind my knees for protection. If he puts his hands on me, there's nowhere for me to go. I can't run. There's no one to help.

"Hey, no. I'm sorry," the boy rushes to say. I can admit that he sounds friendly. Jolly, even. And not in a sporting way. "I'm Wes," he goes on. "From the other night. Remember?"

"Wes," I say slowly.

He acts like we've known each other before. By now he's moved out of the fog and I can see him clearly. And it's true, there's something warm and familiar about him. Tall, much taller than Herschel. Taller even than Papa. Sandy-colored, with freckles. But he's in ill-fitting short pants, which is puzzling considering his age, and no waistcoat. He'd look like a beggar, in such clothes, if he weren't so clean. He's cleaner than me, even. The skin of his face is scrubbed and pink, beardless, and his hair stands up in a mop like Herschel's. I like it better than the oiled-down look that so many men affect. He's not even wearing a hat.

"Yeah. Um. I was here with that other guy? Filming the séance. Last week?" He looks into my eyes, hunting for recognition. He seems like he really wants me to remember. But surely I would remember, meeting this strange boy. *Film* is not a verb, first off. And I certainly haven't been to a "séance," whatever that is. But it's hard to resist his certainty that we're already friends. I feel the pull of him and find myself wanting to remember. Unless of course, and this is a distinct possibility, this boy does not exist at all. In fact, there is quite a decent chance that this boy is a figment of my imagination, who I have conjured out of the mist because I am lonely, and that he's familiar because he's just a part of my mind. If that's true, which it almost certainly is, then it's doubly rude to send him away. Not only rude, but foolish, since who knows if I'd be able to conjure up anyone else?

"The séance," I repeat as though I know what he's talking about. Then I make my best show of remembering. "Oh yes! I remember. Of course."

He looks worried. The figment of my imagination is sensitive.

"Are you okay?" the boy asks.

"Okay?" I echo. What does that mean? Am I . . . what? "I was just waiting," I correct him.

"I was actually hoping I'd see you again," he says, moving nearer.

The figment of my imagination is also charming. I smile prettily at him. Silly figment.

"You were?" I say.

"Definitely," Wes insists with what I imagine he thinks is great authority. "In fact, it was absolutely imperative that I find you. Did you know that?"

"Aw," I say, lowering my lashes to let him know that I'm on to his tricks. "You're teasing me. You're not really here."

"Sure I am." He looks hurt.

As if to prove a point he comes over and sits on the stoop, his knees drawn up next to mine. His shoes are odd. I'm trying to figure out what makes them so odd when he interrupts me by digging his elbow into my ribs.

"See?" he says.

It certainly feels like a real elbow. I look at him warily. I'm not sure if I want him to be real or not. There's something disconcerting, about being so at ease with a boy I've just met. But then, if he *is* real, perhaps he can help me sort out what's going on. He doesn't seem troubled by the fog in the slightest. Fog does happen, from time to time. And it can be very disorienting. Ships dash themselves on rocks all the time, when they get lost in the fog. What if nothing is wrong with me at all? What if I'm experiencing nothing more odious than the strange intersection of weather and Madeira after a night's revels?

A slender thread of relief unwinds inside me, as if he'd found the loose end and is pulling to unravel an ugly shawl in my soul. I laugh at the pleasure of it, and poke him in the ribs in return.

"So how did you find me?" I want to know. "Wes."

I certainly haven't heard his name before. It sounds strange to me, or made up, but then a lot of the boys and girls in other neighborhoods have names that sound strange to someone whose family was English or Dutch. I'd never heard the name Herschel before, either.

"It wasn't easy," he says, leaning in as if to draw me into a conspiracy. "Given that I don't know your name."

Oh, figment. You think you are so clever.

"Wes," I repeat, to let him know that I see through his transparent ruse. "Is that a nickname?"

"Maybe," he replies, and waggles his eyebrows like the villain in a play.

I look him full in the face, smiling, not saying anything, letting him know in no uncertain terms that I expect him to tell me his real name before I tell him mine. But he's waiting, too, and looking back at me just as frankly. A long challenging minute passes with us staring into each other's eyes. The minute goes on too long, begins to make me nervous, but then we both collapse in laughter.

"So, listen," he says. "This may sound really weird, but I did have to find you."

"Weird?" I say, puzzled. I'm not used to hearing that word used so casually. Weird means magical, like the weird sisters in *Macbeth*.

He doesn't see why I'm confused, though.

"I mean. It's not a big deal or anything," he continues, mollifying me. But his manner of speaking sounds odd, to my ears. I know the words he uses, but they seem wrong somehow.

He produces a funny-looking saddlebag, fastened in a way I haven't seen. He opens it and roots around inside. After a minute he produces a sheet of notepaper and he attempts to smooth out the creases before handing it to me.

"I just need you to sign this. I'm sorry. I should have done it when I was here before."

I stare at the paper. It looks something like a bill of sale, not that I've ever had to sign one before. It uses the word "whereas" a lot, and talks about rights to "the image, now and in perpetuity, in any manner of storage or retrieval now extant or devised in the future."

But the words aren't the strangest part.

The words are *typeset*.

Papa's bank contracts are well drawn by his clerks, but they're never typeset. And the paper is so smooth and white it doesn't look real.

I have no idea what it means. I look at him quizzically.

"I mean"—his cheeks are burning bright pink, which I find rather charming—"I'm just as glad I didn't. Remember to get you to sign it, I mean. Before. Because then I had to . . ."

He can't finish his thought, so caught up is he in staring at me. Herschel wouldn't like it, seeing another boy stare at me so. I shouldn't like it, either. But I do. I feel like I glisten when Wes looks at me like that. I wait, not sure what I should do.

"Anyway," Wes continues in a rush, breaking his gaze and turning back to his saddlebag for escape. "Here."

He produces a funny little object that's like one of Mother's gilt pencils, only not made of wood. It's not made of metal, either. I weigh it in my hand. It's light, like a stripped quill, only without any ink. A pen, clearly, but of some kind I haven't seen.

"Sign?" I say. As if my signing anything would make any difference to anyone. Under the law, I'm not even a person. "But what is it?"

I must look more perturbed than I even realize, because all at once his gray eyes darken, and he looks around us quickly as though we're being watched. My scalp tightens with sudden anxiety. I think fleetingly of the contract signed in Marlowe's *The Tragical History of the Life and Death of Doctor Faustus*. Typical, of a young girl being dramatic, I chastise myself.

"Seriously. Is everything okay?" he whispers in my ear.

I stare at him, baffled by this question. That word again.

"Is . . . everything . . . okay." I try out the words for myself. "Oh. Kay."

He presses himself nearer to me, and his skin feels warm next to mine. It feels good, having him here with me. Safe.

"Is it?" he insists. He puts an arm around my shoulder and gives me a squeeze, the kind of squeeze that would be too familiar if it were from almost anyone else. "You can trust me. It's okay."

I don't know why, but this boy feels wonderfully necessary. He looks at me with such soft attention, and when he leans in close to me, I don't worry so much about the fog. I don't feel so lost. I don't even care if he's imaginary.

A smile spreads across my face and I say, "It caps the climax. Got any ink?"

Now it's his turn to look confused. My figment doesn't use idioms, apparently. It could be that my figment isn't very bright. "Um. What?"

"Ink?" I wave the stripped quill at him. "You want me to sign it, don't you?"

"Well, yeah, but . . . ," he stammers, as if he doesn't know how to answer my incredibly obvious question.

"Annatje?" I almost hear someone call from inside the house. The faint sound, fainter than a leaf falling on the ground, sends a chill across the back of my neck, down my spine, all the way to my slippers on the paving stones.

I sit stock-still, my ears straining to decipher if I really heard it, or if it's another game my mind is playing with itself.

"Are you—" Wes starts to say, but I can't have him talking to me until I discover if I heard my name. I make a hushing sound and silence him with my fingertips against his lips. They are warm and soft.

"Shhh," I whisper. Obediently he stops, eyebrows raised with curiosity.

My ears ring with the strain of listening through the silence, and I stare hard at Ed's bedroom window upstairs.

The window sash is open, and the corner of a gauzy curtain drifts over the lip of the window and waves slowly in the air like a hand.

Inside the house, I hear the faintest sounds of movement. Footsteps, or the scraping of a chair across the floor. It's not even a sound, exactly, more a vibration. I can tell that they're inside. They're inside!

And then I hear it again.

"Annatje?" my mother clearly calls. I hear her through Ed's window, as though she's looking for me upstairs.

I leap to my feet.

"I'm sorry," I stammer to my disappointed-looking figment. His eyebrows have risen higher and are meeting in a sorry little point above his nose. "I'm sorry, Wes, I've got to go. That's my mother."

"Your—what?" He glances quickly at the façade of my town house with a look of utter confusion.

I'm already at the front door. It's as real and solid and wooden as ever it was. There's even a chip in the black paint left by the knifepoint, showing the raw wood underneath. But the note has disappeared. I have my hand on the knob, and it's unlocked, and I have one foot on the doorsill.

Wes has scrambled to his feet.

"My mother," I explain, impatient. "I'm sorry, I have to go."

"But—" Wes's voice breaks, and he reaches a hand toward me. "Hey. Listen. I'm sorry, look, I know you don't know me, but I really need your help with this."

I pause, the door open, and it seems impossible that I can still be talking to him when I have to go inside right now and see my mother.

"Help?" I say.

"Annatje!" my mother shouts down the curve of the staircase, sharper and more urgently. "I need you right now!"

I glance up to where she'll appear on the stair any minute. It's clear something is wrong. It must be the letter. Papa's read the letter.

"Please?" wheedles my figment.

In a flash I'm angry with him. Can't he see that I have to go? But he's such a warm figment, and the corners of his eyes look moist and his eyelashes are trembling.

"I . . ." I hesitate, unsure what to do.

"Look," he reasons. "If you have to go right now, I can just wait. Okay? You go do whatever, and I'll just wait down here. It's no big deal. I mean. You won't be long, right?"

"Um . . ." I can't tell how long I'll be. How can I know? I hear my mother's footsteps in the hall overhead, and the door to my father's study slam. Running feet in the hallway between my siblings' rooms. It's the day of the letter, and I have to go.

"Please?" Wes whispers to me. His eyes are yearning, his hand crumpling the paper that he was trying to show me.

I'm inside the front hall now, my hand on the banister, and the hall is just as it should be, with the hat stand and the carpet runner. Perhaps I won't be as long as all that. I have to go see Herschel before we flee to Hudson Square, because Herschel hasn't given me the cameo yet. If Wes walks with me, I'll be safer, in the street. And the truth is, I crave that stolid boy warmth next to me. That crinkling smile of his. His funny wrong words. Is it wrong, to be escorted through the streets by one boy on the way to meet another?

"All right," I whisper to him so that Mother won't hear.

The one time Mother spied me talking to Herschel, I spent two days locked in my bedroom and Beattie slept on the trundle in Mother's room. I still have a pale stripe on my left hip, from where the welt healed. I can't have her see me talking to some strange overgrown boy in short pants.

"Wait down there," I say in my lowest voice. "I'll be back as soon as I can."

"Okay." Wes grins in a way both winning and foolish, like a puppy with a pullet in its mouth. I grin back. So maybe Wes shouldn't walk me *all* the way to Herschel's shop. Maybe he can take me 'til I'm a block away, and I can carry on alone thereafter. "Okay. I'll be right here."

My feet newly light, I start up the stairs to where my mother is waiting.

"Wait!" Wes shouts, and I freeze where I'm standing and give him a deadly look. I can't have Mother and Papa knowing about him. He has to be quiet.

"I don't know your name." The words tumble out of my figment in a rush of explanation and excuse. "What's your name?"

I consider the question, and then bestow on him my most excellent smile.

"Annie," I whisper. "I'm Annie."

I just have time to see his entire face break open in a dazzling grin.

Then the door slams behind me on a passing breeze, shaking the walls of the town house as I hurry up the stairs.

"Mother!" I shout. "Mother, I'm here!"

CHAPTER 5

Mother's face is pale and drawn when she looks down at me over the banister. She's just come out of Papa's study.

"There you are," she says, and her grip tightens on the handrail.

"I'm sorry," I rush to apologize, but I don't know what I'm apologizing for.

Mother's eyes narrow at me, and when I reach the top of the stairs she takes hold of my sleeve and pushes me up against the wall.

"Listen to me," she says in a voice so quiet it fills me with dread. "I want you to go into your bedroom and help your sister pack."

"Pack?" I repeat, but of course I know exactly what she's talking about. She's talking about the letter. "Is Lottie helping her?"

"Lottie's gone home," Mother says.

"Home?" I ask. "But for how long?"

Lottie is from a mean smattering of huts in the countryside far up the island, a hardscrabble village named Seneca. No one knows why it has an Indian name, since I don't think any Indians live there. I've never actually been, and Lottie won't tell me about it. She hates to go back home, though she'll never say why. Lottie doesn't like talking about herself with us as a rule. Winston is from there, too, though, and goes home some Sundays, when Mother and Papa let him get away. Sometimes his wife's owner will let her and the children go there, too, but rarely. Winston gets a faraway look on his face, when one of those home-going Sundays is coming. He has a small parcel of land of his own, with a tiny house that he built, covered with wooden shingles that he split. Winston is free, and always was, as far as I know, but not so many freedmen can buy land. Even land no one else wants but the Irish.

"I don't know," Mother hisses through clenched teeth. "Now hurry. Winston's going to drive us in half an hour."

She shoves me through the door of my bedroom and then hurries down the hall back to Papa's study.

Beattie is nowhere to be seen, though there's a heap of finery and coats on our still-listing bed. I hear drawers opening and closing in Ed's room next door. I stand alone in the center of the room, my skirts in my hands, vibrating with indecision.

"Dammit, Eleanor!" an angry male voice shouts through closed doors.

My mouth goes dry.

I never knew what the letter said. But in this shadow version of my past, this bizarre reliving of a day that already happened, perhaps I can find out.

On silent cat feet, I creep out of my bedroom and down the hall, careful to avoid the creaky board at the head of the stairs. Papa's study is at the front of the house, overlooking First Street, next to Ed's room. I reach his closed door and, holding my breath, lean down until my ear hovers just next to the keyhole. One hand tucks my pigtail behind my ear.

Papa and Mother are both inside, with at least two other men.

". . . let them threaten us like this," Papa is in the middle of saying.

"Peter," my mother says in her cold and reasonable voice. "Nothing has to change. The flotilla is underway. The celebration will go on. Nothing will stop it."

"Do you know what the governor will do, if he hears the threats are escalating?" one of the unseen men says.

"There's nothing to do," my mother insists. "The canal will open. The corporation will succeed. There's no stopping it, even if the governor wanted to. Which he does not."

"I don't know," my father says.

He sounds weary. There's a creak, as of someone sitting down heavily in a desk chair. Footsteps cross the room, and a shadow moves over my face where I hover, listening.

"In any case," another male voice says, "they'll soon see it's for the best. These agitators act from fear. They're essentially ignorant."

"Indeed," my father agrees. A long pause wears by while we all wait to hear what he might say next.

"When they see how cheap corn gets, the violence will stop. It stands to benefit the paupers most of all, anyhow," the other man remarks.

"We might tell the governor in any case," my father says at length.

A thrumming of tension swells throughout the room.

"But, Mr. Van Sinderen," the younger of the two men says. "We don't want to distract him. It's only your . . ." He stops himself, aware that my mother is listening to him with icy attention. He clears his throat. "I'm sorry, madam. But it's only your family that's received the threats."

"What are you suggesting?" my father growls.

"Well," the unseen man demurs. "It's possible that the . . . don't you at least think that perhaps . . ."

"Spit it out already!" my father shouts.

"He thinks it's a private quarrel, Peter," my mother says, and the timbre of her voice turns me to glass. "That this . . . brotherhood, or whatever it is . . . isn't trying to scuttle the corporation. They're trying to scuttle you."

Another creak as my father rises from his seat and stalks across the room.

"In which case," his young corporation colleague continues, "we see no reason to bother the governor. Provided your family's security is sure, of course."

"Which we're prepared to arrange," the other corporation functionary hastens to add. "At our expense. At least until the canal is officially open."

"These crackbrains!" my father explodes, pounding his fist onto the roll-front desk with a thud.

"I've already sent a message to Mehitable," my mother rushes to soothe him. "She says we can stay in Hudson Square as long as we like. And it's only another week 'til the celebration. Then we'll be out of danger."

"Oh, splendid," my father says, molassesey with sarcasm. "Mehitable, no less. She's as giddy as these dashed Luddites. Crackbrains all of them!"

"I'll add, Mrs. Van Sinderen, that the corporation's investigating the threats," the authoritative young man says. "We'll find the culprits in ample time."

"And what happens then?" Mother asks.

Papa laughs mirthlessly, joined by the other two men.

"Ragtag and bobtails," my father mutters. "Sons of whores. What difference does it make?"

I catch my breath, and clap my hand over my mouth.

The figures on the other side of the door all freeze, listening. A moment of anxious silence settles on the second floor of our town house. We all lean in, listening to each other without breathing.

Without warning, footsteps rush across the study floor and the door flings open. I hurry to stand up and appear as though I were happening by on my way to Ed's room, but my mother's pinched face, pale with rage, tells me that my ruse has failed. Behind her I spy my father standing at a chaotic desk, purple-black bags under his eyes, flanked by two younger men in tight waistcoats, their hair slicked down where their high hats usually are. One of them is holding a knife. It's the same knife I saw the stranger use to stab the note onto our front door. They all look up at me, startled into silence.

"Dash it all, Annatje!" my father shouts. "You heard your mother! Get your things together!"

"We're going to Aunt Mehitable's," Mother reiterates, her voice artificially calm.

"Yes, Mother," I say.

I crane my neck over her shoulder, to see if I can glimpse the note. The young man holding the knife sees me looking, and hides the blade behind his back. My father catches up the note and stuffs it into his pocket before looking with lowered brows out the window.

"Don't forget the dress we picked for you to wear for the festivities," Mother reminds me. "And your slippers. Tell Beattie. The newspapers will be there."

"All right." I hesitate.

Should I invent an excuse to leave? But what lie can I spin that would persuade her to let me go?

My eyes shift between her and Papa and the panic-faced corporation men. Papa turns his back to me, fingertips rubbing over his forehead, and one of the men whispers in my father's ear.

I can slip out. Lottie's already left, and Winston won't say anything. If I pretend I'm going right to my room, they'll stay in the study hatching their schemes, and I can get away to see Herschel.

Just for a minute. If I've lived this day before, as I'm increasingly certain I have, then I have to find a way for him to give me the cameo.

I ache for it.

For the cameo, and for how he stares at me beneath his studied brows, and for what he says when he slides it on my finger. His eyes look soft, when he stares at me. Like Wes's eyes, I think in passing.

I arrange my features into a semblance of filial piety. Mother glares at me. She knows me too well.

"I'll tell Beatrice," I say, keeping all excitement out of my voice. "We'll be ready."

"Good girl." Mother dismisses me and then shuts the door in my face.

The conversation recommences the moment the door is shut.

I slip back to my bedroom and find Beattie digging through the pile of dresses and underthings that she left on the bed. An open trunk has been dragged over next to it, and the trunk vomits stockings over its edge and onto the floor.

"There you are!" Beattie breathes. "Did Mother tell you?" Her eyes shine bright with impish excitement.

"That we're going to Aunt Mehitable's? Yes," I say, darting from shelf to mantel to dressing table, grabbing the odd item to toss into the trunk so it will look like I've packed to anyone curious.

"Did she tell you why?" Beattie singsongs, dancing by with a scarf wrapped around her head.

"I saw. Papa got a note."

"We're all going to be killed!" Ed chirps from the doorway between our rooms. His arms are full of sweaters and he's beaming at me from behind them. "We have to flee. Papa said."

"What?" I freeze, my hand wrapped around a spool of thread from

164

Herschel's shop. It's a pale dove gray. I like the color so much that I keep the spool on my dressing table, where I can see it every day. No one knows why. I won't let Beattie touch it.

"It's true," Beatrice says, stuffing the scarf into the trunk. "I heard Mother and them talking about it, before she made me come pack."

"Is Papa still in his study?" Ed interrupts, cramming the sweaters into the trunk and then flopping on his back on our bed. "I want to ask if I should bring my speller."

"Killed? Are you sure?" I repeat.

They wouldn't have let Beattie see the note, certainly.

"Mother thinks it's a ruse," Beattie says in her eminently reasonable way.

"A ruse for what?"

"To scare Papa." She shrugs.

A missing glove is hunted up and then Beattie lays the pair atop the sweaters with care.

"But why would anyone want to scare Papa?" I ask.

"How should I know?" Beattie says. Which is a good point.

I frown, thinking.

"You should pack," my sister says mildly. "Mother said we're leaving in half an hour."

"Yes," I say, staring off into space.

My siblings watch me, waiting for me to leap to attention and start hurling dresses into the trunk like I'm expected to.

"I . . . ," I start to say, and then trail off.

What are Luddites? Could they really mean to kill us?

Does the note say when?

I shake myself awake and smile at Beattie.

"Annie?" she asks, looking curiously at my face. "Are you quite well?"

"But of course I am," I say. "I'm just going to have a quick word with Winston. I'll be right back."

"With Winston?" My sister looks confused.

"Can I come?" pipes my brother from the bed.

He's been expressly forbidden from bothering Winston, as for a period of three months he trailed on the poor man's heels every hour of the day, until one Sunday Ed announced he was going to go live in Seneca and be one of Winston's children instead. Mother put a stop to it then. He's been banned from below stairs without Beattie or me to watch him.

"No," I say. "You have to stay here and help Beatrice. Here, you can be in charge of making sure my evening dress is packed. The one with the puffed sleeves and the velvet flounce."

"Me?" Ed lifts his head. He likes being put in charge of things.

"Yes," I say. "Beattie will show you which one. It's in the wardrobe. Don't forget, it needs the right drawers and stockings, too. So it's important you pay close attention. I'll just run and ask Winston something, and I'll be right back. You won't even miss me."

"All right," my sister says uncertainly.

Ed has already leapt to his feet and climbed into the wardrobe, his two feet sticking out behind him as he roots through the clothes inside.

"I found one shoe already!" he cries in triumph, voice muffled by layers of cotton and wool.

Beattie raises a hand as if she were going to stop me, but I shake my head once, firm.

With a look of silent commiseration at my sister, I vanish out the door of our bedroom as quietly as I can go.

CHAPTER 6

I ease open the front door. And I wait.

I can still hear muffled arguing coming from Papa's study upstairs, and in the instant when the argument boils into shouting, I slip through unobserved and click the front door closed behind me.

The fog has finally burned away, and I take a long inhale, surveying up and down First Street. Crisp autumn sun blinks down onto the Bowery, and a lone seagull wheels by overhead, riding the salty harbor air with a cry.

I look to where I left Wes waiting for me on the stoop, and see that he's gone.

"Dash it," I say under my breath.

Why didn't he wait for me? I said I was coming right back! Now I'll have to walk the Bowery by myself. I don't have much time. They'll be missing me any minute.

Looking left and right, knowing neighbor women are observing me from behind panes of glass, I hurry away from our town house. I can make the walk in a quarter hour, if I'm not held up. Fifteen minutes to Herschel's store, and fifteen back. I can just make it.

I round the corner to the Bowery and hunch my shoulders up,

avoiding eye contact with the various men lounging in the coffee-houses and beer halls. I feel very small, sometimes, when I walk on the avenue. Some of the buildings are six stories tall, with everyone packed together jaw to jaw, people crammed into every cellar and windowless back room and under the eaves and spilling out into the street. Papa says the governor thinks one day the entire island will be filled. I wonder where all the people will go, when that happens. Already there're so many people here that listening at any open window will reveal six other conversations.

I squeeze my naked ring finger between the opposite finger and thumb as I walk, not meeting anyone's eye.

The last time that I lived this day, I didn't know what was going to happen. I didn't know what Herschel was going to say to me. I wonder if I can keep my secret, when he tells me this time. But in a way, I knew it already the first time, too. I feel a twinge of misgiving, having flirted with Wes on my stoop on the very day Herschel gives me the cameo. But I resolve that if Wes were as good as all that, he wouldn't have abandoned me. I don't care if I never see him again.

Maybe.

I've only been alone with Herschel a handful of times. And even then, we're never really alone. No one is ever alone, in the city. Sometimes down by the waterfront, flecks of cotton from all the unloaded bales drift through the air like snow, dotting Herschel's eyelashes and making him sneeze. Between the shipyards and forests of masts with their nets of rigging, sailors straddling the spars and looking down with envy at our idleness, where the children swim on hot days, we lose ourselves in the crowd of other people our age and younger, screaming and laughing and splashing water. He first took my hand on one of those summer afternoons, and no one saw. But I felt it, when he squeezed my hand, and it thrilled me to the roots of my hair.

We've walked at night, the few times we could both sneak away.

Once we stole enough time to ride the Brooklyn ferry over the moon-lit river, stars scattering in the waves before the prow of the boat as we pressed against the railing, the dotted lamps lining Manhattan's wharves receding behind us, enclosing us in darkness. Herschel drew his thumb along my jaw and moved his fingers into my hair and then he kissed me, his young beard chafing my cheeks as he touched his lips to mine, first nervously, trembling, and then with hunger.

I'm lost in a daydream of Herschel, the feel of his mouth on mine, the smell of his skin, and the prickling and trembling in my body when I think about him. I'm deaf to the catcalls from the men loung-ing on the Bowery.

I cross Houston Street, pulse thudding in my throat. I'll be there in seven minutes. I've counted. Seven minutes until I see him. Seven minutes until he gives me the cameo and tells me his plan.

A rumbling noise approaches behind me in the street, and then a carriage thunders by of a like I've never seen. It veers so close I'm pushed aside by the breeze of its passing. Frightened, I scream, and thrust my knuckles into my mouth. The carriage is painted a vibrant butterfly yellow, and it spits like a chimney from under the chassis.

And there's no horse.

"Did you see that?" I shout, reaching out and grabbing the first sleeve in the crowd, which proves to belong to a young mother, only a bit older than me, her face shaded by a fashionable bonnet with a bow under her chin, her hands on the shoulders of a small boy.

"See what?" she cries, looking around with alarm.

"I thought I saw . . ." I trail off.

But I've lost sight of it, between the landaus and wagons, pulled by snorting horses, driven by harassed-looking boys.

The young matron gives me a wary look and steers her boy away in the crowd.

I carry on. Only now I'm unable to daydream. My feet bring

me downtown, and under my feet, I feel an unfamiliar rumbling, as though a sleeping giant were turning over with a snore. A cadre of young men in plaid suits plays at cards at a table in the open doors of a beer hall, and though I should know better, I call to them, "What can that rumbling be? Can you hear it?"

They exchange glances among themselves, laughing, and one of them says, "I'll give you a rumbling."

I shake my head, hurrying farther, looking down at the bricked sidewalk as I pick my way between daubs of mud and excrement. In one stretch the bricks have been oddly replaced with what look like narrow iron bars, as if it were the door to a dungeon. No one else notices anything amiss. I edge around it, peering down, and am met with a blast of hot air, like the furnace of hell, and a screeching and groaning such as I've never heard. Lights flicker by, and the rumbling passes again, and I fall backward in confusion, my hands pressed to either side of my head.

"What is that?" I scream.

A few passersby hesitate, deciding whether to offer me help, or if they should summon whatever man has appointed himself guardian of the ward to usher me off the streets, or into a wagon to be hauled off to the House of Refuge.

A German family loiters on the periphery, watching me, and presently the man approaches me with caution at the apparent urging of his wife. He has a friendly face, and his tall hat is new and brushed.

"Miss?" he says, his accented voice low so as not to attract attention. "Is there someone I can help you to be finding?"

I'm confused by this offer. *Herschel,* I think, but I must only be a few blocks away, and it is only his face that I crave.

"N-n-n-o," I stammer, backing away. "Thank you, no."

"You are sure?" the young wife calls.

Without answering her, I turn on my heel and run.

I haven't gone twenty steps before the rumbling returns, and I stop short, gasping, watching in openmouthed horror as the tenement next to me begins, slowly, inexorably, to shake. A wave surges up the building as across the surface of the sea, from its foundations, up to the windows, to the pitched roof.

I see figures in the windows, moving about in shadow, but no one screams.

No figures appear at windows to throw out babies to be caught, no sashes fly open to wave sheets crying for help. No one seems to notice when a brick falls, then another, then a lump of cornice splits off and plunges down to shatter at my feet, followed by a rain of crumbled masonry. The noise becomes deafening, filling my ears and vibrating my entrails. I lift my arms to shield my face as the building slowly, rumblingly dissolves into dust.

No one else on the street seems to notice. They keep moving along in a tide of humanity, clutching their baskets and children as though nothing were amiss while I stand with arms over my head, my eyes saucers of disbelief.

Where the building stood is only a thick cloud of brown dust, roiling on eddies of autumn air.

"What's the matter with you people?" I scream, my face red.

This didn't happen the last time I sneaked from the house to go see Herschel.

A few people waiting at the street corner before picking their way between the wagons and vegetable stalls eye me with suspicion, but say nothing.

Desperate, I run over to a curiously dressed young man, hatless, in what look like tight-fitting work pants and a collarless shirt. I grasp his arm and try to drag him to a stop.

"That building just collapsed!" I scream in his ear. "Go get help!"

He pretends not to hear me, and my fingers slide off his arm as he disappears into the crowd.

"Someone, help! There's people in there!" I shout, pointing at the giant dust cloud.

My shouts cut short when the rumbling begins with renewed malice. I back away from the buildings, wanting to be far away, but I can't step into the street else I'll be trampled to death by the throng of horses and wagons and carriages. I once saw a little boy trampled, and his twisted limbs and dully flattened head haunted my nightmares for months.

The rumbling thickens, intensifies, and I stand stock-still, tears streaming down my face. It's coming from where the tenement stood. The brown dust cloud seems to be circulating, moving, breathing like an ephemeral nightmare animal. It grows and swells, thickening, stretching itself upward to the sky, growing denser and taller and squarer. The rumbling grows so loud that I scream, and my scream is noiseless, swallowed by the sound of the dust cloud. Inside the cloud, something comes ripping up out of the ground, bricks and rocks exploding in every direction as whatever it is comes rocketing toward the sky. I watch it rip skyward, my head falling backward as the thing stretches five, then ten, then fifteen, then twenty—it isn't possible!—stories into the sky.

When the rumbling subsides I'm left staring slack-jawed up at a fantastical edifice, all dressed in glass, stretching higher in the air than anything I've ever seen. It's like a solid cliff face, as steep and forbidding as the cliffs along the Hudson River at Sneden's Landing. Here and there the glass cliff has lights, illuminated inside, and I spy other figures, outlines of furniture, the moving shadows of people just like the ones in the tenement a moment before.

No one notices.

The crowds along the avenue jostle by as busy as ever, unconcerned, unmoved, oblivious. A girl strides by with a baby in a sling on her chest, bare-armed. Some young men in plaid pants sidle by, their eyes hidden with dark spectacles. Appalled, helpless, I stand rooted to my spot, turning around, staring. A horse trots by pulling a carriage with two people who look down at me curiously, the man in a high hat and the woman in a bonnet, and then another trots by on its heels with two more people, unhatted this time, bare-armed, dressed in short pants both of them, one of them holding an odd box to his face. I hear a clicking sound come from the box as the horse clops past.

I'm dizzy. I put my hands on either side of my head and squint my eyes closed. But they fly open again when I hear a loud blare, or honk, and on a puff of air another landau sails by inches from me, long and black and polished and also, incredibly, without a horse.

"Help!" I try to scream, but my mouth is too dry and no sound comes out. I lean over, afraid I'm going to be sick. No one stops; no one pays any attention to me.

"Help," I whisper to the ground, hands on my knees, gasping for breath as hot tears stream down my face and throat and neck. My nose bubbles.

"Hey," a girl's voice says nearby, and I look up in terror.

She's gazing on me curiously, and looks somewhat familiar. In her face, she looks familiar, anyway. She has heavy straight-cut hair over her eyes, and something about her bearing reminds me oddly of Ed. An impish twinkle in the corners of her eyes. She lays a hand on my shoulder and says, "You okay? You need anything? Hungry, maybe?"

She's oddly dressed, too, in frayed short trousers and stockings and a tight bodice with no sleeves, and she has tattoos of leaves along her arms and winding around her neck. I've never seen a woman with tattoos. I've only seen ink like that on the arms of whalers in bawdy houses where I wasn't supposed to be.

"Thirsty," I manage to say, my eyes hunting behind her, afraid that the rumbling will come back.

The street looks the same. Sort of. Does it? Two blocks away another tenement is slowly collapsing, consumed by the same brown dust cloud, while next to it another bizarre glass cliff bursts instantly up out of the ground like a mushroom, reaching impossibly high into the sky. Then another one, a block farther down. And another! The crowds moving in the streets don't even stop. No one screams. No fires break out.

The girl, oblivious, rummages in a paper bag that she's carrying and produces a glass bottle. She twists out the cork—no, there isn't a cork, just a kind of foil cap—and passes it to me.

"Here. Drink up. You look like you need it," she says.

I read the bottle, which has a paper label glued to it that reads COLT 45. I don't understand what this means.

"But . . . what is it?" I ask. Not that beggars can be choosers.

"Go on," the girl with the tattooed leaves says. "Trust me. You look like ass."

She thinks I look like . . . a donkey? I'd be offended, if I weren't so thirsty.

I take a swig from the bottle, and the liquid is an unpleasant, malty beer. But it rinses my mouth. Grateful, I swallow long and hard, feeling the bitter liquid pour into my stomach.

"All right," the girl says. "Take it easy."

I drink deep from the bottle and then wipe my lips on my sleeve. Before I can thank the girl, she's vanished into the throng.

The rumbling is back, or more properly it never left, this time shaking the victualing house next door to the first tenement. Three

174

men sit smoking pipes at a little table in the front window, and a ruddy-cheeked woman is pouring them flagons of beer. In a trice the rumble has consumed them without so much as a whisper. The victualing house folds in on itself as I watch, like a collapsing paper house, and this time my scream comes so loud that some people actually stop to watch. I fling aside the glass bottle, hearing it shatter, and an unseen voice cries, "Hey, watch it!" before I gather up my skirts and flee.

Blinded by tears, I dart and weave between the people. I have to reach Herschel's uncle's shop before the rumbling gets him.

What if I'm too late? What if it isn't there?

What if I never find my cameo?

CHAPTER 7

I dash through the throngs of people, but I can't escape. The figures around me on the street are changing, hats disappearing,
little boys vanishing from gutters, babies appearing pushed in funny
little cradles on wheels. I throw myself into the city, faces upon faces
swimming up together in the crowd, all looking through me. Do they
even know I'm here? Do they even see me?

"Help!" I cry as I run, my feet flying across puddles and over curbs
and through a honking cluster of horseless landaus.

"Outta the way!" someone shouts, and I flinch.

"Help!" I scream again, running up to an old woman in a long
dress, making her way slowly on the arm of a nurse. Neither of them
responds to me at all, and when I try to put my hands on the nurse's
arm, my fingers don't touch anything. The two women just push their
way along the sidewalk, each looking inward at her own worries.

"I don't understand!" I wail, running away from them, dashing up
to a man in a waistcoat, only it's short in back and has no vest. He's
looking at his wrist for some reason, and takes no notice of the Ma-
sonic temple dissolving into dust directly behind him. I scrabble at
his sleeve, screaming, "Help me! Somebody help me, please!"

But he shakes me off, indifferent, and then strides with purpose across the street with a crowd of other people. The landaus all stop and wait for him, though no one is waving to them to stop.

"Can you please help me?" I beg of a girl about Beattie's age, who pays no attention to me, so absorbed is she in looking at some little object she holds in her hands, a few inches from her nose. She giggles at the object and walks away from me.

"What's happening?" I scream, throwing my head back with my arms spread in supplication to the heavens.

The sky is blue and hot, like in summer, and instead of dirt and animal smells I taste something like brimstone in the air. Instead of roasted pears and hot corn, a cart on the street corner offers a sort of fried paste with spices I've never smelled before. The sign is gibberish: It says FALAFEL.

With a guttural cry of terror I tear off down the street, slamming into a young man surrounded on all sides by dogs yapping at his ankles. I fall to my hands and knees, my palms grating bloody on the pavement, and the young man hollers, "Hey, watch where you're going!"

I struggle to get back to my feet, but my skirts are twisted around my legs, and the dogs are all on thongs of leather attached to the man. I'm trapped in a mesh of leather thongs, and the dogs all snarl and snap at me, lunging for my face. I cower, bringing my arms over my head. Then the dogs are pulled roughly off, and the young man goes away cursing at me.

I'm sobbing, and I look down at the bloody scratches all over my hands. I'll never get home in time.

I'm lost.

I haven't found Herschel's shop.

I don't recognize this street at all.

When I get home they'll beat me raw for running off when I was supposed to be packing. I'll make everyone late, and that could be dangerous, if the Brotherhood of Luddites come for us like they say they will. And Lottie will be upset that I've ruined my dress.

My dress . . .

I look down at myself, and I'm not in the dress I put on in the morning. I'm in the evening gown that Ed is supposed to be packing for me to wear to the opening of the canal, on the corporation barge one week from today. The one with the velvet flounce.

I glance up, looking around myself, eyes widening with bafflement and wonder.

I'm in the middle of a quiet, leafy block, standing opposite a metal gate that is locked shut with a giant rusted padlock and chain. As I gaze upon it, the gate seems to shimmer, as though the iron had been dipped in the thinnest layer of gold. It's just a trick of the light, but I move nearer, peering between the bars.

The gate protects a kind of hidden garden, tucked between two buildings, and thrown completely in shadow by the raking afternoon sun. No one is inside. I lift my hand and rest it against the iron bars. They feel cool to the touch, cool and real. It looks so quiet in there. Quiet and safe. It looks like a perfect place to rest. And I'm so tired, all of a sudden. I'm so tired of running, and the rumbling, and being confused and lost and alone, and I can't find my way anywhere I want to go, and I can't get anyone's attention except when I don't want it. If I can only go in there to rest for a little while, everything will be all right.

I lightly touch the iron bars with my hand, and the gate swings obediently open with a welcoming creak. I sigh with relief. I pass through the gate into the shadows, feeling the springy turf under my slippers, the inviting breath of the shade. I just have to sit down. I have to rest, for a minute. A few shapes loom here and there in the darkness, but I don't pay any attention to them. I wander without any special purpose until I find the most perfect, comfortable spot, a tuft of grass and dandelions in full white puff nestled up against the garden wall. With a heavy sigh I sink down to the earth, stretching my legs out in front of me and leaning my weight against the wall. My cheek presses against the coolness there, and I find this portion of the wall is made of marble, surrounded on all sides by brick.

It feels so good, to be sitting here.

I close my eyes.

My breath comes soft and easy.

I sit that way for a long time. I might have drifted off to sleep, but I don't think so. I just want to close my eyes and be quiet for a little while. And so I let myself rest against this wonderful marble wall, which seems like it was made just for me.

After a time the backs of my eyelids glow red, and I feel a warm sunbeam move onto my face. I open my eyes, squinting into the light and rubbing my eyes with my knuckles. I feel better. I listen, and hear no more rumbling. I heave an enormous sigh, the kind Mother pinches me for making in church, and stretch my arms luxuriously over my head. My spine pops, and I roll my head back and forth on my shoulders, stretching this way and that. I'd like to loosen the lacing that's holding my corsetry together, but I can't reach the laces in back. I'll just have to be too tight for now.

The sun has moved, and I realize I'm late, and they'll be missing me at home. I have to get back. I'll get a message to Herschel when we get to Aunt Mehitable's. It'll be all right.

I struggle to my feet, brushing bits of grass and dandelion fluff from the silk of my dress, hoping I haven't made myself too odious.

I'm mid-brush when I notice that the sunbeam is falling across the marble panel in the wall where I'd been leaning my head.

"What?" I say aloud.

I take a step back, and slip on a clod of dirt, almost losing my balance.

There's carving on the marble slab, but it's difficult to make out. It looks like the carving has been there for a long time, and has partly melted away in the rain.

Slowly, tremblingly, I stretch my hand forward to trace the barely legible letters.

They spell **V A N S I N D E R E N**.

"*What?*" I say again, but it's hard to speak because my lower lip is trembling.

My fingertips reach forward, traveling from the shadow where I'm standing into the cheerful sunbeam. When my hand reaches the light, my eyes stretch open as wide as they can go, so wide the tears that spring to their corners dry before they can fall.

As my hand moves into the light, the nails slowly blacken. The skin of my arm grows splotchy, and the deeper my arm reaches into the sun, the higher up the staining travels. As it moves into the sun my puffed silk sleeve deflates, the lace at my elbow dissolves into grayness and tatters. With a shudder I pull my hand back out of the light and hold both my hands up in front of my face, watching in horror as tendrils of smoke begin to coil up from my fingertips. I've pulled back into the shadows, but it's too late: the mud and soot stains continue to creep up both my arms, spreading across my chest and down my dress, tattering the cloth and reeking of smoke and earth. The wave of corruption spreads over my skirt before my eyes, rotting the hem and reaching all the way to my slippers, which turn dishwater gray. In the periphery of my eyes I see the curls over my ears begin to pour smoke, and I smell burning flesh and singed hair.

"But . . . but . . . ," I sputter, looking in horror down at myself.

I'm whimpering, nonsense is pouring out of my mouth, and I start to hyperventilate, but I can't get my breath because my stays are so tight.

"No," I gasp. "This can't be! I have too much to do! This can't . . ."

I glance through the smoke that's drifting up from beneath my feet, and see that gentle wet-gold sheen travel over the V A N S I N D E R E N with a fairylike unapologetic gleam.

I throw my head back and scream.

I scream, and scream, and scream, and scream, because I'm not feverish, and I'm not mad, and this is really happening this is all really happening and I'm not in heaven I am HERE and what do I do?

What am I supposed to do?

My scream goes guttural, like the bellow of a cow having its throat cut, and I fall to my knees in the grass, tears bursting from my eyes, spittle swinging from my open keening mouth.

"No," I moan, my arms wrapping around my stomach as I rock back and forth on my heels in front of that horrible, horrible marble slab. "Oh no no no no no! Herschel! I want to see Herschel! We were supposed to be together! It's not fair!"

I draw a ragged breath and let it back out with a sob of despair.

"Oh, help!" I sob. "Help! Can't anyone help me? Please, someone! ANYONE! HELP!"

The marble cemetery is completely silent, except for one cooing pigeon that watches me with impassive eyes. I'm all alone, and it's not the day we leave for Aunt Mehitable's after all.

It's not the day I sneak away from the house before we flee and Herschel gives me my cameo. The day when he tells me he loves me and he wants to be with me forever. The day that everything changes.

I was just remembering that day.

I was lost.

Overcome, my heart dissolving into dust, I slump over onto my side, weeping, my knees drawn up to my chest and my hands over my face. I let the sobs come, rolling up and breaking over me like ocean waves. Lifting me up and carrying me out to sea.

I don't know how long I lie like that. But I suspect it is a very long while indeed.

The question, I ask myself as I lie in the dandelions, is what do I do now?

Slowly I push myself up to a sitting position. My throat is raw from screaming, and my face feels hot and swollen. But my tears have finally stopped. I've run out. I wonder, actually, if I will ever cry again.

I look around myself with eyes that are newly clear.

I'm sitting in a small cemetery, protected by a locked gate. It looks like it's been locked for a very long time. Beyond the gate, I see passersby going about their business, all as it should be except for the strangeness of their dress. They're all practically naked. I try to conceive of how much time has gone by, but I can't think about it just yet. At least a year, but something tells me it's much more than a year. I can tell from the light and the heavy pressure of the heat that it's summer, so going practically naked is probably a relief.

A boy lopes by in baggy short pants and a loose-fitting shirt with no collar or sleeves. I smile, as his outlandish clothes remind me of my figment.

Wes.

When I think of his name, my eyebrows shoot up.

Wes! Wes came out of the fog to talk to me!

Wes isn't a figment at all. He's real!

His was the first new conversation I've had since my nightmare began.

And Wes can talk to me.

But how do I find him? He didn't wait for me, when I asked him to. I don't know where he went. I could try to find him at my house—the thought of my house causes a wave of nausea to curdle in my stomach—but I don't know where in the city I am, or how I got here.

I struggle to my feet, stumbling on weak legs, and then pace to and fro in front of the marble slab with my name on it. I can't bring myself to look at the name on the slab. I can't bring myself to think about what's inside. That won't do anyone any good. The idea crowds in on me—the monster that I saw in the mirror when I was getting dressed—but I push it away. I have to think. I have to think. I can't succumb to horrifying myself on top of everything else.

When I first tried to leave the house, I was confused by the fog. It turned me around and brought me back where I started. But later, I was able to leave. I could walk the streets. The fog was gone.

Can I leave now?

I tiptoe up to the cemetery gate and peer through the bars. I don't see any fog. Two boys go trotting past, tossing a large orange bouncing ball between them and laughing. I retreat into the shadows of the gate, afraid that they'll see me. I'm afraid of what I might look like.

I reach my hands up slowly and touch my fingertips to my cheeks.

They feel warm and smooth. Like my cheeks always do.

I close my eyes and swallow hard.

I make up my mind that I will at least try. I'm going to leave. Wes can see and hear me. Wes offered me his help. So that's what I'm going to do. I'm going to go find Wes.

Except when I put my hand on the gate and touch it to make it open, it's locked.

"Huh," I say aloud.

Of course, it was locked before, when I got here.

I grab the iron bars and rattle them.

They don't budge.

Drat.

"Hey!" I call to a couple of girls striding by outside, talking together. Their legs are so bare, it's dizzying. "Hey!" I stick my arm between the bars and wave to catch their attention.

They don't see me. My arm droops with dismay as they pass.

I pace back and forth behind the locked cemetery gate, thinking.

Maybe I can climb over the wall.

I go over to the brick wall and stare up at its blank face. It's probably ten feet high. Maybe higher. A few dull windows look down over the alley, and there's a roll of nasty-looking wire coiled along the top of the wall. It looks like it's covered in razors. I suck my teeth, thinking about how much that would hurt. Just to see how hard it would be, I curl my fingertips into the grooves between the bricks and try to lift myself up. I grunt and scrabble with the effort, splitting a nail and then skidding back down the few inches that I gained.

I stick my injured fingertip in my mouth. It tastes of blood.

I prowl the periphery of the cemetery, looking for a door or a loose window or something, anything that might offer a chance of escape.

There's nothing.

I give the gate a sullen kick as I pass, and its chain rattles in response. Then I sit down with a sulk.

I lie down on my back in the grass, a dandelion tickling my ear, my feet sticking out between the bars of the gate. I stare up into the sky overhead. An impossible angel-bird streaks past, leaving a pale cloud-path behind.

One of the stories in my Diedrich Knickerbocker book was about a man who fell asleep in the Catskills while hiding from his nagging wife. He met some giants and played ninepins in the thunderclouds, and then when he awoke he found that twenty years had passed. The revolution had come and gone, his nagging wife was dead, and the world around him was completely changed.

One of the horseless landaus rolls past on the street outside where I'm hiding. But no one comes, and eventually the sunlight fades, becoming thin and gray. More people stride by, laughing and talking and shouting, just like they did in the evenings that I remember.

I close my eyes, thinking about Wes.

I wonder if he knows, about me. Did he know, when he sat with me on my stoop? Wouldn't he be afraid? When I find him, I'll have to be careful not to frighten him.

I feel my tight muscles loosen. Presently the dandelion doesn't tickle anymore, and the sounds in the street outside begin to recede. They feel farther away. I let myself drift, floating, my eyes still closed. A breath of cool air smooths my brow, and the curls around my ears stir softly. My skirts move around my ankles.

Wes, I think.

Wes, where are you? Are you close by? Do you know that I'm looking for you?

I picture him, his mop of dark hair like Herschel's, his wet puppy eyes. I remember how his elbow felt, pressing into my ribs, and how safe he made me feel. I think of looking into him, as he looks into me.

I hunt around for him, in my mind, trying to discern where he might be. He won't be back at my house. Maybe he's tired, like I am tired. Maybe he wants to rest, too.

Wes.

He's not far. I'm certain of it. He's close! How close?

I picture what he might look like, while he's sleeping. Even the cruelest men look innocent in sleep. And Wes isn't cruel. Is he? I don't think he is. I think he must look very sweet, when he's asleep. Like this. If he were asleep, and I found him, he would look just like this. His eyes would be closed, and his hair would be sticking up at funny angles, and he'd have a red pillow crease across his face.

I open my eyes and discover myself standing in a dark room. A

185

few pinpoints of red light wink along the walls, and I can just make out a sleeping form in a narrow bed pushed against the wall.

I am in a boy's bedroom. At night. In the dark.

Mother would kill me.

I laugh grimly to myself at the thought.

Wes?

I hate to wake him. But I have to. I try to ease him awake. He's dreaming, and it's making him move about under the white sheet. I reach a hand out to touch his shoulder, but I hesitate.

He thrashes against the bedclothes, struggling in a nightmare, and I feel sorry for it, because I don't want him to be afraid.

"Wes!" I whisper, leaning to put my lips close to his ear.

He kicks his blankets away, his eyes pressed closed.

"Wes!" I say again, my face breaking into a happy smile, because I've found him.

"Arrrrgh!" he gurgles into his pillow.

I put my hands gently on his shoulders like I used to do when easing Ed out of a nightmare. But I'm so happy and relieved to see him I can't stop myself.

"Wes, wake up!" I say. I dig my fingers into the flesh of his shoulders and rattle him hard. "WES! WAKE UP!"

His eyes open, and he twists away from me, scooting up against the headboard of his bed, pushing pillows out of his way. My smile collapses.

I've frightened him!

"You're . . . you're . . ." He's gasping for air, his face contorted with shock and semi-recognition. When he sees who I am, his eyes fill with horror, and he opens his mouth to scream.

"Shhhhh!" I stop him, putting my finger to my lips.

He gulps back his scream, but only just.

"But . . . how did you . . ."

He's fighting to understand, I can tell. I reach for him, to soothe him maybe, or to reassure myself that he's really there, I'm not sure which. When he sees my hand coming, he cringes away.

"Wes," I say his name. It feels so good, to talk and know that someone can hear me.

"What," he pants, pulling the sheets up to his chest. "What. How did you get in? How did you know where I . . . What are you doing here?"

"I'm sorry," I say. I bite my lip. Maybe I shouldn't have come.

"How did you get in here?" he whispers with a glance across the room, where I observe another boy sprawled on a matching bed, abandoned to sleep.

"What do you mean?" I ask. "But I told you I'd be right back." I'm hurt, that he doesn't remember. He said he'd wait for me, after all.

"What?" he says.

"Wes," I say, and I'm so anxious to feel him there that I impulsively put my hand on his foot and hold it, hard. "Can you help me?" I sound desperate, I know I do, but I can't help it. I'm afraid.

He stares hard at me.

"Please?" I say, my voice shaking. "Could you? I'm sorry to have to ask, but . . ."

"What's going on?" he asks.

"I don't know," I say with urgency.

"What do you mean?" He puts a hand atop mine, and it feels so warm and reassuring that it's all I can do not to sob with relief. I don't know where to begin. I don't know how to make him see.

"I," I stammer. "I've lost my cameo."

I show him my naked hand.

"You've . . . what?" He doesn't understand.

"I don't know!" I wail, burying my face in my hands and letting the sobs come. I didn't think I could have any more tears, after today, but they spring into being anyway, filling my hands.

"Oh, hey, don't do that," Wes says, and before I know what's happening he's put his arms around me and pulled me to his naked chest. I weep into his neck, coiling my arms around his waist. His skin feels smooth and warm.

"It's okay," he soothes me. His fingers comb through my hair.

I can't stop my sobbing. I'm too overcome to talk.

"What's going on, Annie?" he says, and I hear his voice through his chest.

I can't say it. I can't make the words that are the truth. Instead I say the only thing I can bring myself to admit.

"I've lost my cameo!" I wail.

"Okay," Wes says, concerned but uncomprehending. "We'll find it. Okay? We'll find it."

I disentangle myself from him, wiping my nose on the back of my wrist. My cheeks are hot from weeping.

"I said I'd come right back," I plead. "Why didn't you wait for me?"

He just stares into me, his eyes stricken.

"Wes," I gasp. "I came right back."

PART THREE

WES AND ANNIE

CHAPTER 1

I'm a Rip van Winkle," Annie says dully, sprawled on her back on my bed, feet dangling just above the floor, staring up at the ceiling of my dorm room. Her eyes are so dazed that she could be counting the divots.

"What do you mean?" I ask.

She kicks one foot and then the other, letting them swing. The dawn is starting to break outside, and the pigeon that's nested on my air conditioner for the past couple of weeks coos as she stirs awake. We're talking quietly, so as not to wake up Eastlin. I don't think he'll freak, finding some random girl in our room, but you never can tell.

"You know. Rip van Winkle. From the Knickerbocker book."

"You mean, like, Washington Irving? The guy who fell asleep?" I ask, half remembering a story I read as a kid. A picture book of a guy in breeches and long shaggy hair.

"Yes," she says, closing her eyes and putting her hands over them. "The guy who fell asleep."

I'm sitting on the bed next to her, hiding my boxer-shorted self under a pillow. It's completely awkward, having a girl wake you up when you're not expecting it. I reach down to find a T-shirt to pull on, since it's kind of weird to just be sitting here with only my boxers on while she's in a crazy dress. How the hell did she get into my room?

Eastlin rolls over, groaning. He's probably even more hungover than I am.

Annie and I freeze, watching to see if he's going to wake up.

He pulls a pillow over his head and sighs. Then he lies still.

"Annie," I venture, figuring I can ask now that she's calmed down a little. "No offense or anything, but how did you get in here?"

"What do you mean?" She looks at me curiously.

"I mean," I say, ticking a list off on my fingers. "One, you don't know where I live. Two, even if you did know which dorm was mine, you don't know which room, and three, you have to swipe downstairs to get in. Also, four, the door was locked. Like with a dead bolt. How the hell did you get in?"

Her lower lip is trembling again, and her eyes start welling with tears.

"I . . . I don't know!" she snivels. "Wes, I don't know anything! I don't understand anything! I just need your help!"

"Okay, okay. Look. You probably know more than you think you do. Right? Let's start from the beginning. So you've lost your cameo."

She nods, wiping her face with the corner of one of my sheets.

"All right," I say, edging nearer to her on the bed. "So. Question one. What's a cameo?"

She peeks at me from behind the sheet with disbelief.

"Come on," she says. "You're kidding."

"As far as I know, a cameo is a guest appearance by a movie star on a TV show," I point out.

She sits up, pushing her curls out of her way, and stretches her hands out in front of my face.

"Guest appearance," she mutters. "That's funny."

"Sorry," I say.

"A cameo"—she points to her bare finger—"is like a little carving, made out of shell. Usually they're someone's face. You wear them. Like jewelry. Mine was of Persephone. On a ring, set in gold. Herschel gave it to me."

Eastlin rustles under his sheet, pressing a forearm to the pillow over his head, his hand in a fist. I glance at him, and lower my voice further.

"Herschel. What is he, like, your boyfriend?" I say more sourly than I mean. She called me that name, the other day. A flush of jealousy burns my cheeks.

"He's—" she starts to say, but is interrupted by Eastlin shouting, "God, will you SHUT UP already?"

Annie shrinks to the back of my bed, her eyes full of fear. Eastlin throws the pillow off his head and gets up. Without looking at us he stalks to the door.

"Wes, for serious, I am really freaking tired. Okay? Do you think you could stop talking for two seconds? It's practically tomorrow."

I open my mouth to protest, but Eastlin has already slammed the door behind him.

Slowly I turn to look at Annie. She shrugs.

"I guess we were too loud," I say.

She gives me a tiny smile.

I grin back at her.

"So. Where do you last remember having it?" I ask her.

She furrows her dark brows, thinking. The light in the room is growing more pale, and I can see her clearly now. Her fingers are knitted over her belly, slippered feet swinging. Her head is propped against my dorm room wall where she lies on her back on my bed. She chews the inside of her lip, and it twists her mouth in a funny way, making her mole move.

"I was wearing it at the Grand Aquatic Display," she says. "That's the last thing I remember. I definitely had it on then."

"Um. Okay," I say, not really clear on what a Grand Aquatic Display is, unless maybe it's some kind of hipster summer sprinkler party in Red Hook that I wasn't invited to. Which is probably what it is. "And when was that?"

Annie gets a vague, faraway look in her black eyes. Something about that look frightens me. She's on the point of answering when Eastlin slams back into the room and stalks back to his bed.

". . . swear to God, Wes," he's saying, as if continuing a stream of invective that started in our room, followed him into the bathroom, and then back down the hall to our room unbroken, even though I wasn't there to hear it. "You could be just a little more considerate, you know? Do you have any *idea* how tired I am? Between classes, and my job, and I realize you don't *have* a job"—he walks right past me and Annie without glancing in our direction—"but it's six in the morning, and I don't have to be at the store until ten. I could be asleep, right now."

Annie and I both watch him stalk about the room in nothing but his boxer briefs. I can tell from Annie's expression that she's pretty shocked. Like maybe she's never seen a guy in just his underwear before. Or maybe she just thinks he's hot, I don't know. Eastlin is ripped, I'll give him that. God, I should give her a towel to wipe the drool off her chin.

"I'm sorry, I was just—" I start to apologize, with one eye on Annie.

"I know you're, like, an artist, or whatever, but that doesn't give you license to sit there jabbering in the middle of the night," he interrupts me. "God. Screw this. I'm going to the gym."

He pulls on a pair of gym shorts and leans down to glance in the mirror on his desk. The gym is kind of a pickup scene, he's told me, so I guess he has to make sure he looks good even at six in the morning. As if anyone could look good at six in the morning. From where Annie and I are sitting on my bed we can see his face reflected in the mirror. He peers in close, examining a nascent pimple on his otherwise flawless chin. His eyes shift focus from his chin to us in the background.

"Holy shit!" he says, stumbling backward and staring at Annie.

I have to suppress a smile, but Annie looks between us, worried. She's sitting up now, curled in a little ball with her knees drawn up.

"Where the hell did she come from?" Eastlin demands, pointing at Annie.

"Eastlin," I say, ready to placate him.

"You had a girl in here?" he asks me with a flash of annoyance. While I watch, though the annoyance changes shape. "Jesus," he says, pulling his T-shirt over his head. "You should've said something. Scared the crap out of me. Have you been here the whole time?"

"I'm sorry," Annie says, her voice small.

"Don't be sorry. Christ. I should be thanking you," Eastlin says with a wry smile at me. "Saved me the trouble."

"Man. Come on. Shut up." I give him my best approximation of Clint Eastwood in *High Plains Drifter*.

"This is her, right?" he says. "Hello." He sticks his hand out.

Annie hesitates, then extends her own hand. They shake. She looks sort of shell-shocked by the whole exchange. "We really didn't mean to wake you up," she says. "Did we, Wes?"

"No," I say. "Definitely not."

He watches us both. I think he can tell something weird is going on. He's smiling, but it's an uneasy smile.

"It's no problem," he says, eyeing Annie.

He's looking at her dress. He gets this appraising look in his eye when he's evaluating clothes. A strange expression crosses his face, but he tries to act like everything's normal.

"I was just going to see if Annie wanted to get some breakfast," I say. "Do you?" I turn to her. "Want some breakfast?"

"I guess so." She doesn't sound convinced.

"Great," Eastlin says.

We all sit there for a second, unsure what's supposed to happen next. Eastlin picks up his gym bag and says, "All right. Well. I guess I'll see you later. Nice meeting you . . ." He trails off, giving her time to fill in her name.

"Annatje," she says.

"What?" Eastlin and I say together.

"Sorry. I mean, Annie," she says. She blinks at us without explaining anything.

"Right. Annie." Eastlin nods. He gives me a long look as he heads to the door, but I don't catch what it means.

After he's gone, Annie and I stare at the door. The sun is fully up now, and we can hear morning sounds drifting up from the street. My temples are throbbing, my mouth feels like something crawled inside and died, and all I can think about is pancakes and bacon and coffee.

"Come on," I say, plucking at her skirt. "Let's go eat. Everything looks better after you eat."

"All right," Annie says. She slowly climbs off my bed, testing her weight when she puts her feet to the floor.

My hands twitch for my camera bag, and I pick it up and swing the strap over my head with a practiced motion, feeling fully dressed once I have it on. I gesture to Annie to go out the door first. I'm a gentleman, anyway. Most of the time.

"Annie?" I ask.

"Yes?" She looks up at me with her bottomless black eyes.

"Would you say that your cameo is what you want most in the world?" I smile at her.

. . .

It's early enough that we beat the competitive weekend brunch crowd, and get a table almost immediately at this diner I like down the street. Brunch is like a contact sport in New York, I swear. Everywhere you go you have to wait, like, three hours on a Sunday. A waitress plops us in a booth and throws menus at us like she wants us both dead. Annie sits uncertainly across from me, looking at the menu, flummoxed.

"What?" I ask, glancing at her.

"It's just . . ." Her eyes are wide. "There's so much! I don't even know what a lot of it is."

"Like what don't you know?" I peer at her. Fancy girls don't go to diners, I guess.

"Grits?" she asks me over the top of her menu.

"Um," I demur. Then I grin at her. "You know what? I actually don't know what grits are, either."

She laughs at me, paging through the infinite choices, sounding out some of the words to herself.

The waitress comes back and I ask her for eggs and coffee.

"Beans?" Annie asks hopefully. "And bacon?"

I make a barfed-in-my-mouth face, and echo, "Beans? And bacon?"

Annie nods, looking happy.

"Beans," the waitress says. She gives me a weird look, shoves her pen behind her ear, and leaves us alone.

"All right," I say, leaning forward on my elbows. "So all we have to do is retrace your steps."

Annie's not listening, though. She's gawking. She stares at each person in the diner like they're all from outer space. She's as fascinated by the toddler on a teddy-bear leash as she is by the elderly woman in the tinfoil hat. She stares at the lights. She stares at the linoleum floor. When the food comes, she stares at the food. Maybe she's on something after all. I don't have a lot of drug experience, so it's hard to tell. The one time I smoked a joint at a frat party at UW I got so paranoid that I hid in my closet until morning, petting the sleeves of my shirts. But I feel like people on MDMA act kind of like Annie's acting. Like they want to touch and taste and see everything.

"Hey," I say, reaching across and putting my hand gently on her arm.

"Huh?" She jumps, focusing on me.

"Are you okay? Really?" I ask her, using my serious-dad voice. It's the same one my dad uses on me. I'm starting to get pretty good at it.

"I'm not sure," she says, looking with wonder at the bowl of chili that's been plunked on the table between us. She sniffs the bowl and flares her nostrils with distaste. "No, actually," she reconsiders, leaning her elbows on the table and her forehead in her hands. "No. I'm not. Oh. Kay. I'm Rip van Winkle." She smiles crazily as she says this last part, and that weird crawling chill passes over my neck.

"Listen, do you mind if I record this?" I ask her, because filming it will make me feel less creeped out.

"I don't even know what that means," she says, looking miserably at her breakfast. She picks up a slice of bacon and holds it up to the light.

I rummage in my camera bag, pulling it out and hitting record in one fluid motion. When I look through the viewfinder I zoom in close on Annie's face. I can see every detail of her expression: the mole at the corner of her mouth. The little hairs at the edges of her eyebrows. The redness under her lower lids. She glances up at me, and her black eyes are so intent and glittering that it stops me cold. She's looking straight into me. I swallow, hard.

"Okay," I say. "Retrace your steps. You last had your cameo on at a party, right?"

She nods. Then she lifts the bacon strip again and holds it delicately under her nose, and breathes in the smell. "Do you think I can eat this?" she asks me.

"Sure," I say. "Go ahead." I'm paying for it either way. I hope she eats it. If she doesn't eat it, I will. Maybe I hope she doesn't eat it, actually.

She opens her mouth and makes as though she's going to take the world's tiniest bite. But then she stops herself and drops the bacon strip with irritation.

"I can't," she mutters.

"It's okay," I say, zooming out ever so slightly. "You're sure you had it on?"

"Yes," she says. "At least, I think I did." She's staring down at her fingers like she can't believe they're really there.

"So. Tell me about this party," I urge her. "Where was it?"

She looks at me again, and something is messed up with my focus, so I keep having to fiddle with it. All the zooming in and out makes my hangover pound even worse.

"Downtown," she says.

She's too cool to be all specific. Hipsters never just come right out and tell you where a party was, or who threw it, or what all went down at it. You're supposed to *already know*.

"Like, where downtown?"

Annie picks up a spoon with some hesitation, and stirs the chili. "I asked for beans," she whispers. "But this isn't what I meant."

I've never seen someone look so sad about a stupid bowl of chili. And I've never wanted to protect someone from how sad they're made by a stupid bowl of chili. "Want to send it back? We can send it back," I reassure her. I bet this place gets stuff sent back all the time. Who cares? It's a diner.

"No," she says, laying the spoon aside. "There's no point."

She hides behind her hands for another long minute, and then drops them to stare at me. The camera whirs, and she hazes in and out of focus in a way that makes my eye ache.

"Maybe tell me what you were doing right before you went to the party," I suggest. "Then we can figure out when you last had it on. Were you at home? Getting dressed? What?"

Annie looks up to the ceiling, lost in thought.

"Ummm." She frowns. "I wasn't at home. We had to go to my aunt's house, very suddenly. We all left in a hurry."

"Okay," I say. "So if you left in a hurry, are you sure you remembered to take it with you? Could it just be at your house?"

"My house," Annie repeats. Then her eyes widen as if she's just remembered something. She looks intently at me, and clutches my arm across the table. "My house! Oh my God. Wes," she says, voice low and fierce. "Do you know what a Luddite is?"

"Huh?"

I wonder if Maddie messed with the focus while we were filming her scene for *Most*. I can't get it to stay in place. As soon as I focus on one part of Annie, the rest of her softens out of clarity. I have to keep the camera moving, to even see her. It's super-annoying. I wonder if Tyler would have any suggestions.

"Luddites. Do you know what they are?" She's looking at me so intently that it's making me nervous.

"Um. Sort of? Isn't that, like, someone who hates using computers?" I ask, my fingers on the focus button. Zoom in, zoom out. In, and out. Annie's curls go soft, and then sharpen.

"I don't know," she says, frowning. "I thought maybe you would know." A fleeting look of disappointment crosses her face, and I have a sinking feeling that it's me she's disappointed in. I can't stand the thought of disappointing her.

"Why'd you want to know what a Luddite is?" I ask, framing the shot tightly on Annie's mouth. I'm getting better at getting people to talk, on camera. Sometimes if you just run it long enough, they say what they really mean without even realizing it.

"I . . ." Annie's lips part in my viewfinder, on the point of answering me.

Just then, the pocket of my cargo shorts vibrates. I fish my phone out of my pocket and look down at the screen in my lap. It's from Eastlin.

Not Abraham Mas.

I frown, not sure what he means.

What? I text back.

Something weird going on, he texts back.

What do U mean? I return quickly, eyes still in my lap.

Her dress is handmade, he returns. **All of it. Lace, too.**

So? I answer.

Checked design textbook. It's prolly antique. Not vintage. Antique.

That doesn't make any sense. Why would Eastlin be telling me this? The phone vibrates again.

STOLEN antique.

I glance up with alarm to where Annie's sitting across from me. She's not there. Her bacon sits uneaten, the spoon lying on the table in a smear of chili as if suddenly dropped.

"Hey!" I say.

I look around, but she's nowhere in the diner.

The waitress passes our booth, flipping pages in her order book, and I reach over and take her arm without thinking. "Excuse me," I say. "The girl who was with me. Do you know where she went?"

The waitress gives me a cold look and shakes my hand loose. "The hell you talking about?"

"What?" I say, uncertain. I get to my feet, looking at every face in the diner, faces upon faces upon faces, smiling, talking, chewing, despondent, closed. But none of them are her.

An idea is poking me in the back of my head, but it's too insane for me to face it. I push it away. I push it away really, really hard.

"How the hell did you get into my room, Annie?" I whisper to the empty table.

CHAPTER 2

When I take my hands away from my eyes to look at Wes, I'm met with the figure of a snoring girl, her arms draped down on either side of a scarred wooden table. One of her shoulders peeks out from her dress, which has been loosened in the back. A tankard of beer has been knocked over, making a puddle that runs along the table, along her arm, and drips down her fingers to the floor.

I leap to my feet with a rumption, turning over the bench where I'm sitting. "But," I say, looking to both sides of me in shock.

Wes is gone. The victualing house where we were sitting has vanished.

I'm in a small ground-floor room that's been set up as a beer hall. Half a dozen tables and benches, lamplit, a few posters tacked up on the wall. Men and women hunched over tables, drinking beer, and some of them eating.

I stagger back from the table in confusion.

"Watch it!" cries a woman carrying mugs of beer. I've staggered into her, knocking her sideways, and she only just saved herself from pouring beer down the back of my day dress.

My day dress.

I look down at myself, at my tidy clothes and clean fingernails. No soot. The only smoke that I smell comes from oil lamps on the tables.

What's just happened? I was in the victualing house, I was thinking about eating bacon, I was talking to Wes. Wes was looking at me through his funny looking-box. He asked me something. Something that made me struggle to remember. And I covered my face. And then . . .

"What day is it?" I demand of the room at large.

"Day?" the ruddy beer-hall mistress asks me, her head cocked sideways. "Why, Tuesday, I should think."

"Tuesday," I say. "What Tuesday?"

"What d'you mean, what Tuesday? This one, with her questions." She jerks her chin at me as she sets the beer mugs down in front of four men at the table next to the one where I awoke.

"I mean, when's the Aquatic Display?" I ask. "Has it happened yet?"

When I ask this, two young men in shabby work pants sitting together at the rear of the hall prick up their ears. They're both young, not much older than I am. One of them has curls over his ears, and a skullcap. The other is dark as a Senegalese. They exchange a look.

"Naw," the beer-hall mistress says, giving me a Croaker-eye. "Not 'til day after tomorrow. And the ward boss making me pay for bunting out of my tribute, too."

She eyes the unconscious girl who'd been sharing my table with me, then eyes me, and then folds her arms.

"That beer paid for?"

"Um," I demur.

The girl's obviously not going to pay. I have no idea who she is. I rummage in my pockets, wondering if this strange memory I've stumbled into will supply me with any money. Sure enough, I find a few pennies in my pocket and count them out in my palm.

The woman snatches them out of my hand with a sour look and turns her back on me.

I recognize this beer hall. It's in a basement on Bayard Street, a couple of blocks from Herschel's uncle's store. We used to come here often, though he was always afraid someone would see us. Once, he recognized some young men from his synagogue loafing together in the back, and we turned back at the door.

Tuesday. Two days until the canal opening. Which means my family has absconded to Hudson Square already. What happens today? What am I supposed to do?

I look down at my hands, and find my cameo is still missing.

"Why am I back here?" I whisper to myself, flexing my fingers.

"Why indeed," the beer-hall mistress hollers at me from across the room, and the men she's serving chuckle.

There's a woolen cloak with a beer stain on the sleeve draped over the bench next to the sleeping girl at my table. I feel a twinge of guilt as I reach for it, and then remind myself that this is all dream-stuff, anyway. I tie the cloak under my chin and hurry outside.

It's late afternoon, with a few dead leaves skittering up the center of the street, riding a puff of autumn wind. The light slants low between the buildings, and though life is stirring in doorways and behind windows, for the moment the street is deserted. I pull my stolen cloak around my shoulders against the chill and trot down the block.

At the corner, I hear footsteps behind me, and I stop, ears straining. The sound of horse hooves reaches me from one street over, and a wagon creaking on its struts.

I whip around to look behind me—no one is there.

Just shadows.

"Stop it, Annie," I castigate myself.

I turn the corner and walk faster. Pearl Street falls into shadow as the sun slips behind the buildings, and the darkness chills me deeper. My knuckles are growing numb.

I arrive outside the dry goods store and peer in through the window, shading my eyes with my hands, looking to see if Herschel is behind the counter. If he's not working, I usually walk past. But today, I can't. Today, I have to find him. It's too dark for me to see inside, but the door is propped open. I gird myself and step inside.

"Go away," someone says from a doorway behind the counter. "We're closed."

I can't see who's talking, but I recognize the gravelly, accented voice of Herschel's uncle.

"The door was open," I falter.

"My mistake," the uncle says.

He steps forward out of the darkness, scowling down at me. He's a big man, bigger than Herschel, with curls over his ears and a full beard. Long fringes hang from the waist of his trousers. His shirtsleeves are rolled up, and he's wiping his hands on a cloth. They're stained with something, but I'm not sure what.

"I'll just be a minute," I say, surprising myself with my insistence. He can't frighten me. He's just dream-stuff, too.

The uncle fixes me in a long, steady stare and slowly puts aside the rag in his hands. "Time for more thread already, eh?" he says lightly.

I inhale sharply.

He turns his back to me, browsing through shelves of cloth bolts and rolls of lace.

"Yes," I say. "I do a lot of . . . sewing."

Not exactly true. But I have found myself in desperate need of thread lately.

He grunts, his fingers roaming the shelves behind him.

"That corporation man, the banker, he's your father, yes?" he says without looking around.

I'm taken aback by this question. How would this man, whose name I've never learned, possibly know who my father is?

"Yes," I say, wary.

"They have a big celebration soon," the man continues. "For a big canal. Everything going to change."

I'm not sure what Herschel's uncle is getting at. His tone is strangely hostile.

"Very big," I say, drawing myself up taller in a way that Mother calls imperious. "It's going to transform the city. Papa's been working very hard."

The man snorts. "Hard work, she says. She doesn't know from hard work."

I frown, resenting this man who seems to be enjoying making me feel uncomfortable.

"Is Herschel here?" I ask, my voice cool.

"Not here." The uncle shakes his head.

He sorts through several rolls of thread, finally selecting one particular roll of bright crimson. He holds it up to the light, squinting at it and turning it this way and that.

"But it's Tuesday," I press. "He's usually here, Tuesdays."

"Not here," the uncle reiterates. He plunks the thread onto the counter, then leans forward on his elbow and glares at me. "You know who will benefit, from this canal? Who, besides your father, I mean," he asks, brows lowered over piercing eyes.

I pick up the thread quickly and stuff it in my pocket. Herschel's uncle's gaze is unnerving in its directness.

"Can you tell me where he is? It's very important that I speak to him," I say.

I fish around in my skirt pocket for the necessary pennies to pay for my contraband, and slap them onto the counter between us. Herschel's uncle pays no attention.

"You don't know, do you? Your father and the upstanding corporation *machers* will line their pockets, and for what?" he says, a new fierceness in his eyes. "To give rich men even softer cushions for sitting?"

"I have to find Herschel," I insist. "I have to talk to him. It's very important."

"Herschel's. Not. Here," the uncle says.

I'm so angry, I could spit. But I realize that I have nothing to gain by acting like a child. Of course he won't tell me where his nephew is. He's a hateful man.

"Fine," I say in my coldest voice. "I'll be going then. But when you see Herschel, please tell him I was here."

I turn on my heel, and as I storm out of the dry goods shop, the uncle calls out, "Be careful, Dutch girl who sews so much. I don't think you know what's going to happen."

I'm blinded by anger as I stalk up Pearl Street. What did he mean, talking about my father like that? What did he mean, I don't know what's going to happen? I finger the thread in my pocket, rolling it in my palm. It makes me feel better, having it there.

Lamps are flaming to life as night advances in the ward. I have to get home. If I can. How long will I stay here, in this moment? Can I stay here until I find Herschel, or will I close my eyes and open them and find myself somewhere else completely? Does the advancing night conceal another fog bank that will gather me up into itself and deposit me wherever it likes?

What if it takes me nowhere?

I'm not ready to think about that.

I draw the cloak tighter. I still can't believe how real the cloak feels. How scratchy and oily the felt is where it meets my skin.

I'm mid-muse on the quality of felt when hands clutch my upper arms and I'm hurled against the side of a building. My chin glances across the brick wall, ripping off a strip of skin. I try to scream, but I can't get my breath. Someone's hands are on my shoulders, pushing me against the wall, and I'm instantly afraid that all Mother's warnings about walking alone at night are about to come terribly true.

"There's money in my pocket," I gasp. "You can have it."

"We don't want your money," a young male voice hisses in my ear.

I close my eyes. Oh my God. Please. Please don't.

But instead of fumbling at my skirts, the hands spin me around, pressing my back against the wall. My eyes are shut tight, my fists balled at my sides, ready to fight and kick if I can.

"Why were you asking about the Aquatic Display?" another voice barks.

This is not what I was expecting would happen. I open one eye.

In the darkness, I recognize the contours of the faces of the two young men who were sitting together in the back of the beer hall.

"You followed me," I say.

"Shut up. Why'd you ask about the display, and then go into that shop?" the one in the skullcap demands. He has a metal pin on his lapel, in the shape of a broken spindle.

"What?" I'm confused.

"What do you know about it?" the dark one shouts, flecks of spittle hitting my cheeks.

I cringe away from him, holding my breath.

The other one draws so near to me that I can feel hot air from his nostrils along my cheek.

"What did Herschel tell you?" he whispers.

Herschel!

"Nothing!" I cry. "I haven't seen him!"

"She's lying," the Senegalese boy says. He's missing a tooth, and his nose has been broken at least twice. It zigzags painfully down his face.

"I'm not lying," I say, drawing myself up taller. I lift my bruised chin and stare down my nose at him. "I've been looking for him. I went to the store thinking he'd be there, but he wasn't."

The boys exchange a glower. The one holding me by my cloak tightens his grip, knotting his fists together and pressing me harder against the brick wall.

"You tell us what he told you," the one in the skullcap mutters, his lips almost touching my ear. "You tell us right now. And you'll tell us what your father knows, too."

I squeeze my eyes shut, and scream, "No! You can't hurt me! You can't!"

I raise my fists and flail at the boys, but instead of hitting flesh, my hands hit nothing.

CHAPTER 3

I flop back into the booth, and I can't tell if I'm hurt or angry. She wasn't in the ladies room—I checked. And she's nowhere in the diner. Annie ditched me. And she didn't even eat anything. Finally I swallow a few bites of her cold bacon, just so it doesn't go to complete waste, and now I'm just sitting here seething. It's nine in the morning, and I'm so hurt and confused I could punch a wall.

I lean my head back on the booth, staring up at the ceiling. Why do I always do this? Why do I let people barge into my life, spreading chaos? I let my mom persuade me to get that mushroom haircut that basically ruined junior year of high school. I let my high school girlfriend convince me we'd stay together after college started. Look how well that went. Barely a month into freshman year and I walk in on her tangled up with some Pike brother. In *my* room. I let Tyler convince me his project is some big art masterpiece that I should spend all my time on. I let Maddie drag me into abandoned buildings full of psychotic camera-stealing girls. I let Annie bail on me for no reason, all the time, and I never even say anything to her about it. What, do I not have enough chaos of my own to deal with? And now Eastlin thinks Annie's some kind of thief. Whatever she is, she's clearly completely messed up.

I fiddle with the video camera, reviewing the footage I took of Annie during breakfast. My heart contracts, as I watch it. She fades in an out of focus, my lens roving over her mouth, lingering on her mole. Her black eyes blink at me on digital video, red-rimmed and tired. I try a few different things to see what's wrong with the focus, but I can't figure it out.

I pull out my phone to text Tyler and see what he's doing today. I'm also curious, I admit, to hear how *Shuttered Eyes* went down with the gallery person. I don't want to be attracted by the electric snap of Tyler's imminent success, and yet I am.

There's a new text that came in while I was busy being pissed off. It's from Maddie.

Thanks for last night, it says. **You doing anything later?**

Last night. I can't believe that Maddie was in my room just last night. I feel a sick twinge of guilt as I realize I fell asleep before I could follow up to make sure she got home okay. And I've been awake for hours now and haven't texted her yet.

I am a huge jerk.

Hey, I text back. **Maybe. What are you doing?**

Is that cold? Maybe that's too cold. I frown, and then add, **I had a lot of fun last night, too.**

Better.

Irritated, I shove the phone back in my shorts pocket, leave a heap of dollar bills on the table, and pack my camera into its padded bag. The table is cleared before I even have both legs out from the booth—breakfast rush. Basically kicking me out. Whatever. I shove my hands in my pockets and lope, head down, out of the diner to go find Tyler.

I stop short, though, when I see what's going on outside.

It's Annie. She's got some kind of cloak on, and her back is pressed to the glass front diner window. She's flailing her fists at nothing, thrashing her head, her eyes squinched closed, and she's screaming. People pass her on the sidewalk, but nobody pays her any attention. In her weird frayed dress and cloak thing she probably just looks like a homeless person.

"Hey!" I shout, rushing up to her and putting my hands on her shoulders. "Whoa, Annie! Hey!"

I try to get ahold of her, but she's thrashing so hard that I can't get a good grip. Her shoulders are bony enough that they twist under my hands like eels. We struggle, and before I know what's happened, there's a *crack* and an eruption of stars rains down in my eyes.

"Jesus," I slur, my hands flying to my jaw as I stagger backward. I taste copper on top of bacon grease, and I hock out a glob of metallic spit that lands in a wet red splotch on the pavement. I take my hand away from my jaw and look at my fingertips. They're red with blood.

"Oh!" Annie cries. She's opened her eyes and looks at me with a mixture of terror and concern, like it's taking her a second to place me.

"What the hell, Annie?" I shout. Blood is running from my lower lip down my neck.

"Wes! It's you!" she cries. She flies over to me and flings her arms around my waist. In a flash of blind anger I peel her off me, pushing her away.

"Where the hell did you go, huh?" I shout. "What is this?"

"I'm so sorry," she says, raising a fingertip to my lip and touching it gently. The contact of her skin with mine makes me shiver despite the heat of the sun. "Did I hurt you? I did, didn't I. I'm so sorry."

Instantly I'm ashamed. Because she did hurt me, only not in the way that she means. "You have to stop doing that," I say to her, my voice, catching in my throat. "You can't just bail on me like that!"

"I didn't mean to." Her black eyes plead into mine. There's an explanation in them, but I can't see what it is.

"It's . . ." I falter. "You didn't even eat anything."

"I know," she says. The lower rims of her eyes glimmer with moisture.

I lean my head down until my forehead meets hers. Her skin is cool against mine. I rest my hands on her shoulders to reassure myself that she's really there. She feels so small. Like she's made of paper.

"Listen, I don't care. It's fine. Do whatever you want. I'll help you look for your thing that you lost. Just don't leave me like that again," I whisper. "Please."

My breath stirs the fine curls over her ears. I wait for what I want to hear, which is her promising me that she won't. But she doesn't say anything. She just stands there, pressing her forehead to mine.

Finally I open my eyes and stare hard into hers.

"Please? I hate it. You disappearing on me like that," I confess before I've really thought through whether I want to tell her this or not. Once the words are out there and I can't take them back, I'm sick with fear.

"I'll try," she says. "I will. But . . ."

"But what?" I have to swallow what feels like a lump of rat poison, to get that last word out.

"But I'm a Rip van Winkle," she whispers.

I pull away so she can't see the pain in my face.

"I don't know what that even means," I choke. "What are you even talking about?"

I can't look at her. I'm too hurt. But I feel slim fingers worm their way into my fist, and she takes my hand.

"I'll try to explain. Come with me."

She pulls on my hand, and at first I won't move. But then she pulls again, and I give in and we're walking together. We're holding hands, walking, not saying anything. The streets have started to fill up with people going about their days, and a couple of them do a double take when they see my split lip. We walk for several blocks that way, passing other people in the summer street, not hurrying. I start to calm down. I start to feel like maybe we're making up. If we had a fight, which I feel like we did, but we didn't, exactly. Which is weird, because with my high school girlfriend, there was never any question about when we were fighting. She was a big screamer. Exactly the opposite of Annie. I'm puzzling this out, trying to tease apart the weird ways I feel when I'm standing next to her, when she leads me around a corner into a tiny Village side street and stops us short. On this overlooked stretch of sidewalk, surrounded on all sides by tidy low brownstones and shady trees, we're alone.

Annie's steered me to some kind of disused community garden. It looks weedy and overgrown. The gate is locked with a chain and padlock.

She's acting kind of nervous. I'm worried, but I'm ashamed to realize that I'm sort of excited, too. She's turning to me, for help. She needs me.

"What's this?" I ask, gesturing to the garden with my chin. I've steeled myself. I'm ready for the truth.

Annie's looking everywhere but at me—at her shoes, at the door across the street, at a squirrel watching the action from one of the shade trees overhead.

"Look inside," she says.

Obediently I peer through the bars and into the dark recesses of the garden. I don't see anything, though. Some old statues, but mostly it's all overgrown with weeds.

"What?" I ask. "I don't see anything."

Annie rocks on her feet, anxiety crackling off her like static.

"You can't see it?"

I try again, but it would help if she, like, gave me a hint.

"Why don't you just tell me?" I suggest. The idea is knocking again at the back of my head, but I'm not listening to it.

With a sniff of frustration, Annie points a slender arm through the gate, steering my gaze. "It's right there! In the back. Don't make me read it to you."

"Read *what*?"

Annie stamps her foot, irritation with me boiling over, though I'm at a loss to figure out why she's the one who's angry now, instead of me.

"I'm *a Rip van Winkle*, Wes!" she almost shouts, taking my T-shirt in her fists and bunching it up with insistence. "Do you understand? What do Rip van Winkles do?"

"How should I know?" I look at her with alarm.

"What do they do?" She's almost shaking me.

"I don't know! *Bowl?*" I sputter.

She looks desperately into my face, her nostrils flared, and for a fleeting second I'm worried she's going to hit me on purpose this time.

But instead she drops my shirt and throws her head back and laughs.

When she laughs, her whole body shakes, and she opens her mouth so wide, I can see her molars. I grin out of one side of my mouth, watching, unsure what's going on.

She wraps her arms around her waist, holding herself until her laughter collapses into a fit of hiccups. "Oh my God"—she wipes a tear from her eyes and smiles at me—"they *sleep*, Wes. Rip van Winkles sleep."

I'm still smiling at her, not sure what's so funny. Is she trying to tell me she lives on the street? Does she sleep in this alley?

"Are you saying this is where you . . . sleep?" I ask gently.

Her smile fades.

I knew it.

"Sort of," she says quietly. "You really can't see?"

She's pointing at a marble slab built into the wall of the overgrown garden. There's writing on it, but it's too shady in the park for me to read. I shrug at her, helplessly.

She rolls her eyes. With a long, resigned sigh she sinks to the sidewalk, leaning her back against the locked garden gate with her knees drawn up. She looks up into the sky. A traffic copter goes chopping by overhead, and her eyebrows rise.

I sit down next to her. I've already made up my mind that if she needs me to smuggle her into my dorm for the last week of summer school, it's no problem, and Eastlin can just deal with it. I mean, she may not want to share my bunk or whatever, but I guess I can sleep on the floor for a week. I indulge in a brief fantasy of us together in my bunk, her bare feet pressed to mine, talking about movies under the musky breath of the air conditioner.

"So," she begins, not looking at me. "Remember how I said I last had my cameo at the Grand Aquatic Display?"

"Uh-huh," I say, watching her face.

"You've never heard of that, have you?" she asks the treetops arching over us.

"No," I say. It's not like she has to remind me about parties I wasn't invited to. I am already well aware of all the parties I'm not invited to.

"You don't know anything about it. Not where it was held, what it was for, nothing."

I flush. "I already said I didn't."

"So you don't know when it was," she presses.

"No idea," I say.

She laughs, but it's a dry laugh.

Then she levels her bottomless black eyes at me.

"It was in October. October twenty-seventh."

Huh. That's a while ago. Seems like if her cameo's been lost since then, it's staying lost. "So?" I ask. "It's been lost for a long time. No big deal. We can still try and find it."

"Wes," she says with a sad smile. "The Grand Aquatic Display, which is the last place where I wore my cameo, and which is the last thing I remember being before I woke up in my parents' house? It was a huge celebration put on by my father's company. They'd been planning it for months. The whole city decked out and celebrating, you can't even imagine how big. How many people. All the fireworks, and the lights. Bunting on every building. Newspapers, the governor, the mayor, Aborigines in breechcloths and paint. It was held the night of October twenty-seventh, 1825. Two nights from now."

CHAPTER 4

I feel like I'm on five-minute tape delay. But there the idea is, it's back, and it's burst through a door in my brain and now I see that it's the truth.

That's how she could get into my locked room. She doesn't need a key.

"What?" I ask, struggling to keep up.

"*Asleep*," she says, giving me a meaningful look. Then she glances over her shoulder. "In there. That's what I was trying to tell you."

"You're serious."

I stare at her. Her skin looks translucent in the late morning sun. Flecks of golden light are caught in her hair. I can see her chest rise and fall with her breath, the soft swell of her breasts in that oddly constructed dress she's wearing. She can't be. It's not possible.

"You mean to tell me you're a—"

"Please don't say it." She cuts me off.

"B-b-but—" I sputter.

"Please." She stares into the sky again so she doesn't have to meet my eye. "I'm sorry. I can't have you saying it."

I start to reach over to touch her arm, but something stops me.

I realize that I'm afraid of what will happen, when my hand touches her arm. What will she feel like? Is this even real?

"You're sure," I say, wondering if there is any room for this to be some colossal mistake. It's got to be a mistake. This stuff doesn't really happen. In movies, okay. It's standard. A sheet with eyeholes. A rattling chain. Scooby jumping into Shaggy's arms, yelling, *Zoinks!* Maybe a girl with her hair in her face climbing in sped-up motion out of a Korean well. But not in real life. In real life, when people die, they're just . . . They just . . .

"You don't think there could be some other explanation? I mean, no offense or anything, but what if you're just crazy?" It pops out before I can stop myself, and I immediately clap my mouth shut. Oh my God, I have got to learn how not to have verbal diarrhea. But she laughs.

"I considered that," she says. "But I'm afraid the carving on the marble slab isn't."

I stare at her dumbly.

"It's my name," she clarifies. "My name's on the slab."

She jerks her thumb over her shoulder to indicate the abandoned park. Which I have just realized isn't a park at all. With a sickening shudder I consider that she's in there, right now. She's in there, yet she's right here.

My mouth opens and closes, fishlike, until I realize that I'm not actually saying anything, and I shut it.

"I've found," she says slowly, "that I can't think about it too closely. I can't . . ." She trails off. Then she tries again. "If you look too closely, you'll see too much."

"What do you mean, look too closely?" I whisper.

She watches me out of the corner of her eye. We're both sitting in dappled summer shade, and there's a pool of sunlight splashed on the sidewalk between us.

"Are you sure you want to know?" she asks me.

I don't know what I'm supposed to be sure of. But I say yes, anyway.

She lifts a hand from where it's resting on her knee. Slowly, deliberately, she moves her hand from the dappled shade into the hot pool of sunlight.

When her fingertip reaches the light, I see something begin to change. The very tip of her finger blackens with soot. When her whole hand is in the light, the nails all turn black, the skin scorched and stained. Her arm moves deeper into the sunlight, dark mottling traveling up her skin, and when the lacy edge of sleeve at her elbow reaches the light, I see clearly that it's tattered. Rotting.

I have to turn my head away and swallow a bubble of nausea. It's too much. I can't think about it. I can't look.

Without a word she withdraws her arm and rests her hand back on her knee. In the dappled shade, her skin is buttermilk perfect. Her dress looks old, antique, even, it's true—Eastlin was right! Well, sort of right—but not destroyed. Not . . . rotting.

"The *sun* does that?" I say, horrified.

"No," she says, uncertainly. "Not exactly. It's more the thinking about it that does it. Looking closely. I just used the sunbeam because it's easier to see."

We sit side by side, chewing over this idea. A woman in leggings and huge sunglasses strides past, her heels clacking loudly on the sidewalk. She doesn't say anything to us, but chucks some quarters onto the sidewalk between my sneakers without a backward glance. Confused, I watch her go. Then I hang my head and start picking the quarters up, one at a time. My head buzzes with questions. Like, what is she going to do? How does she move around? What are the rules, for this kind of thing? How long will she be here? They all crowd together in my mouth, each vying to come out first, but then I realize that I'm taking too long to say something, and I should probably say something. She needs me to say something.

"Does it hurt?" I finally ask Annie in a whisper.

Her eye rolls to its corner and stares at me.

"Sometimes," she says.

"But . . . how did it happen?" I ask.

Did she know? Did she feel it? What's she been doing, between then and now?

"I have no idea," she says, her voice so quiet it almost doesn't exist.

"So when you vanish . . . ," I begin, my mind trying to keep up with the sudden fact of the impossible. But I don't know how to finish the thought.

"I don't know," she says. "I've been having trouble with time lately. With knowing where I am."

She faces me and puts her hand on my arm. I have to force myself not to flinch away from her touch, but her hand feels like it always does—cool, real, flesh over delicate bone. Just to be on the safe side, I don't look at it. Instead I look into her black eyes.

"Will you help me?" she asks.

"But I don't know what to do," I confess.

I'm never ready for anything.

I wish I did know.

I wish I were filming this, right now.

"I have to figure out what happened," she says.

I stare at her long and hard.

"What'll happen then? If we figure it out, I mean," I ask.

She reaches over and places her fingertips on my mouth, in that way that she has. Her touch makes my lips feel warm and prickly.

"Shhh," she says. "I can't think about that now. I just know that I can't solve this by myself. And I have no one else to ask. No one else sees me like you can."

I love having her fingers on my mouth. It makes me want to keep talking, so she'll put them there again.

"Okay," I say. "I'll do whatever you want me to do."

As I say it, I hope that I'm telling her the truth.

So she's a . . . Rip van Winkle.

Okay. Maybe.

I eye her as we walk together through the Village, and it's actually sort of fun, watching her look at everything. If it's true, she's never been in a car. That's crazy. Does she even know how big the city is? How does she get from place to place? Right now she's just walking like a normal person. But that's not how she got into my room. She must have gotten in some other way. Can she walk through walls? Can she even control where she goes?

What is she thinking about?

What happens when she disappears?

Is she stuck like this forever?

I have this vague plan that maybe we should go to the library, though the truth is, I'm not a big library guy, so I'm not really sure what we'd accomplish there. But when I suggested it, she brightened up, said, "The Society's still here?"—whatever that means—and so off we went. It made me feel good, that I could come up with a plan. As long as I don't let on that I'm making this up as I go.

Should I be explaining everything to her? Like, this is what an airplane is and stuff? No. Maybe she doesn't want to know. She'll ask, if she wants to know.

God, I wish I were filming this right now.

My phone vibrates in the pocket of my shorts, and I pull it out to take a look. It's a text from Tyler, saying he'll look at my camera if I want him to, and he's around after twelve. I text back that I'm heading to campus, and does he want to get coffee?

Annie watches my thumbs move with a curious smile.

"What's that?" she asks.

"What, my phone?" I say, but calling it a phone doesn't really sum it up.

"Your . . . phone?" She cranes her neck to look at the screen.

"Yeah. You know. Like a telephone. Only small. And no wires."

Annie's looking at me with a smile of complete amusement, and I'm starting to figure out that I maybe should have paid more attention in AP US history. They had telephones back then, didn't they? One look at Annie trying to keep herself from cracking up tells me that of course they didn't.

"It's like a tool," I try again. "You can talk to people, or you can send messages. Like letters, I guess. You can read newspapers, listen to music."

"Read? Like a penny paper?" she asks me.

"Um. I guess?" I say. "It's cool. You wanna see?"

I hold it out so she can see the face of my phone.

"It's cracked," she says.

"Yeah. I dropped it in the subway," I say, and then immediately wonder if I need to explain what a subway is. God, how old are subways? I don't even know.

She peers at it, and then glances up at me.

"How do I make it work?" she asks.

"You just swipe it. Like this." I demonstrate, scrolling through several texts from Tyler, and then accidentally swiping to my text exchange with Maddie. My ears flush pink, and I quickly swipe back to Tyler, but I don't think Annie noticed.

"Here," I say. "You try."

She doesn't take the phone from me, but places her finger on the screen, eyes alight with curiosity. She swipes. She swipes again. Nothing happens.

"Am I doing it wrong?" she asks me.

"Um . . ." I watch her try again, but the screen doesn't change.

Annie tries a few more times, beginning to look crestfallen. When she touches it, the screen doesn't respond. It dawns on me that the phone doesn't know that she's there. It looks like she's here, in the world, standing next to me. But she's not really here.

"Don't worry. Sometimes they just don't work," I say, trying to make it sound like it's not a big deal. I don't want her feelings to get hurt. I shove the phone back in my pocket and take her gently by the elbow, leading her across the street past a row of idling taxicabs and black cars.

"My sister, Beattie, loves letters," she remarks, gazing off into the distance.

"Beattie?" I ask.

"Beatrice," she says. "She's twelve. When she was little I used to post letters to her pretending to be Dietrich Knickerbocker, telling her stories of when Manhattan Island was enchanted. Mermaids in the Collect Pond. Indian spirits along the riverbank. Mysterious ships sailing up the Hudson on dead calm days with no wind. She loved them."

We're strolling up LaGuardia Place, heading for Washington Square Park. Annie watches the face of each passerby, peering at them with interest. Old women, babies, teenagers, it doesn't matter. She looks closely at everyone, and I can tell that she's filing them away, in her mind. Annie remembers things. She's a watcher. Like me.

I bet Annie would really love movies.

"Why'd you stop?" I ask. "Writing imaginary letters for your sister."

Annie's eyes turn sad, and she says, "Mother made me. Said Manhattan was no place for enchantment." She stops and looks at me. "Isn't that an awful thing to say? I always hated her for saying that."

I'm surprised. Annie doesn't seem like the kind of person to use the word *hate* very often. I'm on the point of asking her more, but we've reach the southern edge of the park, and she stops up short, grasping my arm.

"Oh!" she gasps, a huge smile breaking over her face. "Look at it!"

"What?"

I follow her gaze, trying to see what the big deal is. It's just a park. I mainly think of it as the place where they shot Billy Crystal leaving Meg Ryan for the first time in *When Harry Met Sally . . .* It was right by that big arch.

Grinning, she jostles my shoulder. "It's a park!" she exclaims.

"Yeah," I say, trying to be nonchalant. "It's okay, I guess. It's not Central Park, though."

She's so excited she bounces up on the balls of her feet. "The Central Park! They really built it?"

I laugh, baffled. "Well, yeah."

On impulse she throws her arms around my neck and breathes, "Can we go see it?" into my ear.

"Sure!" I say, surprised. "Of course we can. Whatever you want."

She smiles happily to herself, a dreamy look of pleasure on her face. Then, newly resolved, she turns to me and says, "Library first. Then park."

"You're the boss, boss." I grin at her.

"I'm the boss," she repeats, and mock-punches me on the arm.

What a weird girl. She makes being a Rip van Winkle seem almost fun.

We make our way over to the NYU library, which squats on the corner of Washington Square Park like a supervising bulldog. I heard that they put a pattern on the library floor that looks like spikes coming up at you if you look down on it from too high up, to discourage kids from leaping to their deaths down the central atrium. Pretty dark, if you ask me. But I don't know if it's true.

I pull out my summer school ID and prepare to swipe it to get through the turnstile, when I realize that we might have a problem.

"Um," I say, waylaying Annie with a hand on her arm. "Wait a second."

"What?" she asks me, eyes wide.

When we first stepped inside she gawked so hard at how big the building was that her mouth actually fell open. It was pretty cute. I didn't realize people actually did that, when they were surprised.

"I'm not sure how we're going to get you in," I say in a low voice, so the security guard won't hear me.

"What do you mean, get me in? I'll walk." She gestures with a sweep of her hand at the open atrium, which is crowded with people coming and going, the beeps and swipes of bags being checked and book spines being run over demagnetizing strips.

"No," I say. "You have to have an ID."

"A what?" She looks confused.

"An ID. You know, like a driver's license, but for school."

"Like a . . . Wes, what are you talking about?" She folds her arms and stares impatiently at me.

Her mole looks really cute when she's impatient. Okay. So they don't have driver's licenses in the olden days.

"Look," I say, producing my NYU student ID. I hate the picture of me on this, my hair is sticking up and my nose is humongous. I'm grinning so big that I look about fifteen years old. "See? It's got a picture of me and my name and everything. And there's a magnetic strip on the back, so they know it's not fake. It's an ID. You have to have ID for everything here."

She looks wonderingly at the card, brushing a fingertip over the photograph.

"Why, it's a perfect likeness of you," she breathes. "How extraordinary! I've seen credible portrait miniatures, but they were never so like."

"Annie!" I'm getting impatient. I don't have time for her to be all time-traveler about it. It looks pretty suspicious, us loitering out here. They'll call security if we don't act normal.

"And you say I have to have one of these, or they won't let me in? Are you sure?" she asks. But now she's looking at me with an impish expression on her face. A wrinkle forms on the bridge of her nose.

"Yeah. See?" I gesture to the signage over by the security desk, which is very clear about ID and library access and bag searches and all that stuff. Maybe I'm getting paranoid, but I'm pretty sure the guard is staring at us. He's definitely closed his magazine, anyway.

Annie pauses, staring down the security desk and chewing her lower lip.

Then she marches straight over to the security guard.

"You think they won't let me in?" she calls back to me, taunting. Her voice echoes in the library vestibule.

"What are you doing?" I shout-whisper, flapping a hand at hip level to try to beckon her back.

Instead she gives me a lopsided smile, plants her hands on the guard's desk, and leans into his face.

"Hey!" she shouts at him. "You really won't let me in?"

The guard doesn't respond. He's still looking at me, though. He moves his magazine slowly to the side, and folds his hands.

"Annie," I say, getting desperate. "Seriously, stop it!"

She waves her hands in the guard's face, inches from his nose. Then she turns back and smiles at me. I'm about to pass out from anxiety as she climbs up onto the guard's desk on her hands and knees.

"Hey, YOU IN THE HAT," she shouts right up next to the guard's ear. "I'M GOING INTO THE LIBRARY, ALL RIGHT?"

The guard's face remains impassive as he rolls a toothpick from one side of his mouth to the other. With a last long glance at me, he resettles himself in his seat and picks up his magazine. He turns a page with disinterest.

I stifle a laugh of disbelief.

"ALL RIGHT THEN!" she hollers, jumping up and down in front of him. "I'm going in! Here I come! No ID! Just into the library, happy as you please!"

Annie vaults over the turnstile at a run, lands on both feet, dashes into the center of the atrium and turns a completely awkward cartwheel, flashing everyone with old-timey long white bloomers. I can't help myself, and crack up, burying my laughter under my fists. The guard glares at me.

Annie whoops in triumph and yells, "Come on, hurry up!"

She flops to the floor and sprawls on her back in the atrium, lying splayed like a starfish across the tile pattern that's supposed to look like giant spikes. People keep walking past her, stepping right over her, and nobody so much as looks twice.

I try to compose myself, swipe through the turnstile with a polite machine beep, show the guard the inside of my camera bag, and walk over to where Annie is lying, out of breath on the atrium floor, grinning up at me.

CHAPTER 5

"How did you know he couldn't see you?" I whisper as we meander through the library.

She chuckles, skipping alongside me. How can she be so happy? She's . . . She's . . .

I can't bring myself to say it, even inside my own head, where nobody can hear me. Shouldn't she be sad? Or scary? Why am I not scared of her? Okay, sometimes I'm sort of scared of her. But not for the usual reasons.

She glances up at me from under her eyelashes, and her eyes glitter.

"Lucky guess?" she suggests.

I stop and fold my arms. "Come on," I insist. "How'd you know?"

She laughs, and her laughter sends a shiver of pleasure up to the roots of my hair. Whenever she laughs, I find myself staring at her mouth. Her little bow-shaped mouth, with that mole.

Can you kiss people who are . . . who are . . .

Who are Rip van Winkles?

The moment the thought blooms in my mind I try to crush it. That's insane. Right? It couldn't be any more insane. For one thing, she's older than my gran. Actually, she's *way older* than Gran. I cast a quick glance over at her, at the creamy line of her collarbone where it disappears behind velvet ribbon at her shoulder. Then I immediately stare up at the ceiling.

And besides. What about Maddie, who I'm supposed to be seeing later? It's not like she's my girlfriend or anything, but even so. She was just in my room, last night. I flash to a memory of the stark outline of her black lace bra against pale skin in the night shadows of my dorm room. The thought makes me stare even harder at the ceiling.

"For the most part," Annie is saying, "I'm pretty sure nobody can. Not here, anyway."

"But that doesn't make any sense," I insist. "I can see you!"

She looks at me strangely.

"So far, you're the only one," she says, her voice quiet.

"But that can't be right," I insist.

A cute Asian girl in cutoffs and flip-flops walks past us going the opposite direction, her shoulder bag heavy with a laptop and books, and Annie shouts, "Hey! Put some clothes on!" right in her face.

The girl doesn't even so much as glance in our direction.

"See?" Annie says pointedly.

"But I don't get it. Why would I be able to see you, and not her?" I ask, looking back at the girl in flip-flops.

It's not just me, I realize with a rush of certainty. It's also Tyler. And Eastlin. Tyler actually saw her first. I was already thinking about her, the night we filmed the séance for *Shuttered Eyes*, but Tyler's the one who made me go over and ask her to sit down. When I remember the séance, my heart turns over in my chest so hard I have to cough to get it going again.

God. What if she was . . . I don't know. Summoned. Or something. What if that's why she's here? What if it's all my fault?

"Annie," I start to ask her if she knows. Why she's here, right now.

Annie, oblivious to my thoughts, watches the girl in cutoffs over her shoulder, muttering, "Bare legs. In a library." Then she turns back to me. "Why? I don't really know. Maybe they're just not looking right."

She pauses, and I wait to see if she's going to elaborate on this idea. Instead she glances back at me.

"You're always trying to find the right way to look. Aren't you, Wes."

I stare down at her, wanting to finger the soft curls over her ears. But I don't. Instead I swallow, and say, "I guess."

We arrive at a bank of computer terminals, and I wiggle the mouse at one of them to wake it up. Annie is behind me, peering over my shoulder with a mixture of interest and anxiety.

I open up Google.

"So, what was your thing called again? That party you went to?" I ask, ready to type.

Her eyes jump between my fingers and the screen, baffled.

"Um," she says. "The Grand Aquatic Display."

Obediently I type the phrase into the search engine and hit enter. In my ear, Annie whispers, "My goodness. Will you look at that!"

But nothing much comes up. There's a lot of random stuff that doesn't seem to have anything to do with what she's talking about, and a scanned version of some guy's memoir that mainly talks about who all the aldermen were who were involved, and what all the different committees were in charge of, and it's all really dry and boring.

"Is that . . . is that a book?" she asks with wonder, reaching a hand out to touch the computer screen.

"I guess," I say, clicking through the other results. There's nothing much useful, but I'm not sure what else to do.

"Does it talk about anything strange happening, at the Display?" she asks.

"Not really." I frown, scrolling through the dense memoir on

Google Books. "It just says there was some huge party celebrating the opening of the Erie Canal. The Aquatic Display started in Buffalo and came all the way down the canal and then the Hudson to the city. Is that true?"

That's pretty impressive, given that it took, like, a month for anyone to get a letter back then. And no electricity. They basically lived in the Dark Ages. It must have truly sucked.

"Yes. Papa's in charge. They've been preparing for months. It's all anyone can talk about. Yesterday there were these men with him, in his study. And someone stabbed a letter up on our door."

"Someone stabbed a letter onto your front door? Are you serious?" I ask, eyebrows rising. "That's so metal. What'd it say?"

"I don't know," she says. "I never read it. But they panicked. Even Mother. That night we left the house and went to stay with my aunt Mehitable. Just before I found you, I'd sneaked out of the house to talk to Herschel, and tell him we're removing for Hudson Square. But I never found him."

"Hudson Square?" I ask. "Where's that?"

She gives me a wide-eyed, puzzled look. "Why, where it's always been, I imagine."

Great. That's so helpful.

I scroll through a few pages of the guy's memoir, which looks like it was written right around then. He talks about how during the construction of the canal there were a couple of explosions that seemed deliberate, but it didn't hold up the construction any. He doesn't talk about anything weird happening at the Grand Aquatic Display. What a name. They couldn't just call it a barge party? It's kind of stiff, how the memoir's written, but even I can tell it was an epic scene. I imagine I can see it, the flotilla of barges all lit with oil lamps and sparklers, drifting sedately down the river with Indians in canoes on either side, flags flying.

Annie's eyes are wide and blinking as she watches my fingers move on the keyboard, and the changing letters on the screen. It must look like magic to her. I can't wait to take her to see a movie. Maybe I can take her to something tonight. I should rent *The Others* and show it to her! That would be hilarious. No, that might be too intense. We'll go for some big monster CGI-type thing, something that will really blow her mind.

"Let me try something else," I mutter, typing quickly. Maybe I'm showing off, a little.

"You play it like a pianoforte, almost," she says.

This time I try searching her last name, *Van Sinderen*, and *cameo*.

She claps her hands with delight when pages of cameos on eBay and Etsy come up. Some of them are kind of pretty. For the name, there's a street in Brooklyn, and a book award at Yale founded by some dead guy. But nothing that shows both terms together.

I click through pictures of cameos, rings and brooches. They're pretty old-fashioned. But seeing Annie's face alight with pleasure gives me a shiver of satisfaction.

"Are any of these yours?" I ask.

She squints at the screen, her nose inches away.

"No," she says at length. "None of them."

I must look disappointed, because she quickly adds, "They're quite nice, though!"

I drum my fingertips on the desk by the computer, thinking.

"The Society Library always had the daily newspapers for anyone to read. They were laid out on a large table in the center of the reading room. And they'd keep them, for a time. Does this library subscribe to the penny papers?" she asks, her fingertips together in front of her mouth.

I laugh through my nose. Like NYU is going to have newspapers from two hundred years ago, just lying around. I'm sure they were all wrapped around fish and then thrown into the garbage within days. All the newspapers that might tell us what happened are in the bottom of Fresh Kills landfill, or maybe even at the bottom of the sea. Or they've been burned to cinders and we're breathing them right now.

"Annie," I say, trying to be patient. "Do you have any idea what year it is? Right now, I mean. What year I live in."

A weird expression crosses her face, and she moves a little bit away from me. Her hand gropes over to the counter, lands on an abandoned pencil, and picks it up to fiddle with it.

"I think," she says, without looking at me, "that we might ask someone. About the newspapers. I think that's what we should do."

I peer at her. Isn't she curious? That'd be the first thing I'd want to know, if I was a Rip van Winkle.

Maybe she doesn't want to know.

Maybe she can't bear to look at it too closely.

"All right," I say slowly. "We'll do that."

She glances at me, and her eyes are wet.

I reach over and put an arm around her shoulders, pulling her to me until the top of her head tucks under my chin. I can feel the soft cloud of her hair, tickling my throat. Her arms go around my waist. I close my eyes, relishing the rhythm of her breath and the texture of her dress under my hands. It doesn't seem possible. She's so utterly, completely real.

"Hey," whines a voice behind me. "You done yet?"

I glance behind us and find a pimply kid with a mom haircut looking balefully at me. He's holding a spiral notebook.

"Not quite," I say to him. "Sorry." I realize he can't see the girl in my arms. I must look pretty weird standing here, cradling nothing.

The kid gives me a sketchy look and goes away.

"Hey," I whisper into her hair. "It's okay."

She breaks away from me, wiping her nose on the back of her wrist. She nods.

"Newspapers," she says, not meeting my eyes.

"Let me just do one other thing," I say, turning back to the computer terminal. To be honest I haven't used the library for much of anything except checking out DVDs of documentaries that aren't available for streaming. They made all the freshmen do this library orientation thing at UW last year, but I wasn't paying much attention. All I wanted to do was watch movies. And make movies. And watch the movies I made.

I pull up the library home page, and type Annie's last name into the BobCat book search engine thing.

A few books come up by some other guy who's dead, who seems like he was one of those old society gentlemen who sat on lots of committees. But they're all from the twentieth century. Well after Annie's time. I shiver, as that thought passes through me. That even times long ago are after her time.

At the end of the list of stuff by the guy, there's an entry that just says "Ephemera." It's in Special Collections. Sixth floor. On the reference table there's a stack of Xeroxed pages with maps to all the call numbers.

"Annie?" I ask.

"Hmm?" she says, peering over my shoulder.

"What's *ephemera*? Do you know?" I'm embarrassed that I don't know. But, heck. I don't.

"Ummm." She furrows her brows. "I think it just means miscellaneous things. Things that exist? But nearly didn't? Like the noun form of ephemeral."

"Huh," I say. "So—it looks like the library has a box of random stuff that might belong to your family. Unless there's lots of other Van Sinderens out there."

"Really? I don't know any," she reflects. "But then, I'm discovering there's a lot in the world that I don't know."

We exchange dry smiles.

"Want to go see what's in the box? Maybe your cameo's in there!" I suggest.

At this idea, her eyes brighten. "You think?"

"I don't know. Why not?"

"How do we find it?"

I pull out one of the library call number maps, draw a circle around the area that we want, and write the box's call number down in the margin.

"I guess we just go . . . ask for it," I say.

Annie bounces on her toes, like she does when she's excited. Knowing she's excited makes my heart rate trip faster. I love seeing her look hopeful and happy. It makes me excited, too. Now I'm really hoping we find it.

At least, I think I hope we find it.

We ride the elevator to the sixth floor in silence, none of the other students taking notice of the strange girl in the tattered antique dress standing in their midst, eyes glued to the dinging numbers in the elevator overhead just like all of ours.

The doors ping open and Annie and I get off, walking faster than usual down the hall to find what we want. After several minutes of me showing my ID, inventing an independent study topic out of thin air, showing the inside of my bag, promising that I don't have a pen, and being led through a couple of glass doors, I'm finally parked at a long library table covered with foam blocks and told to wait a couple of minutes. All the while Annie stays at my heels, sometimes making faces at me over the shoulder of the reference librarian. Once she strides with exaggerated stiffness and formality over to a disused card catalogue abandoned along one of the reading room walls, puts a finger to her lips, and curls her other finger into the handle of one of the drawers.

Slowly, deliberately, she *pulls the drawer open.* I watch her do it, holding my breath. She skips back to my side giddy with mischief.

"How did you do that?" I whisper to her.

She's laughing so hard she can't answer me at first.

"Annie! Come on! How'd you do that?" I insist.

She's leaning her head on my shoulder, wiping laughter out of her eyes. "I don't know," she says, gasping for breath. "I just did."

"Dude. You're gonna get me kicked out of here," I point out. "Also, I'd tell you that was totally ripped off from a movie I saw from the eighties, except you probably wouldn't know what I was talking about."

"*Dude,*" she says, in a mocking voice. "Come on! It was funny!"

The librarian returns with a medium-size cardboard box, places it on the table in front of me, together with a pair of white cotton gloves, and says, "If you have any questions, I'll be right over there." It's just like a scene in *National Treasure,* except without explosions.

The librarian goes to return to her desk, and sees the card catalogue drawer open. She looks briefly at me, the likeliest culprit. I shrug, trying to look innocent. The librarian gives me the stink-eye and walks over and closes the card catalogue drawer.

Annie is laughing so hard she's having trouble not falling over.

"Shhhh," I say out of the corner of my mouth. "You're going to make me laugh, too!"

"Sorry!" she says. "You're right, you're right."

She smooths her curls out of the corners of her mouth, then settles her hands primly on the table in front of us.

"Wes. May I please see if my cameo is in the box?" she asks with exaggerated care, teasing me for how neurotic I'm being.

"Be my guest," I say.

She gives me a long look.

"What, you can open drawers but not boxes?" I ask, incredulous.

"I don't know! Sometimes I can move stuff, and sometimes I can't. Anyway, I think you should do it." She casts a meaningful glance over her shoulder to where the librarian is sitting.

"All right. You have a point," I say.

I put on the gloves and open the box.

My first impression is that it's full of junk. It's like the box you keep under your bed and forget about until it's time to move, and then you don't know what to do with it, because it seems a shame to throw everything away, but the truth is you never look at it so it might as well not exist. Packets of birthday cards tied together with ribbon, yellowed wedding invitations, a party horn from a 1920s New Year's Eve. Somebody's passport from 1938. A couple of curled photographs of unsmiling 1910s people in dumpy ankle-length dresses and drooping hats. Annie looks into the box with awe while I gingerly start pawing through everything.

Quickly I'm able to see that if there ever was any jewelry in here, it's long gone. Nothing in here has any value. Not jewelry-type value, anyway.

"I don't think we're going to find your cameo here," I say. "I'm sorry."

"I didn't really think we would," she says with a sigh.

I pull out different bundles of correspondence and lay them out on the table one at a time. None of them look old enough to be hers. Most of the stuff in here is from the early twentieth century. Late nineteenth, max, I'm guessing. It's impossible to tell who anyone is, though I spy Annie's last name on some of the cards and letters.

"What's that?" Annie asks, pointing.

I gingerly lift out a piece of paper folded into a tight square, so old that it's turned brown and curling. There's even sealing wax on it, which is crazy—I've never actually seen sealing wax before, except in movies. I guess I knew people really used it, but even so. I lift the paper on my palm and hold it out to Annie so she can see it.

Her eyes open wide, with that bottomless black glimmer they get. She reaches a fingertip over to touch the wax seal. It's stamped in a pattern like a spindle.

"Wes," she breathes. "That's it."

"That's what?" I say.

"The letter. See?" She points to a clean rip in the center of the paper, about an inch long. "What letter?" I'm confused.

"The one they found on our door. The death threat."

I touch the note gently with my gloved finger. It doesn't look like much.

"Open it!" she cries. "Please! Please, you have to open it."

"Okay, okay," I say. "Hang on. I don't want to tear it."

Annie's vibrating with urgency in her seat. I move my thumb along the edge of the paper, and the waxed seal lifts up cleanly, where it was broken long ago. I unfold one leaf. Then I unfold the other. The pattern of cuts made by one knife through all the complex folds is starlike, reminding me of when we'd make paper snowflakes in elementary school.

Trembling, Annie reaches over and takes the paper from me. I'm astonished, that she can hold it. She cradles the letter delicately in her hands, looking down at it.

"That's all?" she asks, her voice catching.

I don't know if she's talking to me, necessarily. I think maybe she's asking the universe. I stare at Annie's face, lit strangely by the fluorescent library lights. Something about her skin has changed. It's like instead of the light shining on her, it's shining in her. No, that's not right.

It's shining *through her*.

"Annie?" I whisper.

She doesn't seem to hear me. Or if she does, she doesn't answer.

"That's all it says? Why would it say this?" she says, but her voice sounds sort of hollow. It's hard for me to hear, and not just because she's whispering.

"Annie!" I hiss, glancing over my shoulder to make sure the librarian doesn't hear me.

She's *fading*. A pit of terror and panic yawns open in my stomach. I don't know what I'm supposed to do. Is she doing it on purpose? Does she know it's happening? I can actually see the tabletop through her arms, as if the substance of her forearms has thinned, faded like an overexposed photograph. The paper almost looks like it's floating a couple of inches off the library table, because Annie's hands underneath it are disappearing.

"Wes?" she asks.

But her voice is so far away that I'm not actually hearing it, in my ears. I'm just hearing it in my head.

"Wes!" she calls again, but the faint rosebud outline of her mouth doesn't move. I only see the outlines of her eyes widen with surprise.

Wes.

"Wait!" I burst, reaching for her, and the librarian glances up at me with curiosity.

I grasp at nothing. The paper lingers in midair for only a second, as if figuring out that the hands holding it have vanished, and then with a soft sigh the letter begins to drift down to the tabletop. I scramble to get my hands under it, to catch it and keep it safe.

The letter settles in my gloved hands, and I stare down at it. The slip of browned paper, wrinkled with age and riddled with knife cuts, bears just one word, written in spidery old-fashioned handwriting.

CHAPTER 6

I don't understand.

I'm staring down at the letter that Wes has put into my hands, so crisp and yellowed that I can't conceive it's the same letter that I saw stabbed into my front door only yesterday. It seems to have been folded so long it's forgotten how to be unfolded, and the fragile, stubborn creases make it sit uneasily in my hands, like a dead leaf.

I'm trying to decide if I recognize the handwriting.

Slavemonger.

Why would someone levy that accusation on our door?

Why?

We don't own slaves. We never have. Winston's a freeman and gets his wages. I see slaves every so often, on the street or at the market, but Papa's family never had them. And Mother's didn't, either—Mother's from Connecticut. I've heard tell of what it's like, in the Southern states. They publish stories in the papers. Sometimes they run away and try to hide amongst the freemen here, and when they're caught, it gets ugly very fast. That Senegalese boy with the broken nose, he could be a runaway. There was fear, under his rage, I saw. Once I saw a black woman in the street, the top of her dress pulled down, screaming, being flogged by two sunburned white men, and the murmurs in the crowd told me that she'd run away and they'd come for her all the way from Maryland. But we're not like that, here. I've heard Papa say they're going to outlaw it, in New-York. It's even part of his platform. Papa plans on being mayor, not that he's ever discussed it with me, but I've listened at enough keyholes to know.

I finger the sealing wax, with the impressed outline of a spindle. What can that mean? What does a weaver want with us? Why would a weaver pin such a scurrilous lie on our door?

I stare at the hideous word, hard. As I stare, the word seems to twist and slither across the page like a garden snake. *Slavemonger.* I concentrate. The writing blurs, and I have to squint to see it.

"Wes?" I ask.

I'm on the point of asking what he thinks it means, when I glance up and observe a soft, gentle fog drifting into the library reading room. It creeps along the top of the card catalogue, oozing across the floor to the librarian's desk, and pouring over its edge like a waterfall. It flows up the walls and streams across the ceiling, billowing like waves of smoke from a fire undiscovered.

"Oh no," I whisper.

Fingers of fog trail across our table, coiling around my arms, swirling under the letter in my hands. I look at Wes, terrified, wondering if he sees it, too.

"Annie!" I hear him call my name, but it's a distant call, the shout of someone in another room, or at the far end of a block, trying to make himself heard.

I can barely make him out, in the thickness of the fog. I see the outline of his cheek, and the soft mop of his hair, but I can't see his face. The fog wraps itself around him like a blanket, pulling him into itself.

"Wes!" I cry out.

In my hands, the letter grows thinner, harder to see. Transparent, like a leaf caterpillar-eaten out of existence. I can no longer feel its texture in my hands, can't register its weight. It fades until all I see is the last hovering outline of that horrible word, as if written on the air. Then, even that remnant vanishes, like a snake's tail vanishing down a hole.

I bolt to my feet, flailing in the fog. My hands meet nothing. No table, no Wes. Nothing.

"Wes!" I bellow at the top of my lungs, but the noise falls dead on my ears, as though I've shouted into a void.

The fog creeps closer, and I stare at it, forcing my eyes to stay open. Maybe if I stare it down, I can make it go away.

The fog inches nearer the tips of my shoes, and I creep backward.

"Go away!" I shout at the fog.

Still it inches ever closer.

"Go away, I don't want you! I want to stay here!" I shout.

A tendril of fog gently touches my toe, and I kick at it. The fog spreads and dissolves, but then re-forms itself and moves softly, smoothly over the top of my foot, sending a delicate finger up to the hem of my dress.

Tears spring into my eyes. Why must I be pulled away now? I just found the letter! But I don't know what it means! What if this is the end, and I'm not going to be a Rip van Winkle anymore?

What if I never learn what happened?

I struggle to keep my eyelids open, refusing to so much as blink. I don't know why, but I've decided that the fog can't do what it wants to do if I'm watching it.

Softly, smoothly, the fog wraps itself around my legs, moving up to my waist. It doesn't hurt. It feels nice, actually. The fog is warm and easy.

I catch my breath, only then becoming aware that I was holding it. I lift my arms over my head, on instinct, the way I do when wading into the Hudson with Herschel and the other children, putting off diving in until the last possible minute, relishing those last few minutes of dry hands before the inevitable water closes over me.

"Annatje?" Someone is calling my name.

"Is she awake?" another distant voice asks.

"Well, she should be, at this hour," says the first voice, which I recognize as belonging to my mother.

"Is she quite all right?" the second voice asks anxiously. "It's not like her, to malinger. Perhaps she's come over feverish."

A door opens and closes, and I twist where I'm standing, unclear where I am. The fog has formed itself into a dense mass at my back, pressing into me, lifting me up.

My eyes are burning from the strain of staying open. It's no use. I have to blink. But what will happen then?

"Oh, she's fine. It's those books she reads. Reading too much thins the blood. And she's always been a lazy girl."

"Eleanor, really." The second voice belongs to Aunt Mehitable.

"I'm awake!" I call. "I'm here!"

I press my lips together to give myself courage, and I close my eyes. The moment my lids meet, I feel myself falling, gently, softly, as one falls in a dream before starting awake.

I hear footsteps crossing a wooden floor, and then hands are pressing on my shoulders.

"Are you awake, dearest?" Aunt Mehitable asks. I can smell the lemon balm on her breath, which she chews to cover her tobacco habit. Mother thinks ladies using tobacco is undignified, but Aunt Mehitable never cared.

A soft hand pushes the hair back from my brow. I open my eyes a slit, and discover myself tucked in bed in the attic spare room of Aunt Mehitable's house. The bud-rose wallpaper is just as it was, lit orange with morning light. Something warm and purring presses into my stomach—my aunt's patchwork, mouse-hungry house cat.

I open my eyes fully and find the concerned face of Aunt Mehitable bending over me, with my mother looming behind, staring down her nose. You can see that they're sisters, as they have the same sharp Yankee nose and pinched eyes. But Aunt Mehitable's more sedate than Mother. She cares less for fashion. And by "less," I mean she cares not a fig.

"Dearest?" my aunt says, fingering the curls over my ears. "Are you awake?"

"Yes," I say, but my mouth is dry. My eye travels down and observes that I'm in my nightdress. The cat yawns and gives me a knowing look.

"It's late," my aunt continues gently. "We were beginning to worry."

My mother sniffs with disapproval and roams over to the mantel to wind the clock there, her back to us.

I sit up, rubbing my eyes. The cat leaps off me with disdain and wraps himself around my mother's ankles before disappearing out the door.

"I'm sorry," I say to my aunt. "What time is it?"

"After nine," Mother says coolly from her vantage point by the mantel.

"Are you feeling quite all right?" my aunt asks, ignoring my mother. She picks up my wrist and feels my pulse. My aunt sometimes fancies herself a cunning woman. It drives Mother wild. "Your pulse is a trifle weak," Aunt Mehitable announces. "I'll have some licorice tea brought up. Help you get your strength back. Tone the blood."

I can't help but smile at my aunt's solicitousness, given my circumstances. And hers, for that matter. But in this memory in which I find myself, I can at least enjoy her warmth, if not her licorice tea, which I loathe.

"I'm quite well, Aunt," I reassure her. "Thank you."

"Best get up," Mother chastises me. "I shouldn't have to remind you what an important day it is for your father."

I look slack-jawed at my mother. It's today?

It's today. The meeting of the waters is today. Today, the city celebrates the official opening of the Erie Canal.

Tonight is the Grand Aquatic Display.

I only have one day of memories left. I'm running out of time.

My aunt gives me a wan smile and pats the back of my hand. "You're pale, Annatje," she says. "I'll have the tea ready when you come down. Strengthen the blood. You'll see."

She gets up and leaves the room, giving my mother a long warning look.

When she's gone, Mother comes over and yanks the quilt roughly off me.

"I don't know what nonsense you're up to," she says to me in a low voice. "But I won't have you ruining today with your histrionics. Now get up. Breakfast will be cold."

I glare up at her and pull my nightdress down over my legs against the chill in the attic.

"Did they find who left the note yet?" I ask her in an accusing voice.

My mother looks surprised and displeased with my question.

"Never you mind," she says. "We're safe here, and everything's proceeding as planned. Except for my lazy daughter oversleeping. Now get dressed. I've laid out your things in Beattie's room."

"Is Papa here?" I ask.

"Yes. For another half an hour or so. In the drawing room."

Mother gives me one last glare from the doorway.

"What?" I ask her, defiant.

"I don't know what's gotten into you," she says. "But we need you

247

to step in line. We're a family. What's good for one is good for all of us. Don't you forget that."

The door clicks shut behind her, and when it's closed I stick out my tongue.

"What're you doing that for?" Beattie asks.

She's just wandered in through the connecting door to the other attic spare room that she's sharing with Ed, and she's chewing on something. It proves to be a stick of dried beef. She's been dressed up like a fashion doll, the ones they display in the windows of expensive mantua-makers. Even her cheeks are rouged. It's disgusting.

"Come here," I say to her.

She comes over by the side of the bed, saying, "You want some?" and holding out the beef stick.

I shake my head, and roughly wipe the rouge off her cheek with a moistened thumb.

"Hey!" she whines. "Quit it."

"You look like an actress, with that stuff on," I say.

Beattie looks hurt. "Mother said I should look like a lady for the festivities. Why aren't you dressed? Your dress is much lovelier than mine. Mine doesn't have a ribbon."

I can't believe they're going to trot my little sister out like a prop for Papa's benefit. My vision goes red, and I leap out of bed, throwing a shawl around my shoulders.

"Where's Ed?" I bark at her.

"How should I know?" Beattie shrugs.

I hurry across the room and fling open the door.

"Annie! Where are you going?" Beattie cries after me.

I gallop down the narrow stairs of Aunt Mehitable's house. They're so steep they're almost like a ladder, and I've fallen down them more than once. My aunt's house is one of the oldest on the Square, a dim and narrow clapboard contraption in the English style, with a sharp peaked roof and wooden shutters.

"Papa?" I call out.

Mother said he was in the drawing room. I have to catch him before he leaves. I have to ask him about the letter.

I tear past my aunt's housekeeper, who gasps at my wraithlike aspect in white linen nightgown and shawl, curls flying. I land with a stomp at the bottom of the stairs and fling myself into the drawing room.

Startled, my father looks up from a newspaper in his hand and stares at me. I'm taken aback by his appearance. Papa looks thin and drawn, with purple rings under his eyes. Sallow skin hangs from his cheekbones with unfamiliar slackness, and his eyes look black and haunted.

"Annatje," he says, as if reminding himself of my name.

I close the door behind me and walk up to him, pulling the shawl around myself. I stare my father in the face.

I don't spend much time with Papa. Mother shoos us away from him so that we don't irritate his nerves. That's how she puts it, anyway—Papa has a bilious constitution, and we're not to upset him. When we were small, we weren't permitted under any circumstances to make noise while Papa was home. I don't know that he's really cut out for politics. His opinions are changeable, and he tires easily. But it's been Mother's plan for him for as long as I can remember.

"Papa," I say.

"You're not dressed," he remarks.

"I don't care about that!" I exclaim, stamping my bare foot.

There's a falseness to my parents' propriety that exhausts me. A refusal to acknowledge the encroachment of reality. To look at him you'd think my father never dove into the river off the docks as a boy, never bought hot corn and favors from those high-yellow girls in the alleys. You'd think my mother never wrung chicken necks on a farm in Connecticut. Who do they think they're fooling?

A shadow crosses my father's face.

"You'd best care about it," he says, tossing down his newspaper. "Today's an important day. We're due on the dais after the corporation dinner at the governor's house. And then the barge tonight."

"I know that. Are you going over your speech, just now?" I ask, and the words taste bitter in my mouth.

Papa gives me a funny look. "Yes," he says slowly.

I step nearer. "Going to tell all the people of New-York how wonderful the canal will be?" I prod him.

"Why, yes," he says. He looks nervous. His eyes shift left and right, as if grasping for a means of escape from his wild-eyed daughter.

"Will it be wonderful, Papa? Will it bring us all into the modern age?" I ask, my lip curling.

"You know it will," he says.

"We'll be able to go into the wilderness in days instead of weeks. Take that rich land that should belong to us, instead of a few naked savages. Furs! Land! Grain! The whole of the west unfurling at our feet like a rich carpet, just waiting to be plundered!"

"Yes!" my father cries, slamming his fist onto the table. "Just so! Yes! It'd be madness to want it otherwise!"

"Tell me, Papa," I whisper, stepping nearer.

My father looks actually afraid. I've never made either of my parents afraid before, and the sensation is both sickening and exhilarating. My mouth draws into a wolfish smile. I lean close to his ear, and whisper, "Tell me why someone put the word SLAVEMONGER on our door."

My father flings aside his newspaper and stalks to the tall window that looks out on the hubbub of Hudson Square. There's no space between street and housefront to speak of, no pretense at sidewalk, and carriages and carts rattle by close enough for my father to touch, if he weren't imprisoned by the panes of glass. In the window I see his sallow face reflected, a wasted shell of the man he used to be. Or the man I used to imagine he was.

"I . . ." He falters, not meeting my gaze in the reflection. "I don't know."

"You're lying," I marvel.

It's not even the gentle lie of elision that adults are in the habit of inflicting on their children. Those lies I'm used to. I even echo them myself, sometimes, especially when talking to Ed, who is still after all very small. This is a lie of the bald-faced type. A lie with no honor.

My father's shoulders sag. "Annatje," he starts to say.

"Annie," I correct him. I want none of his Dutch pretense anymore.

He turns and faces me, looking wan and desperate. "I don't suppose I can expect you to understand," he says.

"What won't I understand?" I ask.

My father looks stricken, as though begging me to go back to being a little girl, uninterested in the sordid aspect of life that, I increasingly see, has been his purview all along. I suppose he wants to protect me. I can imagine a world where my father thinks his own compromised morality will keep his children safe from the truth.

My moment of triumph wavers. I realize with appalled recognition that I have no wish to see my father this way. I loved him. My banker father, with his noble Dutch roots and political aspirations. My father, who knows important men and discusses important things. I don't want to know that he's just a flawed man, like any other.

"It's . . . it's complicated," he falters.

"Try me," I say, folding my arms over my chest.

"The government," he says. "They couldn't put up all the money.

You see? It's a huge project, the canal. You can't even imagine how big. No one's ever attempted anything like it. It's like . . . it's like asking the governor to pay for a slingshot to send some argonaut to the moon. Who'd invest in such folly? Who'd explain to the people why their taxes should be spent on such things? Don't even have enough to eat, most of them. The common man lacks vision, Annie. He can't look any further than tomorrow. Sometimes not even that far."

"I don't think that's true, Papa," I say.

He smiles drily at me. "Of course you don't. Oh, my dear. How young you are."

He moves away from the window, which has become blocked anyway by the back of a ragged woman begging with a child at her breast. My father crosses the room to me, and places his hands on my shoulders.

"We formed a corporation, to solicit private investment. We had to raise the money some way, don't you see?" He's using his now-let's-be-reasonable voice. Nothing drives me to greater distraction.

"From whom, Papa? Who did you go to for money?" I demand, staring him in the face.

"Why, from all sorts of people. Businessmen here in town. Some additional syndicates, as well. Syndicates from farther quarters."

"Southern syndicates, you mean," I say. "Plantation owners. Slaveholders. They gave you the money."

He nods. Ever so slightly.

"But what do they care for the canal?" I exclaim. "They're hundreds of miles away!" I try to twist myself free of my father's grip, but he holds me fast.

"The grain, Annie," he says. "The price of grain will plummet once the canal is open. Use your head. Slaves are expensive. They have to eat. Not well, I admit, but eat they must. No planter will let his stock starve to death. They're expensive to buy, and expensive to maintain in bulk. But they'll get cheaper to keep, fed on bread from grain moved on our canal. Have you any idea how cheap these goods will become, once our canal opens? How much harder they can then be made to work? How rich their trade will make this city? The cotton cargo coming through New-York will expand ten times over. Why, my bank alone holds mortgages on hundreds of slaves. We'll triple our investment in a day!"

"These *goods*," I spit, and this time I do break myself free from his grip. "I thought you said you'd outlaw slavery, in the city, when you become mayor!"

"And so I shall, my dear. The laboring classes will insist on it. Free white men need wages, or they'll starve and riot in the streets. They can't compete with slave labor. Look at this." He gestures to the beggar woman outside the window, who's waylaid a stovepipe-hatted young man who's trying to shake her loose from his sleeve. "Can't you see how they'll benefit? And in any case, they vote. In this city, abolition is what the masses want to hear, so that's what I sell them. And if cotton stays cheap, why, so much the better."

I'm so revolted by what my father's saying that I fear I'm going to be sick.

"But, Papa," I say through the bubble of disgust quickening in my chest. "They're not goods. They're people."

He looks on me with pity, and shakes his head.

"Not like we are," he says with finality.

The stovepipe-hatted man outside shoves the beggar woman off him and shouts loudly enough that we can hear it through the glass. She rains a hail of curses on him the likes of which are surprising, even for someone who's accustomed to the Bowery.

I start backing away, one foot at a time.

"Come now," my father says, seeing the horror in my face. "It's all to the good, don't you see? Tonight the entire city will celebrate.

Some radicals may have tried to shut it down, but they've failed. This canal will bring all the country together, and into the future."

"No," I whisper. "No, it's not to the good."

"Annie, be reasonable. In any case, it'll never be outlawed entirely, no matter what your mother's ladies' group likes to think. Your mother agrees with me. She knows how important slave money is to our enterprise."

Mother knows?

But of course, Mother knows. And she doesn't care, either. She just sees the money, and the political opportunity. She just sees what she wants to see.

I grope for the ceramic base of the large palmetto plant in my aunt's drawing room, bend double at the waist, and heave into it. My stomach is empty. Nothing comes out but bile. I spit, to get the awful taste of the truth out of my mouth.

"Annie!" my father cries.

Slavemonger. That's what the note said. With a flourish at the end, like the tail on a snake. But maybe the flourish was really an *S*. *SlavemongerS.*

I look up from the planter, my mouth hanging open, a rivulet of saliva hanging from my chin. My father is looking down on me with a mixture of fear and concern. He's stopped just short of resting a hand on my back.

I was in the library with Wes. And I read the note with that awful word. I was upset, desperately upset. And then . . .

I glance up at my father's horrified face, and I begin to laugh.

CHAPTER 7

O h my God. Oh my God. Oh my God!

She just disappeared! What the hell am I supposed to do?

I look around in a panic, but it's not like anyone is going to know that anything's happened. I feel like I'm supposed to be doing something. Like I need to spring into action. But what? Who do you call when your . . . when your . . . when someone just disappears?

I look back down at the note.

Slavemonger. She seemed really upset by that. But why?

"Is everything okay?" someone asks behind me, and I jump so hard I almost drop the paper, which would be bad since it's, like, an antique and everything. The librarian is standing there looking at me like I've grown two noses.

"WHAT? Oh yeah. I'm fine." I try to cover how completely freaked out I am by the fact that this girl who's been stalking my every waking moment has just literally disappeared into thin air.

"You're sweating," the librarian points out.

Gingerly I reassemble the note into its little origami square and place it back in the library box without meeting the librarian's eyes. Yeah. I'm sweating. You bet I am. It's all I can do not to barf right in this library box.

"Yeah, well. It's super hot out." I give her a big fake cartoon character smile. "July in New York. Am I right?"

The fact is, the air-conditioning in here makes it completely arctic. She's even wearing long sleeves. The librarian gives me a funny look, and says, "Uh-huh. Just let me know when you're done with those materials, okay?"

"Sure," I say. "I will."

She goes back to her desk, leaving me to try not to hyperventilate while I think about what I should do. I should figure out a way to get her back. Right? But how would I even start to think about doing that? What even brought her here in the first place? Should I keep looking for the cameo myself? Where in the hell is it? HOW SHOULD I KNOW?

Listen, I reason with myself. She's a . . . You know what she is. Right? So there's a chance that, if she's gone now, that's the end of it. There's no helping her. You have to just chalk this up to one of those experiences you never tell anyone about, ever, except when you're an old guy in the home and no one will believe you anyway.

But what if she comes back? I don't want to let her down. She seems to come and go as she pleases. But no, that's not right. She didn't want to go. She called out to me. So she comes and goes, and she can't necessarily control it.

Where is she?

I stand up at the library table, as though I'm going to leap into action. But I have no idea what action to leap into.

I sit back down again.

Maybe I should wait. When she showed up in my room, she said, "I came right back." Right? What if she comes looking for me here? I should make myself easy for her to find, if she can. Right? Yeah. In that case, I should just sit here and wait.

But it's not like she'd ever been to my room before. Maybe she can find me wherever I am. Maybe it's *me*, not where I am in space, or time, or . . . whatever. In that case I should keep trying to figure out what happened to her, to help her. And trust she'll just catch up with me whenever. She'll come back for me. Right?

She has to.

She can't just leave me hanging like this. This can't be *it*.

Gradually I become aware that I'm rocking back and forth in my seat, staring into space at nothing. I must look like a crazy person.

A hand claps me on the back at the very second a young male voice says, "Hey, man," and I'm so startled I actually shriek.

"Dude!" Tyler exclaims, laughing. "Jumpy much?"

The librarian looks at me with an I'm-about-to-call-security face.

"Sorry!" I call to her. "Sorry," I say to Tyler, between trying to catch my breath. "Jesus. You scared the crap out of me."

"I guess! Sorry about that. What's up?" Tyler drapes himself over the back of a library chair and gives me a lopsided smile. He looks happy. He's even wearing less eyeliner. Oh no, wait. It's just blue to-day, instead of black. Daytime eyeliner. My mistake.

"Oh, man," I say, leaning my head in my hands. "I've had the weirdest of all possible days."

Should I tell him the truth? He'll think I've lost my mind. But, so what if he does? If he thinks I'm crazy, then who cares? I'm going back to Madison in a week anyway. I never have to see Tyler again if I don't want to. I can vanish. Forever.

"You look like crap," Tyler says helpfully while pulling the box over for a look. "What's all this stuff?"

"Oh," I say. "Nothing. It's for a project."

"You need a release, if you want to shoot in the library," he points out. "I know. I checked."

"Not that kind of project," I mutter.

Tyler's already moved on, picking up my bag and pulling my

camera out for a look. "So what's the problem with your camera?" he says, taking the lens cap off and powering it up. He plants the view-finder in his eye and looks at the library through a digital lens. "You said the focus was messed up?"

"Yeah," I say, leaning back and staring up at the ceiling. "I was shooting some more footage for *Most*, and I couldn't get the focus to hold. I don't know why."

More acoustical tile divots. Too many to count.

"More footage? Of what?" he asks me with interest.

"You remember that girl? The one you needed a release for? In *Shuttered Eyes*," I say.

"Sure," he says, swinging the camera onto me and grinning.

"So, I got together with her."

"What?" Tyler's grin spreads, and he drops the camera from his face. "You mean, *got together* got together?"

"God! No." I wave him off.

"Pfffft." Tyler laughs, bringing the camera back up. "Eastlin's so right about you."

"Listen," I say. "This is serious."

"I'm listening. Go on," Tyler says.

"Are you finished with this?" a voice interrupts us.

It's the librarian, gesturing to the open box of Van Sinderen ephemera. I glance at all the unlabeled photos and letters and birth-day cards and things. Generations of Van Sinderens that Annie never knew. I feel like I should have gotten more out of it. More than one word on some star-cut letter.

"I guess," I say.

"Find what you need?" she asks me. She's probably wondering what two film guys are doing messing up her archive. She's probably ready to get rid of me.

"Sort of," I say, unable to hide my disappointment. "Actually, no. Not really."

"What were you looking for?" she asks. She sounds like she really wants to know. I'm surprised. Tyler swings the video camera onto her face. "And I'm letting you play with that because I can tell it's not recording, for the record," she adds.

Tyler pulls the camera out of his face, waggles his eyebrows at her, and then puts it back. Like me, he prefers seeing the world through a filter.

"If I wanted to look at really old newspapers, how would I do that?" I ask.

"Like how old?"

"Old. 1820s," I say.

"Sure," she says, like people ask her that all the time. "Microfilm room downstairs."

Tyler groans. "Oh my God," he says. "Microfilm."

That's rich, coming from Mr. 16 millimeter guy. But whatever.

"Or," she says. "You can just check the historic newspapers database."

"There's a database?" I'm stunned.

"Of course there's a database." She smiles at me. "What do you think this is? 1977?" She beckons me to follow her to her desk. "You can do this at any terminal," she remarks, fingers flying over the keyboard. In less than a minute she swivels the screen around to face me.

New York Times. Boston Globe. And a bunch of ones I'd never heard of, that probably went out of business. Everything. It's all there.

"Wow," Tyler says, peering over my shoulder. "I've figured out your focus, by the way," he says to me.

"Great," I say to him. To the librarian, I say, "And this will show me the actual newspapers? Like, I can read them this way?"

"I'll do you one better," she says, smiling. "What're you looking for?"

"I want to know if some kind of accident happened a long time ago," I say. "Or an assassination, maybe. Something bad."

"Date?"

"October twenty-seventh, 1825."

Tyler lowers the camera and stares at me. "You in a history class I don't know about or something?" he asks. "No wonder you're so stressed out."

"No," I say, irritated. "I'll explain in a minute."

"Okay," the librarian says, typing so fast it's like magic. "Ooooo! The opening of the Erie Canal! Very cool."

"Boring," Tyler singsongs. "Come on, man, let's go. I've got tons to tell you."

"Wait a minute." I wave him off. To the librarian, I say, "Yes, right. There was this big party for it. On the water. The Grand Aquatic Display. Is there anything about that? Something bad during that."

"Let's see." The librarian frowns at her screen, paging through various results. "You know," she remarks. "You're more than capable of doing this yourself."

"I know," I say, sheepish.

"Hmmmm," she says. "Oh! Yep. Here we go."

She clicks the mouse, and clicks again.

"What?" I say, bouncing on my toes the way Annie does when she's excited. "What happened?"

"A fire," she says.

Her printer fires up without warning, deafening in the silence of the reading room, spitting out a few pages in quick succession. She plucks them from the top of the printer pile and hands them to me.

I shuffle through them, frowning. She's printed out, like, four different articles, all about some kind of explosion and fire on a barge.

One reports that it's happened, and then there are a couple follow-up articles about them trying to figure out why.

"Wow," I say, impressed. "This is awesome. Thank you."

"No problem," she says. "Lucky for you, it's slow in here today."

I move away from her desk, hunting through the still printer-warm pages for any mention of Annie.

"Dude." Tyler plucks at my shirt. "Come on."

"Wait, wait!" I exclaim. I want to read the articles. I have to find out what happened.

"Wes. It already happened, right? They're not going anywhere. Come on. I'm starving, and I want to tell you about what's going on with Gavin Brown."

"Tyler! Will you just wait one goddam minute? I need to read this." It comes out louder than I intended it to. I can tell, because Tyler's eyebrows shoot up.

"Sure. Jeez. Have a stroke about it, why don't you." Tyler wanders over to the table and flops back into a chair to fiddle more with my camera while I scuttle to a corner by a bookshelf to read the articles away from prying eyes.

Unfortunately, they don't tell me all that much. They're written in this weird, overblown old-fashioned style. Basically, there was a huge party, and they spend about a million years listing all the civic groups who were there. Finally, they get to the good part. The governor poured a bunch of water from different rivers all over the world into the harbor, and all these fireworks went off, and while that was happening, one of the barges went up in flames.

There was screaming. They could hear it all across the harbor, under the sound of the flames. At first no one did anything, because they thought it was part of the fireworks show. But then people on-shore noticed the silhouettes of people on the barge, running back and forth, jumping into the water with their clothes on fire.

I swallow. Hard.

The Canal Corporation won't comment—that must be Annie's dad's company—and the harbormaster thinks some bunting caught fire by accident. It was a great tragedy, the only mar on an otherwise triumphant day.

"God," I whisper, haunted by the soot crawling up Annie's arms and face when she reached her hand into the sunlight by that tiny, awful park that's not really a park.

I can't think about it. I can't.

One of the articles has a strange coda. It says that the United Brotherhood of Luddites has claimed responsibility for the fire on the barge.

Maybe it wasn't an accident.

"United Brotherhood of . . . Huh." I pause, thinking. Where have I heard that before? Luddites . . . Ludditz . . . the graffiti in Maddie's squat. But something else . . .

I rush back over to the librarian's desk. She smiles pleasantly up at me.

"Find something good?" she asks.

"Maybe," I say. "Listen, I know you're busy and everything, but could I use your computer for, like, two seconds?"

"Why don't you go downstairs? Plenty of terminals there," she points out.

"No, I know. But my friend's waiting for me, and I just . . . I promise, it'll only take a second."

"You said two seconds. Which is it?" She arches an eyebrow at me.

"All right," I confess. "Two. But not a second more."

She gestures with her head for me to come around behind her desk. When I get there I open up her browser.

"Google? God, you're killing me," she says.

"Sorry," I mutter.

I search "United Brotherhood of Luddites."

In the pages and pages of random stuff, most of it irrelevant, I spot one thing that chills me so deeply my fingers practically go numb.

It's a nineteenth-century engraving. A trademark, maybe, or like something you'd see on a letterhead.

The engraving is of a spindle.

Just like the one on the sealing wax.

"That's it!" I exclaim, looking excitedly at the librarian.

"What's it?" she asks me, clearly amused at my excitement.

"They're going to blow up her parents! On the barge!" I almost shout. "I have to tell her! Tyler!" I holler across the reading room at my friend, who glances up from my camera.

"What?" he calls.

"Let's go!" I'm gathering all the newspaper printouts in my arms and dropping them everywhere instead. "Can I print this out real quick?"

"Sure," the librarian says, voice mild with amusement. She clicks the mouse and the printer spits out a poorly scaled, fat-pixelled image of the spindle engraving. It's from some outdated blog about the history of anarchism in Britain and the United States.

While I'm doing that, Tyler's come over and is looking curiously at me.

"All right, there you have it." The librarian grins. "Good luck."

"Thanks!" I say, stuffing the image of the spindle engraving into the sheaf of papers under my arm and steering Tyler away with me.

I'm preoccupied as we scurry to the elevator. I have to tell Annie not to get on the barge. Anarchists are going to blow it up and kill her parents. I have to figure out how to find her again, but how?

"Wes?" Tyler interrupts my train of thought.

"What?" I say, irritated.

He looks surprised and hurt, like he's not used to being the one to follow along behind me, rather than vice versa.

"Just," he says, "I was looking at your camera. There's nothing wrong with your focus. It works totally fine. It holds the settings and everything."

"Are you sure?" I say, surprised.

"Positive." He gives me a long, strange look.

The elevator dings open, startling us both. We step in and punch the button for the main floor. There's no one else in the elevator, and we both stare up at the floor numbers lighting up one at a time over our heads.

"I watched some of your footage, while I was waiting," Tyler says, without looking at me.

"Yeah?" I say, glancing at him sidelong.

He laughs once, through his nose. "Yeah," he says.

The elevator arrives at the ground floor and whooshes open.

"Typical," Tyler says before we step out.

"What's typical?" I ask.

"You, you jerk," he says with a lopsided smile. "Leave it to the documentary guy to film a truly transcendent state. I should've known."

I eye him to see if he's angry, or teasing me, but I can tell that he's not. I think he's just begrudgingly impressed.

"Well," I point out. "She showed up for you first."

He nods, unconvinced. "*Shuttered Eyes*," he agrees. "Yeah, well, whatever. But if you'll notice, each time, she was really there looking for you."

My cheeks flush. I don't know what to say to this. All I know is that if I don't see her again, I'm going to . . . I'm going to . . .

I cannot accept the idea that I might not see her again.

"I can't believe it," Tyler continues. "All the time, I thought it would be the people there who'd be the most interesting for my film. I never once thought of catching a real—"

"Don't say it," I cut him off.

"Don't say it? Why not?" he asks.

"Just don't. It really bothers her."

He laughs, tossing his head back.

"It *bothers* her! Oh, man." Tyler is marveling at my weirdness, I can tell.

"What?" I say. "It does. She's very sensitive about it. Wouldn't you be?" I ask him as we weave our way toward the security desk.

"I guess I would," he admits.

We open our bags for inspection, and the guard pages through my Xeroxes to make sure I don't have any stolen copies of the Bill of Rights tucked in there or whatever, and then we're outside in the summer afternoon sunshine.

"If I help you find her, will you tell me how you figured out what she really was?" Tyler asks me quietly. "Will you let me talk to her?"

"Um," I demur.

It's not that I don't want him to meet Annie, it's just that I'm not sure it'll work. Will he be able to see her? Other than on film, I mean. Or through a mirror.

While I'm waiting for a response to come out of my mouth, my cell phone vibrates in my cargo shorts pocket with a text message received. I pull it out and squint at the screen in the glare of the sunshine.

Maddie.

She wants to know what we're doing tonight.

A knot of guilt ties itself in my stomach. It's a pretty unfamiliar feeling, too, given that for most of high school girls didn't seem to know I existed. I was always the guy that girls would take to dances as friends when the guy they were really interested in was going with someone else. If my high school girlfriend knew I was now juggling two girls at once she'd laugh so hard she'd probably get a nosebleed. I text back with my left hand that I can meet her at the same bar we went to before if she wants.

When? She wants to know.

I chew my lip, and then suggest seven. Tyler's looking over my shoulder, but in the glare I don't think he can see what I'm doing.

"Well?" he prods me.

I shove the phone back in my pocket and smile.

"All right," I say. "Sure. Come on."

I stride away from the library, turning right and heading downtown, away from Washington Square.

"Where're we going?" Tyler asks as he trots alongside me.

"I think," I say, "that she's able to find me, no matter where I am. She showed up in my room late last night, but I'd never told her where I was staying."

"She did? Wow. Did you freak?" Tyler asks with a grin. "Was it like that scene in that movie, where the woman's floating over the guy with her hair streaming behind her and then she goes invisible and then his belt starts undoing itself and his eyes roll up in the back of his head?"

"God! No! Shut up!" I smack him on the arm, laughing. "Jeez."

Tyler laughs.

"But that's me assuming she has control over where she goes," I say. "Right? And we don't know for sure that she does. So let's say she doesn't. She wouldn't just show up somewhere random, would she? No. She'd show up where she's comfortable."

Tyler's nodding along with my logic, his hands shoved in the pockets of his skinny black jeans. "So. Where's she most comfortable?" he asks.

We're making good time now, and we jog across Broadway to Great Jones Street, heading for the Bowery. I look at Tyler, somehow completely certain that I'm right.

And I say, "She'd go home."

CHAPTER 8

I am laughing so hard I almost can't catch my breath. My whole
body is shaking with it, and I'm starting to get a stitch in my side.
Oh, it's perfect! I can't believe I didn't figure it out sooner. How can
I have been so stupid?

My father looks down on me, his sallow face twisted.

"Annatje, get ahold of yourself," he says, eyes shifting left and
right as though afraid someone's going to burst in on us and accuse
him of something.

"What for?" I cry, laughing so hard that tears are squeezing out of
my eyes and rolling down my cheeks. "Are you afraid, Papa?"

"What! No!" he raises his voice and grabs hold of my upper arm
as though to shake me back to my senses. The beggar woman outside
the drawing room window shades her eyes with her hands to peer in
at the commotion.

The laughter rises in my chest until I'm screeching, hyena-like, at
the peeling plaster rosettes that decorate Aunt Mehitable's drawing
room ceiling.

"Stop it!" he shouts, rattling me back and forth. "Stop it this
instant!"

I swallow my guffaws and smile prettily up at him. "They were right, about you," I tell him.

The drawing room door flies open and we're met with the shocked face of my aunt. Her eyes jump between my father and me, and quickly land on the woman spying in on us through the window.

"What's all this, then?" she asks. "Mr. Van Sinderen? Is everything all right?"

My father releases my upper arm, and I stagger sideways with the force of it, reaching up to rub the bruise that's been pressed into the flesh under my nightgown sleeve. My aunt hurries to the window and slaps the curtains closed. She folds her arms and stares accusingly at us.

"Yes. Thank you, Mehitable." Papa always calls my aunt by her first name, because he knows she hates it.

"Annatje. Come. I've got that tea you asked for." She gives me a pointed look.

Still hiccupping with my hysterical laughter, I manage to say, "Thank you, Aunt."

She moves over and positions me somewhat behind her, steering me to the door with her body between me and my father. I glare at him over her protecting shoulder.

He stands uncertainly, flexing the fingers of his right hand.

"You'll have her ready to join us on the dais, I trust," he says to my aunt.

"Indeed. It's quite a day, today. One we won't soon forget," my aunt says before shutting the door on him with finality.

When we're alone in the dark front hallway, my aunt peers into my face.

"What's wrong? You can tell me, you know," she whispers. She tucks my puff of curls behind my ear with her fingers and plucks here and there at my nightgown with concern.

"Auntie," I say, searching into her face. "Was Mother always this way?"

My aunt glances with alarm up the narrow staircase, I suppose seeing if we're being observed. Then she sighs.

"She was, in fact," Mehitable says. "Eleanor's an ambitious woman. Always was. Why do you think she came down to New-York? You think she'd have been happy as a Connecticut farmwife? Chapped hands? A dozen children underfoot? Up before the dawn? Can you see Eleanor content with morning milking, and nothing more elegant than summers of church picnics and winter sleighing parties? Come now. You know her better than that."

It's true. I do know her better than that.

"And why did you come?" I ask, drawing my shawl over my shoulders. My aunt always did like a good sleighing party. And I did, too.

My aunt looks up at the ceiling for a long minute, and shrugs. "She brought me down with her. As a chaperone, you know. When we were girls, after your grandparents died. You don't get to meet the likes of the Van Sinderens without you have a chaperone to come along. Else, they're liable to think . . ."

She trails off, and then gives me a wan smile.

"Well. In any case. You'll be married yourself, soon enough. And just think of the prospects you'll have, if her plans all come together. Mind you wear that dress we laid out for you today. How lovely you'll look. Why, we'll have you married off before Lent."

She gives my cheek an affectionate pinch, but can't stop herself from glancing worriedly at the door that hides my father.

"All right," I say, feigning acquiescence. "I will."

"That's my girl," she says. "Now, shoo." She flaps the backs of her hands at me to scatter me back up the stairs where I belong.

I slowly haul myself up the staircase. But I won't be going to my room. I know exactly where I'm going to go. I've finally figured it out.

269

It occurs to me that if my guess is correct, I might not see my aunt Mehitable again. I pause, my hand clutching the banister, and gaze down the stairs at her compact Yankee form, in its many-times-repurposed mantua and practical cap. She's staring at the drawing-room door with a worried look on her face.

I stare at her. I want to tell her how much I love her. How much I loved visiting her funny little house, when I was small. How much I'll miss her.

But when I try to form the words, a hot lump stops in my throat, and all I can do is smile at her. As if sensing that there is something that I want to say, my aging little aunt glances up at me and gives me a bright smile.

"You go on, now," she insists. "Stop dillydallying. It's time to get ready. Past time."

We look, smiling, on each other for a long minute.

"Yes," I say finally. "I know."

When I reach the landing outside my bedroom door, I huddle into a dark corner. I can hear Beattie in one of the bedrooms, humming. Ed's out running wild with some of the neighborhood boys. Mother's upstairs writing letters, Papa is locked in the drawing room.

I'm alone.

I retreat into the shadows, concealing myself behind a disused hall stand, my shawl tight over my shoulders. I flatten into the wall as if I could disappear into the burls of the woodwork.

I close my eyes, and behind my eyelids I conjure a picture of the old-fashioned spindle that I saw stamped into the sealing wax on the letter Wes found in the library. I hold the image perfectly in my mind's eye, as though I were looking at the letter again in my hands, examining every tiny detail.

And then I think about Herschel. I think about his soft brown eyes, with black lashes heavy like silk fringe. I think about the way that his eyes shine when he looks at me. I imagine that I can feel the cameo on my finger. As these thoughts pass through my mind, a cool breath of air brushes over my cheeks, and the curls over my ears stir in its eddies.

Yes. I focus more closely. The grooves of the wax, stamped into the shape of a spindle. A spindle like the ones the English Luddites smashed ten years ago.

Luddites.

A secret society of anarchists.

They're right. They're right, about my father. My father the slave-monger, building an empire on the backs of people he pretends to want to free. He's a liar. The Luddites know that the canal will line the pockets of the rich and hurt people it pretends to help. Even people far away from New-York. The future will grind them up like grist in the mill.

But I don't know what the Luddites are planning at the Grand Aquatic Display.

I have to talk to them.

My eyes still closed, I stretch a hand forward, groping to where I would expect to find the hall stand.

My hand touches nothing.

A huge smile breaks across my face.

Eyes squinted shut, I take one step forward, away from the wall, and stretch out both arms on either side of myself. I stand, poised over an abyss, touching nothing, my head thrown back, feeling the air move about my body, my fingers stretching as if they could reach into the void.

I draw the deepest of breaths, hovering, and then I let myself fall backward. But instead of falling against the wall, or tumbling over the railing and plunging down the stairwell of my aunt's house, I sink into a soft cloud of nothing. I float, arms and legs splayed, nightdress billowing around my ankles. My shawl unwinds from me and slips away. I'm floating, drifting like a leaf in some in-between space. But it's a soft drifting, comfortable. I can swim into different orientations, drawing my knees up to my chest and then coiling around to drift on my belly, my curls hanging down over my ears. I reach my arms forward, as I used to do when breast-stroking in the Hudson with Herschel, but this time there's no weightiness of water in my clothes dragging me down.

I can move.

My guess was right.

I've figured out how to get where I need to go.

Now, I have to find out what happened on that barge.

CHAPTER 9

We stop short on the stoop outside the no-name pizzeria, and Tyler looks at me with surprise. Its windows are open to catch any passing breeze, not that there is any to catch. A couple of kids, their mouths full of cheesy pizza deliciousness, pause their chewing long enough to stare at us. The pizza of curiosity.

"What're we doing here?" he asks.

"This was her house," I explain. "That's why she showed up here first. She lived here."

"Get out," he says, staring up at the redbrick town house. "For real?"

"Yeah," I say.

"The whole thing was her *house*? You're kidding."

"Well, there weren't as many people here then. They probably had more room," I say.

"Don't kid yourself," Tyler says with a roll of his eyes.

"What do you mean? There weren't. The city basically stopped at Washington Square. She told me," I insist.

"Yeah," he says. "But do you have any idea how many people had to live all crammed together back then? You have no idea. My dad says when he was growing up in Chinatown, there were still tenements with, like, two whole families sharing two rooms, and a bathroom in the hall. And that was in the fifties. In the nineteenth century, forget it. It was disgusting."

"Really?" I look up with new eyes at what had been Annie's house, trying to wrap my head around what it must have looked like then. The pizzeria and the glass door make it really hard to imagine. No matter how hard I look, I just see a run-down apartment building on the brink of being condemned.

"For real. Her folks must've been loaded." Tyler sounds impressed. "Are you sure she's really a . . . ?"

I cut him off with a sharp look.

"Sorry," he says, shrugging his shoulders to fend off whatever it is I'm about to yell at him.

"It's okay," I say. "Come on."

We make our way up the steps and ring the buzzer marked FATIMA.

A long minute passes where nothing happens. I'm starting to get worried. What if the palm reader went out of business since Tyler and I were here? It wouldn't surprise me. I mean, seriously, how much money can those people make? The neon sign is turned off, and the cheap velvet curtains are closed.

Just then the buzzer crackles to life and an irritated woman's voice barks, "What?"

"Um. Madame Blavatsky?" I ask, putting my mouth close to the speaker.

"Who wants to know?" the speaker crackles back to me.

"Ah. This is Wes Auckerman? I was here last week. Helping on the film?" I'm trying not to sound like I'm apologizing, but it's not working.

"Oh, for Pete's sake," Tyler says, elbowing me aside.

"What?" I say, raising my hands in self-defense.

"Madame Blavatsky," Tyler shouts into the speaker, "we're here from the NYU security office, and we believe you to be in illegal possession of some sound equipment. Now, we'd hate to have to involve the police, and we're sure you'd rather keep this matter private. So if you'll just let us up, we can settle this quickly and let you get on with your day."

There's a long, anxious pause while the speaker seems to consider what Tyler just said.

Then the door buzzes to let us in.

"Nice work!" I say to Tyler, impressed.

"I remembered I left a mike behind by accident. Just a cheap one. No big deal. She's so shady, though, I was sure she didn't try to, like, return it or anything." Tyler grins at me.

The door on the second floor landing, the one covered over in black construction paper, is propped open on the dead bolt. We nudge it open and step inside. The room reeks of burnt candle wax and cigarette smoke. No wonder she had to use so much incense last time.

"How was I supposed to know that was your microphone?" growls a withered woman in a cheap polyester kimono. Her hair is plastic-carrot orange, and it's hard to recognize her without her turban.

"Have you got it?" Tyler says.

I'm impressed that he's managed to maintain an air of authority, even when it's obvious that we're not with NYU security. We're two nineteen-year-old guys in summer school, and one of us is wearing cargo shorts.

"Oh yeah," she says, waving an unlit cigarette at us. "It's over there somewhere. Help yourself."

Tyler gives me a now-ask-her-whatever-it-is-we-came-here-for look, and moves off to the corner she vaguely indicated to hunt down his forgotten equipment.

"Um. Madame Blavatsky?" I start. My hands are shoved deep in my pockets, because I never know what to do with them when I'm nervous, and being here most definitely makes me nervous.

"Sheila," she corrects me. "Sheila MacDougall."

"Sheila. Sorry. I was hoping I could ask you something." I don't know how to phrase my question without sounding totally nuts. But then, given the kind of stuff people must say to her, she's probably heard everything before.

"Shoot," she says, drifting over to one of the folding chairs by the card table and settling into it with a sigh. She pulls a lighter out of her kimono sleeve—neat trick—and sparks her cigarette. She draws on it long and hard, holds her breath while looking down her nose at me, and then lets it out in a steady stream around the words "You don't mind if I smoke, do you?"

I suppress a cough.

"Found it," Tyler calls from the back of the room.

"So, listen," I start to say.

"They're shutting me down, you know," the medium says conversationally.

"They are?" I ask. "Why?"

"Gonna tear the building down, they said. Build condos. Just what we need in the Village. More condos full of yuppies. You should've seen it when I first got here, in '75. St. Marks Place. The Bowery. This building was full of musicians back then. Couple of artists, too, made stuff out of scrap metal they found in the street. Two drag queens shared the back parlor room. Oh my God, their parties. I saw Warhol at one of them, one time." She takes a long drag, squinting one eye at me against the smoke. "The Guaraldis and me are the only ones left. They bought everyone else out. Forget it. Over."

She plants her cigarette between her teeth and leans back in the chair, balancing on its back legs. It looks precarious, and I'm afraid the kimono might fall open.

"They're tearing it down? When?" I ask, thinking about Maddie, who was squatting here. And Annie. I wonder if Annie knows they're going to tear down her house.

"How should I know? Soon. Next week? Tomorrow? All the same to me." She stretches her arms up over her head, the kimono sleeves sliding down to her shoulders. I imagine I can see the outline of the girl she used to be, when she arrived in New York from wherever she came from. Golden hair, in a 1970s Farrah flip. Sharp, aquiline nose. She would've been beautiful.

I wonder if all old people really just feel like young people trapped in old bodies.

"Where will you go?" Tyler asks. He's carrying the microphone and its wire all balled up in his hand.

"Florida! My sister's down there. Get some sun. Warm up. Finally. These winters, I tell ya." She somehow yawns without dropping the cigarette. Also a neat trick.

Tyler and I exchange a look, and he lifts his chin a fraction of an inch to prod me to ask my question.

"Sheila. I'm . . . I need to find someone I met here. When we were filming," I begin.

"Oh yeah? I usually tell my clients that everything's confidential." She takes the cigarette between finger and thumb like Marlene Dietrich, taps the ash onto the floor, and then plants it back in her mouth and folds her arms.

"I'm not talking about a client," I say. I move over and pull up another folding chair across from her at the card table. I lean forward on my elbows and give her my most sincere, Midwestern-nice-guy puppy-dog eyes. They're one of the only tricks I've got.

She eyes me with suspicion.

"I don't know what you heard," she says. "But I don't deal out of here anymore."

Tyler stifles a laugh.

"No, no!" I say, embarrassed. "Not that, either."

"So, what then?" She looks away, irritated.

I glance at Tyler for reassurance, and he says, "Go on. Tell her."

I swallow hard. "What's the deal with spirits?" I ask.

"What do you mean, what's the deal?" she mocks my earnest-sounding non-accent in a way that makes my ears burn red.

"Like, somebody dies, right? And then what happens? Do they show up as a spirit right away?" I lean forward.

She eyes me warily. "There's different theories. Usually, they have to wait around awhile first. 'Til someone special comes along. Someone with the sight."

"The sight," I repeat. "What's that mean?"

She looks at me like she can't quite believe I'm as stupid as I look.

"You know. *Sight*. Someone who cares enough to see them," she explains. Which doesn't explain anything at all, but whatever.

"Okay. So, once they show up. How long've they got?" I press.

"Depends"—she takes another long drag of her cigarette—"on what they've done. Or what they're trying to do."

"What do you mean?" Tyler asks, and I'm surprised to hear him sound worried.

"Most people," Sheila says, interrupting herself with a hacking cough. "Everybody does stuff they regret, in life. But sometimes, there's that one special thing. That one thing that stands out from the rest. Something you've got to resolve. And that need to make things right, is even stronger than death. But you don't get a lot of time to do it."

"Why not?" I ask, my eyelids blinking rapidly as I start to understand the gravity of what she's saying.

"How long do most important things take, in life? An hour? A day? A week, tops?" Sheila says with a shrug that exposes a few more inches of sun-stained shoulder inside the kimono. "You don't get any longer in the afterward than you did the first time around."

Tyler and I exchange a look, and I can see in his face that he knows what I know.

Annie is running out of time.

"What happens if you can't do it?" I ask, trying not to choke on the words. "Like, what happens if you can't fix whatever that thing is, that you did?"

Sheila's penciled eyebrows go up.

"Then you're stuck," she says.

"What does 'you're stuck' mean, in this context?" Tyler presses her.

The medium smiles slowly, and says, "You should really be paying me, for this."

"Listen," I say, digging in my shorts pocket for my wallet, hoping twenty bucks and a coupon for a free fro-yo will be enough of a bribe. "I need you to hold a séance." I lean nearer, until my nose is only a few inches from her face. So close that I can smell the cigarette on her breath. "Please?"

Sheila MacDougall stares long and hard at me, and then throws her head back with a braying laugh. She's missing a couple of teeth.

"Oh, honey!" she says, placing a mottled hand on my arm. "You poor dumb jerk."

I exchange a worried glance with Tyler, who looks as confused as I am.

"What?" I say.

"Kid," she says. "It's a scam! Come on." She aims her next comment at Tyler, which is, "You knew that, right?"

Tyler looks panicky. "What do you mean?" he asks, his voice tight.

"A scam! You know. Tricks. There's a button on the floor, turns the candles on and off. See?"

Without warning, all the candles in the sconces along the wall flame into life. I'm so startled that I jump. I can smell a whiff of natural gas. In the clear truth of daylight her tricks look obvious and cheap.

"But what about all those people I filmed?" Tyler asks. He sounds genuinely distraught. After all, he wanted to film people in transcendent states. That was his whole project.

"Who, them? Oh, what difference does it make." Sheila MacDougall grinds her cigarette out on the sole of her bedroom slipper, and drops the squashed butt on the floor. "People believe what they want. If I didn't take their money, somebody else would."

"Okay," I say, trying to keep my voice steady. "But the thing is, what if it actually worked, one time?"

"What do you mean, worked?" She gives me a suspicious glare.

"I mean," I say, dropping my voice. "It *worked*. I have proof. And I need you to do it again."

She gives me a long look, presumably to see if I'm joking. I try to make myself look authoritative and serious.

"We'll pay you," Tyler breaks in.

She glances at him.

"Those're the magic words," she says. "Hit the lights."

For a long while, nothing much seems to be happening. We're sitting around the card table in a watery darkness, because the summer afternoon sun is creeping in around the edges of the velvet curtains. Tyler and I are holding hands, which is weird, but then I'm also holding hands with a desiccated 1970s downtown type, so who's to say what's weird anymore. Sheila MacDougall is chanting, and Tyler's eyes are closed. Tyler's less afraid of seeming foolish than I am, I have to give him that. He throws himself into stuff, full throttle. My default, when I'm uncomfortable, is to get really self-conscious. And I'm uncomfortable most of the time. That's why the camera makes everything easier. It gets my attention off myself.

My eyes keep drifting to the ceiling in boredom.

Divots. Too dark to count, though.

I'm starting to think this was a stupid idea. I should've just waited for Annie in the library. Anyway, how do I know she's even coming back?

But she has to come back. The cameo, that's her regret. She's got to find it. And she's got to find it soon. That's the key, somehow.

She's got to come back.

She's got to.

I fidget in my seat. Sheila grips my hand harder, as though trying to hold me in place.

Sheila's chanting grows louder. At my insistence she busted out the crystals and the Ouija pointer thing and everything, and I let my gaze come to rest on these stupid toys on the table between the three of us. Why am I doing this? I could just as easily be waiting for her in Washington Square. Sitting in the afternoon sun on a park bench, watching terriers and spaniels parade by on their way to the dog run. Pigeons pecking around. A few roses clinging to thornbushes, their petals starting to crisp and brown at the edges.

Annie's mouth, her lips like pale rose petals. I picture it, the tiniest of smiles pulling at her mole. Her weird curled hair. That delicious, musky smell she has.

I smile privately to myself.

"Psssst." A faint whisper brushes up alongside my ear, so faint I think I might have imagined it. The fine hairs along the back of my neck stand up.

I crack open my eyes, peeking between my eyelashes. I can just make out the silhouette of Sheila chanting, her head drooping to one side with the half-assed-ness of it, and Tyler with his shoulders hunched up and his eyes squeezed tight as though anticipating someone hitting him in the face. I don't see anything else.

My heart rate has sped up, though.

I hold perfectly still, listening.

The whisper, if that's what it is, moves along the back of my neck and down my right arm. My nerves tingle with the aliveness of it, and I can feel a static electric current lift my arm hairs and move up the surface of my skin, all the way up to the roots of my hair.

"Annie?" I mouth the word, barely whispering it so that the others won't hear.

"Wes?" the whisper answers me. It's somewhere behind me, or to the right.

I move my eyes slowly in their sockets, hunting for her shape. But it's too dark; I can't see anything.

I stare long and hard at a point off to the right. I imagine I hear the faintest laughter, moving around the periphery of the room.

"What are you doing?" the whisper asks, this time brushing against my left ear. I have to fight the urge to let go of Tyler's hand and reach up to scratch my ear.

"I was trying to find you," I breathe.

Tyler's hand tightens on mine. I guess he can hear me. I hope I don't sound stupid.

The faint laughter intensifies.

I look across the table at Sheila, who's kept on chanting like it's nobody's business, totally indifferent to whatever Tyler or I might think.

Is that . . . ?

Wait. Is it?

It is.

Ha!

Standing behind Sheila's chair is the barest outline of a young girl, about seventeen, with curls combed forward over her ears. She's in her same dress, with the low neckline with the bow in the middle, and loosely gathered elbow-length sleeves, the one Eastlin thought was stolen. As I stare she becomes more distinct, as if she were being reconstituted one atom at a time, growing gradually denser and more real.

Her eyes are bottomless pools of black, and she's smiling at me.

She holds a finger up to her lips.

Then, behind the medium's head, she waves her fingers and forms her mouth into an O, as if she were saying *Woooooo!* She tiptoes around in a circle, exaggerating like a mime, pointing at the medium and making faces at me.

I can't help it. I start cracking up. I press my lips together tightly to keep myself from laughing out loud.

Annie sees me fighting not to laugh and then covers her mouth with one hand, pointing at me with the other. She swans around, pretending like she's wearing a sheet. Then she mock-rattles some imaginary chains, rolling her eyes and moaning.

"Dude," I burst through my laughter, my eyes tearing up. I let go of the others' hands and collapse, laughing on the table.

Sheila must have noticed that I've stopped participating or something, because all at once the lights flood on and Tyler screams, "Holy crap!"

He staggers to his feet and reels backward, a hand on his chest like he's having a heart attack.

"What's going on? What are you trying to pull?" Sheila shrieks at us.

Annie's frozen in the middle of the room, arms raised, like she's playing freeze tag.

Tyler is gaping at her, his eyes so wide I can see the whites around his irises.

"Holy crap!" he cries again. "You were serious!"

"Who was serious? What're you talking about?" Sheila MacDougall says, gathering her little crystals and stuff to her chest as if she were worried we're going to steal them.

My eyes bounce between Tyler's horrified-yet-fascinated face, and Annie's smiling one. She's let herself become un-pretend-frozen, and is shaking out her skirts and patting her hair back in place. Sheila, though, is just looking at Tyler.

In a flash I figure it out.

Sheila doesn't see her. *But Tyler does.*

"Hi, Annie," I say aloud.

"Hey, Wes," she says sweetly. She comes over and perches on the card table next to me. She leans her mouth close to my ear, and with a mock-concerned look at Tyler says, "Is your friend okay?"

"Annie?" Sheila spits, getting to her feet. "What, Annie? What is this? Are you putting me on?"

Tyler's face has gone ashen.

"Oh my God," Tyler says. Then he says it again a couple more times, for good measure.

"I told you it wasn't just me who could see you," I say to Annie.

"You were right." She nods. "How did you know? I think he might need a glass of water."

"You boys get out of here," the medium shouts, her voice getting strident.

"Sheila," I say, pulling my video camera out of my shoulder bag and powering it up. "Here."

I pass it to her and indicate the viewfinder.

"What the hell is this? Don't try to con me, kid." She glares at me.

"I'm not," I assure her. "Just look. Maybe start with the shot on Tyler, and then pan slowly over to me."

Tyler's collapsed to the floor, staring openmouthed at Annie and me.

"She's the one in my movie," he finally manages to say. "She kept moving around. In the different scenes. She was never . . . I could never get her to . . . Oh my God."

"I'm sorry he's acting so weird," I say to her. "He's okay once you get to know him."

She nudges me with her elbow. "It's all right. How did you know he'd see me, too?" she asks, eyebrows raised.

Meanwhile, Sheila has accepted my video camera with a cross look and is training it on Tyler.

"Wow," she remarks. "This one's nice. How much this set you back, anyway?"

"It was something you said, actually," I say to Annie.

Sheila pans from Tyler, sitting cross-legged on the floor and trying to catch his breath, and I can hear from the sounds of the focus that she's zooming in. She reaches me, and then she pans a little farther.

Then she says, "Great God in Heaven," and slowly lowers the camera to her lap. Her mouth falls open, and her eyes well with tears.

I turn to Annie and smile. She reaches forward and brushes the mop of hair off my forehead, grinning.

"It's possible to see the truth," I say. "You just can't look at it too closely."

CHAPTER 10

Sheila MacDougall refused to accept our money, which I could tell was a first for her. But she was really, really anxious for us to leave. She hustled us out so fast I had to hang on to the banister because I was worried I'd trip and fall down the stairs. She slammed the door after us, and we could all hear the dead bolt thrown once it was closed.

"Are you freaking SERIOUS?" Tyler is shouting when we all land on the stoop outside.

I'm hugging Annie to my chest, feeling the soft tickle of her curls against my neck.

"I was afraid I wasn't going to see you again," I whisper in the shell pink of her ear while Tyler freaks out in the background.

"I know," she says into my shirt. Her arms go tighter around my waist.

"This cannot be freaking HAPPENING," Tyler shouts, his eyes bright with excitement.

I cup the back of Annie's head in my hand. Her hair is so soft. Underneath the familiar musk of her hair, I can smell the gunpowder on her, like she's been sitting too close to a campfire. That smoky-clothes smell. I close my eyes and breathe her in.

I'm distracted by a tugging at my shoulder, and open my eyes to find Tyler rummaging in my camera bag. "What're you doing?" I ask him.

"I'm sorry, man," he says. "But there is no way I'm not filming this. I don't even care. This is freaking amazing." He glances at Annie with a shy look and laughs with disbelief.

Settings done, recording button on, Tyler fixes my camera to his eye and trains it on us. Annie withdraws against me, but laughs while she does it.

"Does your friend know there's blueing all around his eyes?"

"Yes," I say directly into the camera. "He knows. He thinks he's Billy Idol."

"Please," Tyler says. "Billy *Corgan*. But you guys! Do you realize you basically just gave that medium, like, a reason to live?"

"What's he talking about?" Annie asks out of the side of her mouth.

"You," I answer. "That woman thought she was just a scam artist, but it turns out she's really talented. She totally brought you back when we asked her to. God, her face! Did you see it? You scared the crap out of her!"

"Ha!" Annie says, rather than laughs. "She did not either."

"Are you guys hungry?" Tyler asks, then to Annie he says, "Can you even eat?"

Annie's eyebrows go up. "You don't waste any time, do you?" she says.

"No. I'm Tyler," he says, camera still in his face, sticking his hand out for her to shake.

"How do you do, Tyler." Annie seems amused. "I'm Annie." She takes his hand and pumps it up and down mock-manfully.

I realize I'm holding her to me with my arm around her shoulders, clutching her to me, and I haven't let go just yet.

I should probably let go.

But I don't.

"This is amazing!" Tyler's going on. "I admit, I didn't believe it. Not at first. God! And you're in *Shuttered Eyes*! That's incredible. Wait 'til I tell the gallery. They're going to freak, I swear. Wes, you have to put her in *Most*. For serious. There's never been a documentary like that before. Not a real one. Just let them try and not let you transfer, if you actually put her in *Most*."

"Gallery? *Shuttered Eyes*?" Annie's looking between him and me, but she's smiling like it doesn't matter that she doesn't know what he's talking about. She's just glad to be here. With us.

With me?

"Hey. Let's get pizza," I say, and it feels like the most reasonable thing anyone has ever said in the history of ever. The pizza of reason.

"Definitely. God. Or a drink," Tyler says.

At the thought of a drink, my stomach sinks.

Maddie. I'm supposed to meet her in—I check the time on my phone—a little over an hour. Assuming they're still not carding. She can totally pass for over twenty-one, but the only way I get into bars is by chance when there's no bouncer. I'm meeting her there, in any case. Well, what's the big deal? I didn't tell her it would be just the two of us. I'll just bring Tyler and Annie. We'll hang out in a group. Weirder things have probably happened in New York.

"Pizza first," I say.

"Definitely," Tyler agrees. "Do you like pizza? Have you ever had it? Just you wait. It's awesome."

By the time we're all squared away with slices and sitting around one of the aluminum tables near the back of the no-name pizzeria in the former drawing room of Annie's house, Tyler's started to calm down a little. Long enough to put the camera down on the table, anyway, and get some pizza into his mouth.

Annie keeps looking around herself with an expression that I can only describe as mild shock. I've bought her a slice of pepperoni. She's probably never had pizza before. I wonder what she'll think of it.

I wonder if she can eat.

Tyler's wolfing his down and all three of his slices are gone in about two seconds.

"God," he says, shaking his head. "I was starving. I must've burned through a week's worth of adrenaline up there. You scared the pants off me, I'm not gonna lie. Jesus. I just about pissed myself."

Annie smiles sweetly at him. "Did I? I'm sorry," she says.

She takes my hand under the table, her thumb tucked against my palm in an oddly intimate way, and I feel the customary shiver that tells me she's close by.

"No, no! It's cool. I was just surprised, is all." He grins at her. "It's incredible. Wes, isn't it incredible?"

"No question," I say, catching Annie's eye. "Incredible."

"So? How does this work, anyway?" Tyler asks, firing up the camcorder again. If anyone else in the pizzeria notices that he seems to be filming an empty chair, they don't let on. *Kids,* they're probably thinking. Making an art film. Who knows why kids do what they do.

Annie blushes. "Um . . ." She glances at me, nervous. "I'm just starting to figure it out. But one thing I know for sure is, that woman you paid didn't do anything."

"She didn't?" He's surprised.

"No. I didn't even know she was there 'til I got there. Is that her business or something?"

"Kind of," I say.

"She pretends she can find . . ." Annie hesitates. "People like me?" A glimmer of sadness passes across her face.

"There's no one like you," I whisper to her.

Tyler makes a retching sound. When I glance up to glare at him, he grins at me.

"So? How'd you find us? Where were you? Were you there the whole time?" Tyler peppers her with questions, the red eye of the camcorder blinking with interest.

"Dude!" I exclaim.

But Annie's laughing, and I love the sound of her laughter so I have to stop talking and watch her while she does it.

"I was kind of . . . Gosh. It's hard to explain," she says, frowning.

"Try us," I urge her, my pinkie finger brushing accidentally on purpose against her sleeve.

"Yeah," agrees Tyler, making minute adjustments to the focus. She must be looking hazy to him through the camera, the way she did to me. "Just tell it to us like it's a story. Don't worry if it doesn't make any sense. We'll edit it down later." He grins to show he's just kidding, but he's probably not.

"Well." She leans on her elbows, gazing at the slice of pepperoni pizza between them. "For a long while I wasn't quite sure where I was. In time."

"What do you mean?" I ask, putting my fingertips on her arm. It feels warm and fleshy. I still can't wrap my head around the fact that she's . . . she's . . . a Rip van Winkle.

"I woke up standing in my mother's bedroom. I thought it was the next day. But everything was strange. Not like my mother's bedroom usually is. More like a dream of my mother's bedroom. I don't know how long I stood there, but I couldn't move, the way you sometimes can't, in dreams. And after a time, the room started to change. Then all at once I heard Wes say *Listen*. Since then I'm pretty sure I've been sort of . . . both places at once. Here, with you. Right now. But also . . . Then. Like in a memory." She sounds uncertain.

"A memory?" Tyler asks, entranced. I have the passing thought that if nothing else, this experience is definitely going to turn Tyler from art film to documentary. The idea of it makes me feel pleased with myself.

"Sort of," she says. "I think, when he touched my elbow, Wes sort of pulled me out of where I was. But I was afraid, and I screamed, and I think being afraid makes me go somewhere else, because next thing I knew I woke up in bed with my sister, like it was any other day. Except it was a day I'd already lived. And sometimes I fall— that's not the right word, but it feels that way—back into now. My memory days are all days I've lived before, but they're happening differently from how they happened the first time. I can do things I didn't do before." Annie stares at us, begging us to understand with her eyes. I wish I could. Right now, it's what I want most in the world.

Tyler looks lost in thought, weighing what she's said. "You know," he remarks. "Memories always change."

"What do you mean?" she asks.

"They've proved it. Like with science. Brain imaging, or whatever. I'm serious, I read about it. We think we record a memory in our brains, like me recording this conversation on video, right now. But that's not actually how it works."

"It isn't?" I ask. How does Tyler know all this stuff? I'm starting to think I should subscribe to *Discovery* or something, just so I can make inane small talk as well as he does.

"Yeah. Didn't you read that? It was in the *Times*. I remember be- cause it made me think about filmmaking. Every memory we have changes slightly each time we think about it. We add stuff we learn in other places, or we forget stuff that doesn't seem important anymore. Or you think you remember something, like from your childhood, but actually you've just seen so many pictures of it, and your parents have told you about it, so you think you remember it, but you don't. A memory is a process. Instead of a thing. Like a story we tell ourselves that changes from the standpoint we're looking at it."

Annie considers this long and hard. And so do I. The idea frightens me. Do I actually remember my life? Is this moment, happening right now, with Annie and Tyler in the pizzeria, and that same guy I filmed for *Most* working behind the counter and pretending like he doesn't remember me, is this all that's ever happened? The pizza of forever?

I grip Annie's hand tight under the table, and she squeezes back.

"Which days have you been seeing?" I ask. But the moment I form the question, I know what days she means. And if Sheila MacDougall is right, and they only get as long the second time around as they did the first, then I'm about to find out how much time we have left before she's screwed.

She levels her gaze at me, and there's sadness in the corners of her eyes.

"The days just before the Grand Aquatic Display," she says. "I've been reliving them. In order. But a little differently each time."

I swallow, hard.

"How many do you have left?" I ask, and there's an almost physical pain in my throat when I say it. "Before that night."

She waits a long minute.

"I just left my aunt's house," she says. "On the morning of."

"Christ," I say, burying my head in my hands.

Tyler's excited because he's catching this all on tape. I can tell he wants to be stage-managing this conversation, for heightened dramatic impact, and he's having trouble restraining himself.

"What's the Grand Aquatic Display? Sounds like an off-brand SeaWorld." He laughs at his own joke, but Annie and I don't join in.

"It's—" she starts to explain.

"It's a party," I rush in, speaking over her. I don't mean to be a jerk and interrupt, but I don't want her to have to talk about it for Tyler.

I don't want her to have to look too closely.

"So, what you're saying is, we only have one day left," I say to Annie.

Wordlessly, she looks at me and nods her head.

"Okay," I say. "That's not much time to find your cameo."

"What cameo?" Tyler interrupts, but we ignore him. "Like a guest appearance?"

"Jesus," I say. Her grip on my hand tightens under the table. I don't want her to know how hard this will be, but I can't hide it. I'm a filmmaker, not an actor. "So, wait," I continue. "Before, when you'd disappear. What made that happen?"

She frowns, and says, "It would happen when I got afraid. Or upset. I'd just . . . I don't know. I can't explain it."

"So that's why you vanished while we were looking at the note," I say, my eyes widening.

She nods.

"What note?" Tyler prompts me so I won't forget to explain to the camera what's happening.

Irritated, I look the camera in the eye. "The week before the Grand Aquatic Display, someone left a death threat on Annie's door. Or, they thought it was a death threat."

"But it wasn't," Annie adds.

"And we found it in the library. Wait—" I turn to Annie, confused. "It wasn't?"

She shakes her head. "I don't think so."

"What did the note say?" Tyler breaks in.

"Slavemongers," Annie says.

My ears prick up when I hear the added *s* on the end.

"You don't think it was a threat?" I ask.

"No," she says, dropping her voice to a whisper. "Wes. I think it was a warning."

"To who? About what?" I'm confused.

Maybe it's my imagination, but it looks to me like she goes a shade more pale. If that's even possible.

"To me," she says.

Just then some short kids in bright white sneakers come in carrying a huge boom box. I didn't even realize they still made those things. It's massive, with gigantic speakers, and it's blaring Kanye. The kids plop it down onto the floor like it's no big thing and all stare at the pizzeria menu, adjusting their athletic shorts and shifting their weight back and forth.

"Hey! Turn that crap down!" hollers the guy behind the counter, Paul, who yelled at me for loitering that day that I thought Annie ditched me. The kids mutter and resist, but eventually turn it down, sulking. The promise of pizza outweighs the promise of *Yeezus*.

"It was from the United Brotherhood of Luddites, Annie," I say.

I rummage in my camera bag for the newspaper articles that the librarian helped me find, and fan them out on the table in front of us. Annie leans over and peers at them with interest.

"You found them!" she exclaims.

"Oh yeah. It was easy," I say. Okay, it wasn't easy, exactly, but I want Annie to be impressed.

She reaches a tentative finger forward and traces it down the crumpled surface of the printouts. I can hear the whir of Tyler's zooming in for a close-up on her face while she reads. While she looks over the newspaper articles, I feel my phone vibrate in my shorts.

"Dammit," I mutter, pulling it out for a quick look.

Crap. It's Maddie.

Where R U?

I don't mean that, obviously. I'm excited to see her. I just didn't notice how much time had gone by. I was supposed to meet her fifteen minutes ago.

"You guys," I say. "Come on. We have to go." I'm quickly texting her back that I'm sorry, I'm right around the corner, and I'll be there in five minutes.

"Go?" Tyler asks from behind the camera. I don't think he's turned it off once. I wonder how much memory I've got in there.

"Where are we going?" Annie asks.

"I have to meet someone. It'll only take a minute. She's cool, you'll like her." As I say this, I wonder if it's true. I mean, I don't know that it's *not* true. But sometimes it's hard to tell, with girls. Especially girls you think would have a lot in common. They can sometimes ricochet off each other like identical pool balls.

"Oooooooh," Tyler says, understanding how much trouble I might be in right about now.

I give him a warning look from under the flop of hair on my forehead.

"No, really," Tyler tries to cover for me. "She's cool. You guys will totally hit it off." To me, he says, "We going back to the same place?"

"Yeah," I say.

"We late?" he asks, arching an eyebrow.

"Yeah," I say, stuffing the newspaper articles back into my bag and clearing the paper plates and napkins and everything into a heap and into the garbage.

Tyler stops recording and looks between Annie and me.

"All right, kids," he says with a smile. "Into the abyss."

CHAPTER 11

When we get to the street outside, Annie stops me with a hand on my arm, and says, "Wait."

I'm worried about making Maddie wait any longer, but I don't know how you get a girl like Annie to hurry. The normal rules don't apply to her.

"Please?" I urge. "We're already late."

"Wes, just wait a minute," she says, and the rosebud upper lip of hers hides a subtle tremor.

I lean over so Tyler won't hear what we're saying. "What is it?" I whisper.

"I don't know. It's just that . . ."

She trails off, looking up at the shuttered face of the condemned town house. The palm reader's neon sign is off. There's no life behind the windows at all. I watch her as she stares up at the building's empty windows. She's studying it, hard, her dark brows furrowed, as though she were trying to memorize it.

"I finally figured it out," she whispers to me. "How I can control where I go. If I'm afraid, I'll think about what will make me less afraid, then I can make myself go there. Sometimes." She glances up at me from under her eyelashes. "That was how I found my way back to you. Each time."

I swallow, my ears burning pink under her admission.

"But it also brought me back here," she continues, looking back up at the dilapidated building that used to be her house. "It brought me back home."

I put my arm around her shoulders and fold her into me. We stand like that for a long minute, hidden in the shadows.

"You guys!" Tyler shouts from a little ways up the block. "Come on! Let's go!"

I pull apart from Annie and look down at her. How do you leave home, knowing you can never go back again? I think about Madison, my parents' house, my freshman dorm room at UW. I think about how even if I go back after this summer, even if they've all stayed the same, I'll still be different. I've already left home. And so has she.

I guess the only way to do it, is to do it.

"You ready?" I ask her.

She wipes her fingertips under her eyes, smiles bravely, and says yes.

We turn away, clasping our hands and walking together without looking back.

Tyler's bopping down the street through the fading afternoon, and lights are winking on ahead of the coming city night. It's that moment in New York City summer dusk when it looks like the air should be getting cooler, but it's not. I pluck at the bottom of my T-shirt to peel it away from my skin.

I glance at Annie, wondering if she feels as hot as I do. I notice beads of sweat on her upper lip. So the answer must be yes. What must it feel like, to be inside her skin right now? Not just in her mind, but in her body? Is her dress heavy? If she thinks too hard about what she is, does it hurt? Is she sad?

What does she think about me?

I have to tell her about Maddie. But I don't know what I'm sup-posed to say. It's weird enough, having two girls notice me at all.

"This girl we're meeting . . . ," I start to say. But then I don't know where I'm going with it.

Annie looks at me curiously.

"She's . . . ," I try again.

Annie waits, and when I continue not to say anything, she gives me a wry smile.

"Don't worry," she says after a time.

I'm not sure what she means by that, but I exhale all the same. Anyway, aren't we looking for some cameo that another guy gave her? Maybe she only likes me as a friend. My stomach sinks at this idea, and I edge away from her slightly on the sidewalk, doing my best to pretend like I don't much care one way or the other. If Annie notices any change in the air between us, she doesn't let on.

We get to the bar, and it's early enough that there's nobody at the door yet.

It's not as crowded as it was the other night, and when I don't find Maddie right away I push through the clusters of sweaty kids laughing and clutching beer glasses to the garden in the back. It's warm enough outside that the garden is sparsely populated, and most of the people back there don't have laurel leaves tattooed on their necks. In fact, only one of them does.

She's sitting at a wooden picnic table, looking down into her wine-glass as though reading tea leaves. The garden isn't much to look at—brick patio, strung with Christmas lights, and someone's set up an industrial fan to stir around the summer heat.

Tyler spots Maddie first and stops, waiting to see how I'm going to handle showing up for what's basically a date with another girl and guy in tow. The truth is, I have no idea how I'm going to explain the whole Annie situation. Should I make Maddie look through the video camera so she can see her? But what if that freaks her out, like it did Sheila? Should I remind her about signing the release form? Will she even believe me, or will she think we're all pranking her? I'm already on her jerk list for being late. Basically, there's no good way for this to go.

While I'm hesitating, trying to decide what to say, Maddie glances up as if sensing that she's being watched. When she sees us, she breaks into a smile.

"Oh, hey!" she says brightly to . . . Annie? "Hi, Tyler. Hey, Wes. Perfect timing. I'm about ready for a refill."

"Hi!" Annie says. She climbs over the picnic table bench to sit down next to Maddie, pulling all her skirts and everything out of the way, flashing everyone a long bloomer leg.

"Hey, you. How're things?" Maddie asks.

"Good, I guess? Better," Annie says. "How are you doing?"

My head swims. In my peripheral vision, though, I can see Tyler about ready to explode with laughter.

"You guys . . . you know each other?" I stammer.

"Sure," Maddie says, smiling at Annie. "From around."

Annie smiles at me and shrugs. "She gave me a beer, one time."

"She . . . what?" My head is spinning.

Tyler meanwhile announces, "Yeah, so. I'm gonna get us a round," and disappears. Helpful.

"Also we used to crash in the same squat," Maddie says. When Annie looks surprised at this, Maddie explains, "Yeah. You remember. That place over on First? I saw you there a couple of times. But we didn't talk or anything."

"That was you I heard?" Annie asks, eyebrows bowed upward in perfect half-moons.

Slowly, feeling like my feet are detached from my body, I float over to the picnic table and drift down onto the bench across from them. I'm staring at them so hard that I'm worried a thread of drool is going to drip off my face.

When you put them right next to each other, it's sort of uncanny. The slope in their cheeks. An uncertain shape around the outside of their eyes. Maddie's hair is dyed inky black, but I think back to that photo I saw on her defunct high school Facebook account, and her real hair is light brown. But it was probably a pale flossy blond when she was really young.

Maddie's old Facebook picture showed up when I did an image search of Annie's film still. Google's facial recognition software has no idea how good it is.

They're talking together amiably, the way girls do when they know a guy is watching. There's a performative quality to it. They're being friendly, that much is true, but it's an exaggerated friendly, somewhat for my benefit, to show that they are funny and cool to hang out with, and I should be happy to be there with them. There's a lot of laughing and tossing of hair.

"That beer was really good," Annie is saying. "Thank you. I was in an awfully strange place just then."

"Beer?" I echo. "How is it even possible that you gave her a beer?"

"I saw her on the street the other day," Maddie says. "The day I ran into you, actually. She looked really strung out." To Annie, she says, "So where you crashing now? I've got a cooperative going, if you need somewhere to go. You'll have to share with my friend Janeanna. She's kind of crazy. But, yeah. She's basically okay."

"Crashing?" Annie asks, her head to the side.

"Yeah, you know," Maddie says. "Where're you staying?"

"Maddie," I interrupt.

"Hmm?" She arches her eyebrows at me. If she's thrown by my showing up with some other girl, she's making sure I don't get to see it. Which means she's probably really, really thrown, and she thinks I'm an asshole.

"What's your last name?" I say.

A shadow crosses her face, and she brushes her bangs back off her forehead. "My *street* name," she says primly, "is Madcinderz." To Annie, she continues, "Our co-op is fregan. So you've got to be cool with no meat unless it's free. Same for technology. If you're in the collective you can't use Facebook or anything, because technology is government's way of keeping us all enslaved. We're DIY. And we collectivize everything. What's mine is ours."

"I know that's your street name," I interject at the same moment that Annie says, "What's a face book? I don't think I have one. You'd really let me stay with you?"

Tyler picks that minute to show up with four dripping mugs of beer, which he plonks down on the picnic table between us. Maddie curls a lip—she was drinking wine—but accepts the beer anyway. Fregan, I guess.

"Sure," says Maddie. Annie grins.

"So," Tyler says, grinning like a cat with sparrow feathers in his mouth. "You guys really know each other?"

"Maddie," I press, ignoring the interruption. "Your last name. Come on. What is it?"

Maddie fixes me with a vicious glare. She picks up her beer glass and slurps off the foam.

"What's the big deal?" I ask

"God, Wes. Why do you even care?" she says.

Annie's looking back and forth between us, but I can't read the expression in her black eyes. All at once a gleam of wonder and understanding passes through them, and she rests a hand on Maddie's shoulder.

"Mine's Van Sinderen," Annie says quietly.

Maddie freezes, beer halfway down her throat. She's so surprised that she coughs beer up her nose and has to put the mug down and blow her nose into a paper napkin.

"Awesome," Tyler says.

She hacks, gasping for breath. Annie pounds her back gently.

"Are you messing with me?" Maddie asks once she can get her breath back.

"No," Annie says.

Maddie looks at me. "This is a put-on. What the hell do you think you're doing, huh?"

"I'm not doing anything, I swear," I say.

"You knew that was my last name. How did you know?" Maddie seems pretty angry. Her knuckles are white where they're gripping the beer mug handle.

"Well," I hedge. "Cinders isn't that big of a leap to Van Sinderen. Why don't you want anyone to know your last name?"

Maddie looks like she's thinking about leaving. Her lips are pressed together, and some of the color has gone out of her face.

Annie leans in closer, and runs her hand softly down Maddie's arm. "He's not teasing. I promise. That's really my name. It's yours, too, isn't it?"

Maddie looks wonderingly at Annie, studying her face. Slowly, she nods.

"And what's your real first name?" Annie asks.

Maddie swallows, and something in her face changes to make her look younger. Like she's afraid she's going to get into trouble. Tyler and I both lean forward, listening.

"It's Malou," she whispers.

"But you tell people it's Maddie. You like that better?" Annie presses.

"Malou's Dutch," she mutters, getting all shifty-eyed. "Embarrassing. And, anyway. My family sucks. They're basically bad people. They've always been basically bad people. Why would I want to have the same name as them?"

Annie laughs, that excellent mouth-open laugh she has. Then she throws her arms around Maddie's neck, crushes her lips to Maddie's ear, and says, "I do the exact same thing."

"What?" Maddie gasps.

"I'm Annatje," Annie explains. "And I hate it! It's too old fashioned. I made them all start calling me Annie, and everyone did it just to please me, except Mother. She calls me Annatje out of spite, because she knows how much I hate it."

Maddie's eyebrows bow upward in shock, and then she, too, starts laughing. They collapse onto each other and with their old-fashioned hair and strangely sloped cheeks, they could pass for sisters.

Tyler's leaning in to me to whisper, "Maddie could *see* her? Without a camera or anything? How's that possible?"

"I guess so," I say, mind whirring trying to keep up with what this might mean. "In the house. But on the street, too, it sounds like."

"That's crazy," Tyler says, staring at them from behind the shelter of his beer glass.

"Maybe it's not crazy, if they're related," I whisper to him, watching the girls giggling over something that I can't hear. They've sunk immediately into an intense whispered conversation. When girls get like that, it's like they're speaking in code.

"Related?" Tyler repeats.

"Sure. Why not? How many other people in New York have that name?" I insist. The moment I say it out loud I'm sure I'm right. "Maybe Annie was . . . I don't know . . . haunting her? Without knowing it?"

"Come on," Tyler says.

"Well? Why not? How should she know? She doesn't make the rules."

They're leaning their heads together and whispering. I catch Annie point at me, and Maddie glances at me quickly before hiding her face in Annie's shoulder and laughing.

What's so funny?

"Hey!" I say too loudly, my ears purple under their stares.

"Wes," Annie says, gulping her laughter back. "Guess what? Maddie's going to help us find it."

"Find what?" I can't keep up. Things are happening too fast.

"Her cameo," Maddie says. "But we've got to get out of here. You guys ready?"

Tyler and I exchange a fast glance.

"I already paid." Tyler shrugs.

"All right," Maddie says, getting to her feet. "But I'd better call and let them know."

Them? I mouth to Tyler.

He just grins and shoulders my camera bag. Annie flashes me a delighted smile, links arms with Maddie, and they stroll out of the garden together.

"Come on," Tyler says, gesturing with his head for us to follow them. "Listen. You don't have another thumb drive, do you? This one's running out of memory."

It's hard to believe, but in the six weeks I've been in summer school I haven't set foot on Park Avenue even once. I never had any reason to go. I mean, I'd heard it was the super fancy part of town, so maybe I would have gone before summer school was over, just to check it out. Now that I'm here, I'm not that impressed. If I didn't know better, I'd say the entire street was abandoned. Lights in the buildings are off. Doormen linger just inside the doors, in the air-conditioning. There's not even a cab. It's so empty our footfalls seem to echo on the sidewalk.

"Maddie," I whisper, trotting along on her heels. "Where is everyone?"

She sniffs at my ignorance and doesn't answer.

"They're probably all in the Hamptons," Tyler mutters to me. He's trying to hide the fact that he's impressed, but it's not working. He keeps craning his neck back, looking up at the sedate brick faces of the plush apartment buildings. Marble entryways. Polished brass. Carved nameplates for plastic surgeons and psychiatrists. Annie's gawking, too, her head tipped back on her shoulders like she's never seen buildings so tall before. She sticks close to Maddie's side, their arms looped together. It was a long ride from the Village, past Gramercy Park, and Annie's eyes only got wider the farther uptown we went, murmuring once about how fast we could go without a horse to pull us. She cuddles closer to Maddie, matching her footfalls to Maddie's boot stomps, and more than once I catch myself looking at them with a pained expression on my face. I wanted to be the one to show Annie everything.

We finally arrive at a building that initially looks modest, with a forest-green awning and polite casement windows.

"I don't know what the Hamptons are," I say to Tyler as we all stop and stare up at the face of the building.

"Now, listen," Maddie says. "They'll probably try to talk to you guys. But don't say anything, okay? Just ignore them."

Tyler and I exchange a glance. Who is she talking about?

"Okay?" Maddie presses us.

"Sure," I say uncertainly. "Okay."

Annie and Tyler both nod.

We walk up to the door, and on our approach it is silently opened by a short, barrel-y guy dressed in a navy uniform coat and peaked hat.

"Good evening, Miss Van Sinderen," the doorman says in Russian-accented English.

"Good evening," Maddie and Annie say in unison, then look at each other and burst out giggling.

The doorman, who I can only assume doesn't see or hear Annie, and so is watching a punked-out teenage girl laughing by herself with two sketchy-looking guys walking two steps behind her, stays stone-faced. Like he sees everything and nothing all at once.

Tyler and I walk past him stiffly, both of us pretending like we're totally comfortable in this situation. I see the flicker of a smirk on the doorman's mouth as we pass.

"Dude," Tyler whispers to me out of the side of his mouth. "What is it with you and the fancy girls?"

"Shut up," I hiss back. The truth is, I'm worried I'm having a panic attack. My heart is racing, and I can feel sweat dribbling down my rib cage. My parents' house has wall-to-wall carpeting and a huge TV over the fireplace. Every year my mom puts an original of our holiday card photo in a silver frame that she buys at TJ Maxx, and she yells at me and my sister if we get fingerprints on them. I grew up thinking that our house was pretty nice. I had no idea what I was talking about.

This must be where Maddie had to go, when she left my room the other night. For her curfew. God, this place is plush. Why would she want to stay in abandoned buildings, if this is what she's accustomed to? How does it even feel to be accustomed to a marble-hallway kind of life?

We stop in front of an old-fashioned cage-style elevator, and Maddie presses the button. With a creak and groan the mechanism starts up, and an old analog floor indicator, the kind that's shaped like a fan with the floor numbers on the edge, with an arrow pointer, grinds to life. Lights indicate that the elevator was on the top floor, the ninth. After a long pause while the elevator tries to remember what it's supposed to do, it slowly oofs down to the first floor and the door opens to reveal an impossibly old guy dressed in livery that matches the doorman's.

"Good evening, Clarence," Maddie says.

When she speaks in here, her voice sounds different. Smoother. More polished.

Rich.

"Good evening, miss," the old guy says.

We all pile into the elevator, which is so small and made of such delicate metal scrollwork that I'm frankly shocked it can handle all our weight. Maddie doesn't even tell him what floor she's on. Tyler and I both notice this absent detail at the same time, and Tyler's lined eyes are popping so hard they might fall out. Annie, meanwhile, is so busy marveling at the elevator that she's not paying any attention to us.

"Amazing," I hear her whisper to herself. "It's like a climbing machine."

The elevator rings to a stop on the eighth floor, and the operator cranks the doors open.

"Eighth floor," he announces, as if we didn't know it, and we all load off.

"Maloulou? Is that you?" a woman's voice trills from very far away.

The elevator has opened directly into a softly lit foyer, painted dove gray with white egg-and-dart trim (Gran would be so proud of me, remembering that's what it's called). There's a worn Oriental carpet in the middle of the room, over a polished black-wood floor, with no furniture at all except a huge circular white marble table with a crystal bowl spilling white peonies over its lip. The flowers are fresh, and they fill the air with a fragrance that's just a shade too sweet to be pleasant.

"Yes," Maddie shouts too loudly. To us, she barks, "Come on."

She strides straight across the room, leaving a trail of city grime behind from her combat boots. Tyler and I edge closer together, in the instinctive resistance of middle-class guys to environments in which they might break something expensive. I'm worried about even breathing in here.

"Maloulou? Darling?" the woman's voice calls, having drawn a room or two nearer.

"Dammit," Maddie mutters.

We've only made it halfway down a hall that seems infinitely long, lined at sedate intervals by small gilt-framed landscape paintings, each lit with its own special spotlight. They're mostly images of the Hudson River or pastoral scenes of sad-looking Indians posed against the sky atop a dizzying waterfall.

A woman appears from some secret room and gives us all a look that she probably intends to be welcoming. She's dressed in cream slacks, a cashmere cardigan, and ballet flats that probably cost six hundred dollars, and her hair is the same shade of blond I saw on those women in Eastlin's shop. Like, the exact same shade.

"Well! Are these your friends?" the woman says. A tiny hand hovers under her chin like a hummingbird.

"Uh-huh," Maddie says without breaking stride.

"Hi," Tyler says, not making eye contact, and ducking under the woman's gaze like he's cheating at limbo.

"Hello, ma'am," I say, sticking my hand out. "I'm Wes Auckerman."

She stares at my hand with faint shock and distaste. She doesn't say anything.

"Um . . . ," I say, not sure what I'm supposed to be doing differently. Something, obviously.

"We're going in the living room," Maddie shouts. "Don't bother us."

"Oh!" the woman exclaims. "All right."

Annie moseys by her with an arched eyebrow, but the woman doesn't acknowledge her. She probably can't see her. Then again, she didn't acknowledge me, and I'm not a Rip van Winkle.

"I'll have Etta bring in some sandwiches." The woman's voice follows us down the hall, uncertainly.

"God," Maddie grumbles as we arrive at the end of the impossible hallway. She stomps around, slapping on lights.

"Is that your mom?" I ask, hesitating by the entryway. It's flanked on both sides by Doric columns, and the entire opposite wall is casement windows with a staggering view of the tops of the trees along Park Avenue.

"Please," Maddie says, rolling her eyes. "*Step.* Number two."

Tyler and Annie and I file into the room as Maddie pulls light chains here and there. I'm taking in everything—the chintz, the Lalique, the claw feet, and polished wood. Her living room looks like a hotel lobby. Except way nicer. It feels as big as a hotel lobby, too. Tyler can't contain himself, poking around, touching things. I'm afraid to even sit down. The couches look so deep and professionally fluffed that I might fall into them and never escape.

Finally, Maddie hits a light that floods a large portrait hanging over the fireplace.

"Annie," she says, beckoning. "Come see."

Annie's rooted in place. I can't tell if she's as struck by the sumptuousness of it all as Tyler and I are, or what. But she's frozen stock-still in front of the fireplace, staring up at the portrait with her rosebud mouth trembling.

It's a family group, a man, a woman, two girls, and a boy, gathered around a table covered by maps of New York State. The man

309

wears a dour expression, with a fat belly and gold watch chain, and he's pointing at the maps on the table. His wife looks just as awful. She has a pinched face, and sits across from him in a red satin high-waisted dress, resting a proprietary hand on his coat sleeve. One of the girls is seated between them, younger than we are now, with her hair done up in a weird pointy arrangement. The other girl stands behind them, with her hand on the first girl's shoulder. The little boy stands next to the seated man, dressed in forest-green velvet knee pants and a waistcoat, one foot crossed in front of the other, staring out at the artist with a challenging expression in his face. His elbow rests on his father's back, with his fingers hanging down.

Annie just stares, her hands balled in fists at her sides.

Maddie stands below the painting, arms crossed over her chest, staring up at it, too. "I didn't recognize you," Maddie says.

I'm staring at Annie as she gazes at the painting, watching the minute expressions on her face change from surprise to confusion to mild wonder. I hear rather than see Tyler pull my video camera out of its bag and fire it up, making a record of the scene.

"That's . . . ," Annie starts to say, but she trails off. She turns to Maddie in wonder. "We had this done last year. The corporation paid. It was to hang in Papa's office at the bank." She steps nearer, reaching out as though to touch the canvas.

"Dude," Tyler breathes from behind the camera.

"Wait a minute," I say. "Is that supposed to be you?"

Annie turns to me, and my eyes jump between the real-life appa-rition in front of me and the waxy effigy in the painting. Annie, with her flushed cheeks and bottomless black eyes and delectable mole, looks nothing like the girl in the picture resting her hand on her sis-ter's shoulder. There's no mole. There's no vibrancy at all.

"That's my great-whatever-grandfather," Maddie says, pointing. "Who dug the Erie Canal. That's where the money came from. At first, anyway. Later it came from shipping. And subways; they owned part of the IRT. I always thought he looked like kind of an asshole. And that's his son, my great-whatever-grandfather minus one. I don't remember their names. But I know they all died together, except for the boy."

Annie's eyes go wide, and she steps nearer. "Eddie," she whispers.

We all peer closer at the little boy, with his jaunty foot and impish smile.

On the index finger of his right hand, where it dangles down along his father's back, is an oval smear of red paint, with tiny flecks of gold.

"Oh my God, that's it!" Annie cries, pointing. "Look!" She rocks up on her toes, excitement vibrating off her, as though invisible fireworks are going off over her head.

"Wait. Are you sure?" I say, hurrying forward to see. I squint at the painting, trying to make the blur of paint resolve into a recognizable shape.

"Sure I'm sure," she says excitedly. "It's my cameo!"

"But you said it was painted last year," I point out. "You didn't have the cameo then."

"Daddy had it restored at the Met conservation lab a couple years ago," Maddie says, sounding sheepish. "They told us the boy had been repainted. Changed the color of his suit. Maybe he added the ring later?"

"Eddie." Annie smiles, her eyes going soft. "It wouldn't surprise me, him being vain. And the cameo would've been too big for him to wear on the proper finger. He'd wear it that way instead. I must have given it to him." She looks at me. "But why? Why wouldn't I give it to Beatrice? It doesn't make any sense. And what happened to them?" Annie paces back and forth in front of Maddie's fireplace, her fists pressed to either side of her head.

We all climb into the chintz sofas to think. Tyler starts to put a Chuck Taylor on one of the antique coffee tables, but stops himself.

"So, if Maddie's great-whatever-grandfather got the cameo," Tyler mulls, my camera in his lap, "does that mean Maddie's mom would have it now?"

"Actually," Maddie says, avoiding eye contact with all of us. "No. Not exactly."

At that moment a bent-backed uniformed woman shuffles in carrying a heavy tray heaped with sandwiches.

"Good evening, Miss Malou," the woman says with a raspy smoker's voice. She's as old as the elevator guy. I'm concerned the tray is too heavy for her to carry. My instinct is to get up and help, but that doesn't seem like what I'm supposed to do, so instead I sit and do nothing and feel like a jerk.

"Thanks, Etta," Maddie says, not getting up from where she's slouched down in the sofa, boots splayed and in the way.

The woman sets the sandwich tray down on the coffee table with a grunt, and then shuffles back out without acknowledging any of us.

Tyler picks up one of the sandwiches and sniffs it. He makes a face.

I pick one up and stuff it into my mouth without hesitating, which is a mistake. I suppress a gag. It's cucumber. And mayonnaise. And nothing else.

Maddie eyes me, laughing silently.

"So," I say through a mouthful of sandwich. "What does 'not exactly' mean?"

Maddie sighs and stares up at the ceiling.

"Don't laugh," she warns.

Tyler and Annie and I all look at one another and nod.

Maddie sinks lower into the cushions.

"I bet it's at the New-York Historical Society," she says. She waggles one booted foot thoughtfully.

"What?" I say, rather intelligently, I think.

312

"My dad loaned them a ton of stuff last year. All these papers and crap, I don't know. Junk. Stuff his WIFE"—she yells that last word—"didn't want."

"Crap," Tyler says.

"And my mom doesn't have it, 'cause she lives on Antigua with her tennis instructor," Maddie says to one of her boots. "Dad took back the family jewels in the divorce."

Tyler snorts on *family jewels*, but doesn't say anything.

Annie keeps staring up at the painting. I can't imagine what it must feel like, to see such a wrong painting of yourself. Especially after you're . . . after you're . . . Anyway.

"Great," I say, leaning my head back on the sofa and staring at the ceiling.

Perfectly smooth plaster patterned in delicate florets.

No divots.

"How the hell are we going to get it out?" Tyler asks the room at large.

"Depends on their security," I say. "Like, is it more *Thomas Crown Affair*, or more *Ocean's Eleven*?"

"Please. *Thomas Crown* is bullshit. They're not going to have sliding metal doors on the walls. Now, *Pink Panther*, on the other hand," Tyler says. "They might have lasers. Lasers are way cheap now. With motion sensors."

"*The Italian Job!*" I add, getting excited. "The remake, though. The original sucks."

"Mmmmm." Tyler sighs in a Homer Simpson voice. "Charlize Theron."

"But where are we going to get equipment?" I say. To Maddie, I ask, "Is there, like, a spy gear store around here? Or police supplies?"

"You need ID to buy at the police supply place. What about an REI? They'd have grappling equipment," Tyler points out.

Maddie is watching us, disbelieving.

"Are you guys insane?" she asks. To Annie, she says, "They're insane, right?"

Annie suppresses a giggle. "At least I know what an ID is now," she remarks. "Everything else, I'm just guessing. What does 'spy gear' mean?"

"Huh?" I say.

"I can just go pick it up tomorrow," Maddie explains.

"You . . . what?" Tyler looks disappointed.

"Duh. I turned eighteen last week. And thanks for the flowers, by the way," she says pointedly at me. "And the card and the pony."

"I had a pony." Annie sighs, but nobody pays any attention.

"So you can just go get it?" I ask, incredulous.

"Yeah. Pretty sure. Anything that's on deposit that's ours, I can just go pick up."

Tyler and I stare at each other, and then we both look at Annie.

"We can go get my cameo?" Annie says. "Tomorrow?"

"Sure," Maddie says. "There's just one thing."

"What?" I ask her.

Maddie casts a baleful eye down on her clothes: ragged cutoffs, ripped fishnets, white ribbed undershirt.

"I think I need a costume change," she says, arching a penciled eyebrow. "When I moved to the squat, I sold my other clothes."

"I know just who to call," I announce, feeling pleased with myself and pulling out my phone. "And he doesn't have to be at Abraham Mas until ten."

CHAPTER 12

Outside on the street, so far uptown that I have trouble reconciling myself to the fact that we're not standing on a wooded stretch of the post road under the watchful eyes of cows, I stare up at the face of Malou's tenement building, trying not to be afraid.

Wes and Tyler are conferring between themselves, as boys are wont to do. I don't know if they're not including me in their conversation out of habit, or for fear that I'm such a being out of time that I can't conceive of whatever it is that they're saying. The funny part of that is, though it's bigger than I would have expected, and taller, and better lit, and with fewer horses, it's not after all so very different. The pace is the same. The crowded streets, the smell of food and spirits, the thrum and noise and crush.

New-York is always New-York.

Though the air in Malou's house was exquisitely cold. Like a perfect fall day, all the time. Amazing.

Malou is going to take me with her tomorrow to the historical society, which she thinks holds the cameo Herschel gave me, which at some point I must give to Ed, and Ed to his wife, and his wife to his son, and so on for longer than I can think about. I haven't tried to discern what we are to each other, Malou—Maddie—and I. Those tattoos. She looks like a whaler. She's beautiful, though, for all her ink. I see in her cheeks and in the corners of her eyes contours rather like Ed's and Beattie's. She's like my sister, if we weren't separated by so much distance and time.

Ed. Ed grows up, and marries. I wonder who.

I wonder where he is, right now.

And Beattie. Where is she? She looked so sad, in the painting. And not at all like I remember her. She dies with me and our parents, Maddie said. But why?

Wes and Tyler's conversation is intensifying. It's almost an argument. Malou told us to come back tomorrow morning at nine, and I think they're trying to decide what to do with me until then. I've considered absenting myself, but I don't know how much memory I have left to explore, if I try to go back.

I don't want to run out of time.

"Are you crazy?" Tyler's saying.

"No way," Wes answers. "Forget it. Give it back."

They're arguing about the little camera box that Wes has. He says it's a way of taking down images and keeping them forever. He's very particular about it. I guess Wes wants it back, but I'm bored by their posturing. I realize that their encounter with me, in my peculiar circumstances, will qualify as one of the more memorable experiences of their short lives. But I'd venture to say, that in my short (or is it long?) life, the circumstance looms rather larger.

"Wes?" I interrupt, placing a hand on his arm. His skin is warm to the touch, burned from summer sun.

They stop their arguing. It's well and truly night now, though I don't know the time. I step into the pool of light thrown by a street-lamp, and glance down at myself. The tatters in my dress go into stark relief, a whiff of smoke escaping from under my feet, and I cast no shadow. I close my eyes quickly, not looking. I'm here, I tell myself, I'm here right now.

"What is it, Annie?" he asks me.

When he looks at me, his eyes go soft and tender, and I feel they see deeper into me than eyes usually should. I feel guilty, if I'm honest with myself, when I see him look at me that way.

"Do you think you could take me to see the Central Park?" I ask quietly.

He gives me a long, pained look that I don't much like.

"You want to go to the park?" he asks. "Now?"

I nod.

Tyler and Wes exchange a look. Then Tyler turns the camera over to Wes without further argument.

"You think I can meet you guys tomorrow morning?" Tyler asks. "I wanna see what happens."

"I guess," Wes says. "Is that okay with you, Annie?"

Okay, he says. They both say it, all the time. I've finally started to figure out what it means. It means "yes" and "all right." It also means less than all right, and a begrudging no. It means everything, and nothing, all at once.

"Sure." I smile at Tyler.

He's not a bad sort, this Tyler, though the shortness of his hair still surprises me. He doesn't wear a braid, like the Celestial men I've known, but it seems that no one does anymore. I can see that he and Wes are friends, in the way that boys sometimes compete more closely with their friends than they do with their enemies. I've watched Herschel argue with his friends in the same way. They flash their feathers at each other like roosters.

"Okay," Tyler says. *Okay,* again. "Nine o'clock. I'll see you guys then."

"Right," Wes says. "See you."

Tyler fixes me in a strange stare, his eyes sliding down my form in a way that makes me cross my arms over my chest. Then he grins, and jogs off backward with a wave. Wes and I wave back.

"It's dark," Wes remarks, and he sounds nervous. "Are you sure you want to go into the park now?"

I can't help but laugh at him. First, at his idea of dark. The night lights here are so harsh and glaring that I can see every divot on his nose.

"What do you think's going to happen?" I chide him. "You afraid the boys from the Bowery will come cut your watch fob? Come on. Walk with me."

Wes laughs, too, perhaps realizing that whatever he might fear for himself, I, at least, have nothing to fear in the Central Park tonight.

My fear waits for me tomorrow.

There are street signs on the lampposts, a splendid invention. They tell us that we are on the corner of Seventy-Second Street and Park Avenue. Imagine, the city reaches this far uptown.

I take Wes by the hand and lead him west. The streetlights mark our way as friendly and safe, and there's even a sliver of moon overhead. There's almost no one about. This quarter seems rich enough that I imagine everyone has a country seat where they retreat in the summer, avoiding the cholera. Perhaps up by the Bronck's. I knew a girl whose parents had a house nearby where I imagine we are, when it was hilly countryside shot through here and there with streams and apple trees. I wonder if she knows her country house is paved over and gone.

Wes allows me to pull him along, holding my hand pressed between both of his as if he's afraid I'm going to float away. His hands are hot around mine.

"So," Wes says.

"Hmmmm?" I ask. I'm enjoying the walk, staring up at the

bright-lit windows. Here and there I spy silhouettes of people behind the curtains. I like that I can see them, and they don't know I'm here.

"Tell me about this Herschel guy," he tries to say it lightly.

I glance at him, and he's looking at me with naked eyes. I have to be careful, how this unfolds.

"Well," I say slowly. "What do you want to know?"

"How long have you known him?" Wes struggles to get the words out.

"We met when I was fifteen," I say.

"How old are you now?"

I laugh. "Why, seventeen, I should think. Depending how you count."

"Really?" He's surprised, but I can't tell why.

"Why, how old are you?" I ask.

"Nineteen," he says, his voice sounding kind of strangled.

"Herschel's nineteen, too," I say.

The afternoon I wandered into his uncle's dry goods store by mistake, having gotten lost and missed the store two blocks over that Mother wanted me to visit, I must've lounged on the counter talking with him for over an hour. His uncle was sick that day, so he was running the store by himself. I'd never seen a boy with brown eyes as heavily fringed as his. And he was funny. He had this way of talking, this order to his words that made light of everything I said. I was laughing so hard my ribs hurt, and my cheeks got sore from smiling. I coiled a curl around my finger and leaned forward, and when I saw his gaze accidently slip to the lace at my chest, a thrill thundered through me so hard that I couldn't breathe.

He looked away immediately, and sold me some thread.

His hands were shaking.

I came back the next day.

I knew I wasn't supposed to.

He tried to explain. That it had nothing to do with me, but that it would be impossible. His family would never allow it. I must see how impossible it would be.

I didn't care.

The first time we sneaked out together was two weeks later. It was a Sunday afternoon, and I was supposed to be home with a fever. Mother, Papa, Beatrice, Ed, and Lottie were all at church, and Winston was up in Seneca. Our house was empty, and I rattled around in it, pacing the floors, chewing the nail off my thumb, wearing a path in the leftover scrubbing sand.

Then, I left. It was the middle of the day, autumn.

I forgot my hat.

I didn't even wear a shawl.

I went and stood outside his uncle's shop, staring in the window. His back was to me, he was putting something away on a high shelf, but he felt me there, watching him. I saw his back stiffen, and he turned. He stared back at me, into me, with those fringed eyes. Without a word, he came outside, locked up, and we stole away. I came home disheveled, with leaves clinging to my dress, and everyone wondering where I'd gotten to. But I think my mother knew.

I glance at Wes. He's waiting for me to tell him something, but I can see in his earnest, boyish face this isn't what he wants to hear.

We pause at the avenue crossing, watching the yellow horseless carriages go sailing by, and the sign over our head reads MADISON. Like Maddie. I smile, thinking about that strange, angry sort-of-sister. I wonder if that's where she got the name that she really wanted. And Cinders! Like Cinderella. I wish I'd thought of it.

"Annie?" Wes says. "Are you all right?"

This corner, where we're standing, used to have a small wooden house, with a grassy hillside behind it dotted with sheep. I don't know how I know this with such certainty, but I do. I can see it, without seeing it. Like I can see the impression it left behind. It's there, underneath the surface of the buildings and asphalt. They'd trade with travelers rolling on cartback down to the city from Hartford or Boston. And even this far inland, their yard was ringed with crushed oyster shells.

Wes pulls on my hand, bringing me back to myself.

"Am I?" I ask him.

He squeezes my hand and we hurry across the street, the lamps on the landaus throwing him into stark relief in the dark. His shadow stretches long against the stone walls of the buildings as we pass them. His shadow moves alone.

Fifth Avenue, when we reach it, is awash with carriages and people, the urgent rush that I'm used to. The carriages come equipped with horns, replacing—or sometimes adding to—the shouts of drivers scattering passersby out of the way. I feel a jolt of excitement, seeing the black outline of the trees against the night sky across the avenue.

"They've been talking about this, you know," I say to Wes, marveling. "I heard Papa and some gentlemen from the committee."

"About what?" Wes asks.

"About having a park," I say. "There's no parks, where I live. Have you noticed that?"

"I never really thought about it," Wes says, sounding surprised. "Why not?"

I shrug. "I don't know. But on hot days, like this, it means we all go to the waterfront."

"Really?" He makes a face.

"Oh yes. The sailors and ropemakers all hate it, because we're underfoot, and the boys steal things to sell at the pawnshops. When the sun is hot and bright, like it was today, it makes a corona around your head, if you stare at yourself in the river. A halo, that follows you wherever you move. Have you ever done that?" I ask him.

"Yes," Wes says softly.

The carriages all stop at once, following the command of some complex system of lamps, and we dash hand in hand across the street, running for no reason.

It's cooler when we reach the park, and the darkness makes me feel safe. I can tell the opposite is true of Wes, though. Anxiety vibrates in him like an over-tuned fiddle string.

"How did you meet him?" Wes presses me.

"At his uncle's store," I say without looking at him. I feel him stiffen next to me, with a new awkward hitch in his walk.

"So, is he, like, your boyfriend or something?" Wes asks.

We move deeper into the park, wending our way along a roadside. We're not alone. Couples wander with us, people walking little dogs on leads. Children weave around us on funny toys with wheels. We cross over a bridge, and off to the right spy a wide plaza leading down to a lake so perfect it almost doesn't seem real. A fountain plashes in the center of the plaza, and under the bridge I hear a lone violinist playing music that sounds both beautiful and sad.

"I don't know how to answer that," I say, looking at Wes.

"It's a pretty basic question," he says, a line forming between his eyebrows under that sweet mop of hair on his forehead.

We keep walking, turning down a long promenade lined with trees so tall they meet overhead. Benches line the promenade, and people from all walks of life rest on them, watching us pass. Old women with wire baskets at their feet, tiny babies in wheeled carriages, men dressed only in undershirts. A family walks by, and the man has a cap on the back of his head like Herschel used to wear. He's young, and so is his pretty wife in her modest clothes. Three children, two girls and boy in a cap, too, romp around their feet.

I have to look away.

"Tell me," Wes says. "I need to know. Please?"

"We'd steal away to be together . . ." I hesitate. "But we weren't allowed."

Wes abruptly releases my hand, and as soon as the pressure is gone, I miss it.

"Two years," Wes says, sounding almost angry as he walks next to me. He's thrust his hands in his pockets. "That's a long time."

"I guess," I say. I don't know what to do with my own hands now. I wrap them around myself and cup my elbows.

"What's the deal with the cameo, then?" he asks me.

I look down at my naked left hand. The next time I go back, I'll find it. Finally. I wonder what will happen then.

"He gave it to me," I whisper. "The last time I saw him. Been saving up for it, he said. Asked one of his cousins, a jeweler, to hold it for him, 'til he could pay."

Wes greets this bit of information with scathing silence.

"We . . ." I pause.

Should I tell him?

"Go on," Wes says. A chill runs down the back of my neck even in the heat of the summer night, when I hear how he sounds.

"We'd talked about running away," I say at last.

It's true. We did. In a roundabout sort of way. Like we were daring each other to say it. Seeing who could hold out the longest. At first we talked about it by not talking about it at all. And then we talked about it as though playing an imaginary game. If we ran away, which we weren't, because it was impossible, but *if* we were, how would we go about it? What would we do for money? How long before they knew we were gone?

My cousin's cart, Herschel says in my mind, a summer afternoon lazing next to me on the riverbank, shading his eyes from the sun. *It'd be a while, before he missed it. We'd drive until the wheels fell off.*

But where? I hear myself ask. *Not south, surely. North? How far north?*

I don't know, Herschel replies.

He couldn't imagine what would happen next any more than I could. I think about Wes's friend Tyler, all that stuff he said about memories. That they're always changing, each time we think about them. We think they stay the same, but they never do.

Is that really what Herschel said, about taking the cart until the wheels fell off? Or is it what I wanted him to say?

"So. Why didn't you, then?" Wes asks, his hands digging deeper into his pockets.

We turn off the mall, leaving the watching eyes of New-York and disappearing along a winding path through the trees, meandering down to the artificial lake. I want to find Wes's hand again. I feel safer, with him holding me here.

The lake is so calm in the moonlight that it perfectly reflects the outline of the trees on the opposite shore, like an ink stain on folded paper. The moon has moved higher in the night sky, and through the white glow of the city around us, I can make out two distant stars.

"He said"—I'm thinking, while I tell Wes this—"there was something he had to do first."

"Oh? And what was that?" Wes asks, trying to make the question sound curious, but instead it comes out irritated.

"He wouldn't tell me." I hear myself say the words, and I have to stop walking.

What did Herschel tell you? the Senegalese Luddite boy shouted at me in the street. *What do you know?*

Of course. Of course! Herschel was Luddite! And his uncle, too, probably, the one who told me I had no idea what was coming.

"Wes," I gasp, reaching for his sleeve.

"What is it?" He stops when he feels my hand, close enough that I can smell his boyish skin. It's hard to make out his features, now that we're away from the streetlights.

"The Grand Aquatic Display," I say, my grip tightening. "I know what happens."

I expect him to be excited, but he's not. Even in the shadows I can see his face contort in misery.

"Annie," he says. His voice catches in what almost sounds like a sob. "I know what happens, too, okay? I already know. And I don't want you to go. I don't want you to go back."

I slide my hand down his arm, and take his hand in mine. They're trembling, our hands. But I'm not sure if the trembling is his or mine.

"You don't?" I whisper.

"Sometimes?" He blinks quickly, clearing the tears from his eyes. "I wish I'd never met you. Then I'd just be able to do my film, and take the time to make it really good, and I'd transfer and get everything I wanted. It would've been so much easier!"

The bottom falls out of my heart, and all that's left inside me is a whistling emptiness.

"I'm sorry," I force the words out.

"Why me, anyway?" he says. "Why'd you have to come here and . . ." He trails off. "Why'd you have to come to me?"

I step closer, close enough to press my lips to his cheek. It's damp, and I taste tears. I move my lips up to the corner of his eye, kissing the tear away, my lips touching his skin with the softness of butterfly feet. His arms go around my waist, crushing me to his chest, and I grasp his shirt in my fists, pressing my face into his neck.

"I'm here, right now," I say, my voice muffled by his skin. "I'm here. With you."

He shudders against me, his own face buried in the curls over my ear.

"I have to tell you something," Wes whispers fiercely.

"Wait," I whisper back. "Wait."

A little ways away, through a screen of trees, we discover a filigreed summerhouse, an open patio with a roof for shade, and benches down close to the water. A warm breeze trips along the lake surface, ruffling the reflected city. I lead Wes by the hand down the path to the summerhouse. He knits his fingers around my palm.

"Do you think . . . ," Wes says, and I can feel his pulse thrumming fast under his skin. "Annie. Do you think it's possible to love more than one person?"

I stare long and hard at him. That word hangs in the air between us.

Did he say it?

Did I hear it?

Or is it what I wanted him to say?

It's impossible to see his expression in the dark. I can only see the outline of his hair, his jaw, and his shoulders as he turns to me. A knot unties itself inside my chest.

I whisper, "Yes."

Then Wes's fingers are in my hair, and he's pulling me to him. His mouth meets mine, soft and warm at first. Hesitant. Herschel is the only other boy I've kissed, and his mouth was more insistent, rougher, thinner lipped, and salty. Wes tastes of mint, and his lips are smoother, softer. Richer. I close my eyes, feeling an electric spark where our lips connect, like the rays of the sun in a corona over our heads when we stare into the waters of the Hudson on a sunny afternoon.

We kiss for a long time, hungry for each other, Wes's hand on my thigh, firm and sure of itself, his other arm around my waist, and at times I gasp for breath, throwing my head back so that his lips can find my throat, my neck, the hollow of my collarbone. The moon rises higher, and the sound of the city recedes behind the sheltering branches that hide the summerhouse where we coil ourselves together.

I am here. I am here, right now.

CHAPTER 13

When I open my eyes, the light is thin and gray, and tiny sparrows are bickering in the branches overhead. My cheek rests on my arm along the back of the bench, my feet drawn up underneath me. Wes's head lies in my lap, heavy with sleep, one arm still encircling my waist while the other hangs to the ground. He lets out a soft snore, and burrows his nose into a fold of my dress.

It's today.

Today is my last day.

I don't want to wake Wes just yet. His face is smooth in sleep. I rub my eyes with a yawn and stretch my arms overhead until my spine cracks. My stays will be leaving red marks on my rib cage.

The park around us rolls gradually out of sleep, birds and squirrels beginning their morning ablutions, and on the far side of the lake, girls not much older than me go prancing past like racehorses, wearing nothing but stockings and tight shirts and shaded spectacles, their pigtails swinging. The city hums to life while I watch, the sky brightening through the treetops, sounds of carriage horns and crying babies and conversations, the honk of ducks paddling by on the pond at our feet.

"Wes," I say, cupping his cheek in my hand. His beard is coming in, and his cheek is rough.

"Mmmmrrrfff," Wes says, pulling my skirt hem over his eyes and rolling onto his side on the bench.

I smile down at him, and gently poke his shoulder. "Wes," I say. "It's morning."

"So what," he says from under my skirt.

"So," I say, "we're supposed to meet back at Maddie's soon."

"What time is it?" he moans. He rummages in the pocket of his short pants and pulls out his little glass slab. He pokes one eye out from my petticoat hem and peers at the object.

"Argh," he says.

"What, argh?" I ask.

"Battery's dead. Do you know what time it is?" He looks up at me with a bright, warm smile.

"Nigh on morning. There's people about."

Wes disentangles himself from me and plants a sweet kiss on the corner of my mouth. His beard is scratchy, but I drink in the kiss all the same.

"I love your mole," he says out of nowhere. "Your mole tastes perfect."

I laugh, as it's doubtless the oddest compliment I've ever gotten. I never thought much about my mole, though Beattie used to sometimes wake me up by poking it with her finger, as though I were a doll whose eyes could be opened by pressing a button.

Wes takes one of my curls and rubs it thoughtfully between finger and thumb. I reach up and trace a fingertip along one of his eyebrows. It feels silky to the touch. We stare at each other, unwilling to shatter the fragile silence that holds us together, protected from the rest of the world.

"Mommy, there's a man here!" a tiny voice cries, and we break apart, startled.

A small child in a sailor suit is pointing at Wes, and its mother appears behind it, pushing a wheeled baby carriage with a resigned expression on her face.

"Keep going, Aiden." She sighs without a word in our direction, heaving the carriage around a corner in the path. The child in the sailor suit scampers after her.

Wes looks at me.

"I guess we should be getting back," he says.

I nod. I wrap my right thumb around my bare left ring finger.

Today. I'll find my cameo today.

Hand in hand Wes and I emerge from the park, passing carts selling pastries and coffee on the street corners. He stops to buy a cruller and some coffee in a paper cup that says, "We are happy to serve you" on it in faux-Greek font. The cruller looks good, warm and shining with sugar. I wish I could taste it. With a twinge of sadness I think of the roasted-pear seller I used to frequent on First Street, the fruits syrupy with sugar.

Wes is wiping sugar from his lips with his wrist when we arrive back at Maddie's building. A different man stands guard at the door today, and before he'll let us up he has to talk into some sort of oddly shaped speaking tube to obtain our approval.

"Eighth floor," he informs us once approval is granted.

He has an accent I've never heard before—not French, German, or Portuguese, not Carolina, Chinese, or Dutch. A stranger among strangers. I smile at him, but he doesn't see me.

When the lifting machine deposits us back in Maddie's foyer, we are met with boisterous noise from deep within the apartment. A pair of large men's shoes sits under the table in the center of the foyer, together with a satchel.

"There is no WAY I'm wearing this!" Maddie hollers.

Wes and I exchange a look. We're late. Maddie's already getting dressed.

"Hello?" Wes calls.

"In here!" a young male voice answers, and Wes and I grope our way down an infinite hallway, looking in at doors—a linen closet first, then a room seemingly designated only for bathing, then a room with nothing but books and a large wooden desk, like Papa's study—before we finally choose the right one. We open it to an explosion of finery, and Maddie standing poised with a boot held high over her head, a boy cowering at her feet. The room is all done up in florals and pastels, and looks nothing like Maddie at all. With some surprise I see that the bed is the exact same one that I used to share with Beatrice. But it's been painted white and is piled high with so many pillows it's hard to imagine there's any room for sleep.

"Eastlin?" Wes says, and the boy kneeling on the floor glances over at us with a smile.

"Will you tell her how gorgeous she looks?" cries the cowering boy. "She won't listen to me."

He's the same boy who was asleep in Wes's room, the one I scared by accident. He's beautiful, which isn't a word I often use to describe boys, but it's the only word for him. His skin is peach smooth and perfect, and though I find his manner of dress alien, the worthiness of his form is undeniable. Wes dresses like a boy, to hide his male shape. But this one—Eastlin?—has no such compunction. He's like the Bowery bloods, lounging on street corners with nipped-in trousers and perfectly cut coats.

"You look—" Wes starts to say to Maddie, but he stops himself when he catches me looking at him.

Maddie whirls on us and chucks the boot in our direction, but we both duck and it whomps ineffectually against the doorjamb.

"I look ridiculous!" she shouts.

She's wearing a dress that at first glance looks something like mine. It's a rich brick-red, of a color to make her skin look dipped in buttermilk. It falls in sumptuous layers to just below her knees.

"Not at all!" I say, rushing up to mollify her.

Maddie turns away, wrinkling her nose. But I see her looking at me from underneath her eyelashes in the same hopeful, expectant way Beattie and I use on each other when we feel anxious and want to be complimented.

"You look lovely," I say, resting a hand on her arm. In a whisper, I add, "Truly."

The tiniest of smiles pulls at Maddie's cheek, and she whispers back, "Really?"

"You do," Wes manages to say.

I don't look at him when he says it.

"What I've *been* saying," Eastlin grumbles. "Now sit down over there."

He steers Maddie over to a cushioned stool at a dressing table, and brushes a finger along the side of her neck, over the lattice of her tattoos.

"How long have you been here?" Wes asks Eastlin. He goes over to Maddie's—my—Maddie's bed and flops onto it.

"Not long. Maybe half an hour," Eastlin says, casting an appraising look at the laurel leaves staining Maddie's neck. "Why in God's name would you get a neck tattoo, huh? What are you, a Hell's Angel?"

"I'm an anarchist," Maddie says, lifting her nose in an imperious way. "My body is mine, and I'll do what I want. I don't have to bow to your capitalist definitions of beauty."

I stifle a laugh, gazing on Maddie in the mirror.

"The man begs me to come over here and make you look respectable, and that's what I'm going to do. Now be quiet," Eastlin says, reaching for a tub of some dun-colored cream. He dips in a finger and starts dabbing it on Maddie's neck. "Too dark," he mutters to himself, wiping it off with a cotton ball. He puts the tub down and rummages for a different one.

"Yo! I'm here!" a boy hollers from the front vestibule. "Did I miss anything?"

It's Tyler, who bursts through the bedroom door with a grin on his face, carrying a giant bag bulging with what I imagine to be recording equipment.

"God!" Maddie says. "What is this, *Extreme Makeover, Maddie Edition?*"

Tyler has fixed a recording box to his face and creeps up to where Maddie's sitting. "Annie, you look awesome," he says.

"Maddie," Maddie corrects him. "Annie's over there. And I look like a bourgeois sellout."

"No," Eastlin says with exaggerated patience. "You look like a lady. Now hold still."

Maddie rolls her eyes and looks pleadingly at me. "You see what I have to go through?"

I rub the sore spot on my side where my stays are digging in, and say nothing.

"Where'd you get all that stuff, anyway?" Tyler asks, aiming the camera at Eastlin's potions and boxes of clothes.

"Abraham Mas did their first show for Fashion Week this year," he says through his nose as he draws a careful line along Maddie's eyelid. "Kind of on a shoestring, though. I helped dress the models. This stuff is leftover from that."

"Oh my God," Tyler moans. "You got to touch real models, and you don't even appreciate it."

Eastlin smirks without moving his hands, drawing a delicate line on Maddie's other eyelid. "I appreciated it more than you would," he says.

"Maddie," Wes asks from his vantage point in the bed. "This is a pretty sweet apartment."

She grumbles, but doesn't say anything, as Tyler adds, "Seriously."

"Why would you want to stay in some squat, if you could stay here?" He drops his voice to a conspiratorial whisper. "Did they throw you out or something?"

Maddie huffs in annoyance and bats Eastlin away from her face, turning her back on the boys in her plush little girl's bedroom, her hands on her cheeks. She stares at herself in the mirror, and in her reflection she meets my gaze. She looks older, dressed up in this way. I can see the outlines of the woman they're planning for her to be. It's a trap they've laid. They cosset you, and pet you, and tighten the screws so slowly you don't even feel them sink into your skin.

I know exactly how that feels.

Who's going to offer to drive her away on a stolen cart until the wheels falls off? Whose secret cameo will invite her into a world of her own making?

I rest a hand on her shoulder. I'm looking at her hard so that I don't have to look at myself. I don't trust mirrors.

"Because . . . ," Maddie starts. She swallows the tears that are welling up in the lower lids of her painted eyes.

"Because they're slavemongers, aren't they," I whisper in her ear.

Maddie closes her mouth and nods. She looks down into her lap as Eastlin steps away and studies his handiwork.

"Not bad," he says. "If I do say so myself." To Maddie, he adds, "While you're gone I'm just going to burn these fishnets, okay? You don't mind, do you?"

Maddie wipes a tear out from under her eye and makes a face at him, but the glower subsides into a smile. She gets to her feet, smoothing the front of the dress down with her hands.

The transformation is remarkable. Her tattoos are hidden under flesh-colored paint, like actresses use, and her eyes have less soot around them. He's urged her dyed hair into a low chignon, and the dress skims her form most becomingly. It must be so much more comfortable, wearing dresses like that, with no lacing.

"What do you think? Is it all right?" she asks me, eyes wide, hunting for my approval.

I smile at her. "I know it's not to your taste," I say. "But I think you're lovely."

"Do I look respectable? I have to, or they won't let me in," Maddie says. "They'll, like, call the cops or something."

"You look a perfect lady," I say.

"All right!" Tyler interrupts, hopping from one foot to the other. "Let's get this show on the road! Can we all fit in one cab? Should we Uber it? Where is this place anyway?"

Maddie loops her arm through mine and smiles regally into Tyler's camera.

"Sorry," she says. "It's just Annie and me, going."

Wes clambers off the bed and moves over to us, hovering between us and the door. "Are you sure? Maybe I should come with," he says.

"No," Maddie says.

A flash of panic illuminates Wes's eyes, but he's trying mightily not to show it.

"But," he says to me, his voice tighter than usual, "what if something happens? When you find it?"

Maddie and I exchange a look.

"We won't put it on until we get back," Maddie suggests. "How about that?"

"Yes," I say, and now it's my turn to waver. "I'll do it when we're all together."

Wes looks carefully at me while Tyler moans, "Oh, man! But I got extra batteries and everything!"

"Where do you want to do it?" Eastlin asks quietly as he puts his various tools away.

I look over my shoulder at him. He hasn't looked fully at me since I walked in with Wes. I can tell that my very being here sets his teeth on edge. As it should. I don't belong here.

"I don't know," I falter.

"Maybe back at your house?" Wes suggests.

It's a logical idea, but something about it makes me afraid. I don't know what's going to happen. I don't know where I'm going to go. I think of our front door melting before my eyes, and can't conceive of seeing that happen again.

"They're about to open," Maddie prods us. "We should get going. I don't know if I have to fill out any paperwork, or whatever."

Eastlin closes a case full of paints and powders with a decisive snap and says, "You guys go. We'll text you where to meet us. Okay?"

"Fine," Maddie says.

"All right," I agree.

Maddie hauls me to the door and my eyes stay locked on Wes, who reaches a hand out as though to stop me. But then we're gone.

My head is still spinning from the incredible speed of the horseless landau when Maddie presses an unmarked buzzer outside an imposing marble façade across the Central Park from her building. It looks to me like a mansion, but of a scale I hadn't heretofore imagined.

What wealth there must be in New-York now! Dizzying wealth, like the kings of France in the old regime, with their gilded walls, alabaster peacocks, and bowlsful of jewels. Our town house could fit inside this one seven times over or more. I follow close on her heels as Maddie heads inside, trotting to keep up with her as she strides past an airy art gallery, through an unmarked door secured with another buzzer, down a long hallway filled with false light, and at last through a modest glass vestibule deep in the building's entrails.

There's a young woman perched behind a desk, and her demeanor is serious and businesslike. Her beauty staggers me. Everyone has such perfect teeth, such smooth and unblemished skin. Even Mother, for all her vanity and social ambition, has pox scars on her cheeks and a brown front tooth.

"You must be Miss Van Sinderen," the woman says to Maddie.

I peer unseen over Maddie's shoulder to watch their exchange. I still prick up my ears and begin to respond when I hear someone say my name.

But I might as well not even be here.

"Yes," Maddie says with an imperiousness that reminds me of Mother. "I've come to pick up an item my father placed on deposit here a few months ago. This piece wasn't meant to be put on loan."

"I'm so sorry," the young woman says with an evenness that belies her sorriness. "What a blunder. Here, come this way."

She leads us into a narrow room lined with filing cabinets, with a felt-covered table in the center. Maddie seats herself at the head of the table and folds her hands, tapping her thumbs together.

"Are you sure they'll just give it to you?" I whisper in her ear.

"Shh," Maddie shushes me out of the side of her mouth. "Just act normal."

I gather she's saying that mainly for her own benefit, as I can act however I like with impunity. But I'm too nervous to try playing pranks on the young woman from the historical society. I'm afraid that she'll somehow snatch away my last chance without even knowing what she's done.

This woman has the power to damn me for eternity, and doesn't even know it.

"Now then," the young woman says, reappearing from a vestibule carrying a large book under her arm. She sets it on the table in front of us and opens it to the first page. "This is our finding aid for the collection. You don't know the acquisition number, do you?"

"No," Maddie says tightly. "It's a piece of jewelry. A cameo."

"A cameo," the woman repeats.

She runs a finger down a long list. Then she flips a page.

She flips another page.

I'm so nervous and afraid that I fear I'm going to scream, and if I scream, what if somehow the woman will be able to hear me? My ability to effect change in the world waxes and wanes. Sometimes I can touch things, and sometimes I can't. I can be seen in certain glimpses, but not in others. My feelings can sometimes bring me into sharper relief. As when I rattled the bars of the cemetery gate: My horror brought my hands into firm-enough condition that I could grasp the bars and make them move.

As I'm thinking these things, the young woman's head snaps up, and she looks straight at me. I freeze, thumbnail in mouth, holding my breath.

She stares right at the spot where I'm standing, but her eyes aren't focused on me.

"Is everything okay?" Maddie asks, her gaze jumping between me and the woman.

The woman frowns.

Then she turns slowly back to the book.

"Yes," she says. "I'm just jumpy."

I exhale as silently as I can, and while the woman's attention is distracted, Maddie glares quickly at me, telling me with her eyes to keep quiet. I shrug, and mouth, *I didn't do anything!* Maddie shakes her head.

"All right," the woman says. "It looks like we have a few cameos in the Van Sinderen collection. Do you know which one it is?"

"Um," Maddie says, biting a lip. She looks at me, eyebrows shooting up in inquiry.

"It's red," I whisper. "A ring. With Persephone on it."

"Is there a . . . red one?" Maddie asks.

"Hrm," the woman says. "Doesn't say. Why don't I just bring them all out?"

"All right," Maddie says.

A few minutes pass while the young woman disappears into wherever it is that she goes. I pace to and fro behind Maddie's chair, a finger twisting my curls.

"What if it's not here after all?" I say.

"It'll be here," Maddie says, inspecting her fingernails. Eastlin made her wipe off the chipped black polish.

I hear a faint buzzing sound, like a tiny bee caught behind a wardrobe door. Maddie reaches into her bag and pulls out a little glass box like the one Wes carries. She peers at it critically. Then she grins.

"That's a great idea," she says aloud.

"What is?" I ask, rushing to look over her shoulder.

"The boys have decided where we should meet for you to put the ring on, when we find it," she says to me, her head cocked to one side.

"Where?" I ask, worrying my hands together

"You'll see," Maddie says.

Just then the woman reappears carrying a tray with a few small boxes on it of varying degrees of antiquity. She sets the tray in front of

Maddie and seats herself at the table. I tiptoe up behind the woman and peer over her shoulder.

"So," she says. "This one's been dated to 1867." She passes a large brooch to Maddie, with a woman's face in profile, alabaster on ebony. The nose looks a bit like Beattie's, but that could be my imagination.

Maddie glances at me, and I shake my head.

"That's not it," Maddie says. "I'm looking for one that's older."

"Hmmm," says the woman, consulting her finding aid. "What about this one? Estimated to be 1840s."

She opens a small leather box and reveals another brooch surrounded by gold filigree. It's another woman, with delicate white curls against a pale blue background.

Maddie raises her eyebrows at me. This time, the woman follows Maddie's gaze over her shoulder, and stares again at the space where I'm standing. I hold perfectly still, not even daring to breathe. Then I shake my head with the tiniest movement I can manage.

"Nope," Maddie says, startling the woman, who jumps in her seat.

A sheen of sweat has formed on the historical society woman's forehead. It gleams under the artificial lights.

"Is it cold in here?" the woman asks uneasily.

"Not that I've noticed," Maddie says. But she also is looking nervous.

I retreat a few steps away, withdrawing into a shadow cast by one of the filing cabinets.

"Which is the oldest one?" Maddie asks, stirring the boxes in the tray. She picks up a tiny cardboard one and opens it. There's a tuft of cotton wool inside, and Maddie starts to peel it away.

"Here, let me," the historical society woman says, reaching for it.

"But it's mine," Maddie says, pulling the box away. The woman's hand knocks against the box, and in the struggle the box slips out of Maddie's hand and falls to the floor.

The box lands hard and something small comes flying out, skittering across the floor like a skipped pebble until it comes to a rest against the toe of my slipper.

The gold band is dented and crushed into almost an oval shape, and a thick layer of grime lines the setting that holds the red sliver of shell in place. The carving is less fine than I remember, the white form of Persephone dulled and chipped in places. The shell-red background has faded to a burnished oaken brown. But there's no question.

It's mine.

My cameo.

My heart lurches in my chest, a rising pressure as the memory of Herschel floods my limbs, flushing my skin. I catch my breath to choke back a sob.

"Be careful!" the woman remonstrates Maddie, getting to her feet and hurrying to pick the trinket off the floor where it rests against my toe.

She kneels at my feet, her finger and thumb grasping the gold band. She freezes. She's staring at my shoe, it's unmistakable. From my shoe she stares in dawning horror at the hem of my dress, up my skirts, tipping her head back to look up to my face, when she lets out a throaty scream.

I flee into the shadows, bringing my fist to my mouth to force myself silent, leaving a coil of burnt smoke in my wake.

The archivist falls back on her heels and stumbles haltingly to her feet.

"Are you all right?" Maddie asks, eyeing her warily.

The archivist is shaking. With a trembling hand, she puts the ring into Maddie's waiting palm.

"I . . . I . . . I'm . . ." The archivist is staring hard into the shadows where I'm hiding.

Maddie holds the ring up to the light, turning it this way and that. "Persephone!" she says brightly. "This is it. Thank you."

She slides the ring onto her right ring finger. It fits perfectly.

The archivist's breath is coming quickly, and a bead of sweat is trickling down her hairline.

"Do you need me to sign anything?" Maddie asks. "Or can I just go?"

"I . . . that is, you should really . . . Um . . . ," the archivist stammers. She's staring into the shadows where I fled, looking to see if I'm really there. I bite down on my thumb, forcing myself not to move.

"Listen, I'm in kind of a hurry," Maddie says, pushing her chair away from the table and standing up. "You can just handle any paperwork for me, right? You don't really need me to sign anything."

She looks coolly at the panicked woman cowering at the table, who nods fiercely.

"Y-y-y-yes, that would be fine," the archivist says. "Go. Please."

Maddie's shoulders shake with silent laughter, and she winks at me. When she does, my fear vanishes. I let myself smile, and step out of the shadows.

"Great! Thanks. You've been a big help." Maddie strides over to me, loops her arm through mine, and indicating the archivist with her chin, says, "Say thank you, Annie."

"Thank you!" I chirp as sweetly as I can.

But the archivist doesn't hear me over her wretched scream.

CHAPTER 14

"Where the hell are they?" I ask no one in particular. I am seriously starting to freak out, and there's no sign of them yet. What if something happened? What if she went away without me?

A woman jostling by with two small kids in tow, all wearing matching I ♥ NY sweatshirts, gives me the hairy eyeball as she passes me on her way to the observation deck.

"They'll be here," Tyler assures me, keeping the camera trained, for some reason, on my feet. Typical art guy. For some reason they love carving the body up into its constituent parts. He's promised me I can use this footage for *Most*, so my documentary is going to have a seriously arty look for a change.

"Relax, Wesley," Eastlin says from his vantage point leaning against the wall.

"How can I relax?" I say, gripping the mop of hair over my forehead and giving it another tug. "You relax! There. See how that sounds?"

"You have to keep it together, man," Tyler remarks. He pans over to Eastlin and zooms in on his face. Eastlin's eyes are closed.

"Maddie's sure they got the right one?" I ask.

"Mmm-hmmm," Eastlin says.

A whole group of kids on a band trip or something all descend on us en masse. They're like fourteen or fifteen, all new breasts and big teeth and big feet, and they're in identical lime-green T-shirts. On the back of the T-shirts I see that they're from Madison, and they go to my rival high school. They whoop and holler, shoving one another like puppies as they mass at the door to the outdoor deck, and then go spurting through it with a squeal. I shudder as I watch them go. God. All I want in the world is to get into NYU.

Well. Not all. Perhaps not even most, anymore.

"Ugh." Eastlin rolls his eyes. "Kids."

Eastlin is twenty.

"They're sure, though? Annie recognized it?" I press. When we were looking at them on the internet, they basically all looked the same to me. Different colors and whatever, but that's it. What if they got the wrong one?

"Dude," Tyler says, swinging the camera back around to my face. "They got it."

I can't hold still. I wander over to the window by where Eastlin's leaning and press my forehead to the glass. I have never felt more anxious in my entire life. I'm so anxious there's a good chance I'm going to explode, and then Eastlin and Tyler will have to clean my intestines off this plate-glass window.

"She said they were in a cab," Eastlin says. "It should just be a couple more minutes."

"Why don't you go out and have a look?" Tyler says. "You haven't been here yet, right?"

Tyler has appointed himself ambassador to my rube's awakening in Manhattan. He's even talking about making me to go a Broadway

343

show, before I leave at the end of summer school. *Wicked* or something. Except I hate musicals, and I hate heights, and I don't want to leave, and all I can think about is what's going to happen when Annie finally puts her cameo ring back on.

I'm supposed to go home in four days. Four days is nothing. Four days to fit in everything I haven't done. I haven't walked the full length of Broadway. I haven't been to a punk show in the East Village. I've only been to Brooklyn, like, twice, both times with Tyler. I haven't been to Yankee Stadium, or Chelsea Piers, and I've only been to the High Line once, and it was so crowded I could barely move.

I've done everything in Madison a million times. When I think about Madison now, it's all in tones of gray and beige. New York unspools before me in Technicolor, those saturated reds and blues of expensive film stock and flickering lights. I want to go backstage at the Abraham Mas show and watch Eastlin dress girls of such impossible thinness and beauty they seem almost like insects. I want to go to the gallery in Chelsea and see *Shuttered Eyes* installed in one of those white rooms with concrete floors that make everything, no matter how mundane, look rare and expensive. I want to collaborate with Tyler on his next film project, and maybe see my own work projected in one of those galleries. I want to see where Maddie moves after the squat she shares with Janeanna gets bulldozed for new condos. I want Tibetan dumplings in Jackson Heights and knishes on the Lower East Side and barbecue in Harlem and congee in Chinatown and pupusas in Washington Heights and eggs at four in the morning no matter where you are. I want Preston Sturges retrospectives at Film Forum and shuffleboard in Brooklyn and EDM in a warehouse in Red Hook that I'll never find again. I want to live New York City. Not live in it, but live *it*. I want to be alive, right here. Right now.

It's what I want most in all the world.

A finger pokes my upper arm, startling me out of my obsessing. It's Tyler, who says, "Come on. They're here."

I turn around and spot two young women with similar faces, both in tattered burgundy dresses and old-fashioned hair, making their way slowly through the crowd. Maddie is leading Annie by the hand, and Annie has her other hand over her eyes like a blindfold. She's grinning. As Maddie approaches, she presses a finger to her lips to keep us from saying anything.

Tyler fires up the video camera, and Eastlin pushes himself off the wall where he was leaning. We gather around Maddie and Annie.

"Okay," Maddie whispers. "Keep them closed. Promise?"

"I promise," Annie says.

A short family, a mom, a dad, and three little kids, all five feet tall or less, circle past us, talking together in Spanish. The mom pushes the glass door open to the observation deck, and a chill breeze blows into the room where we've been waiting, carrying with it the sounds of car horns and shouting school children.

"Where are we?" Annie asks.

"It's a surprise," Maddie says. "Come on. Eastlin, you help me steer her."

Eastlin blanches and doesn't move. It's funny to me that he's so suave and jacked, but when it comes to Annie and her . . . situation . . . Eastlin's afraid.

"Here, let me," I say, circling my arm around Annie's waist.

At my touch, Annie catches her breath, and her body shivers against mine.

"Trust me," Maddie murmurs into her ear. "This is perfect."

We three walk haltingly to the door. God, I hate heights. I really, really don't want to be doing this. Tyler steps in close with the camera to catch the expression on Annie's face, and he bumps into me without really meaning to. It makes something in me snap.

"Will you watch it?" I shout at him.

He glances at me over the eyepiece of his camera, giving me a hurt look. "Yeesh. Sorry."

Maddie, meanwhile, has pushed open the glass door and is steering us out onto the observation platform, right up close to the fencing that curves up and back over our heads. I swallow to get rid of the sickening dizziness snaking through my body.

"Ready?" she whispers to Annie.

Annie nods. "I'm ready."

"Okay. Look," Maddie says, giving Annie an encouraging squeeze.

Annie drops her hand from her eyes and stands frozen, unbreathing, looking down at the immense tapestry of the city spreading south from beneath her feet.

We're on the main observation deck of the Empire State Building, a place I know only from *Sleepless in Seattle* and *King Kong* (the original, not the remake). From here we can see all the way to the Battery, the skyscrapers of downtown looking like children's toys clustered together at the point at the bottom of the island. Seagulls wheel by in the distance, and the Hudson is dotted with sailboats and ferries. The sun burns high overhead, and its light glints off the glass of the skyscrapers. Summer haze clings to the shore of New Jersey, obscuring our view of Jersey City, so Manhattan floats in a cloud by itself, hemmed in on both sides by imaginary rivers. Yellow taxis creep up and down the veins of Manhattan, pedestrians crawl along the street so far below us that they look like pill bugs.

"Oh my goodness," Annie breathes. She rests her hands on the diamond-patterned bars of the observation deck, leaning her forehead against it, like she's straining to break free.

"Come on," Eastlin urges me to step closer. "You've never seen it, either."

My mouth has gone bone dry. Visions of *Vertigo* and plunging down hundreds of stories to my death crowd in around me, and I get light-headed and Eastlin has to catch hold of my elbow. God, I'm a wuss.

"I can't," I say, my voice sounding strangled.

Annie turns to me and smiles. The breeze stirs the curls over her ears and makes the lace along her neckline flutter. She holds a hand out to me.

It's me. She wants me, next to her.

I hesitate, and then I grasp her hand tightly, swallow once very hard, and step to the edge of the observation deck.

"Look at this," she whispers to me. "Look at all of those people, living. Just look at it all."

Clutching her hand in mine, I grip my free hand on the bars and peer over the edge. I tremble with terror, and press myself against her. Annie doesn't look afraid. Her bottomless eyes are bright, her rosebud lips parted, as though she were drinking it all in.

"I can see it all, Wes," she breathes, staring with wonder down at the city. "I can see the blocks where they've plotted out the streets, but no houses are built yet. Look! I can see the cow fields and the streams glistening through the hills. There's the Five Points. I can see our town house. There's Brooklyn ferry landing, down by Herschel's uncle shop, I can see it between the wooden masts and the rigging. There's the steeple of Trinity Church! I can see everything!"

"Annie. Aren't you scared?" I whisper into her hair.

But she fixes me with a delighted smile and says, "No. There's nothing to be scared of."

I'm distracted by the whir of Tyler filming us, poking the camera over our shoulders and peering down the edge of the skyscraper. More children thunder by behind us, and I hear Maddie say, "Whoa!" and giggle as she nearly gets knocked over by the wave of them. I'm distracted by an elderly man escorting a woman with support hose

347

rolled up under her knees, digging through his pockets to find a quarter to feed into one of those owl-shaped telescopes. It's too much to take in all at once. It's happening too fast.

Annie lets go my hand and stretches her arms out on either side of her, closing her eyes and breathing in the wind.

"Look at her," Tyler whispers, perhaps without knowing he's doing it.

Her smile broadens, and she opens her eyes. "Maddie," she says. "I'm ready."

Maddie rummages in her bag and pulls out a tiny, battered cameo ring. After all that fuss to find it, it's nothing like I pictured. It looks old and worn-out.

"Are you sure?" Maddie asks, holding the ring between finger and thumb.

"I'm sure," Annie says, starting to reach forward to take the trinket from Maddie.

I'm overwhelmed with an insane desire to tear the ring out of Maddie's hand and fling it over the edge of the observation deck. I could get arrested, if I did that, but the image burns in my mind, the sunlight sparkling off the gold as it falls, falls, falls and shatters on the pavement below into a thousand shards of reddish shell. Then she'd have to stay here. I want her to stay here!

"Wait! Don't! Please!" I cry, choking back a sob. I don't care that Tyler and Eastlin and Maddie are here to see. I don't care if they'll think I suck. I don't care! I want her to stay here!

Annie pauses, hand poised in midair.

"What's going to happen?" I babble crazily. "When you get back. What are you going to do? What's going to happen?"

"I'm going to help the United Brotherhood of Luddites blow up the corporation barge at the Grand Aquatic Display," Annie says smoothly, her brow serene.

"What?" I shout "No!"

"They're slavemongers, Wes," she continues. "My father. The corporation. All of them. They're using slave money to finance the canal. It'll flatten the wilderness and line their pockets, while fooling the poor into thinking it's good for them, too. The Luddites are right. We have to make people see the canal is a mistake. That's what I'm going to do."

"Damn," Tyler says under his breath, his camera training an unblinking eye on the crazed girl in her tattered dress who's holding my hand, her curls blowing like a corona around her head.

"Luddites!" Maddie exclaims, her eyes bright with happiness. "Wait! You're one, too?"

"What?" I say, going cross-eyed with confusion. Tyler zooms into a tight shot on Annie, Maddie, and me.

Annie throws her head back, laughing, and says, "You all are amazing, you New Yorkers of the future. I love you." She looks straight at me. An electric shock statics through the air, and my hair stands on end. A spark flies off my hand where it grips the metal railing, and I let go with a squeal of pain.

Before I can stop her, Annie plucks the cameo from Maddie's waiting fingers and slides it onto the ring finger of her left hand.

For a split second, nothing happens.

Then beams of light pour out from underneath the ring where it meets her skin, and the static electricity in the air gets so thick I can hear it snap.

"Wait!" I scream in a panic. "No! Wait!"

But I'm too late, she's already—

CHAPTER 15

The sky spins over my head and the observation deck drops from under my feet, and I hear an incredible roaring in my ears, louder than any sound I've ever heard, as the skyscraper beneath me pulls apart and vanishes into nothing. The sun burns brighter, and I close my eyes against it as I start to fall, seeing nothing but the red behind my eyelids, feeling wind rush through my hair, ripping the pins out of my pigtails. A slipper flies off, and my stockinged toes stretch into the void, my hands reaching out into thin air. Herschel's ring burns into the skin of my finger, and it's like there's a light growing up from deep inside the shell, the figure of Persephone bending and moving as if she were as alive as I am.

I open my eyes and find myself plunging into fresh dusk, the sky below me ribboned with red clouds. Faster and faster, I pass a seagull, then a pigeon flutters off screaming in a cloud of feathers. The ground is speeding up to meet me, and I'm afraid I'm going to hit the cobblestones and that will be the end. I fling my arms up in front of my face to ward off the coming blow, but it's no use, I open my mouth and take a breath to scream . . .

But instead of the shattering of my bones, I plunge into a soft pillowing, as though my body were a leaf fallen from an oak tree in autumn. The air catches me, cupping me in its palm, and I drift through a gap in the world until my feet come softly to rest on the ground. My eyes are still closed, but everything is silent. I stand immobile, listening.

Then, as though I were an image in one of Wes's captured moving pictures that's been frozen and is now speeding forward, a wall of sound comes bearing down on me. I cringe in fear, but when I open my eyes I see that the terrific noise is local Ward 4 fire brigade's brass band and bass drum, and I'm standing on a dais next to Mother and Papa, with Beatrice cradling one of my hands and Ed dragging down the other like a sea anchor. Throngs of New Yorkers are crushing forward to reach the platform, all brightly lit by lanterns and torches throwing all our faces into jack-o'-lantern shadow. The firemen parade by in formation, whiskered cheeks puffed out with effort blowing into their horns, tall hats and fringed epaulets gleaming, and the governor stands at the podium next to us, clapping his white-gloved hands and grinning.

My father looks beefy-faced and blurry from too much gin, and Mother stands next to him, propping him up with the crook of her arm, beaming in her proprietary way across the heads of the people parading below her. The dais has been set up in front of the town hall, which is almost completely obscured with billowing bunting in red, white, and blue, and on the heels of the band come uniformed private police mounted on painted horses, trotting high, their tails flicking. When the policemen pass the governor, they raise their arms in salute, and the governor acknowledges them with a happy return. My father salutes them back, sloppily, leaning with his free elbow on the banister.

I glance around, trying to get my bearings. Everywhere faces throng together, tired or leery, bright-eyed, excited, painted, hot-cheeked, drunk. Voices babble and shout in all different languages,

351

German, Spanish, Portuguese, English, French, Arabic, Chinese. A fresh horn section bears down on the platform, flanked by children tracing bright sparklers and streamers through the air, followed by the boys from Columbia College, all decked out in woolen academic robes and tasseled hats.

"Wave," my mother hisses to me, grinding her foot on my toe.

I look around myself in panic, and Ed drags on my arm, trying to hide behind me. My left ring finger burns with the heat from Herschel's cameo, and my senses are alive with the need to find him. I hunt over the heads of the crowd, searching. Desperate.

And then I see him.

He's there, a few shoulders back in the crowd at the foot of the stage, staring at me, his face pale under his dark-rimmed hat, his ear curls tucked up out of sight. When I spot him his eyes widen, and his whole face brightens in a smile, and he starts fighting his way through the throng to get nearer to me.

"Herschel!" I breathe, and Beattie hears me and stands on her tiptoes to see.

"He's here?" she whispers in my ear as the college boys parading past in the street are supplanted by robed young men from the College of Physicians and Surgeons. Two different brass bands blare warring themes from opposite ends of the green in front of the Town Hall, bass drums throbbing in syncopated disunion.

"What? How do you know about Herschel?" I hiss at her.

"Come on, Annie"—my sister looks at me from the corners of her eyelashes—"everyone knows. You act like no one sees you when you go walking in New-York."

"I have to talk to him," I say, trying to drop Ed's hand. He clings to me like molasses.

"Don't go!" my brother pleads. "It's so loud! Stay here!"

"What are you doing?" Beattie says with urgency. "You can't go!"

"You don't understand!" I cry to her. "I have to!"

We're interrupted by a tattoo from a trumpeter, and the crowd simmers to a roar as the governor waves his hands for their attention. The sunset flames across the sky over Manhattan, turning the shop windows into red mirrors. I hear a sharp rapport, like a gunshot, and jump as a mob of children scatters laughing before an exploding string of firecrackers. The air smells rancid with gunpowder.

"Welcome, one and all, on this historic occasion in the City of New-York, and indeed, the world over!" Governor Clinton booms through a speaking tube, arms held wide as though he could embrace all the rabble and gather them to his noble chest. "Welcome to the flotilla newly arrived from Buffalo with their Aborigine guides, and welcome to the esteemed members of the Canal Corporation, whose vision and achievement this is!"

Applause smatters across the crowd as my father and a few other men, waistcoats too tight and hats too tall, attempt to bow in a way both puffed with noblesse oblige, yet sufficiently modest as to win the votes of sailors and draymen. Everyone fails, with my father's secretary even losing his hat in the crowd to a quick-fingered urchin. The bronzed Aborigine standing behind the secretary, in a tight plaid suit and hat but with long black plaits over his shoulders, has to smother a laugh.

"We gather tonight to celebrate the union of the waters of Lake Erie with the waters of the mighty Atlantic Ocean," the governor continues, thumbs behind his lapels.

"Look at them," I whisper to Beattie, glaring at Mother and Papa, both of them beaming out over the crowd, my mother's gloved hand waving at no one. "They'll say anything to the crowd to get what they want. The canal's corrupt, Beattie. The corporation took money from the slave traders to get it built. And they're going to rip open the Indian lands, too. It's rotten, and it's wrong, and these people should know it's all a scheme to fatten up the slavers, and fatten ourselves to boot. Look."

Beattie follows my gaze, and I see a glimmer in her eyes of beginning comprehension. Monsters aren't these fairy things in storybooks. They're not pumpkin-headed ghouls galloping through the night in old Knickerbocker stories. They're people like this, who bend others' suffering to their own gain, and smile and wave while they do it.

"The note—" Beattie starts to say.

"Herschel put it on our door," I whisper, my breath hot on her ear. "*Herschel did.* It was a message from the Luddites. To warn me, about our parents. Don't you see?"

Beattie's eyes are widening with panic, and Ed has edged nearer to us. My mother opens her mouth to laugh, her face long and distorted like a marionette's.

"Now," the governor booms into the night, "the assembled company shall process down to the Battery for the Grand Aquatic Display, wherein the waters of all the greatest rivers in the world shall be joined together as one. It's a new world, a new dawn for the City of New-York!"

The bands all bellow in semi-unison, jarring enough to make ears bleed, as a bevy of carriages rolls through the massed crowd, liveried drivers scattering beggar women here and there with a brandishment of the horsewhip. A dark woman with her head wrapped in a scarf trips as she backs out of a horse's way, and she collapses on the cobblestones with a scream. Hands grasp her arms and dress and haul her out of the way. A hoof clops down on the stone where her head lay an instant before, and the horse whinnies against the shouts of the crowd.

"Come, children," Mother calls to us as she steers Papa to the edge of the dais and toward the waiting carriage. Its door is open, and a small child with no shoes on and a muddy face hangs gawking on its window.

"What are you going to do?" Beattie asks me.

Mother gestures to us impatiently as the carriage driver fights off the throng from dragging on the horses' reins. Beattie's eyes jump between our parents and me, and Ed clings to her waist, trying hard not to cry.

I've lost sight of Herschel. He's been swallowed by the crowd, or worse, what if he's been trampled? I crane my neck, rising on tiptoes to try to get a better look, but the light is failing, and the flames of torches make the shadows of the mob duck and dance crazily in the street.

"Annatje! Beatrice! Edward! Get in the carriage!" Mother commands.

"Annie, we have to go," Beattie says. "We can't stop now."

Then I see him. Herschel's stepped up where one of the liverymen should be standing, on the trunk platform at the rear of our carriage. He catches my eye with a quick wave of his hand, and he gestures with his chin over his shoulder. I see the other two boys from the Luddites, the ones who frightened me in the street, attached to other carriages in the procession, here's the one in the skullcap sitting up next to the driver, there's the broken-nosed Senegalese holding a horse's bridle in his fist. There're probably others I don't know and can't see.

I think of the painting in Maddie's house as my eye falls on a quivering-lipped Ed. The barge. Must they all be on it but him? They were before. But must they now?

Can memories be made to change?

I nod and hustle my brother and sister to the waiting carriage door. As I take Beattie's hand to bundle her in next to Mother, I clutch her wrist and force her to look me in the eye.

"Listen to me," I say, digging into her skin with my fingernails. "Listen. Whatever you do, *do not get on that barge*. Understand?"

"What? Why?" Beattie asks, Ed peering moonfaced over her shoulder from inside the carriage.

"Don't you let Ed get on, either. Neither of you gets on the corporation barge. Got it?" I shake her.

Ed and Beattie nod silently as Mother shouts, "Get in the carriage! Now!"

I glance at Herschel perched on the rear of the coach, who leans in close to me and says, "Annie. Get in. I'll be right here."

His voice. Oh, his voice. That's what it sounds like. I feel like I haven't heard it in decades, even though I only saw him last week. My skin shivers with pleasure, waves running along my limbs to the tips of my fingers and toes. The ring on my finger glows at the sound of it, and my heart swells so that I fear everyone will see, as though light might come streaming off my face.

I climb inside, and Herschel slams the carriage door closed and raps on the roof, signaling to the distracted driver up front that we're ready to go. Another loud series of pops as more firecrackers go off *rat-tat-tat* on the cobblestones, causing a horse on the carriage in front of ours to rear, clawing the night with his hooves. Our horse backs up, too, throwing me into my mother and then cracking my temple against the door handle. Stars explode behind my eyes, and the reek of gunpowder gets even thicker.

Cries of "Let's go!" and "Walk on!" and the carriages lurch one at a time into the rolling river of people who walk, some carrying little makeshift Stars and Stripes, some dressed to the nines and others in rags, bands marching past the carriage windows, trombones and cornets blurting their sounds over the heads of the passersby as we all flow in a river of humanity down Broadway to the Battery.

I twist my skirts in my fists. Papa is laughing, his head rolling on his shoulders, and Mother is waving across his great belly out the window, keeping her hand just out of reach of the beggars.

"What are you going to do?" Beattie leans forward to whisper in my ear as we bounce over a curb.

"New-York has to see what the canal will do," I whisper back. "We have to show them."

"But, Annie," Beattie says. "You can't stop it now. The canal's finished. They're going to dump the water of Ganges and the Hudson and the Amazon all into the sea, and then it'll be open."

"It doesn't matter," I say, setting my jaw. "When they see what the canal really means, there'll be riots in the streets. I'm going to give them a grand display they'll never forget."

We roll with drumbeats and fanfare and torches all down along the water's edge, the crowd finally growing so thick that the carriages can go no farther. The governor has gotten out of his carriage ahead of ours and wades through the populace, escorted on either side by rough-looking young men with hats pulled low over their eyes. The Battery is thronged with crowds the likes of which I've never seen, the waterfront bristling with masts in silhouette against the darkening sky, and more ships floating at anchor here and there in the harbor, with low black rowboats sculling back and forth between them. Lanterns hang from every mast and spar, smoke belching out of smokestacks and casting the night in a burning haze. We're nearly there. How can I keep them off the boat?

Mother and Papa are fumbling at the carriage door when a drunk sticks his head through the window and cries, "Canal Day! Issss Canal Day! Huzzah!"

He thrusts a bottle in through the window, and in a trice I knock the bottle out of his hand, dumping foul-smelling liquid in Papa's lap.

With a bellow Papa jumps to stand up and brush the spillage off him, cracking his head hard on the landau roof. He collapses with a groan back into the seat, his head lolling, eyes rolled up in their sockets.

"Peter?" my mother asks, resting a concerned hand on his chest. She shakes his lapel, and he slumps over senseless to the side, leaning on Beattie, who struggles to right him. Ed cuddles closer to me, the tears having overflown their dams.

Now who's the crackbrain, I think wickedly.

"Mr. Van Sinderen?" a young corporation lackey cries into the carriage window after hustling the drunk away. "Are you quite all right, sir?"

The bands outside are striking up again, and a lone firework goes off with a whine and glittering pop over the water. Someone bellows through a speaking tube that all parties expected on the barge should make their way to the gangplank.

Mother shakes Papa more roughly. "Peter!" she shouts in his ear. "We're going to miss the boat! Wake up!"

"Mr. Van Sinderen?" the lackey says again. "They're calling people to the barges, sir."

"Peter, dammit!" Mother says, pulling off her glove and slapping Papa across the face. The force from her blow flops his head over to the other side, but his eyes are glassy and he doesn't reply.

Cursing, the lackey wrestles the carriage door open and leans in, thrusting a small container of ammonium salts under Papa's nose. Mother catches a whiff of it and coughs, shouting, "Be careful where you put that, for God's sake!"

Meanwhile, the door on my side of the carriage opens softly, and I feel a gentle hand on my arm.

"Annie," Herschel says to me levelly. "It's time to go."

My lover stands before me full of life, and my heart quails at the sight. I push Ed into Beattie's arms, take Herschel's proffered hand,

and step out of the carriage. I feel as light as a leaf, as though beams of light were shining out of my head.

"No!" Beattie screams. "Wait!"

I turn to my struggling family in the carriage, Mother gagging on the ammonia stench as she and the secretary try to rouse the dead weight of my drunken, head-stunned father, Beattie wedged in next to them, her arms full of my bawling little brother. I lean back into the carriage and plant a kiss on Beattie's cheek.

"Don't you worry," I say with a smile, tucking a hank of her hair behind her ear. "You keep them here. Watch Ed. I'll be back soon as I can."

I'm lying to her. We both know it. Tears start to fill Beattie's lower lids.

"Ed?" I say to the sniveling creature cowering on the carriage bench in his new suit. He rubs his eyes and stares at me.

"Here," I say, pulling the cameo of Persephone off my finger. It glows faintly in the oncoming night. I bring it to my lips for a fast kiss and then slide it quickly onto my brother's thumb. "You hold this for me while I'm on the barge. Keep it safe. That's your job. All right?"

He looks down at the trinket with fresh interest. "All right," he acquiesces. "But only 'til you come back."

"Fair enough." I smile. "Now whatever you do, stay here, with Mother and Papa. All right?"

My siblings nod dumbly, and a strange golden glimmer seems to pass over the scene, the fairy wash of light I saw at the park. Like a leaf showing its underside on a breeze. A subtle change.

"Annie . . . ," Beattie starts to say. Her face crumples and she can't finish.

"I know. Me, too," I reply.

Herschel's hand is around mine, and it's time for me to go. I slam the carriage door against my mother's muffled cry of "Where does she think she's going?" We take off at a dead run, weaving through the crowd.

"They're going to cast off!" Herschel cries. "We have to hurry!"

The gangplank is thronged with so many people that we'll never be able to fight our way on. The barge sags low in the water, heavy with bunting and bands and milling people, streamers dropping between the gunwales and the shore. A few rowboats bump up against the hull, full of more people laughing, tossing streamers, a few uninvited young men trying to vault aboard.

"We can get on from the stern," I shout to Herschel, pointing.

He nods, and we dash through the crowd away from the gangplank to the shade of a tree near the end of the Battery, its branches trailing streamers like a weeping willow. We skid to a stop as a rough-looking young man steps forward from the shadows, clutching a weathered leather bag to his chest. The leather has been branded with the pattern of a spindle.

"That's Claude," Herschel explains. "It's all right. He's with us."

"Here, take it," the man says, thrusting the bag into Herschel's arms. He has a thick Creole accent. Another contraband. "You sure you're ready?"

"I'm ready," Herschel says.

"What she be doing here?" The man gives me a suspicious look, taking in my fancy dress and my prissy curls.

"It's okay. I'm in the Brotherhood," I say, fixing him with my steeliest stare.

"*Okay?*" the rough-looking Creole repeats as though he's never heard the expression before, and I smile to myself.

Herschel is startled to hear this pledge of revolutionary allegiance from me, but when the suspicious man eyes him for confirmation, he nods, squeezing his shoulder in reassurance. "It's perfect," Herschel insists to him. "Her father's in the corporation. She's kept us apprised of their plans all along." He peers at me closely, and then adds with a smile, "It's *oll korrect.*"

I grin at him.

The young man's suspicion morphs into a begrudging respect, and he crosses his arms over his chest. "All right," he says. "Remember. Paint the letters big. Big as you possibly can. It's pointless if no one ashore can see."

"Right," Herschel says, peering into the leather satchel to confirm its contents and then slinging it over his shoulder.

"Paint?" I echo. "What do you mean, paint?"

"A slogan of liberation. On the barge," Herschel says, and the tone of his voice suggests he's reminding me of something I already know.

"Wait. We're not blowing it up?" I ask.

"Blowing it up?" He laughs. "Of course not! The original Luddites smashed the cotton machines. But if we smash the machines of oppression, they just build more. Our Brotherhood is different. We're here to change their minds instead. Come on!"

I'm giddy. We're not blowing it up! This time *is* different! Maybe . . . maybe . . . But I can't let myself think about that now.

Herschel takes up my hand. My skin flames to life when he touches me, and we go flying across the Battery as fast as our feet can carry us.

Private police from the Second Ward, retained by the corporation for the evening, have started herding people away from the gangplank, and we sneak unobserved to the stern of the barge where it's moored not far from the West Battery peninsula. A thick hemp docking line groans under the drag of the barge as revelers mass on the port side to wave to the people on shore. Night is gathering quickly in the shadows of the Battery, and no one observes us as we creep to the dock edge. The stern of the boat bobs about ten feet away.

"We can shimmy across on the dock line," Herschel suggests. "Can you do that in a dress?"

I grin at him through the dark, plant my hands on his cheeks, and kiss him full on the mouth. He's surprised, his young lips trembling. Then his lips warm under my pressure, and he kisses me back.

A pop and explosion from a child's firecracker startles us apart, and I break away from him, taking a few steps back. I hoist my skirts up over my knees, bloomers exposed, take a deep breath, and then I start to run.

"*Gott im Himmel!*" I think I hear Herschel exclaim, but it's too late to stop now. My foot plants hard on the edge of the dock, the light-spangled waves below me, and I jump.

I vault up as high as I can go into the air, my feet kicking, and then I land on the deck, collapsing in a heap of skirts over my head. Some other young people on the barge applaud and cheer, and a few young men rush over to help me to my feet, slapping me on the back and shaking my hand.

While they're congratulating me there's another thunk and it's Herschel, sprawled out on the deck on his stomach, one leg in the water, scrabbling his way aboard. They've thrown the dock lines off and the barge is slowly starting to make its way into the current. Several young men haul Herschel to safety by the back of his jacket. He's lost his hat in the leap, and when the young men see his ear curls, they drop his jacket and move away.

"Jew," one of them mutters under his breath.

I rush over to help him to his feet, glaring back at the strangers who've vanished into the throng. The music has reached deafening levels, and I can't get Herschel to hear me over the horns. I ascertain that he's not hurt, only winded and hatless.

As the barge pulls away from shore, I spy my parents' carriage rolling to a stop at the foot of the gangplank, and my father lurches out of the carriage door with my mother close on his heels. They're waving their arms and shouting, but I can't hear them.

Herschel moves with stealth behind the band in the stern, making sure of the leather bag, until we reach the lee side of the cabin. We're alone. Most of the corporation crowd has gathered on the larboard side, where they can watch the city lanterns recede into glittering dots along the shore. The barge will pull away from land and swing around into the current in a wide semicircle until the starboard side faces the city, and that's when the governor on his barge nearby will pour the waters into the harbor, and they'll light the fireworks.

We don't have much time.

Herschel fumbles the leather bag open and pulls out a couple of cans, some brushes, and a pocketknife. Swearing with effort he struggles to pry the cans open. Finally he gets one done, dips a brush, and sets to work.

I grab another of the brushes and dip it into the paint, but it's old and congealed so thick I almost can't get the brush in.

"Herschel," I whisper, tugging at the hem of his coat.

"What?" he whispers back.

"It's too thick. I can't get enough on my brush," I say.

"Add some turpentine," he says, jerking open the other canister. "That'll thin it out. Here." He dumps some bitter-smelling liquid into the paint, sloshes it around inside with the handle of his brush, and sets back to work. Some of the turpentine spills on my dress and slippers, but I don't pay any attention.

We work quickly, making the letters as big as we can, covering the entire side of the cabin. Smoke belches from the stacks in the center of the barge, and a long horn sounds as the boat slowly begins to change direction. I feel the wind shift, blowing my skirts out to the side.

"Should I sign it?" he asks me, smiling his crooked smile.

I laugh. "Maybe not with your name," I say.

Herschel leans down and signs the brotherhood's name with a flourish, but he gets the spelling wrong.

"Ludditz?" I ask, teasing him.

He chucks the paintbrush into the sea and comes over to take me in his arms. "Hey now. I didn't have a fancy tutor like you," he says, nuzzling my ear.

The barge's wide circle continues, the steam engine groaning under the weight of so many people. We pass through the shimmering white pathway of moonlight stretching across New-York harbor, and Herschel holds me closer to him. I can feel his heart beating in his chest, and the rhythm of mine matches his.

"After this, when it's all over, can we go away in your brother's cart like you said?" I ask, my breath hot on his neck.

He nods.

The barge continues its slow, laboring turn, and a distant voice echoes through a speaking tube across the water, announcing that at the conclusion of the drumroll, the governor will pour the combined waters of the Hudson, Ganges, Amazon, Mississippi, Lake Erie, and all the major waterways of the world into the harbor of New-York City, and a new age will be upon us. Rattling snares begin on the governor's barge a few rods away, and the snares on our corporation barge roll to life, drumming deep in my body, in my veins, in my heart.

Herschel and I cling together, and in the split second between the drum's abrupt silence and the distant plash of river water, Herschel whispers, "'Til the wheels fall off."

I turn my face up to kiss him, and our mouths find each other as the first firework goes off overhead with a whistle and pop and rain of sparks. One after the other fireworks launch, a row of sparklers sizzles to life along the edge of the gunwale, and in the sudden illumination of every corner of the boat the assembled corporation folk gasp.

Behind us, on the barge cabin, written in letters as tall as me, is the wet bloodred slogan PROGRESS WITH SLAVERY ISN'T PROGRESS. Underneath is signed UNITED BROTHERHOOD OF LUDDITZ, with a long flourish on the z.

The company on board immediately bursts into appalled gasps, tittering among themselves and cries of "What?" and "Who did this?"

The slow flame of chaos starts to lick through the crowd, as shouts of "But what do they mean?" echo through the night. Onshore the onlookers gasp and start arguing amongst themselves.

"Annie!" I think I hear my father shout. "Is she aboard? Wait! Annie!"

Amid the heat thrown off by the gunwale sparklers, the letters of our fresh-painted statement begin to smoke. The turpentine in the paint. It's flammable. The letters start to bubble.

But I'm not paying any attention. I'm wrapped up in Herschel's arms, in the longest, most exquisite kiss I've ever imagined. I feel myself enveloped in him, in the perfect warmth of his presence, of his mouth and mine together, his hand gently cupping my cheek.

"I love you," I murmur into his neck. "I love you."

"I love you, too," he breathes into the curls over my ears.

I don't even notice when the letters in PROGRESS burst into hot blue flame.

CHAPTER 16

"Y ou gonna to answer that?" Eastlin asks.

I burrow my head into my pillow with a sullen groan.

He sighs and I hear him get up and pad over to where my phone sits plugged into its charger, ringing its head off, and probably showing one million missed calls.

I don't care.

"Hello?" Eastlin says. "Uh-huh. No, this is his roommate."

A pause.

"What? Oh, okay."

A pause.

"Uh-huh."

Another pause.

"Hang on a sec. I'll see if he's back yet." Eastlin muffles the phone against his shirt. "Wesley. It's your dad. Again."

Oh. Great. My dad.

"Tell him I'll call him back," I groan.

"Mr. Auckerman? Yeah, he's right here. Hang on."

Then the phone is in my hands and Eastlin is laughing at me from his twin bed on the other side of the room.

Asshole.

"Hi, Dad," I say into the phone, struggling into a seated position with my hair sticking up.

"Hey, Sport," Dad says, causing me to flinch. There never was a guy less sporty than me. "How's tricks?"

"Um. Okay, I guess." My gaze floats up to the ceiling. I wonder how many divots I'll count before I can end this conversation. I definitely don't want it to go on longer than twenty divots.

"That your roommate? He sounds like a good guy."

"Yeah." I eye said roommate, who somehow, despite the fact that it's the middle of the afternoon on a Saturday, looks ready to shoot an aftershave commercial. "He's all right."

Eastlin hears this and makes a flex face, Hulk Hogan style. I roll my eyes and try not to audibly laugh.

"Your mother was telling me that you've made some nice friends there," Dad continues. "I hope we'll get to meet some of them tomorrow."

"Uh-huh," I say.

There's a pause, I guess while Dad waits to see if I'm going to elaborate on this.

I'm not.

"Well . . . ," he falters. "She said you'd met a girl? That true?"

I flop onto my back on the dorm bed with a fresh groan. *Dad, you have no idea.*

Hearing my groan, my father chuckles. "I ever tell you about the waitress I crashed with, back when I was in New York in '75?"

"Yeah," I say.

"I met her waiting on line at CBGB for tickets to see Television. Oh my God. She was hot."

"Uh-huh," I say.

"Let me crash at her pad in the East Village," he continues. "She used to love it when I . . ."

"*Dad.*" I blanch. "God! Her *pad*? Give me a break."

"Touchy, touchy" he says. "Sorry. So, listen." He's going to ask me what time documentary workshop is tomorrow. And he's going to pretend like there isn't a bunch of paperwork that I wanted him to sign. He's either going to pretend he didn't get it and we're never going to talk about it again, or he's calling so he can disappoint me now instead of face-to-face. It's a classic Steve Auckerman move.

"What?" I say, unable to keep the challenge out of my voice.

"Your mother and I are all settled in here at the hotel," he says. "Not too bad. We used miles."

"Great," I say.

"What time you say the screening started? Two?"

I've only said that about one million times since he hinted that they were thinking of flying in. So yes, Dad. It's at two. Still. "Yeah," I say, editing out all the first part.

I'm up to fifty-one divots.

"Terrific. We want to take you and your friends out for a steak after it's all over. You think maybe you could pick a place? And not a cast of thousands, you know. I work for a living. Just, you know. Two. Three, max."

"Sure, Dad," I say. Seventy-eight divots.

"Great." There's a pause while my father clears his throat, and I hear my mother's voice say something in the background. "Oh," Dad says, as if he's only just remembered something, and Mom didn't totally just prod him. "And some forms came for you. To the house."

Well. Score one for Wes. Dad opened the envelope.

"And?" I say, daring him to tell it to me straight.

"Well, the truth is, your mother had some doubts. She doesn't like the idea of you being so far away."

I groan in annoyance. Sure, it's *Mom* who doesn't want me to do it. Way to pass the buck, jerk. It's not that he's jealous I get to be the one who's young and making art in New York instead of him.

"Great," I say, making clear how pissed off I am.

"But then I took her to lunch with your gran. She says hello, by the way."

"What?" I say, sitting up on my elbows.

Eastlin arches his eyebrow at me from across the room.

"Your gran. Says hello. She's very fond of you, you know. You ever send her a thank-you note, Wes? It's the right thing to do."

"GOD. Yes. What happened at lunch?" I say, divot totals forgotten. Fairy dust is sparkling in the corners of my field of vision.

"Well, the three of us had a good long talk," Dad says. "And the upshot is, we think it's a great idea. We've signed the forms for you to transfer."

What?

What?

"YES," I shout, getting to my feet and holding my arms over my head like a prizefighter after the knockout. Eastlin jumps up and echoes my yes in a quiet whisper, then does a disco victory lap around the room. "Oh my God. DAD. Thank you! Thank you thank you thank you thank you thank you!"

"I'll bring them by your screening tomorrow. Then you can get everything in before we leave," Dad says. Mom's voice in the background adds something, and he says, "You're going to have to help out, though. Depending on your aid package. You'll probably have to get a job during the school year."

"I know. That's okay," I say in a rush, already thinking I can ask Professor Krauss if she needs a research assistant. Or, hell, maybe Eastlin can get me a job at Abraham Mas. Then I can dress skinny Upper East Side girls, too. Or, screw it, I'll work at Tyler's dad's dry cleaning shop, I don't care.

"That's assuming you get in. Let's just hope this film of yours is good, huh, Sport?"

All the air rushes out of me like a popped balloon. As if I needed another reminder about how important workshop is. Steven Auckerman, undermining for the win.

"I think"—I pause for dramatic effect—"I think *Most* is going to be different from anything they've seen. I know it."

"All right then. So, listen. Your mom and I will see you at the screening tomorrow, and you can't make her feel bad if she cries, got it?"

"Got it," I say, and I become aware that I am grinning. In fact, I'm grinning so hard I'm a little concerned the corners of my mouth will meet around the back of my head and the top of my head will fall off. "Okay, Dad. See you."

"Bye."

Click, and Eastlin is already standing on his bunk in an attitude of supreme pre-celebration. "OH MY GOD," I shout, tossing my phone on the bed and gawking empty-handed at Eastlin.

"Spill!" my roommate demands.

"I'm transferring. I'm going to NYU," I say. "If *Most* is good enough, I'm going to NYU!"

I'm worried I'm going to cry, I'm so excited.

"I KNEW IT," he says. "That's awesome!"

Eastlin comes in for a fist bump, which turns into a bro-hug with a lot of back pounding.

"Yeah," I say, my eyes glazed.

I have to tell Tyler.

And Maddie. I really have to tell Maddie.

"Oh, stop begging," Eastlin says.

"What?" I say, reaching for my phone already so I can text them. Oh my God. Oh my God. It has to be good enough. Right? It has to be. I can't have come this far, learned this much, only to have it all fall apart when I'm on the cusp of getting everything I want. Can I?

I'm completely freaking out. Completely.

"About rooming for next year. I mean, stop begging already. It demeans us both," Eastlin says lightly.

I grin at him.

"Okay," I say.

Eastlin smiles at me. Then he shrugs like he's pretending not to care. "I've gotta be losing my mind," he sighs, shaking his head. "Straight boys never pick up after themselves."

Tyler's keys are jingling again, his leg all jumpy, and for a second it feels like no time has gone by at all, except Deepti's cheering section has taken the day off.

I'm back in the screening room, and I'm staring at the ceiling to make sure that if I actually do throw up, I will at least choke to death on my own vomit rather than embarrass myself by getting it all over the floor. I made my parents sit in the back instead of with me, because I just couldn't handle the look on my dad's face if Professor Krauss rips my film. Cannot. Possibly. Handle it.

"It's tight, Wes," Tyler whispers to me.

I grunt in response, because I'm too nervous to talk.

I'm feeling good about *Most*. I think.

Mostly.

Ha! Hilarious, Wes. I am hilarious.

I remind myself that I don't really know any of these people. Not really. If it turns out that *Most* sucks, then who cares? I'll get a C, I'll go back to Madison, I'll finish my communications degree, and then . . . and then I'll . . .

Then I'll work in a shoe store and spend the rest of my life reliving the moment I almost had everything I wanted.

Well, it doesn't matter, because none of these people will be there, whatever I do, and in a year nobody will care that some kid from the Midwest showed a crappy, self-indulgent documentary film during his summer film school workshop screening. Only I will know.

Somehow this thought doesn't do anything to calm me down.

"Okay, simmer down, kids," Professor Krauss says from the podium. We're all restless, the faculty as well as the students. Summer is winding down to an end. "Our first victim is Mr. Diegetic Sound himself, Wes Auckerman, with a digital video documentary he's calling *Most*. Hit it."

That's all? No intro, no welcoming parent blather, nothing? We're just going to . . . watch it?

Remember, I tell myself. *You don't actually know any of these people. If they hate it, it doesn't matter.*

But nothing I can say to myself will make any difference. The fear is there, and it's eating at my entrails like a parasite, and I want so badly for the movie to be amazing and I'm so afraid that they will laugh, and nothing I can do now will make any difference. The lights go down, my classmates settle into a hush, the numbered countdown begins (I cut it in, because it's my movie, and I'll do it how I want it done). And then, the screen lights up with what should be a hazy, out-of-focus shot of Annie's face. That perfect mole, those bottomless black eyes. I hold my breath, and my classmates do, too.

But the screen only shows the empty bench by the lake where Annie van Sinderen told me what she wanted the most in the world.

EPILOGUE

I'm still laughing when I step out of Professor Krauss's office and peer at my phone and find a text from Maddie.

U coming over? it asks.

Yes, I reply. **What time?**

How's now?

Perfect, I respond, and stuff the phone in the pocket of my cargo shorts.

I pause in the vestibule of the film department, looking up and down the hallways lined with posters of movies made by Tisch grads. A couple of girls walk by, giggling under their hands and pointing at me. I don't recognize either of them. After a second of debating back and forth, they come up and one of them goes, "Um, excuse me, but are you the guy?"

I can't stop myself from grinning.

"Um. Yeah," I say, tugging at my Ramones T-shirt. "I'm the guy."

"Oh my God," one of the girls says, laying a hand on my arm. "I could not believe what people were saying about your film."

"Aw," I say, waiting to feel myself blush, but not feeling it. "Thanks."

"Seriously," the other girl says. "I was at the screening, 'cause my girlfriend was in your class? And it was awesome. I mean, I loved all the people you talked to, but I kinda felt like the voids were the best part, you know? In the park, and in the pizzeria. They gave it a really terrific pace, you know? Like a meditative break, to give us time to reflect on desire?"

"Aw," I say. There's the blush. I knew it was in there somewhere. The pizza of embarrassment. "That's really cool of you to say."

"What did Krauss think?" the first girl asks.

"It was epic," the second girl says to the first. "She totally freaked-out-loved it. Like, I didn't know she ever gave A's for anything. Seriously." To me, she goes on, "So are you taking advanced documentary workshop in the fall? I'm going to be in that one. I think you and I should form a study group."

"That would be awesome," I say. "Yeah. I'm definitely taking that class. Study group, totally. That would be amazing." I'm nodding while I'm talking, and I'm grinning, and while I give the documentary girl—whose name proves to be Jordan—my cell number so we can get in touch in September, which is only four weeks away, I feel myself growing taller and lighter. Yeah, I am going to be in that class.

Because Krauss just told me my transfer went through.

I shove my hands in my pockets and lope to the elevators.

Where R U? I text Maddie while I wait. The elevators here take forever, I'm not even kidding. She told me she and Janeanna were scoping a new squat, about ten minutes from the film department. But I haven't seen it yet.

My parents, the phone vibrates back. **Come pick me up?**

My eyebrows shoot up.

OK, I respond. But the thought of facing those sepulchers on Park Avenue fills me with a sick sort of dread.

You remember the address? the phone trills.

Park Ave, right? What number? By now I'm inside the elevator, and it's creaking its way to the lobby.

LOL!!!! Maddie texts back. **U so funny. I'll show you the new squat after.**

The elevator doors groan open.

How am I funny? I text her as I head out to the street to hail a cab. Going to the Upper East Side is like taking a trek to the Himalayas, practically.

A cab pulls up just as her response vibrates in my hand. **Duh. It's Jane Street. 341. Hurry up!**

"What?" I say aloud, staring down at my phone in bafflement. Is the star of cracks in my phone screen making me unable to read? Jane Street? But that's in the West Village.

"In or out!" the cab driver shouts at me. A black car behind him lays on the horn.

"Sorry," I say, getting flustered. "Never mind. It's okay. I'll walk."

"Asshole!" The cab driver flips me off. But I'm too busy staring at my phone to get upset about it.

I cross Washington Square Park, heading west. Is she messing with me? Maybe she's kidding.

You're *sure* it's not Park Ave? I text as I pass Waverly Place and cut north.

Um. Yeah? she texts back, followed by a bunch of emojis with their tongues sticking out and their eyes crossed. I laugh and stuff the phone in my pocket.

I pass a bodega and remember the rules of Maddie's Luddite fregan collective. I pick up some potato chips, a tray of barbecue tofu and broccoli, a thing of bananas, and a six-pack of Colt 45.

The sun's dropped lower by the time I get to Jane Street, and my arms are tired from carrying groceries. The building number she gave me proves to belong to a modest brownstone with a nail place downstairs. I'm pulling out my phone to text her that I'm there when the door opens and she's there, biting a lip.

"Your hair," I say without thinking.

"What?" she says, reaching a finger up to touch it.

Maddie looks amazing. Amazing, and . . . nervous? She smiles down at me from the doorway, fingering the folds of her dress. She's still punked out, but with a slightly softer edge. Maybe a little more grunge than punk. She's in a soft floral dress with her combat boots today, and her hair is down, instead of in the beehive.

Her hair is blue. Blue as ashes.

"You changed it," I say.

She smiles at me uncertainly. "Um. No. I didn't?"

"Um," I say, staring at her. The stare goes on just a little too long, and then I remember that my arms are tired because I've been carrying this grocery bag, so I say, "Hey, listen, so I brought some groceries. For the collective. All vegan. I think."

Her eyes brighten. "Oh! Really? That's nice of you."

But she doesn't make a move to, like, come take the bag from me, or invite me in, or anything.

"Yeah," I say, unsure. "There's, um. Some tofu, and some bananas, and—"

"Maloulou? Is that him?" a resonant male voice calls, and then a middle-aged guy appears in the doorway behind her. He's in a painter smock and his graying hair is in a ponytail.

"I thought your dad was a banker?" It spills out of me, while Maddie and her father exchange an amused glance.

"He's as smooth as you said," Maddie's dad remarks.

"Sorry," I mumble. "Mr. Van Sinderen, I'm just sort of . . ." I don't know what I'm trying to explain, because nothing about this seems familiar. Or rather, it does, but I can't shake this feeling that something is off. Something's changed.

"You guys dropping stuff off at the collective?" he asks Maddie. "If you see Janeanna, tell her her dad's almost done with the plans for the community garden."

"Sure, Dad," Maddie says with a roll of her eyes.

"Um—" I start to add, but I don't know where I'm going with it.

"Do you want to leave?" Maddie interrupts before I can embarrass myself further.

"Leave?" I'm confused.

Her dad laughs, says, "You kids have fun," and disappears back upstairs.

"Well," Maddie says, looking up at the sky. "It's nice out. I thought maybe we could go to the park."

She's right. The sky has this soft, lovely grayness to it, cloudless, but pale bluish white. Like a moonstone.

"All right," I say, and Maddie smiles a huge grin and comes tripping down the stairs like a kid, landing next to me with a stomp of her boots.

By the time we get back to Washington Square, my arms are really killing me. We settle on one of the benches in the park, not far from where I filmed that guy for *Most*. The one who was obsessed with flying on the Concorde, even though it doesn't exist anymore.

Wordlessly Maddie fitzes open two bottles of Colt, handing one to me in a brown paper bag. We sit in silence, sipping our terrible malt liquor, watching the life of the park pass us by. Moms in yoga pants with babies in strollers, teenage girls about to start high school, an old Korean man holding his wife by the arm, both bent nearly in half with age. Dogs tussle in the dog run, and a young guy breaks it up. In the distance, someone turns on a radio. Vintage Beastie Boys. "Intergalactic." It's all as it should be. And yet, different.

"So, guess what?" I say, leaning on the bench with an arm along the seatback, behind Maddie's shoulders, but in a casual way.

"What?" she asks. She settles herself into my arm, and I feel a brush of the flesh of her shoulder against the crook of my elbow. Where our skin meets, the patch of my skin starts to tingle.

"I'm transferring," I say. I'm keeping it light. I'm not looking at her. That way, if she doesn't react, it's okay.

"Oh yeah?" she says, just as lightly. "To Tisch?"

"Mmm-hmmm," I say. I take a swig of my malt liquor and have to stop myself from spitting it out. Damn, that stuff is nasty.

"Huh," she says. "So it went through?"

I allow myself a sidelong glance in her direction.

She's smiling.

"Yeah," I say.

I'm smiling, too.

"Yeah, well. Guess what? I'm starting next semester at City College," she says. "So. I'll be around. The collective's got another space lined up for September. In Brooklyn, I'm pretty sure Janeanna said."

Also without looking at me. Instead she's twisting a ring on her finger. Some kind of dark brown carved shell. A terrier has his paws up on the chain-link fence across from us and wags, and Maddie smiles and waves at him. The gold band glints in the sun.

"Arlo!" a woman calls from inside the dog park, and the terrier disappears.

"Yeah?" I say. Maddie glances quickly at me, as if gauging to see if I consider her starting at City College to be good news.

"Yeah," she says.

We're staring at each other now, and a moment of static electricity passes in the space between us. Her eyes are wide and black and nearly bottomless, the lashes trembling.

"Good," I say, and I take her cheeks in my palms. I study her, to make sure this is okay, and then I lean in and kiss her.

We stay like that, locked together, tofu on our laps and my hands holding her cheeks, our lips pressed together. My glass Colt 45 bottle rolls unheeded off the park bench next to me and cracks in two on the cobblestones. It's probably only a minute that we sit like that, a still point frozen in the swirling eddies of life in Washington Square Park.

But a minute can be an eternity, sometimes.

AUTHOR'S NOTE

A few months ago, a man from my insurance company came to inspect my New England house. This is one of those grown-up responsibilities one never thinks about in high school; it turns out that a lot of adulthood involves thinking about things like gutters and doctor's appointments and paperwork. But I digress. The man nosed around my rickety old house, taking measurements, checking smoke detectors, and before long he noticed a lot of books on the shelves with my name on the spine. It came out that I was a novelist, and he asked me what I was working on just then—I was working on this book, as it happens—and I told him I was writing a ghost story that never used the word *ghost*. He nodded sagely and informed me without a trace of irony that I didn't have to worry—my house wasn't haunted. He'd been in ones that were, of course. Sad houses with thick presence. Houses that wear the misery in their pasts like winding sheets.

Ghosts are hard to categorize, but scratch the surface of reason and you'll find that most of us harbor secret beliefs about them. While writing this book, I heard innumerable stories from friends, neighbors, and strangers of inexplicable footprints, eerie sensations, and crawling skin. At a cocktail party at a southern university where I was teaching fiction one semester, a woman mused to me that she didn't see how you could be a Christian and *not* believe in ghosts. She herself had, at one point, been awakened in the night by the specter of her mother.

For such a young country, the United States is an unusually haunted place. Sociologist Judith Richardson points to the Hudson River valley from Manhattan up to Albany as a uniquely haunted sphere, one steeped in literature and folklore even beyond the persistent headless horseman of Sleepy Hollow fame. Ghosts are both remnants of history and witnesses to it. In a region like New York, marked by nonstop waves of immigration and change, in which it can be argued, as Richardson does, that the signal experience is of a stranger newly arrived in a forbidding landscape, ghosts both invite our terror and reassure us that others have trod our path before. In that sense, the ghost represents a curious contradiction in terms: extant and illusory, terrifying and reassuring. Their spectrality enables them to contain several ideas at once, embodying our slippery, overlapping cultural feelings about history, place, and time.

Ghosts are tied inextricably to a specific place, oftentimes a site of transition and change. Folklore regularly locates ghosts in conveyances—at a crossroads, on a bridge, near a river, in the backseat of a car. But the most haunted realms in literature are, of course, houses, sometimes of such specific character that they bear names themselves: Usher, Hill House, Bly. Houses imprison ghosts, perhaps, as bodies contain souls; *ghost* is the name we give to an innervating sense of an object's, or place's, persistence through time. Ghost stories are how we forgive houses for daring to outlive us.

In the same way, certain places can be said to be haunted by our imaginations of them. Both Annie (whose Dutch name, Annatje, is an homage to the folktale of a murdered servant dragged screaming behind a horse in the Hudson River valley) and Wes move through a New York City that is in some sense impossible to see. Annie sees the city as she remembers it being, while Wes sees the city alternately as his father has told him about it and as he's experienced it in movies. Memories, while true, are impermanent, and film, while permanent, is untrue. The real place lies somewhere between these layered images, these overlapping specters of the city as it never was.

History, too, struggles with ghostly narratives, as forgotten and overlooked ideas refuse to disappear completely, instead bubbling just under the surface of that which is remembered. New York's financial involvement with slavery, for example, was something of a historical ghost until recent excavations have returned that fact to light. Academic history, even when revisionist, is typically bound by a rhetoric of power. Only select perspectives last: perspectives of the literate, the rich, the powerful. But silenced voices have a way of refusing to lie dormant as our culture marches away from their moment in time. They instead become folded into us, lingering on the periphery of our experience. Haunting us.

The haunted self, the haunted house, and the haunted city: When we talk about ghosts, then, we're not just dealing with sheets and chains and Scooby-Doo. Ghosts are the language we have come up with for talking about ideas that influence us even in the absence of our conscious awareness. A whiff of cologne might conjure the specter of our first love, a certain quality of light in summer might be the ghost of our childhood home, and something as innocuous as a traffic pattern might be the lingering scar of a city's entire reason for being. We can all point to things that have made us what we are, but there are many more things we can't point to, because they are invisible. We're surrounded by ghosts all the time. In a sense, we're ghosts ourselves.

As I showed the home inspector to the door after he declined my offer of coffee, he reassured me once again that I had nothing to be worried about. Some ineffable quality of my house met with his experienced approval, which of course made me happy. But as I shut the door behind him, I had to reflect that in a way he was wrong. Certain smells will always transport me to July 4 celebrations in this house. Its staircase was moved by people I never met, to a place of their choosing, for reasons of their own. It stands on a street with a name changed out of revolutionary zeal over two hundred years ago.

My house is definitely haunted. And I bet yours is, too.

ACKNOWLEDGMENTS

I would like to thank first and foremost my incredible editor, Jennifer Besser, for guiding this project from its inception through many close revisions into the weird and wonderful story it has become. I'm grateful also to my agent, Suzanne Gluck, for whom I would take a bullet, together with all her colleagues at William Morris Endeavor, most particularly Clio Seraphim, Laura Bonner, and Ashley Fox. I feel so fortunate to be published by the incredible group at Penguin, whose commitment to quality literature for young adults makes our culture better. My thanks to all of them, but especially Don Weisberg, Marisa Russell, and the amazing Andrea Lam over at Penguin for grown readers.

A number of people graciously lent their expertise to this story so that I could attempt to write with authority about things of which I understand but little. Kaye Dyja provided laser-eyed commentary on teenage slang and point of view. Professor Rosanne Limoncelli graciously took the time to show me around Tisch and give me insight into the in-jokes and everyday lives of the NYU film program (but I hasten to add that any mistakes, be they technical or psychological, are mine). The excellent Andrew Semans read and reread chapters to correct my misapprehensions about films and the teenage boys who make them.

Many friends and colleagues supported me during the writing of this project, and I'm grateful to all of them for keeping me sane. Particular thanks are owed to Sibyl Allston, Irina Arnault, Sandy Barry, Julia Bates, Shaine Cassim, Michael Deckard, Heather Folsom Prison Blues, Julia Glass, Connie

Goodwin, Will Heinrich, Jon Harrison, Eric Idsvoog (my secret weapon), Juliet Mabey, Veronica McComb, Jane Mendle, Ginger Myhaver, Matthew Pearl, Brian Pellinen, Eric Reid (my weapon of secrets), Colleen Rowley, and George Spisak. Thanks also to Annabel Teague for being an early teen reader, Eli Hyman for crushing the 10 percent, Phyllis Bloom for being my tireless street team of one, and Ruth Ferguson and Peter Wright for telling me about the footsteps in the dust on their stairs to nowhere. My love and thanks also to the denizens of the Springfield Street Table, the Tuesdayistas, the Ménage, the Third Sarah Battle Whist Club of Boston (Ithaca Chapter), and End Times Island, without whom my year would be a bleak vista indeed.

A number of institutions and scholars also made the historical aspects of this book possible. I would like to recognize in particular the New-York Historical Society's exhibition *Slavery in New York* from 2005, and its attendant exhibition catalogue and website, as well as the Metropolitan Museum of Art's 2001 *Art and the Empire City*. The Merchant's House Museum's meticulously preserved 1830s interior allowed me a clear imagination of the inside of Annie's house, and I'm grateful to them for working to preserve the rare heritage of nineteenth-century architecture in New York City. Both the New York Marble Cemetery and the New York City Marble Cemetery remind us of all the New Yorkers who have trod the streets before us. I'm grateful also to Judith Richardson for her terrific book *Possessions: The Uses of Haunting in the Hudson River Valley*, which first spurred my interest in thinking about ghosts in New York, and to Siddhartha Lokanandi for bringing it to my attention.

Thank you to Rand Brandes and the Lenoir-Rhyne Visiting Writers series for hosting me as writer in residence during the final edits and revisions of this book, and to the American studies program at Cornell for offering me the opportunity to teach a class on ghosts in American culture as this book was first percolating. My most profound thanks to the undergrads at Lenoir-Rhyne University and Cornell who consented to think, talk, and write about ghost stories with me, and to the readers kind enough to encourage me to keep writing.

Finally, my gratitude as always to my parents, George and Katherine S. Howe, for meeting my career choice with just the right combination of bemusement and pride, and of course, to Louis Hyman. Boo.